Mockingbird Diary of St. Helena Island

Deborah Serravalle

CACTUS RAIN
PUBLISHING

Arizona USA

Mockingbird Diary of St. Helena Island

Published by Cactus Rain Publishing, LLC
San Tan Valley, Arizona, USA
www.CactusRainPublishing.com

ISBN: 978-1-947646-20-9

Proofreading by Certified Proofreader Anita Beery:
        ExpertProofreading@Yahoo.com
Cover Photo by Ali Purse
        Nova Scotia Canada
Author photo by Andrew Maxwell

Published September 15, 2025
Published in the United States of America

Mockingbird Diary
of
St. Helena Island

Deborah Serravalle

Dedication

This story is dedicated to the memory of the freedmen of
St. Helena Island, South Carolina,
and the teachers who walked alongside them.

"Education is the most powerful weapon
which you can use
to change the world."

Nelson Mandela

❧ ❧ ❧

Mockingbird Diary
of
St. Helena Island

Deborah Serravalle

Chapter 1

Henrietta
St. Helena Island, South Carolina
April, 1908

A mockingbird warbled, cheeped, and chirped at the moon all night. Even now, at sun-up, his lusty performance shows no sign of abating. Miss Ellen once told me to take pity on these nightlong marathon singers, as they may be mourning the death of their mate. Out of respect for Miss Ellen and her loss, I continue to refrain from rebuking him. Instead, I roll out of bed, rub my throbbing temples, and glare at the window. His stuttered whistles glide into a sweet trill. Did a Carolina wren take his place? My ear isn't that keen. Not like Miss Ellen's.

I sling on my dressing gown, tiptoe closer, and draw back the curtain. At my appearance the winged creature takes flight. I search the magnolia branches high and low. All that remains are quivering leaves, the suggestion of feathers, and a thin, stray sunbeam.

Where did Maum Cat hunker down last night? That ancient woman, like her namesake, curls up and sleeps anywhere, anytime. No patch of sunlight is safe.

I check the parlor for Maum, but the horsehair armchair is vacant, my plush settee as well. No makeshift quilt pallet graces the corner. I shuffle through the room, tug open the screen door, and cringe at the squeal of rusty hinges. On the porch, I expect to find Maum Cat swaddled in a blanket on the swing, but do not. Nor is she out front, camped beneath the sorrowful oak.

When she arrived yesterday afternoon, we planned to pick oysters today and roast them for dinner. I cross my arms and take a sweeping glance around the property. I shrug and go inside.

I burn the coffee and stub my toe while dressing. My crinkly, curly mane cannot be contained, and the swath of gray I try to hide insists on a front-row seat. Then the blue headscarf I tie on won't stay put. I reach for one more vibrant than Joseph's coat of many colors and stop.

Maum Cat, for all her roaming and unannounced visits, never fails to bid me well and say goodbye. Abandoning the scarf, I grab my buzzard rock from the dresser, pocket it, and put on my gloves. At the front door I step into my boots and head out to locate the old woman.

I'll begin at the Plantation House. Partial to the padded, deep swing on that screened porch, Maum Cat often visits my childhood home for a snooze. While I'm there, I can ask Miss Ellen about the bird's song.

On the road to Frogmore House the temperature rises and the morning dew evaporates. At a break in the trees, I admire the broad, cloudless sky and spy a great blue heron gliding into the marsh. The sun glints off the water like thousands of sequins. With a *sploosh* the heron settles amongst the grass stalks, only their spring-green tips visible above the rising tide.

Sudden movement ahead captures my attention. One, two, then three dogs hurtle out from the scrub. The last, a young hound, stops on the road. He inclines his head my way, sniffs and then lopes off after the others who have already disappeared into the bracken and reeds. Animals are good that way. Most times, unless you threaten them, they don't bother you, unlike people. My jawbone aches with vague memories of hurtful people. Ignoring the pain, I carry on.

Rather than turn at Seaside Drive, I veer off and tromp through the woods to a footpath that will bring me out near Frogmore House. The shortcut also means I'll avoid passing Jakob's cabin.

ૐ ૐ ૐ

A quarter of an hour later, I emerge from the woods, cross the road and walk the short distance to Frogmore. Once inside the shaded laneway, I pause to admire the parallel stretch of pines and draw a deep breath. Their invigorating scent says "home." A longing blooms in my chest and my scalp tingles. I quicken my pace.

On the screened porch, the vacant swing sways and creaks in the sea breeze. No Maum Cat. I pull open the back door to step inside. All is silent. Goose pimples flush my arms; my breath quickens. No whiff of brewed coffee or toasted bread lingers. Miss Ellen rises early. More so since our Miss Laura passed, leaving her a widow in all but name. I rush from room to room, but find no one.

"You here?" I call out, bounding the stairs to her bedchamber. Finding the door ajar, I push in. "Miss Ellen?"

It takes a moment for my eyes to adjust in the dim light. At first I can only discern the outline of the canopied bed. Then, seated bedside, Maum Cat materializes.

"There you are," I whisper.

Releasing Miss Ellen's hands, Maum braces the chair's arms to stand, hobbles behind it, and waves me over.

Inside the bed curtains, Miss Ellen lies pale and immobile on the mattress, the covers drawn up to her chest. Eyes closed, her mouth gapes, slack-jawed.

"Is she ill?" The back of my throat aches and a sour taste floods my mouth.

Maum shakes her head and points at the chair. "Sit."

My whole body commences trembling and I make my way on shaky legs. Once seated, Maum rests a hand on my shoulder.

"She gone in she sleep, Henrietta."

I stare up at Maum. A host of questions scrambles around my mind, yet I am unable to bring forth the words to make a single query—a relapse of an old affliction. Instead, I peel off my gloves and reach for Miss Ellen's hand, a hand that lovingly cared for me throughout most of my childhood. Hands that never hesitated to help me, or my brother, Fountain. Her white skin feels papery and cool; her once delicate knuckles are knobbly with age and all the more dear for it. I thread my fingers through hers; mine a smooth, dark shadow. I lay my forehead atop our clasped fists.

No vision appears. No rush of emotion or wave of memory. The one time I reach for my dreaded gift, I am abandoned.

A choking sob bubbles in my throat and bursts out, followed by another and another. Maum strokes my back and offers me a handkerchief.

I straighten up and dry my eyes. "What happened?"

"She go to be with her Lawd," says Maum.

"I can see that." I shrug her hand from my shoulder.

"You mamas together again," says Maum.

"Why are you here?" I stand, pull on my gloves, and pace the room.

"Same as you," says Maum. "Miz Ellen need me, so I come."

"No, I never sensed she needed me." I shake my head. "I woke up and you were gone. I came looking for *you*."

"Why here?" asks Maum.

I stop my pacing and return to the chair. The bedroom clock punctuates the silence. I do not know how to answer. The reason I told myself before setting out no longer rings true. Rather than venture all the way here to search for Maum, she had other favored spots closer to my cottage or along the route.

Maum Cat tilts her head. I have lost my words. I close my eyes, and in my mind listen to the bird that sang outside my window. *Carolina wren or mockingbird?* I must accept the day without an answer.

༚ ༚ ༚

Chapter 2

Henrietta

My footsteps echo throughout the sanctuary of the Brick Church. April sunshine streams through the paned windows, casting a honey glow on the pews. Some folks may find comfort in this and perhaps see it as a sign of God's grace. Not me.

Taking my seat in our pew at the front, I fiddle with my Sunday best gloves and avoid looking at Miss Ellen's casket resting on a dais near the pulpit. Maum Cat displays no such reluctance and dodders over to lay both hands flat upon the burnished wood. Eyes closed, her lips move. Is she muttering a Christian prayer or an old African incantation? One never knows, since Maum dips into either well as she sees fit.

I slide over and leave the aisle seat for her. Fountain and his family will fill the remainder of the pew. My brother's pragmatic nature alleviated much of the practicalities associated with Miss Ellen's death. Without complaint, he spoke with the pastor, organized the funeral and community tribute, and notified our mother's northern family of her passing. *Passing.* Such a tender, benign word; its utterance a mere puff of air. *Death,* on the other hand, requires a forceful push of tongue and lisping hiss, like the soul-stealing viper responsible for its creation.

Maum returns, wiggles in beside me, and bows her head.

"Henrietta." Fountain's voice is pitched low.

I rise to greet him and my pocketed buzzard rock bumps against my leg. A tightness between my shoulders eases. Maum remains seated in prayerful repose. Like me, she can disappear in plain sight.

My brother's eyes are bloodshot. I put aside my own grief, step into the aisle, and accept his warm embrace. He clings a tad longer than I expect; his body shudders.

"Hush now," I mumble into his ear, and rub his back like I did when he first joined our family. He pulls away, nods, and dries his eyes. A pinprick of light to penetrate my dark cocoon.

Fountain's wife, Olivia, waits at a distance. Her straw hat is new. Fountain beckons and she approaches.

"We be here for you, Henrietta." Olivia blinks and wrings her handkerchief.

My niece and nephew cross paths and stumble as they approach. He huffs a laugh while my niece's eyes widen. In a heartbeat they regroup and move forward united. In turns, they kiss my cheek. Fountain and his family then settle in our pew and face forward. I also sit down, grip Maum Cat's hand, and wait for the service to begin.

Today will not be Miss Ellen's final disposition. We, her St. Helena family, will celebrate her life and then relinquish her mortal remains to her sister, Hattie. Tomorrow, her body will begin the long journey north to Pennsylvania, where Aunt Hattie and Uncle Edwin reside.

The click of shoe heels on floorboards, scuffing footsteps and muttering tell me the sanctuary is filling with mourners. As does the rising temperature and murmurs of sorrow. I gulp down the ache in my throat and check my wristwatch.

Will Jakob come with his daughter, Esme?

I resist the temptation to turn and seek out his face.

"Further up. No. Closer. There." The volume of my friend Fairy's demands are a distinct contrast to the muted babble.

I put my head down and despite all, smile, imagining the embarrassed expression on her husband, One-Armed-Tommy's face.

The sanctuary thrums in expectation by the time our pastor takes the pulpit. Spreading his arms like Jesus on the cross, he indicates we must stand. Musicians behind him commence playing a hymn. The pastor leads off:

> *As I went down in the river to pray*
> *Studying about that good ol' way*
> *And who shall wear the starry crown*
> *Good Lord, show me the way…*

I am in no mood to celebrate the Lord or ask for His direction. Beside me, Maum Cat raises her hands and voice. *How could she offer praise when He took my mother?* I grieved Miss Laura, but did not experience her loss to the extent I do Miss Ellen's. I grit my teeth through the final stanza. Just before the hymn ends, I think I hear Jakob's bass voice.

In that mawkish tone common to White clergymen, the pastor thanks everyone for coming to pay their last respects, reads passages from both Testaments, and then offers a prayer of thanks. Head erect, my eyes remain open. In the sermon that follows, he chronicles why Miss Ellen came to live here on St. Helena Island, how she and Miss Laura established the Penn School, and their eventual adoption of Fountain and me. In doing so, he refers to Miss Laura as her "good friend." Anyone with eyes saw they were so much more to each other.

The pastor steps aside and our friend Kit approaches the pulpit. His voice is the deep, rich baritone you associate with a man twice his size. He adored Miss Ellen, and she him. I glance at Maum. Kit is her great-grandson. Affection smooths the ravages of time on her face.

Amazing Grace, how sweet the sound
That saved a wretch like me…

A jagged sob chokes me. Miss Ellen loved this hymn. The lyrics conjure a bittersweet yearning within me. Defiant tears stream down my face. Behind me, sniffles give way to sobs; a woman wails, another keens.

Kit returns to his seat. I press a handkerchief to my eyes, dab my wet cheeks. The pastor thanks him and announces that an esteemed colleague of Miss Ellen's will share words of remembrance.

My back stiffens. *O Lord, not her replacement, Miss Cooley.*

I draw a quick breath. Not Miss Cooley. The school board's representative, the Reverend Doctor Hollis Frissell, makes his way to the pulpit. My gaze pivots to Miss Ellen's casket. Would she be angry or honored? I lean forward and peer down the pew at Fountain. He stares straight ahead, paying me no mind. Maum places a hand on my thigh. I sit back and hope for the best. Dr. Frissell sets down a sheaf of papers with care and scans the mostly Black congregants. His glance alights on one person then another, and he greets them with a nod or a smile. And then his gray eyes meet mine. In them, sorrow glistens bright and true. Taken aback, I lower my gaze.

He clears his throat. "For years, I attempted to bring Penn School under the auspices of the Hampton Institute," he says, "as I believed our amalgamation would strengthen our shared goal: to train up Black educators and citizens." He smiles and shakes his head. "More than once I ventured to Frogmore House with this request and left empty-handed, defeated by Miss Ellen and Miss Laura's desire for Penn to remain independent."

His comments elicit a flurry of subdued chuckles, a few *Mmmhms* and a couple of *Amens* from the mourners, most of whom are Penn graduates.

Dr. Frissell then moves his story forward, to the time just before Miss Laura's death. "On one of my final visits, Miss Laura relented. She wanted to assure the continuation of Penn School after her passing, and Miss Ellen's place as principal."

His face reveals no trace of irony. Does his conviction blind him?

The weight of these memories fills my chest. I struggle to breathe. Dr. Frissell's sentences echo and fade. I catch only the odd phrase, a few words—*courage, commitment, legacy.*

I return to my senses to discover Dr. Frissell has completed his tribute. Kit is once again at the pulpit, and the congregation is on their feet singing…

…whatever my lot, thou has taught me to say,
It is well, it is well with my soul…

Kit's hymn ends and the pastor offers a final prayer and benediction. I try to stand, but Maum Cat pins me to the pew with a frown. Moments later, the rustle of clothing and hum of voices thin out as the sanctuary empties.

Friends, neighbors, and colleagues will wait outside the church doors to offer my brother and me their condolences. Afterwards, we will cross the road and gather on the grounds of Penn School to celebrate Miss Ellen's life with food and praise songs. The people of St. Helena will share stories. And tomorrow, when it is time to deliver her casket to the wharf, our people will form a procession. The songs of those who knew her well and loved her best will follow her out to sea.

Fountain slides close to me. "Would you like to walk out with us?"

"No, but thank you." I briefly take his calloused hand in my gloved one. "I'll stay for a bit. Let the sanctuary empty."

Am I doing this to avoid the crowd, or to allow space for Jakob to find me?

Fountain looks back at Olivia and the children. They have exited the pew from the other end, and stand waiting for him. He hesitates, but then moves to join them.

I turn back to face Maum Cat, and discover Tommy and Fairy standing in the aisle.

"When you're ready," she says, "come on over to the school grounds. We'll be waiting for you. Your students as well."

My children. I smile and nod.

Once they leave, I am no longer able to resist the urge to discover if Jakob and Esme came.

"Lookin' for sumptin'?" Maum arches one grizzled brow.

I scowl at her.

She crosses her arms and scowls right back at me. "You kick a hungry dog 'nuf, even he let you be."

≈ ≈ ≈

After Miss Ellen's funeral and celebration on the Penn School grounds, Fountain drives Maum and me to Frogmore House where I will stay for a time. Miss Ellen's affairs must be seen to and her belongings sorted. This task falls to me.

Rather than journey the length of the laneway, I ask Fountain to drop us at the entrance.

"Why?" His nose wrinkles. "I don't mind driving you in."

"I know," I say. "But I want to stretch my legs."

Olivia puts a hand on Fountain's arm, stopping any further protest.

Maum Cat has climbed down. Her back to us, she waves and commences down the lane. None of us question her abrupt departure. The poor old woman may desire a moment to herself, away from the undertow of our grief.

After I step down from the wagon, Olivia joins me. Without a word, she pulls me into an embrace and the tension within me loosens a fraction. My niece and nephew likewise hop off.

"Bye, Auntie." They each hug me. I close my eyes and savor the youthful, lively feel of them. They won't be children for much longer. She's grown rounder and softer; but he's taller, with bony clavicles that remind me of a coat hanger.

The children clamber aboard the wagon. Olivia has joined Fountain, who calls out, "I'll see you tomorrow." With a click of his tongue he urges the horse onward.

Olivia and the children twist in their seats and wave goodbye. Moments later, the wagon turns at the crossroad and disappears. With an ache in my throat, I turn and follow Maum Cat's trail.

Soon I catch up to her and we stroll arm-in-arm down the lane and out, onto the lawn of the old plantation property. I don't want this day, Miss Ellen's day, to end. After tonight, I must face all my tomorrows without her.

"Look!" I stop and point at the mother-of-pearl horizon. On this evening, the sky outshines the setting sun.

Maum gazes at the glory crowning the marshland.

The huge globe drops from view. "That there's Miz Ellen's goodbye," says she.

"Seems fitting." I smile at Maum. "She loved this island."

"Sure did." Maum gives me a single nod and turns to go.

We round the back corner of the house as the porch's screen door screeches and slams.

Maum and I look at each and wait to see who'll appear.

"Henrietta." Jakob strides toward us.

Without a word, Maum Cat releases my arm and trudges forward. Jakob is so intent on me, he doesn't acknowledge Maum as they cross paths.

"I hope I didn't startle you."

"What are you doing here?" We speak over each other.

How did he manage to arrive here ahead of us? The last time I saw him was just before Maum and I left the Penn School grounds. He and Esme were talking to a neighbor.

"Can we sit?" His eyes skim the house.

I nod and lead the way. His scent drifts over to me—a blend of sea pine and salt that sets my heart to racing. I am ashamed at the joyful flutter in my belly, and Miss Ellen not yet in her grave.

Inside the porch, he sits across from me on a wicker chair not made for a man of his height. Elbows resting on splayed knees, he clasps and unclasps his hands.

"I'm sorry for showing up this way." He shrugs and his lips curl into a smile. "I needed to see you."

"But we were together only a little while ago at the gathering for Miss Ellen." I remove one glove and fumble in my pocket for my buzzard rock.

He tilts his head and narrows his eyes.

Sweat prickles my brow. "What I mean is, if you wished to speak to me you could have done so there."

He heaves a sigh.

I squeeze the rock and glower at him. "Your daughter spoke to me!"

His brows shoot up. "You implying I should have approached you at the gathering?" He springs from his seat, throws his hands in the air, and paces. "You think I didn't want to go to you today? To comfort you? Here's the truth: Folks know about us." His face contorts, he turns, and hangs his head.

I jump up and reach out. "Jakob—"

He turns around. Seeing my extended arm his eyes widen.

Heat flashes my face and neck. "Please," I point a finger at his chair. "Sit back down."

We return to our seats. He toys with a button on his shirt.

Drawing a deep breath, I reach for the memory of his betrayal, an event more surprising than our first kiss. For both our sakes, I must end this once and for all.

I clear my throat. "I am glad you came—"

Jakob bridges the space between us in a flash. Crouched at my feet, he pries the buzzard rock from my closed fist. I blink back the light sparking on the periphery of my vision. He places the buzzard rock on the table beside me. Slipping my glove back on I clear my throat, ready to make an excuse for the rock's presence.

Jakob stops me with a *Shussh*. "It's fine," he says, "I know that rock eases your anxiety." He takes my hand. "You said all I need to hear, that you're happy I'm here. You've had a long day so I won't stay. I'll see you tomorrow." His knees complain loudly when he stands and he chuckles. "Neither of us getting any younger, Henrietta."

I know Jakob means more than his creaking joints.

He brushes my scarred cheek with the back of his hand. I close my eyes and clench my jaw.

After he leaves I go inside and find Maum Cat in the parlor, tucked in Miss Ellen's favorite chair, her feet resting on the pouffe.

"Jake gone?" asks Maum.

"Mmhmm." I circle the room, stopping to run my gloved hand along the back of the old Chesterfield. "He'll be back."

"'Course he will," says Maum. "Ain't neber too late—"

"Please, Maum. Not now."

I wander to the secretary desk and pick up a silver-framed photograph of Miss Laura.

Are my mothers together again?

With a sigh, I replace the photo and open the desk's drop-shelf. The cubbyholes are lined with an assortment of folded letters, envelopes, and cards.

"I best go through these papers soon and find out if there's anything that needs seeing to."

The first three drawers of the desk's lower half contain an assortment of files, ledgers, and writing instruments. The bottom drawer won't open.

I straighten up. "Last one's locked." I search inside the desk and other drawers for the key, but can't find it. "That's odd."

"Try de picture," says Maum.

"Picture?"

Maum shakes her head and, rising with a grunt, clomps over to the desk. Picking up Miss Laura's photograph, she begins to work free the frame's backing.

"Wait—" I take a step forward.

Maum stops and looks at me, head cocked.

"What makes you think the key is inside the frame?"

"You want to open de drawer?"

"Yes...it's just..." I shrug and walk to the desk. "I feel odd going through her personal papers."

"Henrietta," Maum cups my chin. "It be fine."

I nod.

Maum peels off the backing and a tiny brass key pops out. She passes it to me and returns to her chair.

"Thank you!" I blink at the key resting in my palm. I think to ask how she knew where to find it, but reconsider. Maum's ways are Maum's ways.

"You gonna open dat drawer?" She leans forward.

I squat down, insert the key and turn it. *Click!* The drawer sticks, so I give it a firm pull and it opens.

I sense Maum's eyes boring into my back.

Inside are five notebooks: ordinary, except for one. Larger than the others, it's bound in leather. A mockingbird, stained lowcountry sky-blue, is tooled onto the cover. I gather up the lot, peek into the drawer, and sweep my hand around the edges. Nothing more. I push the drawer shut.

I stand and my knees crick like Jakob's did earlier. I stow thoughts of him to the back of my mind and turn around.

"Just notebooks." I cross the room and stand in front of Maum. "This one is pretty." I hold up the mockingbird book for her to see and then return it to the bottom of the group.

"What's in 'em?"

I open the top notebook. Inscribed on the first page are dates, August, 1861—December, 1862.

I look at Maum. "They're Miss Ellen's diaries." Her loss presses on me like a weight.

Suddenly, I am assailed by a raging fire within. Jakob's right, we're growing old. I slap shut the notebook and tuck the lot into the crook of my arm.

"Come on," I say, "it's cooler on the porch."

Outside, I take in a lungful of the evening air and fan myself with a notebook. It takes a moment, but the hot flush eases.

Maum Cat arrives a moment later and lowers herself onto the swing.

Taking the wicker chair nearest her, I set the top book on my lap and place the rest on the side table.

"Do you think she'd mind me opening these?" I ask Maum.

"'Course not," says she. "That's why she left 'em."

"I don't know that's true. Neither do you."

"Henrietta, why else she write down what she thinkin' in dem books and keep `em if she don' want you to know what's in `em?"

"I suppose."

"Hand me dat quilt." Maum points to the shelf under my side table.

I pass her the blanket and sit back.

Maum shuffles, squirms, and after a moment, settles. "Well?"

With a trembling hand, I open the notebook and read the inscription page...

This book belongs to:
Ellen Murray, Newport, Rhode Island
August, 1861 to June, 1862

The next sheet is filled with Miss Ellen's energetic, cursive script.

"You gonna read dem books or use de gift God gave you?"

"Curse, you mean?"

Maum shakes her head. "God don' curse de beloved."

I'm in no mood to argue with Maum. And truth be told, the thought of experiencing the finer points of Miss Ellen's life through her eyes holds great appeal. If ever there was a time to put my ability—be it gift or curse—to good use, it is now. I peel off my gloves and with a fingertip I trace the notation on the title page. In a hollow swoosh and rush of opalescent light, Frogmore's screened porch recedes.

૨ ૨ ૨

Chapter 3

Ellen
Newport, Rhode Island
August, 1861

Four pairs of hands wove needles in, out and around the quilt pieces for Lila Butler's ever-expanding trousseau. If a husband wasn't found soon, either Lila or her cedar chest would become unhinged. I'd prefer to be at home with a gripping novel than in her parlor.

"Ow!" I stuck the tip of my pricked finger into my mouth.

"Ellen Murray, pay attention," Lila said in a singsong voice. "Needles are sharp."

I wish the same could be said of you.

I sucked harder on my fingertip to stanch a flow of blood and sarcasm.

"Are y-you all right?" Thelma asked.

"Yes, thank you." I accepted the hankie Sally passed.

"Now where was I?" Lila tilted her blonde head as though trying to remember.

I cleared my throat. "Ladies, have you read anything interesting lately?"

"My father would love you," Lila said. "He always suggests I read something or other from his library. Thank goodness Mother discourages him."

"Why would she do that?" I asked.

"She says reading will give you outrageous ideas," Lila said. "Needlework is a more a suitable endeavor for a young lady."

It took effort not to roll my eyes. "What books did your father suggest?"

"Oh, I don't recall," Lila's brows drew together. "One about an uncle and his shack in the woods? It didn't interest me in the least."

"Uncle Tom's Cabin?" I asked.

Lila shrugged.

Thelma looked up from her stitching. "I've heard of that story, it romanticizes the Negro slaves." She shook her head back and forth.

"What a lot of silliness," Lila said, "it proves my mother's point."

"It does?" I asked.

"I agree with Lila," Thelma's dark brows furrowed. "There are more pressing problems in this world, like hardworking White folks that don't have enough to eat. Why is that man worried about slaves? At least they're clothed and fed."

"A woman wrote that book, a teacher like me," I said, raising my voice and looking around our circle. "You do realize these people are bought and sold like cattle? Even the children are snatched from their parents and sent to market. Young and old are beaten. Clothed and fed could mean rags and scraps. England abolished slavery. More and more here are questioning it. Especially Black people themselves."

Thelma glanced at Lila who smirked. Sally kept her head down, eyes intent on her needlework.

For the next few minutes, we sewed without talking.

"The reverend spoke about this at church." Thelma placed the quilt patch on her lap. "Now what did he call those people who want to free slaves…"

"Abolitionists?" I asked. Thelma and I attended the same Baptist Church, although, due to a summer cold, I had been absent on Sunday past.

"Yes, abolitionists," Thelma resumed sewing.

"An abo-bo-litionist will be the guest sp-speaker tomorrow evening at the Friends yearly me-meeting," Sally said. Due to her stutter, Sally only speaks when she has something of import to say. I'd forgotten that some of her family belonged to the Society of Friends.

"An abolitionist, you say? At the meeting house on Farewell?" I asked.

Intent on her needlework, Sally nodded.

"Oh look, because of this silly talk, I've snarled my section!" Lila said. "Thelma, will you come over and help me?"

Thelma crossed the room, skirts rustling.

"Goodness, Lila, what have you done?"

I focused on my embroidery, determined to complete it, return home, and ask Mother's permission to attend the abolitionist's talk.

Later that afternoon, over tea, before I could make my request, Mother announced to my sister Hattie and me that she'd accepted a dinner invitation for tomorrow from the Joneses' family. I opened my mouth to say that I couldn't go, then thought better of it.

I picked up the teapot. "More tea?"

As I refilled our cups, I wondered whether Mother would insist I go to the Joneses' if I explained wanting to go to the meeting? Even if she agreed, she might insist I be chaperoned, which would be difficult to arrange at this late date. I set down the pot and put my intentions aside. For now. I had until tomorrow to come up with a plan.

ᘓ ᘓ ᘓ

The following morning, I announced I had a headache. In the early afternoon I took to my bed with a book. The stairs creaked, and I stuffed my novel under the covers. Seconds later, the door opened and Mother walked in with cool compresses and strong tea.

"Perhaps you should stay home this evening and rest." Mother put her hand on my brow. "You're not fevered, but I fear that cold of yours is returning."

The hard spine of the book beneath the blankets dug into my side, reminding me of my subterfuge.

"Don't look so forlorn," Mother patted my hand. "There's always another dinner, another outing. Your health is more important. Hattie and I will offer your regrets."

I sank deeper into my pillows.

Later, after Mother and Hattie left for the Joneses' dinner party, I completed my toilette and headed downstairs. I'd written a note explaining my sudden recovery and that, feeling restless, I planned to walk to church and hear a speaker, neglecting to mention what church and which speaker. I placed the note on the hall table and hesitated.

The clock chimed.

I grabbed my plainest shawl, rushed out the front door and dashed down the path. As I ran, a sudden gust caught my skirts. Hoping this didn't portend another storm, I closed the gate and scurried down the street, careful to avoid the puddles from the last round of rain. What if foul weather descended upon my return home? Certainly it would be dark, something I hadn't considered until now. I walked faster.

Twenty minutes later, I arrived at the Meeting House. Inside the entrance I paused, surprised at the immediate and open worship space. Rather than pews, benches lined the room, most full. I moved to one side and stood against the wall. Unlike my Baptist Church where I knew everyone, I spotted no familiar faces. With sweaty palms I clutched my shawl tighter. If I left now I'd—

"May I help?"

"Oh!" I turned to the voice and discovered a woman, slightly shorter than me.

Her dark eyes sparkled, and she grinned. "I didn't mean to startle you."

"No...it's all right." I glanced at the door, then back at the woman.

"You look lost. Are you alone?"

"Yes." I threw up my hands. "I came without thinking through how I'd return home when night falls. I should leave." I sighed. "But I really wanted to hear the speaker."

She chuckled. "In that case, I'll see you home safely. I'm Laura. My seat is near the front, on the women's side."

I peered into the sanctuary. As she said, men occupied one half, women the other.

"There's room for you." She pointed with her chin. "Do you see the vacant seat, there, on the left, just opposite the farthest window?" She smiled. "I'll join you in a moment."

Releasing a breath, I smiled. "Thank you."

Laura hurried off.

I made my way to the space on the pine bench she'd indicated. The tang of turpentine tickled my nose. I willed myself not to sneeze, and looked about. A bespectacled lady, seated close by, wore a plain black dress and a snowy, ruffled cap. As did many other women in the congregation. Across the way, their husbands and sons also wore simple cuts of black or gray. I'd observed the occasional Quaker person out in our community in their simple garb. But here, all together in their place of worship, we visitors stood out like splashes of color on a neutral canvas.

Unlike my church, here no one spoke. Not a whisper. Most heads were lowered in thought or prayer, I couldn't tell. Taking quiet breaths, I sensed we were waiting. For what I had no clue. I closed my eyes and listened to the silence. A peaceful power warmed me from the inside.

At the rustle of skirts and whiff of lavender by my side, I opened my eyes.

Laura smiled and inched closer. "Have you been to a Quaker meeting before?" she whispered.

I shook my head. "I'm Ellen Murray, by the way."

"Nice to meet you." Laura patted my hand, sending a shiver up my arm. "For Friends, Ellen," she continued, "even business is a time for contemplation and worship. That portion of the meeting started earlier. Now they are listening to the leading of God's spirit."

"How do you know all of this?" I had noted Laura's royal blue skirt and white Garibaldi shirt. "I assume you're not a Friend."

"I'm from The First Unitarian Church in Philadelphia. I'm here to—"

The woman beside Laura forced a cough. Laura smiled. We turned from each other and faced the front where a man stood. I noted the absence of a podium, or even a simple lectern.

"Friends, our visitors have been patient this evening while we concluded our business. Now we will move on to something which concerns all of us: the issue of slavery."

On either side of the sanctuary, heads nodded, accompanied by the rumble of mumbling. Laura shifted and sat taller.

"As many of thee know," the man said, "the First Unitarian Church of Philadelphia and the Reverend Henry Furness have taken a vociferous stand against the evils of slavery."

Laura's church.

"Tonight, a member of their congregation raises the question: *What Have I to Do with Slavery?* Welcome, Miss Laura Towne."

I drew a quick breath and turned in my seat. Her brown eyes met mine, widening for an instant, before she stood and walked to the front.

My mind raced to our earlier conversations, casting about for silly things I may have uttered. Deciding I could do little about that now, I settled my thoughts and waited for Laura to begin.

Laura scanned the congregation and, in a loud, clear voice asked, "What have I to do with slavery?" She stopped and again glanced around the room. "It doesn't concern me; I hold no man in bondage." She held up a hand. "This is not a subject that belongs to me, or to you. It is for the South, not us in the North. As for slaves, I forget them as best I can. Why linger on something one cannot alter or affect?"

A collective exhalation filled the sanctuary.

Laura moved closer to her audience.

"Are not my time and energies better spent on that which matters to me most; that which I may influence? Certainly there are not enough hours in the day to attend to all that is wrong within my own sphere. I cannot bear to listen in vain to that which is beyond my influence or control."

I recalled sitting in Lila Butler's parlor where my friends spouted similar arguments regarding slavery. *There are more pressing problems in this world,* Thelma had said. Did Laura's views align with Thelma's? As Laura's eyes moved from one person to another, I gripped the bench and waited for her to continue.

"Friends," she said, "if we are to assume this position, one may also ask, what have I to do with the poor or the hungry? Certainly, no one would consider this argument civilized.

"Ah, I see," Laura nodded. "When we talk of the poor, we refer to those who are White, therefore, South or North matters not. But the case of the poor Negro, bound in chains by us, must be debated and defended."

Laura is correct! None of my friends would object to helping a poor White family. Only a few months ago a tearful Lila had taken up a collection for a German widow with five children.

"It is prejudice which hardens hearts, renders us blind." Her voice raised. "Open your eyes to the Negroes' humanity." She

20

looked around the room. "Open your hearts and ease their suffering. It is within your power to do so."

Men and women leaned forward.

"Are we not a country founded on the principles of freedom?" she asked. "Whether South or North, we are one body. If I injure my foot, I do not refuse to dress the wound because it is not as important as the sliver in my hand. Is it not more sensible to tend to your injury, whether it be foot or hand, North or South?"

She paused, and I released a breath I didn't realize I was holding.

"But not all slaves live in abject poverty." Laura addressed those seated in the front row. "Many are better fed and dressed than poor Whites."

Thelma's words exactly!

I inched forward.

"We take the Black man from his home country, put him aboard a vessel to travel by sea, in the most abhorrent of circumstances. If he survives the journey, we work him for our exclusive benefit and pay him nothing for his labor and then, Friends, we argue, he is better off for our interference. This justification of our behavior is perverse and the enemy of the good that dwells in every one of us, including the Negroes."

Whispers circled the room, raising gooseflesh on my arms. Although I had never given voice to this notion, Laura's assertion resonated: The Black man was no different than me, or anyone else here tonight: a creation of God with a beating heart and soul.

"What have I to do with slavery?" Laura turned and walked back to the front.

"Everything!" she said, her voice raised. "A call to do what is right; to stand against this evil. Not just for the slave, but for our own moral betterment. For our country. That we might join others in the civilized world who have turned their backs on this evil."

"Hear, hear!" someone called out.

"Thank you, one and all, for your kind attention," Laura said.

The moderator approached her. "Well said, Friend Laura. We thank thee for thy wise words. Thou hast given us much to consider."

With a final nod, Laura strode down the aisle.

The moderator looked out at the room, now buzzing with conversation. "Let us take a moment to pray and reflect."

Laura arrived at our bench. My head inclined as though praying, I left my eyes open a slit. She leaned close. Her warm, sweet breath brushed my cheek. "I suppose that was a surprise."

I straightened and I took her hand. "You were wonderful."

ﷺ ﷺ ﷺ

Nearing eleven o'clock that evening, Laura's buggy stuttered to a halt by my front gate. Lamplight from the parlor window pooled and shimmered along the rain-soaked walkway.

"I'll see Miss Murray to the door," Laura said to the driver.

We had sat side-by-side in easy silence on the short drive to my house. Now, thinking perhaps I wouldn't see her again, a knot cramped my belly. The discomfort surprised me.

"I'm in Newport for a few more days," Laura said, as we walked.

The knot loosened. "Oh, how nice—"

The front door whooshed open.

Hand to chest, Mother's eyes bounced between Laura and me. "Ellen, I've been worried."

"Didn't you get my message?" I asked.

Mother held up my note. "Yes, well you never said which—"

I cleared my throat. "Mother, this is Miss Laura Towne. Tonight's guest speaker at The Great Meeting House."

"Please don't be upset with Ellen, Mrs. Murray." Laura stepped forward. "She considered leaving before dark, but I encouraged her to remain and offered her a drive home."

The tight lines at either side of Mother's mouth eased.

Laura turned to me. "Would you be free to tour Newport with me tomorrow?"

"That would be lovely." My pulse quickened. "I'll pack a basket."

"Let's say eleven." Laura smiled at Mother. "Nice to meet you, Mrs. Murray. Good night!" Laura turned and marched down the walkway.

Suppressing a smile, I waited, but Mother made no comment about Laura's unladylike gait.

At the buggy, Laura turned and waved before hopping aboard. The moment the door closed behind us, I turned to Mother. "You have questions, I know, and I'm happy to answer them. But right now I'm tired." I took her hand in mine. "May we talk in the morning?"

She sighed and handed me a lit chamberstick from the hall table. "Off you go."

"Thank you." I kissed her cheek and climbed the staircase to my bedchamber.

ಬ ಬ ಬ

I sat on my bed and petted the cat curled up near my pillow. Where would we go? What would I pack for our picnic? What would I wear?

"Why am I so jittery, Bella?" I rubbed the cat's soft, warm belly.

Staring at me, she purred and stretched.

Snippets of the evening with Laura flashed through my mind...*her clear voice...the brown eyes that crinkled when she smiled...her touch...her scent: a hint of lavender and something else indefinable.*

On one hand, I felt as languid as Bella looked. On the other, this unexplainable restiveness spurred me to move; that, and the heat. I wiped sweat from my brow and rose from the mattress. I moved the chamberstick to my night table, and walked to the window. Pushing it open, I looked down at the dark, empty street. The ocean's roar and briny mist rushed in on a cool, mizzly breeze. Distant thunder rumbled. Confident no one could see me, I unbuttoned the neck of my blouse, I took it off, removed my chemise and stepped out of my skirt, petticoat and bloomers. Leaning slightly out the window, the refreshing drizzle beaded on my face and frizzed my hair. Drops pooled and streamed along my naked body, trickled between my thighs, tickling. Yet a curious heat still burned within me.

Shutting the window, I closed the drapes. Opening a drawer, I chose my thinnest cotton gown. The almost sheer fabric clung to my damp skin. Sitting at my vanity, I unpinned my hair which the salty mist had transformed into a mass of ringlets. Usually the routine of a hundred brush strokes cleared my mind. Not tonight. I felt as wild and different within as I looked at the erect tips of my breasts, hips, and thighs visible through the moistened cotton of my nightdress.

I turned from my reflection. Why had the brief encounter with Laura affected me so? How would I ever sleep?

Warming milk meant going downstairs to the kitchen and drawing attention to myself. Perhaps, if I read for a bit...

Climbing into bed, with pillows propped behind me, I grabbed my novel from the night table and opened it to the bookmarked page. Before the end of the first paragraph, the letters and words blurred to an image of Laura. Where was she now? Was she thinking of me? A shiver ran the length of my body. I shut the book and set it back.

Pushing down the pillows at the headboard, I fluffed them.

Perhaps, at this exact moment, Laura was also preparing for bed.

I raised a hand to my hot cheek. My face, I'm sure, was flushed pink.

Sliding under the covers, my nightgown rode up to my hips. The cool sheets against my bare skin inflamed the singular heat plaguing me. Next, my breasts tightened and tingled.

Lifting my bottom, I straighten my twisted nightgown. The fragrance of my own body and soap wafted up, reminding me of Laura's lavender scent. A pleasurable volt darted between my thighs. I closed my eyes. Flashes of Laura appeared: her sweet, warm breath on my neck as she whispered in my ear at the Meeting House...her full lips and delightful smile.

My eyes opened. Smiling, I once again closed my eyes and with Laura's image as a beacon, drifted into a deep, dreamless sleep.

ᑫ ᑫ ᑫ

I awoke refreshed the next morning, excited to face the day, if not Mother. When I went downstairs, I found Mother and Hattie already seated at the breakfast table with a pot of tea and rack of toast between them.

I took my place across from Hattie. "Good morning," I said, and poured a cup of tea.

"Morning." Hattie stared into her teacup.

Mother nodded.

"Did you hear the thunder during the night? There's something about a storm that's thrilling, don't you think?" I buttered a slice of toast. "It makes the sunshine all the more special in the morning."

Judging from creases on Mother's brow, a storm within her still raged. Hattie drained her cup, opened a book she'd brought to the table, and commenced reading.

"I suppose you're happy it's a fine day," Mother said, "seeing you plan to gad about Newport."

"Gad about?"

"Sorry, I shouldn't have put it that way," Mother said.

I set my toast, and cavalier attitude, aside. Leaving out my little subterfuge regarding the Joneses' dinner party, I shared with Mother how I'd arrived at The Great Meeting House and the way Laura had assisted me; the important points of her antislavery speech, and how they had resonated with me and the audience of Friends and visitors.

"You've insisted that I spend time with others," I said. "For that reason I've subjected myself to the likes of Lila Butler and her crowd." I kept my voice even. "They're fine women, in their own way, but I have little in common with them. Now, when I've met a well-educated woman who has more on her mind than local gossip and landing a husband, you object. Why?"

Hattie looked up from her book. "Ellen does have a point, Mother."

I glanced at my sister, grateful for the support.

Mother exhaled a long, slow breath. "You said it yourself, Ellen, she's not like other women. She's unmarried and travels about giving speeches. I'd wager she's ten years your senior. I worry about her influencing you, especially when you don't have—"

"A husband?" Hattie suggested.

"—your health back." Mother shot a frown at Hattie. "Too much excitement could cause a relapse." She shrugged. "I don't deny I'd like to see you girls settled, with husbands to care for you. What mother wouldn't?"

Hattie made a choking sound. Mother and I looked at her and she waved us off with a hand and pointed at her teacup.

"Humph." Mother crossed her arms.

I gave Hattie a warning glance.

"Perhaps it's my fault." I leaned forward. "Last night you arrived home to an empty house, alarmed and confused regarding my whereabouts, especially since I haven't been well. And then I returned with someone you've never met, from a gathering I attended without your knowledge or consent. Please forgive me."

Mother's knitted brow smoothed.

"But I am so excited to have a new friend, Mother. Please be happy for me and don't allow my poor judgment to influence your opinion of Laura."

The quarter hour sounded and Mother looked at the clock. "Miss Towne is picking you up at eleven. If we're to pack a lunch basket, we'd better get a move on." She stood and pushed in her chair.

"Thank you, Mother."

"Finish your breakfast, Ellen. Your sister and I will manage."

"What?" Hattie said.

Mother began to load the empty tea tray. "I know there's cold chicken and peach pie; there may be some pound cake left over."

᠈᠊ ᠈᠊ ᠈᠊

Chapter 4

Ellen

I closed the front door behind me just as Laura pulled up in a two-wheel cart.

"Good morning, Ellen!" she called out. "A lovely day for a little outing."

"It sure is." and picnic basket in the back, climbed aboard.

"Where are we off to?" Laura asked.

"Would you like to see the harbor?"

"Perfect." Laura smiled. "I confess a fascination with water."

"Me too," I said. "As a child, I lived in New Brunswick, the British colony. My aunt and uncle own property on the St. John River, and we spent a great deal of time on the water."

I pointed in the direction the horse faced. "The harbor isn't too far. Veer left at the end of the street and carry on."

Laura picked up the reins and clicked her tongue. With ease, she maneuvered the cart out to the main road and into traffic.

"I must say, I'm impressed with your driving. Two-wheel carts require more skill than a wagon."

Laura chuckled. "An ability borne of necessity."

"Whoa." Laura slowed the cart as a coupe careened onto the street.

From the window, Lila Butler stared with eyes wide, her mouth an "O."

"Friend of yours?" Laura asked.

"An acquaintance." I chuckled. "Not the kind of gal to ride a cart."

Laura frowned. "I didn't want to inconvenience my hosts and request their wagon again."

I turned in my seat. "Oh my goodness, don't give it a thought. Lila's priorities are not mine."

Laura patted my hand, sending a curious shiver up the underside of my arm. I settled back and we drove on.

We arrived at the harbor and Laura pulled the cart near the water's edge where a selection of catboats, schooners, and small steamships were docked.

"Marvelous," Laura said and removed her bonnet. Closing her eyes, she took a long pull of salty air.

Still and silent, I admired her snub nose and lopsided smile. A puff of wind lifted the loose curls about her temples.

Not a beauty, but beautiful nonetheless.

Following suit, I slid off my bonnet and delighted in the briny breeze.

"Look." I pointed at the shoreline across the way. Amidst a hodgepodge of summer cottages stood a mansion. "I'm fond of the wrought iron widow's walk."

"Lovely," Laura said. "And what a view! Who lives there?"

"It's the summer home of Henry Anthony, our state senator, as far as I know."

"Exactly! There are scores of influential families in Newport," Laura said. "More so in the summer months. That's why I'm here, to sway people like your senator. I'm hoping politicians, industrialists, and businessmen will use their influence for good."

"Forgive my cynicism, but aren't those in politics or business driven by self-interest and profit?"

"You've hit the nail on the proverbial head." Laura's eyes sparkled. "Business and trade is tied to the Southern slave economy.

A gull squawked overhead, swooped down and landed on a moored sloop. Our cart horse raised his head and whinnied.

Laura picked up the reins. "Forgive me," she said, steering the cart back onto the road. "I'm passionate about the Negroes' plight."

"Don't apologize," I said. "I'm interested."

Smiling, Laura gave me a sideways glance. Beneath my breastbone, something fluttered.

"Oh, turn here," I said, putting a hand to my décolletage. "We can picnic at Gravelly Point. It's a good spot to view the lighthouse on Goat Island."

Laura made the turn. "You have me at an advantage, Ellen."

"I do?" I blinked at her.

"Yes," she said with a laugh in her voice. "I know you live with your mother and sister, Hattie, but little else."

I cleared my throat. "Well…I have another sister, Frances; she stays with our Uncle LB, in New Brunswick." I drew a breath. "Let's see…I adore novels and dabble at poetry; I love cats and music."

Laura glanced at my hands. "Do you play?"

"Yes." Following Laura's gaze, I splayed my fingers. "The piano. I'm grateful for it; music can inspire the most willful child. I'm a school teacher. My students bring me no end of joy, and trouble," I laughed.

"Teaching is an admirable profession," Laura said. "I don't have the patience or temperament for it."

At the Point, I set out our food. I wasn't hungry in the least, but to be polite I nibbled on a small square of pound cake and sipped lemonade. Laura, on the other hand, ate with gusto. After her fill of cold chicken and potato salad, I offered her some pie. She hesitated but then said, "Oh, why not!" and settled back, fork and plate in hand.

"You've never married?" Laura said between mouthfuls. "You're an attractive woman. I daresay there have been many a suitor." With the tines of her fork, she gathered stray bits of pastry.

"Gracious!" I said. "You are forthright."

"That I am." Laura laughed. "A character trait that's been called a blessing by some and a curse by others. You needn't answer."

With a chuckle, I said, "I'm inclined to agree with the former assessment." Pausing, I drew a breath. "The truth is, I've avoided any serious entanglements, as I have no desire to give up teaching." I closed my eyes and titled my face to the sun. "And you?" Holding my breath, I waited.

"Likewise. Marriage has never been an option for me," Laura said. "I value my independence and work far too much."

I searched her face. "I cannot tell you how good it feels talk to a like-minded woman." For a brief moment our eyes locked and I felt we were connected beyond words.

A gust of wind ruffled my hair and cooled my face.

She grinned. "Liberating, is it not?"

"Yes, I usually don't remove my bonnet." I smoothed my hair back.

"I mean us being here, together," her eyes glistened, "with a day of adventure and discovery before us." Laura took my hand and squeezed it.

My breath caught and for a moment I considered playing down her enthusiasm. But the warm, inviting hands holding mine bid me otherwise.

❧ ❧ ❧

By the time we had finished our picnic at Gravelly Point and completed a leisurely drive around the harbor, I knew God had answered my prayers and delivered a friend to whom I could relate: a soul mate. Her smile thrilled me, and her touch made me want to hold on and never let go.

Laura stopped the cart by my front door. "Come in for tea," I said. "I've had such an enjoyable time this afternoon, I don't want it to end. Not yet."

She loosened the reins. "I'd like nothing more, but I promised to visit a patient upon my return. My hosts' niece, I can't let them down."

"Patient?" I blurted.

Laura laughed. "We talked so much about 'The Cause' I suppose I forgot to mention that I am first and foremost a doctor."

"A medical doctor?"

"Yes, a homeopath, to be precise."

"What's the difference?" I asked.

"Simply put, allopaths focus on a specific organ or part when offering treatment, whereas homeopaths regard the body as one organism."

"Well!" I chuffed. "It never occurred to me that you had a profession besides abolitionist, but of course you must. Foolish of me not to inquire."

"Nonsense." She took my hands. A flush creeped up my neck. "We have so much to share and precious little time to do it." Laura stared down at our clasped hands. "I'd love to meet with you again before I leave. I have commitments tomorrow afternoon, but I'm free in the evening."

"In that case, please come for dinner," I said. "That'll give Mother plenty of time to fuss with the meal preparations."

Laura's brows lifted. "I don't want to impose."

"You won't," I laughed. "Mother loves any excuse to be in the kitchen. If we're lucky, she'll make her famous clam chowder."

ɜ☙ ɜ☙ ɜ☙

The next evening, over chowder in the dining room, Laura and I took turns telling Mother and Hattie about our outing the previous day. I mentioned Laura's medical training and Mother gave me a look of stunned amazement. From that point forward, though, her expression hardened into something inscrutable.

"Perhaps we should address you as doctor?" Mother asked.

Laura chuckled. "No, I prefer not to advertise my education."

"Oh...very well," Mother said.

"Ellen, you've barely touched your chowder," Mother said. "Are you unwell?"

Laura turned to me, brows gathered.

"Not at all." I spooned some of the thick, creamy broth and offered everyone a smile.

"When do you return to Philadelphia, Miss Towne?" Mother asked.

"I address a group of businessmen in the morning, and I'm booked on the afternoon train," Laura said.

The chowder curdled in my stomach.

"I see." Mother reached for the cornbread.

"I visited Newport earlier this year."

"When?" Hattie asked.

Laura dabbed her lips with a napkin. "I came a few months ago. April 12th, to be precise," Laura said, "when the first shots of the war between North and South were fired. President Lincoln called for volunteers and I vowed to do my part. Since then, I've sewn and sewn for the Union." She laughed. "But I confess, I despise stitchery and needlework of any sort."

"I do too!" I said.

"You appear flushed, Ellen," Mother interjected. "Are you certain you're well?"

"Yes, Mother. I'm perfectly fine."

I turned to my sister.

"Remember that day, Hattie? You and I heard the news during a shopping trip to town." I swiveled to Laura. "How silly, taking you to Gravelly Point when you've already been to Newport."

"Not at all," Laura said. "I never had a chance to view the waterfront on that visit. This trip has been especially gratifying. Aside from the excellent opportunities I've had to advance the antislavery cause, I made new friends." She smiled at Mother and Hattie, her final gaze landing on me.

With a tilt of her head, Mother acknowledged the compliment. "I imagine your doctoring and antislavery work offer many opportunities to meet new people and make friends."

"Acquaintances, certainly." Laura smiled. "Contacts for the cause, definitely. But true friends? No, Mrs. Murray, they are precious and few." Laura lifted her knife and cut some butter. "Don't you agree?"

"I do." Mother nodded.

"It's a shame you couldn't stay a bit longer," I said.

"I have commitments back home." Laura cleared her throat. "Perhaps you'd consider visiting me in Philadelphia, Ellen?"

"That would be wonderful." I leaned forward. "But classes start soon."

"What about Christmas?" Laura's eyes sparkled.

Wearing a thin smile, Mother rose from the table. "Time for cake and coffee. I'll be right back."

After serving up lemon cake, Mother poured the coffee. "Miss Towne," she said, moving from cup to cup. "What are your thoughts on this war dividing our country?"

Laura poured cream into her coffee and stirred. The spoon chimed against the china. "It's certainly a complex problem with no immediate end in sight."

"So you think it will continue for a while?" Mother asked.

"Yes." Laura nodded. "All told, eleven of our fifteen slave states have left the Union. The Confederacy is gaining momentum."

"Surely the Union is stronger," Hattie said.

Laura shrugged. "Perhaps. But overconfidence leads to failure. Our defeat at Bull Run this past spring, for example."

"What are you saying?" Mother poured her own coffee.

"That it isn't going to be easy. Or over swiftly," Laura said. "War hurts all of us. And it forces the issue."

"The issue of slavery—" Hattie said.

Mother cocked her head. "President Lincoln never sought to ban slavery in the South; only to contain it. He didn't want this war."

"You're right," Laura sat back. "But when slavery is threatened, so is the South's way of life."

Mother's brows shot up. "You feel they are right to defend it?"

"No, I believe slavery to be an evil institution and we are behind other nations in addressing it," Laura said. "But resistance is understandable; moral objections are easily dismissed when a way of life is threatened." Laura took a sip of coffee before continuing.

"Slavery drives the South's cotton-based economy. And by extension, the North's mercantile industry. Many Northerners also would like the antislavery genie put back in the bottle. To simply abolish slavery, without forethought, would mean economic suicide for the South and the North." She put down her coffee.

"I'm confused, Miss Towne." Mother toyed with the handle on her cup. "On one hand you're against slavery, on the other you sympathize with its supporters and acknowledge that its abolishment portends disaster."

"I'm saying we need an affordable, sustainable labor alternative for the South's cotton growers," Laura responded.

"That's all very well," Hattie said. "But who, if not the slaves, would do their work?"

"The same people who pick the cotton now," Laura said. "Set them free and then offer fair compensation for their labor."

Hattie huffed. "Why would those in charge pay for labor that is now free?"

"It's not free if you calculate the costs for the upkeep and care of people who do not want to work. Overseers must be hired, slaves—albeit poorly—must still be fed, dressed, and doctored."

Mother's expression remained neutral.

"And," Laura continued, "I daresay, production would go up, not down."

"What if some did not want to work? Or left the plantations to seek their fortune elsewhere?" Mother asked.

"Some will. But there are plenty of poor folks here in the North, White and Black, who, if paid a fair wage, would gladly take their place," Laura said.

The coffee cup's rim hid Mother's mouth. "You believe the Negroes capable of grasping this concept and managing their own affairs?"

A curious question coming from Mother. On our recent trip to New Brunswick, Uncle LB and my sister Fanny had expounded a view close to Laura's and Mother had agreed with them.

"I do," Laura said. "At least eventually. The fact is, they've had no chance to prove themselves. And how could they? They're intentionally held back; independence, for that matter, independent thinking, is discouraged at every turn. Like us, these are skills that must be taught."

Mother nodded. "Not all will believe this possible."

"We don't need *all*; to start, we only need *some*," Laura said.

Right then and there, I made up my mind: I would go to Philadelphia for Christmas.

ᥥ ᥥ ᥥ

At our front door, Laura thanked Mother for her hospitality and Hattie for her company. Laura and I walked in silence to the wagon. A cold dread filled my breast.

"Let's not say goodbye tonight." Laura held my hands. "My train leaves at four o'clock tomorrow afternoon. Meet me at the station." Then she slid her hands up my arms and pulled me to her.

Melting into her embrace, I whispered, "I'll be there."

ᥥ ᥥ ᥥ

The following afternoon Mother knocked at the door of my bedchamber. "A moment?"

"Of course." I glanced at the clock on my night table and put my hairbrush down on the vanity.

She closed the door and sat opposite me on the desk chair. Her lips were pressed together; stern lines bracketed her mouth.

She exhaled slowly, all the while staring at me.

My heart sped up. "What's wrong?"

"I love you, Ellen. I want what's best for you. And for you to be happy—"

Shaking my head, I turned my back.

"O Dear, I don't mean to upset you. Your new friend, Miss Towne. I like her. A great deal, if the truth be told. She's intelligent and compassionate—"

I pivoted around.

Mother smiled. "You look surprised?"

"No...well, yes...I mean, I agree. It's just I thought—"

"I'm not a fool, my dear. You are also a bright young woman. That you should desire a friend who is your equal, who espouses similar values, is understandable—"

"Still, you hesitate."

Mother nodded. For a moment she stared into the middle distance. She took a deep breath and focused her gaze on me. "You're enamored. It concerns me. Miss Towne is several years your senior, I'm sure—"

"Are you suggesting I can't think for myself? Why are you worried about our age difference? I don't see how that matters."

"You are an independent thinker, that's a fact. However, under the right circumstances we can all be swayed."

"Swayed? I still don't understand your objection."

"Ellen, I'm not objecting to your friendship with Miss Towne."

"I'm glad to hear it because—"

Mother stopped me with a hand. "It's *the way* you are taken by her. I'm concerned things will get out of hand. She's an accomplished woman. Being older, Miss Towne has experienced more of life. Likely she's had suitors. You, on the other hand, haven't any experience at all. I trusted that one day you'd meet a young man who would enthrall you—the way Miss Towne has. Perhaps it's that I still hope you'd wed, that you'd have a husband to look after you, a family to love—"

An image of my former piano teacher, Miss Post, popped into my head. I'm about twelve years old and we're in her parlor, both seated on the piano bench. The notes challenge me. She moves closer and leans in, closes her eyes and touches the keys.

Enchanting music spirals round me like a ribbon. A summer breeze floats in through an open window and the scent of lavender dances to the tune. My breath catches and my throat tightens—

"Ellen?"

I blinked. "Yes?"

"I sense your life heading in a direction that concerns me." She threw up her hands.

I grabbed hold and stilled them. "Mother, I do not want a husband."

Eyes shimmering, she nodded, but did not let go.

🍂 🍂 🍂

My talk with Mother had lasted longer than time permitted. I rushed into the train station, anxious and breathless. Would I make it before Laura's train departed?

I hurried onto the platform where the carriage doors stood open. Travelers were already queued up and filing in. It took me a moment to find Laura. She looked dignified in a plum-colored skirt, crisp, snowy shirtwaist and jaunty hat that sported a feather. Turning in my direction, she pressed a palm to her heart and grinned.

I reached her and she blurted, "I'm so glad you're here."

"Surely you never doubted me?" I took hold of her hands.

"I confess it difficult to leave you."

I smiled; I couldn't help myself.

Laura chuckled. "You find my distress amusing?"

"Of course not," I laughed outright. "It's only that I feel the same way." I released Laura's hands and embraced her. I lingered, trying to memorize her scent, her touch, the way she felt against my body.

The train's whistle blew and we drew apart.

Tears glistened in Laura's eyes.

"We'll write," I tried to sound upbeat. "And by Christmas we'll be together again."

"Yes, together." Laura lifted her suitcase.

We made our way over to the carriage door in silence. A young man took Laura's luggage. She disappeared into the cabin. I stepped back to scan the windows. A minute later, three cars down the line, her feathered hat appeared at the window. The train lurched, rolled, and chugged forward. I fixed my gaze on her face coming closer, closer. Our eyes locked and the tips of my fingers tingled. For some time after the engine's smoke cleared and the train had disappeared, I remained on the platform, hand raised, heart aching.

ба ба ба

Chapter 5

Henrietta

The whistle sounds, but rather than receding along with the train, it grows more piercing. Youthful Miss Ellen vanishes, along with the station platform. The whistle continues to scream and I feel as though my head will explode.

"Henrietta…Henrietta—"

Silence snaps, sudden and thick as fog.

My eyes fly open.

Maum Cat stands before me, holding Miss Ellen's journal.

Blinking, I place a hand to my hammering heart. "Goodness gracious, Maum! You can't just pull me away like that."

"You find her? You see Miss Ellen?"

"Yes!" I huff. "But if I'm going to do this you have to let me drift in and out of the visions at my own pace."

"You didn't answer when I call out," says she. Her chin wobbles.

"Ah." I soften my voice. "Did I alarm you?"

She sets the journal down and hobbles back to her swing. Wiggling on, she struggles to fix the blanket.

"You wanted me to use my gift." I walk over and tuck her in. "Remember?"

Maum pulls the covers up to her chin. "Be careful."

"I will. Promise." I smile down at her. "In the meantime, you get some rest."

Settled once more in my chair, I open the journal on my lap and find the spot where I left off. Taking a breath, I place my fingertips on the date Miss Ellen has inscribed. In the space of a heartbeat, I am transported back to Newport, December 1861.

᠉ ᠉ ᠉

Chapter 6

Ellen

After class dismissal, I slumped into the chair at my desk and cradled my throbbing head. A tower of unmarked compositions sat to one side, a smaller stack of reviewed papers on the other. Something low in my throat clawed. Swallowing, I drew my fingertips down the length of my neck.

Please God, I don't want to be sick. Not now, with my Christmas trip to Philadelphia only days away.

If I even alluded to a sore throat, Mother would withdraw her permission that I visit Laura. Sitting straighter, I considered the time it would take to mark the remaining papers. Too long. I'd finish up at home and reward myself afterwards by rereading some of Laura's letters.

Rain, sleet, and snow trailed me home. Shutting out a gust of wind, I clomped into the foyer. Mother rushed in from the kitchen. "I've kept an eye out for you," she said.

I tried to smile, but the corners of my mouth wouldn't cooperate.

"Never mind. You're home now. Here, give me your hat." Mother walked closer. "And I'll take that cloak."

I shrugged the sodden garment from my shoulders and handed it over. Mother shook off the snow. The reek of wet wool filled the small space and soured my stomach.

She hung my cloak on a hook. "Are you okay?" she asked, glancing back. "Your face is blotchy."

"Mmhm," I said, "I've a headache from marking papers."

"Go on then," Mother said. "Take your satchel upstairs while I brew some willow bark tea." She gave my arm a squeeze and then scooted off.

Minutes later, I sat by the hearth, sipping tea. Curled up in the chair opposite, Hattie buried her nose in a book.

"Can I get you something?" Mother asked. "I've prepared a beef stew, but it won't be ready for a while."

The mention of meat inflamed my nausea. Swallowing, I shook my head. "No, thank you."

"I hope this headache isn't a sign you're getting sick again." Mother trained her eyes on me. "Your chest might still be weak from that bout in the spring."

Hattie looked up from her reading. "Any other symptoms?"

I suppressed a cough. "I told you, my head hurts."

"You *are* flushed." Scowling, Mother moved closer.

Fearing Mother would put a palm to my brow, I got up.

"I'll take my tea to my room," I said. "And grade some papers before supper."

ta ta ta

At the top of the stairs I stopped until my breath calmed. I then shuffled along the hall to my bedchamber. Closing the door, I walked past my satchel on the desk, straight to my bed, and put my teacup on the night table. Shivering, I climbed under the top quilt and sank into the mattress. Tears pricked my eyes. If I got ill again, I couldn't travel to Philadelphia for Christmas. Laura's precious letters offered comfort and hope. But I needed to hold her again.

Tears spilled down my cheeks. Sniffing, I leaned over and lifted a handkerchief from the table drawer and dabbed my face. Then I took out the stashed, ribbon-bound packet of letters and eased back onto my pillow. Every night before going to sleep, I re-read at least one. All her letters buoyed my spirits, but none more so than the first.

> *Philadelphia, Pennsylvania*
> *September, 1861*
>
> *My dearest Ellen,*
>
> *Thank you for your lovely letter. I was so heartened to receive it. I confess, on the train ride home, my heart grew heavier with each passing town, knowing I was drawing farther and farther from you…*

As did mine…

> *...By way of distraction, I left the car and took a stroll down the corridor. There I encountered a man who recognized me, a banker from Philadelphia. He explained he had been at the luncheon meeting where I'd spoken before our departure.*
>
> *Unfortunately, he'd been called away before my speech and asked if we might chat presently. Happy for a diversion, I agreed.*
>
> *He immediately stated he believed the framework of American society rested upon class distinction and that slavery's abolishment would bring social and economic chaos, leading to lawlessness and the end of democracy.*
>
> *"Think of a beautiful building, Miss Towne," he'd said, "an architectural delight, if you will. At its base is a plain, serviceable foundation, remove it and the entire structure collapses."*

I stopped for a moment to rest my burning eyes and took a long drink of tea. Despite having read this exchange numerous times, Laura's gumption and her willingness to share with me heartened my spirits

> *...And yet, Ellen, behind this man's bravado I sensed unease. And so I countered his justification with a moral argument. Back and forth we went, from the biblical view of slavery to today's powerful and corrupt slaveholder; from the perpetual state of fear and instability in which the South now finds itself: masters fearing slaves, slaves fearing masters to the viability of free labor. In the end, we parted on friendly terms, but I do not know if he was convinced. For me, however, our meeting and exchange had been just what I needed: A reminder of my purpose.*

I clutched the letter to my chest. For the umpteenth time, I thanked the Lord for bringing me Laura, a woman of substance. Smoothing out the page, I resumed reading.

> My family asked about my impression of Newport. I explained that generally, when I spoke, about half of the people listened; a portion of those folks already entertained abolitionist views. The other half disagreed and believed slavery necessary; a small percentage of these folks were outright hostile. My brother, Will, bless him, worries for my safety. My sister, Lucy, who runs our household, does not understand why I am so driven. In truth, Ellen, I do not know why either; only that I am.
>
> I told them of our serendipitous meeting and of your possible visit at Christmastime. I pray your mother will agree for you to come. This pleasant thought I will take with me now, to bed, and dream of your visit.
>
> Affectionately yours,
> Laura

"Affectionately mine," I whispered. Tucking the letter in with the others, I laid back and closed my eyes. *Just a few minutes—*

≈ ≈ ≈

"My dear, can you hear me?" Mother asked.

What an odd question. I attempted to open my eyes, but failed. I tried to speak, to tell Mother I was fine; no need to raise the alarm, but the adhesive that had fused my lids also fastened my lips. My heart raced and I endeavored to sit up, but a tremendous force tethered me to the mattress.

"Calm yourself, Ellen." Mother's hand smoothed my brow.

"Hattie, fetch a cloth and a bowl of cool water, hurry."

Now a voice. Hattie is reading. I reached to understand the jumble of words, but the tangled snippets faded and disappeared.

I stopped struggling and floated until another voice filtered into my mind.

≈ ≈ ≈

Mockingbird Diary of St. Helena Island

"I'm sure you've heard about the Battle of Port Royal in South Carolina on November 7. The Union Army took Beaufort and the Sea Islands. Apparently, Beaufort is like a ghost town. The majority of White plantation owners fled inland and left everything behind, including their slaves. Most of them are on the islands where the cotton grows. Can you imagine, Ellen! Thousands of slaves are now free. But are they?"

Laura?

I yearn to respond, but I cannot resist the fatigue that consumes me.

A salty breeze cools my face, tendrils of hair brush my cheek, water laps my bare feet; farther off, the roar of waves breaking. But this is not the familiar shore of Newport.

Where am I?

I look down and discover I am wearing a nightgown. A gust of wind ruffles my hem. Confused, I turn left, and then right. Giant shadow trees lurk. Draped upon their branches clinging vines droop like peeled skin. Gooseflesh ripples my body; my teeth chatter. Tidewater pulls at my feet.

And then behind, someone cries my name. I turn and face a clapboard house bathed in moonlight.

A woman rushes down the porch steps—

ཀ ཀ ཀ

With a gasp, I opened my eyes and blinked at the bright light. My room. Only a dream.

I shielded my face from the dazzle of sunlight, and judge the time to be late morning or early afternoon. From outside, harness bells jangled, a horse whinnied; muffled voices drifted from downstairs. I pulled back the bedclothes, and leaning over noticed a makeshift cot on the floor beside my bed. How odd. Did Mother keep vigil?

The windows, the walls, even my desk, tilted and teetered. Bile rose in my throat. Squeezing my eyes shut, I lay back on my pillow.

Scuffling steps echoed in the stairwell. Bella landed on my bed with a *thrump* and *meow*.

"Come back here, you naughty girl," Mother called out.

Purring, Bella settled on the pillow and commenced kneading my scalp.

I opened one eye, then the other. No spinning walls or wobbling furniture.

"Shoo, Bella!" I untangled the cat's paws from my hair and nudged her off the mattress.

Mother entered, followed by Hattie. I fluffed the blankets and pulled myself up against the headboard.

"My goodness, you're awake!" Mother's eyes filled with tears. "I left for but a moment!"

Hattie clapped her hands. Laura appeared at the door, as though conjured by the sound.

I looked from Mother to Hattie. Did they also see her?

"It's about time you woke up!" Laura grinned. "You gave us all a fright."

"You certainly did!" Mother said.

Hattie smiled at Laura.

"You're here," I said to Laura and then looked to Mother and Hattie. "How...why?"

All three drew close to my bed. Laura sat on the edge. Each of them took turns answering my questions and explaining the days of my feverish departure. After I had gone to bed feeling unwell, Mother had checked in and discovered me burning up with fever. Unable to rouse me, she tried to bring my temperature down. Her efforts failed and she called for the doctor, who diagnosed influenza compounded by pneumonia. Nature, he said, would take its course. Mother and Hattie alternated nursing duties, but nothing took hold. Aware of Laura's healing skills, Hattie took it upon herself to send her a telegram and request help.

"And thank goodness she had the presence of mind to do so." Mother reached for Hattie's hand.

"Laura hopped on the first available train," Hattie said.

"You mean to tell me I've been unconscious for days?" I glanced from Hattie to Mother.

They both nodded.

I looked at Laura. "How long have you been here?"

"Three days," she said.

"Laura brought down your fever. I couldn't." Mother reached over and put a hand on Laura's back. "I don't know what we'd have done without her."

Laura smiled at Mother. "Let's try some broth, shall we?"

After Mother and Hattie left the room, Laura walked over to the dresser, poured some water into the washbasin. Taking a fresh cloth from a stack, she rinsed it out and returned to her position beside me on the bed.

She held out the washcloth. "May I?"

I nodded my consent and Laura placed the cool cloth across my brow and down my cheeks. Gooseflesh rose on my arms.

"My, my," I said. "Mother has taken to you."

Drawing the cloth down my neck, Laura loosened the drawstring on my nightgown. "Yes, oft times troubles have a way of pulling family together."

"Is that how you think of us?" My pulse quickened as Laura pressed the washcloth to my clavicles, and then circled around to the base of my scalp.

"I suppose, I do." Laura chuckled. "I hope that's all right by you?"

I took her free hand and held it to my cheek. "More than all right."

Laura stood at the washstand when Mother returned with a tray holding a fragrant bowl of chicken broth. She placed it on my desk. "I'll be back in a bit," she said and closed the door behind her.

Laura retrieved the tray and returned to her spot beside me on the bed. I immediately reached for the bowl.

"Absolutely not." Laura grabbed my wrist. "You're as weak as a kitten." Lifting the bowl and spoon, she said, "Open up."

I laughed. "Yes, ma'am."

"Just a small amount now, and more later. Tomorrow we'll try some solids," Laura said.

"I still can't believe I lay here insensible all that time."

"Neither can I," Laura frowned. "That stubborn fever just wouldn't break. You slept straight through Christmas!"

"Oh no," I pulled away from the stack of pillows at my back. "I ruined the holidays for everyone."

"Nonsense," Laura dipped the spoon into the broth. "Come now, have some more."

I relaxed back into the pillows and sipped the soup Laura offered. "To me it felt like a night's sleep—a solid one, except for odd dreams."

Brows raised, Laura held out another spoonful of broth.

I swallowed. "And voices. Hattie, and sometimes Mother. And then I thought I heard you. I wanted to wake up, but I couldn't."

Laura handed me a napkin.

"Poor Mother, she must have been frantic." I dabbed my lips.

"I'm just grateful Hattie asked for my help." Laura set the bowl aside.

"So am I..."

"I sense a hesitation," she said.

"No! I'm thrilled you're here." I shrugged. "But now I'm awake, you'll be leaving."

"Certainly not," Laura said. "I plan on nursing you back to good health."

"But what about your antislavery work?" I asked. "And your commitment to help the Union Army?"

"Whether I'm in Philadelphia or Newport, I can do my bit," Laura said. "In fact, I've already taken on some of the Army's sewing."

"Sewing?" I giggled.

Laura's eyebrows shot up. "What?"

"You hate needlework."

"I do," Laura shrugged, "but I want to help and that's what's needed."

"But your medical practice, surely—"

Laura stood and picked up the soup bowl. "I'd say I'm putting it to good use right now."

☙ ☙ ☙

Chapter 7

Ellen

Having spent the better part of January convalescing, I now managed small stints in the classroom alongside the substitute teacher. Today, I graded papers in the parlor while Laura put the finishing touches on yet another soldier's shirt. Smiling, she folded the garment and put it onto the completed lot.

After my fever had broken, I insisted Laura abandon the pallet on the floor and share my bed. Hands entwined, we talked. If Laura fell asleep first, I often lay awake, studying her face, the tilt of her nose, the curve of her cheek. I desired to memorize and hold on to her. Drawing closer still, I'd shut my eyes and, cocooned in the delicate scent of her lavender soap, drift off.

Mother walked into the parlor with a full tea tray and interrupted my reverie. Hattie followed her, mail in hand.

"One for you," she chirped, and dropped an envelope on the table beside Laura.

Stomach churning, I stared at the letter. Would this be the one that called her home to Philadelphia?

"Tea! You read my mind." Laura turned to me. "What about you, dear?"

"Yes, please," I said, my voice thick.

Frowning, Laura took the filled cup from Mother. "Is something wrong?" she asked me.

"You must stop spoiling me." I pushed aside the papers I was grading. "How will I ever manage after you're gone?"

"You're leaving?" Mother looked from me to Laura.

"But why?" Hattie asked.

Laura passed me a cup of tea. "I wasn't planning to go anywhere." Her voice rose at the end, turning her statement into a question.

Mother narrowed her eyes. "Ellen?"

I stirred my tea. The chime filled the pause. "I'm gaining strength every day." I sipped tea, head bowed over my cup.

"Soon there'll be no reason for you to stay," I added.

Hattie doled out the biscuits in silence. After a few minutes, Laura set her half-finished cup down and opened the letter.

I drank my tea as Laura read for a few minutes, her expression neutral. With a sniff, she folded the letter, returned it to its envelope and tucked it in her pocket.

I put down my cup. "Anything important?"

"An update from the Freedman's Society in Philadelphia." Laura stood then and, picking up the teapot, refilled everyone's cup and offered more biscuits.

Mother and Hattie chatted with Laura about their sewing. I stared at the pocket containing the letter. Normally, Laura loved to expound on these communications. Why not a word this time?

Laura drained her tea. "My turn to tidy up."

While she collected the empty teacups and saucers, I searched her face, but saw nothing out of the ordinary.

ea ea ea

That evening alone in our room, Laura's eyes shone with excitement. "Close the door," she whispered.

At the click of the snib, she took the letter from her pocket and danced a jig.

I laughed. "Good news?"

"Oh, Ellen! Exciting news to be sure! And an invitation."

I plopped down on the bed. "Go on."

Laura sat opposite, on the desk chair. "Do you recall the Battle of Port Royal in South Carolina last November, when the Union Army captured Beaufort and the Sea Islands?"

I nodded.

"Most of the White landowners deserted, leaving all their belongings—including their slaves." She frowned at the letter and then at me. "Can you imagine? These people are contraband of war! A kind of limbo—not free, but without the means to feed or clothe themselves."

I cringed. "How awful." It dawned on me that Laura's missive from the Freedmen's Society contained more than just an update. "What's to be done, then?"

"The gentlemen affiliated with the American Missionary Association met with President Lincoln. He gave permission to visit the area and assess the situation. That trip resulted in the Port Royal project. The goal is to prepare the Negroes for life as free citizens." Laura glanced from the letter to me. Her eyes glistened. "Don't you see, Ellen? This project is an opportunity to prove that Negroes will labor for a wage, not just the whip." She leaned forward. "I've been invited to be part of a corps of Christian missionaries responsible for distributing food and clothing; to establish and staff schools. What an opportunity!"

"Establish schools? You mean from the ground up?" I spoke around the lump clogging my throat.

"Of course," Laura said. "Nothing exists presently."

"But you're not a teacher."

"These are desperate times, Ellen." Laura shrugged. "The anti-literacy laws prevented enslaved people from learning to read or write. I should be able to manage the fundamentals, and I'm certainly able to dole out supplies."

"I didn't know an actual *law* existed."

"Absolutely. Knowledge is power," Laura said.

I cleared my throat again. "You're considering going then?"

"Would you come with me?" Laura's voice softened. "Imagine establishing your own school! You'd be hard pressed to do that here in the North; at least not without raising considerable funds."

"Go with you?" My heart hammered against my rib cage.

"I've already given it some thought." Laura's eyes shone. "I'll be leaving near the end of March or beginning of April. You can join me when the school year finishes and your contract is fulfilled. By then you'll have regained your strength." She shrugged. "It will likely take that long for the Relief Committee to approve and arrange your passage."

She joined me on the bed and took my hand. "Please say yes. I should be weak without you. We'll be strong together."

I nodded and looked down at my lap. *Breath in, breath out—*

I loved my mother and sister, and my teaching position and students, but my life had been otherwise unremarkable, until Laura. The thought of helping children learn to read and write who'd been denied the opportunity appealed to me. I possessed the skills. This was my chance to make a positive difference in their lives. And mine.

"Will you come?" Laura asked again, her brows crimped.

"I'd have to speak to Mother, and resign from my teaching position," I said as my thoughts darted from one scenario to another: Mother approving; Mother denying permission. Leaving my students or staying the course? Moving to a strange place with unknown dangers. Could I bear it?

"Yes—" I blurted.

Laura threw her arms around me. "I was so worried you'd say no." Laura released me; her eyes shone. "Why did you say those things earlier? Dear Ellen, did you really believe I'd leave you, that I'd allow us to be parted?"

"I suppose. I have no hold on you."

"Is that so?" Laura lifted my hand, kissed it and then held it to her breast. A steady beat thrummed through my fingers, up the length of my arm to my own heart. Soon my pulse slowed and joined Laura's unwavering rhythm.

&a. &a. &a.

The weeks leading up to Laura's journey were challenging for me. One minute I could hardly wait for our future to begin, excited by the teaching opportunities that awaited me. The next moment, I was forlorn at facing the months ahead and waiting my turn alone. By April's onset, alternating joy and dread consumed me. The night before Laura's dawn departure, we retired early. I snuggled down under the covers while Laura checked and double-checked her traveling clothes.

"Come to bed." I threw back the blankets and patted the mattress.

Laura nodded, but continued to stare at the ensemble laid out for the morning.

"Are you all right?" I asked.

Laura picked nonexistent fluff off of her flannel nightdress. "Of course."

"Are you having second thoughts?"

Laura climbed into bed, adjusted her pillow, stretched out. "No."

The lavender-tinged scent of her skin washed over me. A now-familiar hum fluttered low in my belly. I rolled onto my side. "Not exactly an adamant denial."

Laura chuckled and turned to face me. She smoothed the hair from my face, drew the tips of her fingers across the curve of my neck. I wriggled closer.

"You are trying to distract me." I caught hold of her hand.

She turned onto her back. "I'm scared. There you have it. I'm always blustering on about standing up for what we believe, but my knees are weak."

I turned her face to mine. "Only a fool wouldn't be frightened."

Laura's brow creased. "I suppose."

"What frightens you the most?"

"All of it." She sighed. "That I won't be up to the task; that I'll find the climate too hot, too wet, too cold; that the people will be unmanageable; that I'll get sick. But mostly," she said, "that I'll be lonely without you. That your mother won't grant her permission."

"Leave Mother to me." I caressed Laura's cheek.

"It's been weeks now and your mother hasn't agreed," Laura said.

"She will. Trust me." I held her gaze. "This separation is but a moment in time. Before you know it, I'll be in South Carolina, pestering you!"

Laura's eyes glistened with unshed tears, but she smiled.

"That's better." I straightened the blankets around us. "Now, I want you to tell me all that you're looking forward to, your hopes for the people of St. Helena, and for us."

Laura spoke of our future amongst the freedmen of St. Helena, and the clipped pitch of her speech softened. Eventually, the words dissolved and I drifted off to the cadence of her voice.

※ ※ ※

"Wake up, dear. It's nearly time to go."

I blinked and looked around. Light from the chamberstick cast Laura's shadow on the wall. I pulled myself up against the headboard. "You're dressed."

"I couldn't sleep."

I threw my legs over the edge of the mattress.

"The driver will be here soon." Laura turned to the mirror and adjusted her hatpin.

A tornado of longing threatened to carry me off. I clutched the mattress edge and swallowed.

She turned around. "Will you walk out with me?"

"Of course." I brushed away the cobwebs of sleep and pulled my skirt on over my nightdress, pulled on my stockings, and stepped into my shoes. No jacket required. My shawl hung on a hook downstairs. I finished the last button at my waist and looked up to find Laura staring at me.

"Is something wrong?"

Shoulders hunched, she laughed without mirth. "How will I manage without you?" She covered her face and sobbed.

I bridged the space between us, and pulled her to me. "You will manage just fine." I waited until she collected herself. "You are doing this not only for The Cause, but for us; that we might have a life of purpose, together. Focus on that."

Taking a stilted breath, she nodded and lifted her handkerchief from the dressing table to dab her eyes.

I caressed her shoulders and rubbed her upper arms. "Before you know it, we'll be together again. Forever."

The clop of horse hooves and rumble of carriage wheels reverberated from the street.

Laura pulled away and reached for her bag. "Let's go."

I grabbed her wrist, and drew her to me. "Not yet."

Laura stood before me, her brows furrowed. I cupped her cheeks, tilting her chin. Crystal tears glazed her lashes. My heart fluttered, but I hesitated. The urge to memorize her features overrode my desire. Her breath quickened and I leaned in. Soft, full lips met mine with equal intensity. Seconds passed before I could bring myself to pull away.

Breathless, I dropped my hands to her waist, and pressed my forehead to hers. "It's time."

"Yes, it is," she said, her voice flat.

Hoisting the strap of her bag onto her shoulder she said, "Come, Ellen Murray. I refuse to commence this journey without you by my side."

The rising sun streaked the sky pink and blue. I helped Laura into the carriage as the driver secured her luggage. Seated, she touched my face with her fingertips.

"Right, that's everything loaded." The driver climbed aboard and took the reins.

I caught Laura's hand before it slipped away, and kissed the tender spot where her wrist and palm met. Closing the carriage door, I took a step back and gulped air.

The driver made some clucking sounds and the carriage lurched into motion.

Shadowed in dawn's light, Laura leaned out of the window and mouthed, "I love you."

A chill skittered down my spine, freezing me to the spot.

Nothing else mattered. Not this time apart, nor the wait. Not the hardships we may or may not encounter.

Raising my hand, I mouthed back, "I love you more."

୬ ୬ ୬

After several false starts due to paperwork and poor weather, my June departure date for South Carolina arrived. Creamy sunshine and birdsong streamed in through billowed curtains; a good omen. I closed my suitcase and buckled the straps. My trunk, packed and ready for weeks, sat downstairs by the door.

I left my heavy suitcase on the bed for the carriage driver to lug downstairs. I still needed to put Laura's letters in my handbag. They kept Laura close, but they also provided the benefit of her experience.

I lifted April's letters, bound in a yellow ribbon. At the time I'd chosen the color of springtime daffodils to represent our new beginning. Now the bright ribbon reminded me I must not back down, but face what lay ahead with the same courage Laura had demonstrated. I fanned the edges and recalled her arrival in Beaufort, now occupied by the Union Army. She and her two female traveling companions had spent the first few days in town before venturing on to their headquarters and final destination: The Oaks Plantation on St. Helena Island.

I buried the April letters in my handbag and picked up the next batch of May's, bound in green ribbon. Lifting the packet to my nose, I closed my eyes and imagined they held the briny scent of St. Helena. Although I longed to go to The Oaks Plantation, I did fret about the disturbing things Laura related and the many people with whom I'd be required to interact.

The plantation house was split, figuratively and literally, down the middle, between Laura's relief committee, "Gideon's Band,"

and the cotton agent assigned to oversee the 500-acre plantation. The cotton agent prioritized crops, whereas Gideon's Band and The Oaks' superintendent, Mr. Ward Pierce, focused on the well-being of the freedmen.

I picked up Laura's latest missive, still on my desk. This letter explained how these competing interests had erupted in a showdown on Hilton Head Island. Mr. Pierce was there to express his concerns to the military general and encountered the angry cotton agent's assistant at the dock. Unfolding the letter, I ran my fingers over Laura's words.

> ...Oh, dear Ellen, I can heal poor Mr. Pierce's physical wounds, but I fear his spirit is defeated and he has resigned his post. I am so disappointed. Yet, I cannot blame him.
>
> Rather than remove the offending cotton agents and put Mr. Pierce in charge, the plantations have been reorganized. Each will have their own superintendent.
>
> All will report to a man named General Rufus Saxton. Rumor has it he is sympathetic to the freedmen's plight. I hope this is true.
>
> I pray you come soon for I feel my resolve weakening. I need your support and companionship more than ever...

I re-folded the letter and shoved it back into the envelope.

Bella, curled up on my pillow, meowed.

My throat constricted and I went to her. "You're safer here, little one." I petted her soft coat. "Hattie promised to take care of you."

Bella meowed again and jumped off the bed.

I glanced around my room and considered that perhaps I, too, would be safer within these four walls. Yet security without Laura amounted to a prison.

I stuffed the last of Laura's letters into my handbag and followed Bella out the door.

ða ða ða

Chapter 8

Henrietta

Lifting my hand from the first volume, the animated vision of Miss Ellen's past recedes. I draw several deep breaths and open my eyes. The porch is now shrouded in darkness. Thoughts and images of Miss Ellen's kitty, Bella, linger, like the afterglow of a dream. I glance at Maum Cat who remains stretched out on the porch swing, sound asleep. Rather than purr, Maum snores.

I knew my mothers met at the Meeting House in Newport, Rhode Island, where Miss Laura spoke on the abolitionist movement. But that's all. I am touched by Miss Ellen's reaction, to learn of their immediate and intense attraction. Certainly, neither of them spoke of their love for each other. Their bond shone through in how they treated one another, with respect and love. Which makes sense. They lived by James 2:17, "Faith without works is dead." They believed in doing for others and instilled those principles in me and Fountain. *Feelings* aren't something I associate with them.

As a child I never questioned their relationship. If anyone else did, I never got wind of it. Small-town folks are considered terrible gossips; island folks are even worse, I'd wager. Yet Miss Ellen and Miss Laura sashayed all around these parts without a whiff of controversy. Quite the opposite, in fact! Their approval was sought. Even by those who held different ideas about Black education. Like the Reverend Doctor Frissell who spoke today at Miss Ellen's funeral. Folks saw them first and foremost for what they were: relentless advocates for St. Helena's Black community.

To learn that Grandmother questioned their union surprised me. She certainly came around because I never saw any evidence of her disapproval. Quite the contrary. I suppose you never know what's buried in the past.

Thinking, I look down at the remaining diaries on the table beside me. I place my fingertips on the next one's binding. A current darts up my arm and pierces my heart. Are Miss Ellen's secrets calling me?

At that thought, I shiver. The next instant my teeth chatter. I look at Maum, covered in the one skimpy quilt. I recall that Miss Ellen stored a slew of them in the hallway cedar chest. Figuring it's going to be a long, cool night, I step into the house to brew a pot of tea and fetch warm blankets.

After choosing a couple of thick quilts and a knitted afghan for Maum and me, I look up and notice the old picture portrait on the wall above the chest. I don't recall the last time I really looked at it. It's of Miss Ellen and two Penn students—or scholars, as she referred to them. She's still in her twenties, I'd guess. And beautiful, in a wholesome kind of way. She wears a severe pillbox hat, but her hair is pulled back and a mess of ringlets rest on one shoulder. It must be winter because she wears a woolen jacket over a blouse with a big bow tied at the neck. A book sits open on her lap and she points to something on the page for the seated girls. Miss Ellen told me the older one was Puss, and that until she met me, Puss had been her favorite. I wonder whatever happened to her.

Arranging the blankets over one arm, I carry the tea tray to the porch.

Outside, a fat buttery moon shines, and a hail of stars splatter the indigo sky. I tuck the second quilt around Maum Cat. She grunts, rolls over, covers her head, and is snoring again by the time I am seated and wrapped in the wooly afghan. The wind howls and whistles. At the shore, waves crash and roar in retreat. A king tide may wash in with the full moon. Tree frogs join the chorus, with their high-pitched *purrreeeek*. From the pines, a great horned owl stutters, *hoo-h HOO-hoo-hoo*. Years ago, Miss Ellen helped me identify that call mimicking the sound with, *Who Cooks for You?*

It's a wonder I can hear myself think above the din. Yet my surroundings recede as I sip hot tea and consider that about the time my mothers came to St. Helena, I, too, had arrived, but under different circumstances. Unlike them, I didn't choose St. Helena as my home. It chose me.

Maum Cat stirs briefly as my thoughts travel back in time.

Those long-ago days are a jumble. A few details and people I remember; the rest is hazy. It's like trying to pin down a wily dream. Just when you think you have captured it, the memories scurry off to the locked parts of your mind. I am haunted by what I do not know. I *do* know that I left Beaufort sometime after the Big Gun Shoot in 1861, when the Union Army came and all the rich White folks ran for their lives. They say some of them left hot food half-eaten on their dining tables.

One thing I am most certain of is this: My jaw hurt and I couldn't talk. For a long time after, even when it healed up enough and speaking was possible, every time I tried to utter a word my stomach roiled and I'd throw up. That made the pain even worse and the healing time longer. So I stayed silent. Maum Cat got me speaking again, at least some. I clung to silence the way some toddlers cling to a blanket or doll. Maum guessed I was six years old when she brought me here from Beaufort. She gave me a birthday too, November 21. Years later, Maum Cat's daughter, Manners, told me Maum set my birthday for the day she brought me to St. Helena. Can't argue with that logic, I suppose.

First I went to live with Manners and her family. With that brood, I suppose she figured one more wouldn't much matter. Since Maum lived in the next cabin, I spent the better part of most days with her. Clinging to Maum became as natural as being speechless. After the fire that razed both Manners and Maum's cabins, Miss Ellen took me in. Several other folks on the island sheltered Manners and her children until they rebuilt. As for Maum Cat, she's been wandering ever since.

I'm ashamed to say I haven't given Manners a thought in quite some time. She's been dead going on ten years. Sad how we let the memory of those we love fade. Could be that's why folks say *passed away*. With each day that passes the dead get pushed further and further to the back of your mind. Unlike her daughter, Maum Cat appears eternal. She might be the oldest person on St. Helena. I tease her sometimes, asking how many of those nine lives of hers she's got left.

Like she knows I'm thinking about her, Maum snort-snores and scuttles farther down under the quilts. Gulping the remainder of my tea, I place the cup on the tray. I close my eyes, lift the next journal onto my lap and open it. The moment I touch the page, a sudden rush of the cool evening air swirls and grows increasingly warm. A steam whistle blasts and my eyes fly open. The back porch, my chair, and Maum have all vanished. I now stand on the deck of a docked steamer, facing a familiar shoreline.

ᔆ ᔆ ᔆ

Chapter 9

Ellen

Our steamer docked at Hilton Head Island in South Carolina. Clinging to the deck rail I looked out upon a jungle of palmettos, pines, and scrub that snaked the shoreline and beyond. My heart drummed and I struggled to breathe. Perspiration tickled my scalp and trickled between my breasts, yet my mouth was as dry as the coveted Sea Island cotton. I made a mental note of the date: June 8, 1862, that I might record my first impressions later, and said goodbye to the crew on deck. With sea legs and trepidation, I gripped the ropes on either side of the sagging gangplank onto Hilton Head Island.

As though God wished to underscore my anxiety, the moment my feet touched solid ground a great crack of thunder sounded. Everyone on the dock stopped and looked skyward.

A passing sailor slowed. "Nothing to worry about, ma'am. Thunderstorms are common in these parts. They gots lots of bark and no bite." He smiled and carried on.

I took a big breath, a step forward, and stuffed my anxiety into a locked box with no intention of releasing it anytime soon.

Minutes later, boatmen sent from The Oaks arrived to collect my belongings from the wharf. I would travel separately. The men rowed off, singing a pretty refrain, *"De bels done rung, an' we goin' home…"*

Their spiritual encouraged me. In one short boat ride, from Hilton Head to St. Helena Island, I would be at my new home and reunited with Laura. I didn't have to wait long. Soon after, I boarded a small vessel and looked ahead over the water toward my new home.

Approaching St. Helena, I recognized the shoreline from the description Laura shared in her letters. A strip of land jutted out into the ocean like a crooked crone's finger. Soldiers' tents dotted the sandy peninsula, and gangly palmettos, like the ones on Hilton Head, ran hither and thither amongst them.

The moment I set foot on dry land, a Black man stepped forward.

"Miz Ellen?" he said. "Miz Laura send me to fetch you." He took off his wide-brimmed hat and held it against his chest. "Folks call me Hastings."

After begging Mother's permission to come, the lengthy separation, and paperwork postponements, Laura and I would shortly be together again. I wanted to squeal for joy and clap my hands. Or jump up and down. Anything to release this pent-up excitement.

"Nice to meet you, Hastings." I enunciated every word.

"This way, Miz." He motioned with his hand.

I followed Hastings to the cart and fairly skipped aboard. Taking my seat, I steadied my breathing to quash the delightful rush of anticipation making my head spin.

Breathe in, breathe out.

I did this for a bit, while focusing on the rhythm of the horse's hooves. Eventually, my lightheadedness abated and I viewed my surroundings.

The dense forest continued inland, punctuated here and there by open spaces of lush marsh grass.

"What's that smell?" I wrinkled my nose.

Hastings laughed and slowed the cart. "Dat be pluff mud."

Laura had warned me of the vernacular the locals used and assured me I'd come understand. But presently I was in a fix. The only word I recognized was mud.

"Fluff mud?

Hastings chuckled and shook his head. "Pluff."

"Pluff," I repeated. "Why does it reek so?" I asked.

Hastings shrugged. "De marsh brimmin' with life 'n death. Suppose dat be why."

I barked out a laugh. "Oftentimes the simplest answers make the most sense."

Hastings chuckled. "Dat be true 'nuff, Miz Ellen."

Soon the road veered, leaving the open marsh behind. Once again we traveled through dense vegetation. Pines, their rough bark varying shades of shimmering gray and brown, grew on either side of the washboard road.

A flash—followed by a long roll of thunder, sounded. Hastings scowled, tugged the horse's reins and uttered something I couldn't make out. I gripped the edge of my seat.

We turned at yet another crossroad. Our new route was canopied by interlocking tree branches. A greenish-gray, hairy substance hung from the limbs in clusters, creating an eerie, web-like tunnel. This must be the Spanish moss that Laura described in her letters. She wrote that the freedmen believed the trees were haunted by *Greybeards:* spirits trapped as punishment for their sins. I glanced at Hastings. His intense expression led me to think Laura hadn't exaggerated the people's fears.

Suddenly, the heavens opened. I have never witnessed such a deluge!

Hastings stopped the cart amidst a break in the trees in front of a chapel. "Kent go no further," Hastings shouted. He drew a tarpaulin out from under his seat and handed it to me.

"We abide here `til de rain stop." Hastings hollered over the downpour.

My spirits sank at the prospect of a delay.

Hastings ran ahead to the entrance. I followed with the tarp draped over my head. He pulled open the door and a burst of song and wail of organ sprang out that even the pounding rain couldn't drown.

We entered and the music stopped. A small group of men and women seated in the front pews turned in unison. Hastings gathered up the sopping tarpaulin and moved off to the side.

One gentleman stepped out and forward. "Please, come in."

"We were on our way to The Oaks—"

"You must be Ellen Murray! We got word this morning you'd arrived." A woman slid out of a pew and strode forward. Something in the tilt of her head, or perhaps her close scrutiny, reminded me of Lila Butler, back home. I pushed the comparison aside and walked forward.

"Nelly Winsor," she said. "I'm from The Oaks. We'll be roommates."

"Nelly," I said. "Laura told me you're a teacher."

Others followed Nelly's example and filed out of the pews and introduced themselves.

"We all attend The Brick Church," Nelly said. "It's up the road, but we came here after service to try the Episcopalians' new organ. Before we set out, word came you'd arrived. Miss Towne went straight back to The Oaks, not wanting to risk you getting there before her." Nelly chuckled. "And now here you are! You've got to be tired." Nelly drew me into a pew. "Come, sit."

I sat down heavily and prayed the rain would ease so we could continue our journey.

"Have we far to go?" I asked.

Nelly shook her head. "Another three miles."

We both looked out the windows that faced a small graveyard. The storm had passed almost as quickly as it had come upon us. A light drizzle still showered the trees and tombstones.

"Edward Philbrick from Coffin Point offered to take me home." Nelly rolled her eyes. "But now I can hitch a ride back to The Oaks with you and Hastings."

&. &. &.

On the final leg of our journey to The Oaks, the rain clouds evaporated. I clasped my hands together to keep from fidgeting.

Nelly turned to face me. "How did Miss Towne ever talk you into joining her?"

"Pardon me?" I said. "Why would you think I needed to be convinced? Haven't all the volunteers come for the same reason, to participate in the Port Royal project and advance the abolishment of slavery?"

Nelly nodded, her ringlets bouncing. "Yes, yes." She waved a hand. Again reminding me of Lila. "What I mean to say is, coming to this backwoods isn't for everyone. Aside from the obvious, what made you agree to sign on?"

"Likely the same reason as you," I said.

"To escape your family, find adventure, and perhaps a husband?" Nelly said.

I laughed. This young woman resembled Lila in more than looks. "You're certainly frank!"

Smiling, Nelly shrugged. "One of my many charms."

"I'm a teacher," I said. "The prospect of establishing a school for the freedmen, and all that would mean for their future inspired me."

"And Miss Towne?" Again, the head tilt and curious look.

"And Miss Towne." I held her gaze.

"Hmmph." Nelly blinked. "Well, if *establishing* a school means trying to teach illiterate children in a run-down shack with little to no supplies, you won't be disappointed."

We turned at a crossroad and Nelly sat back. "Almost there."

This young woman was like the scent of pluff mud. Fair or foul? I couldn't decide. I supposed time would tell.

A laneway appeared and Hastings turned the cart. "The Oaks be crick-side," he called back.

I craned my neck for sight of the house.

"Crick" was an understatement. Between the heavy rain and a high tide, water encircled the outcrop of land where the plantation house stood. On the left, a line of tall pines, in front a cotton field; to the right, a row of tidy huts, covered in blue blossoms, squatted in the shade of trees.

"That's where the freedmen live," Nelly said, while pointing at the huts.

We pulled into the yard and a collection of children, knee to chest height, swarmed the cart. They giggled and shouted welcome. I waved and called out a hello, while Nelly ignored them. Hastings steered the horse cart, seemingly confident our charmed followers would make way.

Farther in, behind another collection of small dwellings—I surmised the previous quarters of house servants—stood the main house. Tall, square and reasonably new, it boasted a wide, deep front porch, comparable to country houses in the North.

Hastings drew the cart up to the porch stairs and helped Nelly and me down before driving off toward the stables round back. I neared the porch steps and a tall Black woman with golden eyes flew out of the front door. The screen slammed behind her.

"Get, get, get," she called out, clomping down the steps.

The children encircling me scattered like a flock of startled pigeons.

"This is Rina, our housekeeper," Nelly said.

"Thank de Lord you here, Miz Ellen!" Rina said. Our eyes locked.

"Miss Laura hear you comin' she near faint."

"I did no such thing." Laura opened the screen door and stepped onto the porch. "You startled me."

At the sight of Laura, my heart sped up. I longed to hold her close, and judging from her high color, she suppressed a similar, strong emotion.

"Rising suddenly made me faint." Laura walked down the steps toward me.

Rina crossed her arms, but said nothing.

Laura clasped my hand and I detected a slight tremor.

Laura glanced at Nelly. "You arrived together?"

"A downpour forced us to stop in at the chapel," I said. "We met there."

"Quite right," Nelly said. "Now if you'll both excuse me, I'm going to head into the parlor. I've some work to do." She smiled at me, then Laura. "I'll see you both later, at dinner."

"Go on then," Rina said to Laura. "Take Miz Ellen up and show her de room you be sharin'. I gots to see to de chickens."

Laura grabbed my hand. "Come on."

We made our way into the hallway and up the long flight of stairs to the second-floor landing. Pushing open the door to the bedchamber, she closed it behind us. Two single beds faced the door, one in each corner. Clothing hung on hooks.

"The house, although big, is full to the rafters with others like us. This room is *ours*." Arms spread, Laura turned in a circle, stopping in front of me. "One bed is Nelly's; you and I will double up." Laura smiled. "I cannot believe you are actually here!" She took both my hands and spun me around.

"Stop," I said, laughing. "I'm dizzy."

She slowed then, and pulled me close. "Finally, we are together."

Tears sprang to my eyes and I clung to her. "I don't know why I'm crying," I sobbed.

"I do," Laura took me in arms. "We are together now. All will be well."

Before dinner, Laura introduced me to Ted Hooper, St. Helena's General Superintendent. Based at The Oaks, Mr. Hooper managed all the plantations on the island. Well over six feet tall, he had dark bushy eyebrows, one with a bald strip.

I tried not to stare. Or imagine how it got there.

At the dining table, Laura sat opposite Nelly and me. I wanted to ask Nelly about the students, and teaching here in general, but I didn't want to interrupt her conversation with Mr. Hooper. I unfolded my napkin. Later, perhaps.

A tureen of fragrant broth arrived at the table—turtle, of all things!—fried croaker fish, collard greens, and rice. For dessert, Rina served juicy blackberries. Over coffee, Laura announced the freedmen held their praise meetings on Sunday evenings.

She smiled at me. "Would you like to go?"

"I suppose—" I blinked and suppressed a yawn.

"You must be tired, Miss Murray." Mr. Hooper dabbed his mouth with a napkin, "but I promise you'll find the service invigorating. Besides, everyone is curious about you."

"Mr. Hooper is right," Laura said. "The comings and goings of the plantation owners and the armies upended the freedmen's lives. Trust is key. The more accessible and open we are, the better. I think we should go, Ellen, if only for a short time."

❧ ❧ ❧

Chapter 10

Ellen

Along with Mr. Hooper and Nelly, Laura and I crossed the yard to the freedmen's cabins. Rhythmic clapping and singing came from one particular dwelling. Other night sounds—lapping marsh water, hooting owl, and thrumming bullfrogs—joined the chorus. The others told me that this, the "Praise House" cabin, belonged to a woman hailed as the oldest person on the plantation.

Yellow light from kerosene lamps spilled from its open door and windows. Crossing the threshold was like slipping through a portal into another world. Black faces alight with the fervor of worship filled the cramped space, along with the scent of tilled earth, chopped wood, and fried food. A woman, wrapped in remnants of old blankets and shawls, huddled in a corner. One man wore a carpet made up like a poncho. For all that, he strutted about as though swathed in spun gold. The women draped themselves in scarves, layered multicolored skirts and blouses.

In one corner, a wizened lady, her face ornately tattooed, danced.

"That's Dolores," Laura whispered to me, nodding in the direction of a dancer. "She came from Africa as a young woman. Spent years suffering God-knows-what at the hands of an evil man. Her five children all sold off and scattered."

My stomach flip-flopped. Mouth open, I stared at Laura.

"Ma'am?" A young fellow motioned us to open seats.

The singing continued, and eventually I detected a chorus. Three men stood apart to lead and clap. The others shuffled in a circle following one another, turning occasionally, bending their knees, and stamping. The shuffling and stomping reverberated through the thin floorboards, up the legs of my chair and coursed through my body. Eventually, the singing became softer, easing into a chant, then a murmur. The clapping stopped, the circle slowed and the dancers drifted to the side.

A man stood, head bowed, eyes closed, and the room—so filled with music and movement only moments before—stilled.

Laura whispered in my ear, "That's Good Marcus."

"O Lawd, we thank you for dis day!" Good Marcus' quavering voice rumbled.

Here and there people murmured their agreement. Good Marcus called out a litany of things, and people, and offered thanks. After each item, sometimes an individual, other times the group, sounded their agreement with an "Amen," or added commentary.

While I could only understand the odd word or phrase, the reaction of the congregation kept me riveted.

"Christ done set we free!" Good Marcus boomed. "Christ meek we free so dat we gwine be free people fa true. So den, leh we stan scrong an lib de way free people oughta lib."

Eventually, his words drew into formation. He quoted, from memory, and at length, a section of the New Testament, Galatians 5.

Christ hath made us free, and be not entangled again with the yoke of bondage.

The room hushed as he told the story of how he came to be here, at this place; how his first owner sold him to another plantation. My chest tightened as he recalled his beloved wife and child he left behind.

A woman wearing a yellow headscarf called out encouragement. A man with a rope belt next to her joined in. Good Marcus' testimony took several detours through scripture. He held up the circumstances of his life as an analogy, and warning, against spiritual bondage.

"Bot God sperit da mek people good like a tree da grow good fruit. God sperit da mek people lob one noda. E da meek um hab joy een dey haat."

But the fruit of the Spirit is love, joy, peace, long suffering, gentleness, goodness, faith.

I glanced about the room at the people raptly listening, nodding or speaking aloud their desire to move forward, without the burden of bitterness. These people's testimonies put my anguish from my brief and temporary separation from Laura into perspective. My cheeks flushed. I vowed to do better in future when facing my own trials.

Mr. Hooper stood and cleared his throat, preparing to address the assembly. What a challenge after Good Marcus' testimony!

Before Mr. Hooper opened his mouth, two young men burst through the door, carrying a third boy under the arms and at the ankles. Another young fellow trailed behind; in one hand he gripped several long-handled spears, in the other, a wire bucket brimming with bloated, belly-up frogs.

"Hep," the fellow at the injured boy's head, gasped. "Gator come when we jiggin' frogs."

A woman screamed: a piercing, agonized wail. Everyone spoke at once and rushed forward. Mr. Hooper staggered and slumped onto a nearby chair.

"We pull him from de gator's mout," the other boy chimed in.

The boys set their friend on the plank floor and he moaned. Blood pooled around the wounded arm. Or what remained of it. Two jagged bone-ends protruded from bright-red flesh.

The temperature in the cabin soared. Skunky body odor and the cloying note of blood clawed the back of my throat.

Everyone circled the boys. A woman stepped forward, I assumed the injured fellow's mother, and threw herself on the floor beside him, sobbing. The boy's eyes widened, and then rolled into his head. Laura pushed through, and fell to her knees. The friends shuffled back. Crimson bloomed on Laura's pale blue skirt.

"Rina," Laura bellowed. "Get everyone out. Go to the kitchen and boil a kettle of water; fetch vinegar and clean rags, bowls, too. Several sizes. Take everything to the dining room."

Laura's eyes darted about, landing on Nelly. "Go with Rina. Throw a sheet over the table, cover the floor. Then go up to our room. Bring down my black bag and the rectangular case beside it."

Nelly swallowed hard, nodded once and took off.

Laura turned to me. "Will you help?"

"Ye—es," I said, disregarding the tingle at the base of my spine.

Laura called over to Mr. Hooper who now stood at the door. "Ask the men to find a wide plank. We need to transport this fellow up to the house."

Laura laid a hand on the mother's back. "I'll look after him."

The woman in a yellow headscarf helped her up, all the while assuring her we'd save him. I prayed she was right.

"I need to stanch the bleeding," Laura said to me and pointed her chin toward the corner. "That mound of rags, bring them here and then find a tourniquet."

While I rummaged through the heap, the boy's moans turned to sobs.

"What's your name, son?" Laura asked.

I set a strip of fabric beside Laura.

"Tommy." His eyes fluttered.

Laura snatched a few of the rags, folded them under Tommy's upper arm, elevating it.

"Tommy, I'm tying this cloth onto your arm to stop the bleeding," Laura said. "Then we'll take you to the house where I'll close the wound."

Tears slid down the side of his face. My chest tightened. He already faced a challenging future. How would he fare now, so cruelly disabled?

Three men arrived carrying the makeshift stretcher. With care, they transferred Tommy onto it. Outside, torches lit the way to the house.

"You," Laura addressed a slight fellow. "Keep one hand on Tommy; make sure he feels safe." She then secured the rag cushion under the injured arm and instructed Tommy to remain still. She told the two men prepared to bear the stretcher to be swift, but cautious.

With the patient on his way, Laura hiked up her bloodstained skirts and bolted for the door. "Come on, Ellen," she called, flying past me.

$$\approx \approx \approx$$

Winded from our dash to the house, Laura and I rushed into the dining room. Nelly stood by the table. Sheets shrouded it and covered the floor. She'd also thought to bring in extra lighting. Mr. Hooper stood beside the arched doorway.

The men entered with the stretcher carrying Tommy. His eyes flitted everywhere.

"Lay him on the table." Laura waved impatiently. "This way, I want his injured arm nearest the sideboard."

"You two lift him." Laura ordered the stretcher bearers. She supported Tommy's mangled arm. "On the count of three—"

"Ellen and Nelly, stay. Everyone else can leave," Laura said. Ted Hooper backed out.

Rina came into the dining room with a jug of vinegar, bowls, and clean rags. Behind her, Hastings towed a massive kettle of boiled water.

"Where shall I put these?" Nelly held Laura's bag and case aloft.

"On the sideboard," Laura said, adding, "Will you stay and assist?"

Nelly nodded and Laura turned to me. "I'm going to anesthetize the patient, and then have you take over."

I curled my hands into fists. "How?" I swallowed.

"Chloroform." Laura opened her medical bag and withdrew a brown glass bottle. Then she unclasped a rectangular wooden case, lined with various knives, saws, files, and even pliers.

Tommy reached for Laura with his good arm. "Please, ma'am, no, no, no—"

I moved closer and laid what I hoped was a comforting hand on him.

"I'll give you some medicine to put you to sleep, so I can fix your arm without you feeling it," Laura said.

Under my hand, I felt Tommy relax a fraction. "Will it hurt?"

"No." Laura leaned in. "You won't feel a thing. Afterwards you'll be sore, but I'll give you something to help the pain."

In all the shock and confusion, I didn't know if Tommy understood that he'd lost his hand and lower half of his right arm.

Laura straightened up and turned to Nelly. "Stay with him. I need to give Ellen instructions."

She led me into the parlor, grabbed my hands and, in an urgent whisper, explained that she would start the chloroform process, but it would be my job to ensure Tommy stayed insensible throughout the surgery.

"But I need to warn you—" Laura drew a breath. "Too little chloroform and Tommy will suffer, go into shock, or panic and turn the surgery room into chaos. Too much and…well…we could kill him."

"Oh my!" I felt the blood drain from my face.

"Trust your instincts, they're good." Laura squeezed my hands. "And I'll be right beside you."

Back in the dining room, Laura tied a rag around the lower half of my face, Nelly's, and then her own. "We'll be less likely to inhale the chloroform fumes," she explained, and then had us wash and rinse our hands in a bowl of water laced with vinegar.

"All right, Tommy." Laura poured about a teaspoon of clear liquid from the brown bottle into the hollow of a rag, and recapped the bottle.

A treacly scent tickled the inside of my nostrils.

Laura placed the rag about an inch from Tommy's nose and mouth. "Just relax and breathe in."

Tommy closed he eyes and inhaled.

Laura set the rag compress over his nose and mouth. "That's right."

Laura waited until his breathing steadied before passing the bottle to me. "If he stirs, or gives any indication he's waking, add a couple of drops—that's all—and reapply the compress. Understand?"

I nodded and Laura turned to Nelly. "I need you to pass me an item when I ask for it."

Nelly grimaced at the assortment of instruments and tools displayed on the sideboard.

"I'll guide you," Laura encouraged. "You can do this," she turned to include me, "I have faith in both of you. Pray for guidance and ask me for help if you need it."

First, using vinegar, she cleansed the wound. During this procedure, Tommy's eyes remained closed and he snored softly. After examining the jagged, protruding bones, Laura asked for a saw, which could have easily belonged to a carpenter. Laura gripped Tommy's shoulder and bore down on the bones. I focused on Tommy's face, his dark, smooth skin, thick black lashes. I couldn't block out the scraping of steel through bone.

My stomach curdled; saliva filled my mouth. Breathing heavily through my nose, I closed my eyes and swallowed.

Hearing an odd sound, I looked up. Laura wielded a rasp. Back and forth she went over the bone ends. Tommy's breathing changed then; his lips parted. My hand rested on his intact upper arm and although he didn't move, something in him tensed. Beneath closed lids, his eyeballs zigzagged. With a prayer for guidance, I put two drops of chloroform onto the rag and replaced it over Tommy's nose and mouth. The vapors instantly worked their magic.

With a fine, hooked metal needle and black suture, Laura sewed the severed veins inside the wound.

Nelly impressed me. Her face was as pale as the sheets draping the sideboard and floor, but when asked, she passed Laura scissors to cut the sutures. Using fine-nosed pliers, Laura found another vein. I marveled at the skill and speed with which she worked. Only once during this period did I have to reapply the chloroform compress.

Laura exhaled. "Now to close the wound."

Voices from the front porch drifted in. From the volume, I judged the vigil had multiplied.

I checked Tommy's eyes for movement. I stroked his face, but he remained insensible.

Laura folded and stretched a portion of loose skin over the open wound. She struggled to push the needle through the tissue and fat. Sweat beaded her forehead. I asked Nelly to dab it off, lest it run into her eyes.

Soon the bared bone and raw flesh were encased. With some care and a bit of luck, what remained of Tommy's arm would heal.

Beneath my fingertips, Tommy stirred.

"Almost done," Laura called out.

This time I put only one drop onto the compress.

Laura cut and dipped gauze in vinegar. She covered Tommy's stump with these before dressing it with clean rags.

She stepped back. "Good job, ladies. I couldn't have managed without you." Smiling, she rinsed her bloody hands in the vinegar water, and then dried them with a clean rag.

"You're welcome." Nelly smiled and then collapsed onto a chair.

Laura moved up alongside me and laid a light hand on my back. "Ellen, I'm sorry. What a thing to happen on your first day. You didn't sign on for surgery. But I couldn't have done it without you."

I drew a stuttered breath. "I want to be helpful, to make a difference here."

She smiled. "In that case, you already have. Tommy will attest to that when he's able."

The circumstances were horrific and difficult, but seeing the boy's bandaged arm, noting Laura's satisfaction and receiving her praise for a job well done, made it worthwhile. For Tommy, his disfigurement would present challenges, but thanks to Laura, he would live.

Laura removed the chloroform compress and grinned at the young man's relaxed face. She then lifted his intact arm and checked his pulse. "He'll sleep for a while."

I hoped she was right, but Tommy's snoring had stopped.

Laura's smile faded, and she adjusted her hold on his wrist.

My heart stuttered. Had we lost him after all?

🐦 🐦 🐦

Chapter 11

Henrietta

AAAaaaaheee!

My startled re-entry to the present sends the notebook flying out of my hands. It hits the empty teapot which lands with a thud on the floorboards.

Maum Cat bolts upright, swatting the quilts from her head. "Wat's goin' on?" She's bug-eyed and her headscarf hangs over one brow.

High-pitched squealing and chattering rises up from the shore. "Otters fighting, I think." Hand to chest, I take measured breaths to still my racing heart.

With a harrumph, Maum lies down again and yanks the quilts back up and over her head.

"Thanks, I'm fine," I mutter, squatting to pick up the teapot, now sporting a chip on the spout. When I stretch for the journal, my left hamstring muscle cramps. I stand, leg bent like a heron at rest. With caution, I straighten and attempt to bear weight. When my foot hits the floor, the muscle twists anew.

"Aughhh!"

I hobble in a circle.

"Yeowww!"

With the fallen afghan from my lap wound about my feet, I flap my arms like a fledgling. Unable to save myself, I sprawl face-first on the floorboards.

Moaning, I roll over. My head and shoulders lie between the rockers of Miss Ellen's chair, the wooden slats mere inches from my nose. A sudden thunderous clap and flash of light precedes a jolt of pain and pressure in my jaw. Flailing, I try to wriggle out, knowing I must escape or my head will burst.

"Henrietta!"

Maum is beside me, down on her knees. She moves the chair and props me up. I raise a trembling hand to my jawbone. The knife-like sensation now dulled to an ache.

"Wat happen?" asks Maum.

"Leg cramp." The words curl around the pang in my jaw. "I stumbled and fell, hit my back." I glimpse at the rocking chair with its skeletal underbelly.

Maum eases back onto her haunches. "Why you touchin' you face?"

Does she think I'm not telling the truth?

The ache in my jaw vanishes. I open my mouth; close it. Move my jaw from side to side. Nothing. And nothing is what I tell her.

Maum stares at me.

"What?"

Getting to one knee, using me for support, she stands.

"Hey!" Still weak from the fall and fright, I steady myself.

Ignoring me, Maum shuffles back to the swing. I return the teapot to the tray. Then I pick up the notebook with two fingers, snatch the afghan with the other hand, and limp to my chair.

Instead of lying down, Maum stays upright, stretches out her legs and fixes her blankets.

"What scairt you when you was under dat rockin' chair?" asks Maum.

I frown at Miss Ellen's rocker, and sigh. "I don't know. I opened my eyes and saw the backside of the seat. Made me feel strange."

Maum frowns. "How you mean, *strange?*"

"A frightening feeling, like I was trapped or something. Doesn't make sense, it's only a chair." I take a breath and a moment to consider how to explain. "Then I heard thunder, saw a flash of lightning—"

Maum tilts her chin to the night sky.

"I know, not a cloud."

Maum grunts.

"That's when my jaw—"

Maum tenses. "What about you jaw?"

"It hurt." I shrug. "A knife-like pain and for no reason." I throw up my hands. "Could be imaginings getting the better of me, what with the shrieking otters and being in Miss Ellen's journals."

"What'd you learn?" asks Maum.

"How Miss Ellen helped Miss Laura operate on Fairy's husband, Tommy's, injured arm. I knew he lost it to a gator, and I think I knew, or guessed, that Miss Laura stitched him up. But surgery? I wonder if Fairy knows."

"Miz Ellen and Miz Laura save lots o' folks. Keep at dem books, mebbe she save you." Maum yawns, slides down onto the bed of the swing and closes her eyes.

"You mean how she and Miss Laura gave me and Fountain a home?"

I wait, but Maum's done talking, even if I'm not. Seconds later, her shallow breathing deepens to wheezing snores. I do believe Maum Cat could sleep on the edge of a razor.

Between drinking the pot of tea and all the commotion, I am no longer sleepy. The otters have settled their dispute, and the rest of the lively night sounds have abated. Waves no longer assault the shoreline. Rather, the water whooshes and slaps the sand; the clockwork sounds of our sea island. I, too, should get back to the task at hand.

Opening the notebook, I find the page where I left off. But rather than immediately return to Miss Ellen's history, I glance at the rocking chair. I've never been fond of them. The motion makes me dizzy, which turns my stomach. Still, I've never been afraid to sit in one. Why would I? They are hardly dangerous. Stomach aflutter, I force myself to take a hard look at the chair. Gagging, I turn away and take measured breaths.

I want to dismiss my experience as fantasy, conjured by grief at the loss of Miss Ellen; confusion, because of my unsettling conversation with Jakob; or an over-stimulated imagination from delving into Miss Ellen's adventures. But none of these explanations satisfy me.

What if I took another peek underneath?

A brisk breeze picks up. In the lantern's light, dry oak leaves circle on the ground. Faster and faster they rustle and swirl until a column spins only a few feet from the porch. The whirlwind rises and my blood runs cold. I cover my face with both hands and abandon any thought of re-visiting the rocking chair. Seconds pass; the rustling wind recedes. I drop my hands and open my eyes. All is still and quiet.

In that moment, I decide to tell Maum Cat all that happened with the chair. Might be she'll have an explanation. Or find one. She has her ways, strange though they be. I look over at the swing. She's curled like a comma under bedding that surely weighs more than she does.

It'll keep 'til morning.

Standing, I edge over to the rocker and cover it with the afghan. Tucked back into my own chair with a different blanket, I pick up Miss Ellen's notebook and journey back.

ᴥ ᴥ ᴥ

Chapter 12

Ellen

In those few frightful minutes, unsure if Tommy would live or die, Nelly and I stood huddled together. With God's grace, Laura revived Tommy from his chloroform stupor. Finally, she told us his pulse had resumed a normal rhythm.

In the weeks following Tommy's surgery, it appeared everyone at The Oaks, including the patient himself, had accepted the injury and amputation. The residents of St. Helena dealt with extreme hardships on a daily basis. I also understood that priorities were ground to a point: survive. Still, I questioned the apparent blasé attitude.

ટ- ટ- ટ-

Under Ted Hooper's good-natured leadership, our days settled into a comfortable, but exhausting routine. Depending upon Mr. Hooper's obligations at the other plantations, we rose between six and eight. Today was mercifully on the later side of early. Laura visited and fed her pet mockingbirds caged in the yard. After a quick breakfast, we went to the stores where the freedmen purchase goods and clothing at a reasonable price. Before I knew it, noon chimed. After lunch, Laura worked on the books, and I went to teach alongside Nelly in a cabin that served as our schoolroom.

The dirt-floor cabin was full to overflowing with children seated on floorboards raised and balanced atop wooden blocks, and adults who tagged along. Amidst this organized chaos, the scholars heartily recited their ABCs and numbers.

Adults stood at the back or at the entrance. Some even peered through the windows, mouthing words as we pointed to the blackboard. It still astounded me that this fundamental building block to learning was denied them, and codified by law. Good Marcus, the man who had given his testimony at the praise meeting on the eve of my arrival, came regularly. Many young mothers also attended, with babies at their breast and toddlers in tow. Often these women stepped away to tend a needy child, but soon returned, questioning others about what they'd missed.

This afternoon just before school let out at four o'clock, I noticed Tommy hovering by the entrance, the healed stump of his arm exposed. I caught his eye for a moment before he disappeared. Not for the first time, I questioned what would become of him. No formal program existed for Tommy, or any of the other young adults here. I knew how to develop a curriculum and implement a plan. Still, I wanted Laura's opinion. Her experience in the general comings and goings at St. Helena exceeded mine. After dinner we usually visited the freedmen's cabins and saw to their needs, medical or otherwise. Tonight on the drive over, I planned to broach the subject.

We dismissed school and I followed the children out with newfound optimism regarding the people of St. Helena, their future, and my purpose.

꙳ ꙳ ꙳

We had just finished our meal when Mr. Hooper cleared his throat and asked for our attention.

Seriousness in his usual lighthearted tone raised gooseflesh on my arms. Laura and Nelly, both frowning, turned to him.

Mr. Hooper straightened his shoulders and once again cleared his throat. "I've been informed that due to the harsh conditions and ever-present dangers on the island, the Philadelphia Commission is considering abandoning the Port Royal project and withdrawing its financial support."

My breath caught and I looked across the table. Nelly had blanched; Laura sat rigid, her expression inscrutable.

"Our survival hinges on their support," Laura said. "This project isn't a theoretical idea anymore. We've asked the people here to join us, to trust us. To abandon them now is unthinkable!"

"I agree," Mr. Hooper said. "I'm heartsick at the news."

Laura's eyes blazed, but her voice softened. "They were aware of the challenges from the outset. Why the sudden concern?"

Mr. Hooper sighed. "Word had reached the Philadelphia Commission of how the boy's arm was mangled by the alligator." He looked at each of us in turn.

Nelly's eyes bulged. "And for that they may withdraw our funding?"

"It's given the original naysayers reason to reassert their original claim that it is dangerous and that our northern constitutions cannot tolerate the climate." Hooper shook his head. "They argue, as they did before, that the risk is too great."

"Leaving also presents risks," Laura said. "If the North prevails, a plan—both social and economic—is needed to address the inevitable collapse of slavery. This issue is at the heart of the Port Royal Experiment."

"Nothing is final," Mr. Hooper said, "at least not yet. The Commission asked me to provide a report detailing if and why they should continue with the project."

"What do you plan to say?" Laura asked.

"For one, I'll beg them to reconsider," Mr. Hooper said. "I hope you three will help."

"What do you need?" Nelly asked.

"Miss Towne, you mentioned leaving is also risky." He looked at each of us. "If you three shared some examples of why that's the case, it'd help me formulate a rebuttal."

"I can give you a progress report on the children, how eager they are for their ABCs and numbers," Nelly said. "I'll start this evening."

"Around sundown, Ellen and I attend patients on The Hill," Laura said. "Come with us tonight. A visit there will give you plenty of reasons why the Port Royal project must continue."

My plan to educate the young adults of St. Helena would have to wait. Rescuing the entire Port Royal project took priority.

Ted Hooper stood and pushed in his chair. "Let's go."

ঌ ঌ ঌ

Reeling from the news that the Philadelphia Commission might pull our funding, no one spoke on the drive to The Hill. The blazing heat of the afternoon had subsided. The sun, now low in the sky, cast a golden sheen over the marsh grass. Palmetto sprays rustled in the delicate ocean breeze that carried the faint perfume of sea salt and wildflower.

Upon our arrival, we walked down the chain of packed-dirt pathways, which linked the shacks and people within.

Stopping at Aunt Phoebe's cabin Laura said, "I've been treating her for chronic leg ulcers."

Mr. Hooper frowned. "Ulcers?"

"They're open sores that don't heal," Laura said.

Mr. Hooper's mouth curled down. "Poor hygiene?"

"Partially." Laura took a deep breath. "It's complex. Until recently, Aunt Phoebe lived a life of forced, hard labor compounded by poor nutrition, which led to compromised vascular health, and then ulcers. I can clean, wrap, and order rest for those wounds. But the underlying problem is ignorance borne of a reliance on White masters. Ultimately, that's what we're here to address. And why we need to stay."

"I agree, Miss Towne," Mr. Hooper said. "But naysayers argue that plantation owners avoided this island for most of the year for health reasons. I must prove that the benefits of funding the project outweigh the risk to young, White volunteers."

"And Negro lives are worth less than ours?" The question was out of my mouth before I could stop it.

"No, Miss Murray," Mr. Hooper said. "Like you, I believe all lives are precious. But I must substantiate my belief with hard evidence."

My cheeks burned. "I apologize, Mr. Hooper. It's just—"

He smiled. "No need to explain, Miss Murray. I understand your outrage."

"We'd best begin," Laura said. "I'll ask Aunt Phoebe if she minds you attending while I examine her." She knocked on the cabin door and entered.

Moments later, the door swung open and Laura beckoned us inside. It took a minute for my eyes to adjust to the dim lighting.

Huddled in one corner on a makeshift rag bed, under a canopy of sky blue fabric, sat Aunt Phoebe, her hair wrapped in a scarlet scarf. Her shirt and skirts were a clash of hue and pattern. Like all the other freedmen on St. Helena, she chose the brightest, boldest colors and fashions from our store.

"You already know Miss Ellen," Laura said to her. "This is Mr. Hooper, from The Oaks."

Despite being installed on a throne of rags and dependent upon our aid, Aunt Phoebe responded with a regal nod.

Laura launched into a summary of the case. "Aunt Phoebe is, at best guess, 75 years old. She has extensive ulceration and swelling of her left leg."

Laura removed the compress bandages on the old woman's leg. "On previous visits, this swelling was dark bluish and the surface of her foot up to the knee joint was deeply ulcerated. Also, the affected area above the foot writhed with fat maggots."

Mr. Hooper drew a quick breath.

Laura cleared her throat and continued, "Aunt Phoebe's general condition is remarkably better," Laura said.

She put her hand on Aunt Phoebe's leg. "Are you still troubled with burning?"

Aunt Phoebe shook her head.

"Good," Laura cupped the old woman's shoulder.

Laura redressed Aunt Phoebe's leg, elevated her foot with a tattered pillow and then stood. "Continue to rest. I'll be back later in the week."

I stayed to tend to Aunt Phoebe's final needs for the evening while Laura and Mr. Hooper went on ahead to Kisse's cabin.

After the door closed, I asked if she would like me to help her undress for bed.

She shook her head. "De gal be coming."

I nodded and glanced up at the canopy. On previous visits I'd been curious about it, but hadn't asked. "Why have you draped that sheet from the ceiling?"

"To keep de hants away," Aunt Phoebe said.

I had no idea what she meant and it must have shown on my face.

"Dem bad spirits stuck 'tween dis world and de next." She sounded amazed at my ignorance.

"How does a sheet help?"

"It be blue, like de water," she said. "Confuses 'em."

I noticed the window covering was also blue. "I take it the hants can't swim," I chuckled.

"Dat's right." She sounded pleased that I'd caught on.

I frowned. "Why are you worried about the hants?"

She glanced down at her damaged leg. "A boo-hag's ridin' dat done dis."

"Given you ulcer sores?"

"Uh-huh."

"But, you heard Miss Laura—"

Aunt Phoebe scowled. I decided another approach more prudent. "What's a boo-hag?"

She looked about and lowered her voice. "Boo-hag's slippery creature dat shed its skin. Dat's why dey warm, like fresh kill. Dey's de color o' blood, so you cant see 'em when night come. Den de boo-hag slip under you skin and wear you, like a new set of clothes."

My expression must have reflected my disbelief, for she continued.

"One mornin' I woke and dis here leg was burnin'. I tek off de blanket, de stench o' rotten meat 'bout slap my face. Dat's how I know a boo-hag done dis, 'cause de smell."

"But surely you don't think—"

"How else you gonna explain it?" She cocked an eyebrow.

"You've worked hard all your life, often without enough to eat, and now you're getting on in years—"

When I trailed off, she leaned forward. "But *why?* Answer me dat."

I didn't know what to say. I looked at the door. "Well, if there's nothing more you need, I'd better be going."

She fixed the blankets around herself. "No, de gal be coming."

Closing the door of the cabin behind me, I hurried along the worn path to Kisse's cabin. Mr. Hooper waited near the door. I nodded to him before I joined Laura inside.

"Everything all right?" Laura asked.

I nodded.

Laura turned her attention back to Kisse.

On her cot, the new mother unlatched the sleeping child from her breast and covered herself.

Laura held out her arms. "May I examine your girl, Kisse?"

She passed the baby to Laura. The child arched her little back in a big stretch; her thick lashes fluttered, and her eyes opened.

"Your daughter is beautiful," I said.

"What have you named her?" Laura asked.

"Rose," Kisse whispered.

"Lovely," Laura said, and then added, "A gentlemen from The Oaks came with me this evening. I'd like him to meet you and Rose. May we invite him in?"

Kisse adjusted her dress and looked at the door, her expression neutral.

When Laura and I had first attended Kisse, we were baffled by her indifference. Nothing we did or said elicited much of a response. Rina had heard us discussing the young mother-to-be one evening and told us that, owing to Kisse's gentle nature, the master had often singled her out. That was all Rina needed to tell us. The man's reputed penchant for the whipping post preceded him. No doubt the petite hands with thin wrists now clutching a bodice had once been bound to that post.

Kisse continued to hold her silence, and I cleared my throat. Laura looked at me, and I shifted my gaze to the door.

Moments later, Mr. Hooper leaned over Rose, grinning. Laura then handed him the child and he cradled her in the crook of his arm.

I stood beside Mr. Hooper and Baby Rose. Laura sat with Kisse, talking.

Mr. Hooper smiled and cooed at the babe. I drew closer and held a finger out for her to grasp.

"Is she heavy?" I asked. "Do you need me to take her from you?"

"No," Mr. Hooper smiled. "She's as light as a cotton ball."

"I'm glad to hear it," I whispered, stroking Rose's sweet head. "For this child depends upon you to convince the Philadelphia Commission to leave our funding in place."

I sensed Mr. Hooper's hold on her tighten.

After Kisse's place, we made several brief visits to other cabins: the scalded hand was on the mend; the sore throat was better. We rarely heard a query, much less an argument. A regrettable remnant of the freedmen's ingrained deference to Whites, Laura and I had concluded. We hoped the freedmen would become more confident and self-reliant as the Port Royal project advanced. In the meantime, our word was golden. The questions and challenges would come later. I hoped so. Their passive compliance unsettled me.

Mockingbird Diary of St. Helena Island

Mr. Hooper lit the wagon's lantern for the ride home. His back, ramrod straight on the drive here, appeared rounder now. We joggled along the sandy dirt road. Beams of lantern light bounced amidst the live oaks and Spanish moss. By lantern and moonlight, the trailing strands resembled ghostly specters. With a shiver, I turned my attention to Laura and Mr. Hooper's conversation.

"It's unfortunate the Philadelphia Commission heard about Tommy's encounter with the alligator," Laura said. "It can't be denied that dangers and risks exist. Your task is to argue that—"

"The risks are far greater if we leave." Mr. Hooper loosely held the reins. "Agreed. Like you, I believe the North will prevail. As you stated earlier this evening, emancipation is only a matter of time. On St. Helena, we're uniquely positioned to prove freedmen will work for wages and become contributing members of society.

"What is to be gained by leaving?" He turned to look at Laura and me. "If we abandon these people now, Aunt Phoebe, Kisse, Baby Rose, and hundreds of others like them will suffer."

"Children are learning how to read and write." I wiggled forward on my seat in the back. "Tools for the future."

"We wage a different war, Mr. Hooper," Laura interjected. "Ignorance is our battlefield."

"I'm ready to write that response, ladies." Mr. Hooper gave us a curt nod. "Let's pray I'm successful."

❧ ❧ ❧

Chapter 13

Ellen

After the others had retired, Laura called me into the parlor and patted the settee next to her.

I sat down and my heart sped up. Her calm expression often belied a vexing problem.

"Don't look so worried." She smiled. "I just want to chat."

I clasped my hands. "All right."

She turned in her seat to face me. "Last month when the Army evacuated the freedmen from Edisto and brought them here, I couldn't fathom how we'd provide for over a thousand more people. Although presently we were able to give out enough food and clothes, I still woke up in the night worrying about the Philadelphia Commission's threat to end our funding, and the ramifications."

She reached over and took my hand. "You're also not sleeping—" she held up a hand to stop my protest. "You pick at meals."

I took a deep breath. "I despise not knowing what's going to happen."

She frowned.

"If we lose it, the Port Royal project closes and so does our school." Tears pricked my eyes and I put my head down.

"I know," Laura said.

I sat forward and turned to face her. "The children are hungry to learn, and they're capable. They deserve a chance."

"Back in Newport, I witnessed your commitment to your students. What I haven't appreciated is how invested you've become here, on St. Helena."

"The schoolhouse—if you can call it that—can barely accommodate the St. Helena children. Never mind the ones from Edisto." I shook my head. "I don't know how we'll manage."

"What we won't do is sit on our hands while the Philadelphia Commission ponders our future." Laura picked at imaginary fluff on her skirt. A moment later, she drew a deep breath. "Together, we'll find a way, Ellen. Let Nelly and me worry about the younger children. Did you forget that Ted agreed with your idea to expand the enrollment to include older students? That means your responsibility begins and ends with them."

"Part of me feels guilty," I said.

"Whatever for?"

"Living in New England I knew about the slave codes. The limits on travel, owning property, that type thing." I shrugged. "But until we met, I didn't know about the anti-literacy laws that make it illegal for Blacks to learn to read or write. I realized some may be illiterate, like many poor Whites in rural communities. But outlawed!? I need to make amends. Do you think I'm wrong to feel this way?"

Head tilted, she stared at me. "I wouldn't say wrong." She gave my hand a squeeze. "People are uninformed. That's why I went to Newport. Once you understood the evils of slavery you wanted to do your part to end it. That's all anyone can do. Nor are you wrong to be passionate about educating the freedmen. Actually, I'm relieved."

"Relieved? How so?"

"I've harbored the fear that you'd come only for me. What with all the difficulties and turmoil, I worried you might—"

"Might what?"

"Leave," she said. "Or be glad if the funding falls though."

"My goodness!" I clapped a hand to my chest. "I'm glad you spoke up." I nodded, considering her concerns. Laura deserved a fulsome answer. I locked eyes with her.

"Perhaps initially being with you took precedence. But once I arrived and truly understood the need, and the challenges, my motivation and focus expanded."

"I'm happy, and relieved to hear you say so." Laura exhaled and squeezed my hand. "I suppose this waiting has everyone on edge."

"Has Mr. Hooper said when he expects the Commission's response?" I asked.

"No, and he's likely more concerned than us. Dismantling the whole project would fall to him."

"Would you and I have to leave?" I asked.

Laura's brows shot up. "How could we stay? If the Philadelphia Commission struggles to support the project, what chance would two lone women stand?"

"We could try," I said. "My mother might help. Your family? You met wealthy people traveling and speaking up North."

"Let's worry about that if and when the time comes," Laura said.

"Speaking of worries," I sat back on the settee, "assuming our funding remains intact, where will we put all the students come September?"

"I haven't a clue. At least not yet," Laura said.

The clock chimed the hour. Laura yawned. Then reaching up, she cupped the side of my face. "Come now, let's go to bed."

ða ða ða

A week later, Nelly, Laura, Mr. Hooper, and I gathered for dinner. Mr. Hooper glanced up from his soup and said, "Ellen, have you given any thought about the new school year and how we're going to incorporate the Edisto arrivals?"

I set my spoon aside. "I've thought of little else."

Mr. Hooper took a swallow of soup. "It's going to be too crowded in the tiny shack for the younger children. The back room barely holds the older St. Helena students, never mind adding the Edisto lot."

"We don't even know if we'll be here," I said through clenched teeth, "so it may not be an issue."

"Come now, have some faith." Mr. Hooper smiled.

Laura frowned. "Have you new information?"

"I have two pieces of good news." Mr. Hooper dabbed his mouth with a napkin. "First, I received word that the Philadelphia Commission is leaving our funding intact—"

"How marvelous!"

"Thank goodness!"

"When did you hear?"

Our voices tangled over each other.

"Today, of course," Mr. Hooper said. "I might tease you, but I'd never withhold such great news for long."

"That's why you inquired about the school?" I asked.

"Mmhmm." Having finished his soup, Mr. Hooper dug into the fried shrimp and rice Rina had set out.

"I don't mean to cast a shadow on the good news," I said, "but I have no idea where we'll put all the scholars. Like you said, the shack and the back room aren't an option. I suppose we might teach outside in good weather. But when it gets colder, or rains—could the Army lend us a tent?"

"A tent!" Nelly blurted.

"Hold on," Mr. Hooper held up a hand. "That's my second piece of good news." He looked at me. "Shortly after the Edisto refugees arrived, I contacted the governing body of the Baptist Church and explained our circumstances. They've granted your school permission to use the Brick Church until you can secure your own building." He smiled. "Are you pleased?"

"Pleased?" I swallowed the lump in my throat. "I'm thrilled!"

Fork held mid-air, Mr. Hooper said, "Another thing, it occurred to me your school needs a name. You may want to give that some thought before September."

"What about Penn School?" I said.

He chuckled. "You're a step ahead of me, I see!"

My cheeks warmed and I smiled.

"I like it," he said. "To honor William Penn, Pennsylvania's founder."

Laura leaned back grinning. Nelly huffed and crossed her arms.

It was clear that Nelly did not possess a passion for teaching. However, she had been here longer than both Laura and me. We needed her help.

"Nelly, isn't this wonderful news for us?" I emphasized the "us." "It may not be the schoolhouse we'd like, but we'll be in a solid building with a decent amount of space."

Nelly harrumphed. "I'm just pleased I don't have to return to that shack." She resumed her meal.

I glanced from Nelly to Laura. She gave me an almost imperceptible shake of the head and picked up her fork. While I pushed the food around my plate, Mr. Hooper tucked back into his meal.

ða ða ða

September arrived and Penn School transitioned into the Brick Church. The Edisto children displayed a hunger for knowledge equal to that of our St. Helena scholars. Despite being short-staffed and contending with the noisy open space of the church sanctuary, the scholars progressed well. By mid-September we'd fallen into a nice routine.

Mr. Hooper had appointed me presumptive principal, not Nelly. She did her job well, but with little enthusiasm. Although still a valuable asset to our teaching team, more and more she now assisted Mr. Hooper with the administration of the island's cotton plantations.

With funding for the Port Royal project settled, I slept like a stone and my appetite returned with a vengeance.

Tonight Rina served up fried fish with okra, and mouth-watering cornbread. Halfway through our meal Mr. Hooper said, "I have an announcement."

"Good news, I hope." Laura took a sip of water.

"I think so," he answered.

Nelly smiled over at Mr. Hooper. I shot a glance at Laura, who remained expressionless.

"The supervisor at the Eustis Plantation suddenly resigned and returned North, leaving me in dire straits. Nelly has agreed to take the position, effective immediately."

While I sat with my mouth hanging open, thinking of all the ways Nelly's departure would affect Penn School, Laura spoke up.

"Congratulations, Nelly! You will do a wonderful job," Laura said. "We're happy for you, aren't we, Ellen?"

"Yes—" I stammered. "Of course you will be missed at school, and here, at The Oaks. But you'll be an excellent administrator."

"Thank you, Ellen." Nelly offered me a genuine smile. "That means a great deal."

"You're most welcome." Feeling guilty, my forced smiled softened. "I wish you all the best at Eustis Plantation."

Mr. Hooper steepled his fingers and looked fondly upon Nelly. "Our Miss Winsor will be the youngest person appointed superintendent."

"Not to mention the first female," Laura added.

Mr. Hooper chuckled. "That's sure to raise some eyebrows, but I'm not in the least concerned. Nelly has proven herself capable."

"Thank you, Ted," Nelly said. "I am very excited."

"Your departure, however, leaves a gaping hole at Penn School." Mr. Hooper frowned.

I held my breath, praying his good news included a solution.

With a heave of his shoulders and a loud sigh, Mr. Hooper returned his attention to his plate without offering a word.

ۋ ۋ ۋ

Chapter 14

Ellen

A fresh morning breeze streamed in through the open window above my desk. Nigh on winter, the days remained warm, but the evenings cool and—praise God!—the mosquitoes are gone. One more dip of the pen to finish my journal entry.

While I waited for the ink to dry, I reached for my first completed notebook. Fanning the pages, I stopped at an entry before my arrival on St. Helena. Across the top of the page I had printed, *The Black Day, May 12, 1862.* Laura had written to share her outrage at the military's haphazard attempt to train and arm freedmen. Without a proper explanation of why the training required them to go to the camp of Hilton Head, the freedmen feared being sold back into slavery. Frightened, the men resisted. Rather than allay their fears and gain their confidence, the general on Hilton Head ordered them rounded up. The fiasco resulted in confusion and damaged trust on both sides.

I closed the book on that disturbing notation and, after checking the drying ink on my latest entry, filed both journals away.

Thankfully, General Rufus Saxton now oversees the Port Royal project. Tonight he will be our dinner guest, along with a new arrival, Colonel Thomas Higginson. Assigned to train and lead Black regiment recruits, I hope he doesn't repeat the mistakes of his predecessors.

ﻬ ﻬ ﻬ

Dusk descended like a feather. I centered a vase of camellias and rosebuds on the dining table. Stepping back to admire my handiwork, I turned at the clomp of horses' hooves. A lantern beam flashed through the window and swiveled across the sideboard. The gruff rumble of voices preceded the heavy footfall of boots on the porch. I straightened my skirts, smoothed my hair and headed to the foyer. I arrived at the same time as Laura and Mr. Hooper. We opened the door to our guests.

General Saxton introduced Colonel Higginson, whose green eyes held a hint of mischief. He bowed to Laura and me before shaking hands with Mr. Hooper.

Immediately following grace, Rina doled out steaming bowls of vegetable soup with rice. Despite meager pickings, she always produced an impressive spread.

"I understand you teach the Black children," Colonel Higginson addressed Laura. Outspoken and direct, she possessed an air of authority that appealed to men.

"Yes, and the young adults also," Laura answered.

Mr. Hooper looked up from his bowl. "Perhaps bring Colonel Higginson up to date."

Laura dabbed her lips. "Miss Murray is the educator, not me. Already teaching the younger children, she approached us about creating a curriculum for the young adults. Soon after, she offered them classes in the back room, here at The Oaks. If you want to know more, I will defer to her."

Colonel Higginson turned his gaze on me. "How many older students do you have?"

"Well," I smiled, "I started with nine. But then the island's population grew by sixteen hundred in July when the evacuated freedmen of Edisto Island arrived."

Higginson's brows shot up. "However did you manage?"

I smiled. "In September we moved our classes to the Brick Church."

"So you've formed an actual school?" Colonel Higginson said.

"Yes," I smiled. "We're calling ourselves Penn School. I'm the principal-instructor, I teach alongside Miss Towne, who is responsible for the younger scholars."

"There's only the two of you?" The Colonel's voice rose.

"For now," I said. "My original teaching partner recently left to assume a position on the island. In the meantime, Mr. Hooper arranged for a temporary teacher from another plantation school to fill in. Our permanent replacement is due to arrive any day."

"Well done!" Colonel Higginson smiled.

"Thank you." My cheeks warmed. "It's been a team effort."

"But your initiative," Higginson said.

Laura laughed. "You'll have a difficult time getting Miss Murray to accept the credit she's due, Colonel."

I cleared my throat. "Are we ready for the next course?"

Laura rang a handbell to signal Rina.

"Where were you before coming to St. Helena, Colonel Higginson?" I asked.

Rina waltzed into the dining room balancing a platter of fried oysters and a bowl of glistening sweet potatoes.

"With the 51st Massachusetts Black regiment. I left to serve here," Colonel Higginson said. "My primary objective, with General Saxton's help, is to ready the Black men of St. Helena and the surrounding area for combat."

Rina glared at the Colonel, then thumped the platter and bowl onto the table and stomped off. An unintelligible rant rumbled in her wake.

Laura scowled after her.

Higginson's brows puckered and he glanced around.

"You'll have to excuse Rina." All eyes turned to Mr. Hooper at the head. "Not everyone shares your enthusiasm, Colonel. Here on the island, misunderstanding and mishandling of the freedmen's role in the military left people wounded."

"How so?" Higginson asked.

Mr. Hooper summarized the bungled attempt to recruit Black soldiers while Laura doled out food.

Famished despite the solemn discussion, I tucked into my meal. The others soon followed suit.

"Such unnecessary trouble." Colonel Higginson shook his head. "I knew there'd been a half-hearted attempt at recruitment. Your explanation fills in the blanks."

General Saxton snorted. "Perhaps they thought you'd find a way to decline the assignment, if you knew the details."

"That terrible business affected our entire community," Mr. Hooper said.

"That's an understatement." Laura set down her water glass. "The Black Day debacle all but ruined the trust we'd established with the community."

"Perhaps you can understand Rina's reaction," Mr. Hooper continued. "Her nephew was amongst those forcibly marched off to Hilton Head. The freedmen have little reason to believe our word and every reason to doubt it."

"Still," Higginson said, "we mustn't lose sight that arming the Black men is a step toward winning the war and securing their freedom."

"No argument from me. Provided it's properly executed," Mr. Hooper said. "From what I understand, your latest round of recruitment was successful."

Higginson nodded. "The latest, yes, it's a start but—"

"But," Mr. Hooper interrupted, "we must also consider the consequences of your success. There will be fewer men to harvest the cotton crop. Need I remind everyone that the continuation of the Port Royal project hinges on our experiment of free labor being *profitable?* It must be as lucrative, or more so, than its slave labor counterpart. If not, our detractors will pounce upon that."

My heart sped up. We'd managed to avoid one threat of funding withdrawal. I dreaded the thought of another financial crisis and what that would mean for the Penn School, and the Freedmen.

General Saxton, who'd done more listening than talking thus far, spoke up. "Do you have something to that end in mind, Ted?"

All eyes swiveled to Ted Hooper.

"I do, although I confess I cannot claim responsibility. The idea belongs to our latest arrivals from Edisto." Ted paused.

"I'm listening," General Saxton said.

"The Edisto men recognize what's at stake and say they don't wish to limit recruits for the sake of the crop. They claim to have enough manpower for both enterprises, and that they will get in our cotton."

"What about our people?" I asked, feeling a little defensive of the original residents of St. Helena.

"A fair question," Ted said. "But they are newer to the concept of free labor. Some will help harvest the cotton. But many would rather plant their own gardens and reap a reward they can control, versus the *promise* of a wage."

"All the more reason for this undertaking to be successful," General Saxton said.

"Exactly." Ted grinned. "But for now, the Edisto refugees are more experienced. They brought in the cotton on that island, essentially functioning as free men."

"And soon they will be truly free," General Saxton said.

In silent, tacit agreement, the conversation stopped while Rina and her helpers cleared the table. Rina returned shortly thereafter carrying a large apple pie and pot of coffee. Laura thanked her, saying she'd serve dessert.

"You said, *truly free.*" Laura poured the coffee. "May we assume you're referring to Mr. Lincoln's Preliminary Emancipation Proclamation of September?"

"I am." General Saxton nodded.

"And you believe that will be incentive enough?" Laura asked.

"The Rebels must end the fighting and rejoin the Union by New Year's Day, or their slaves will be made free. The Proclamation is brilliant because either way the Confederacy must concede defeat. Without slaves to work the land, the Rebels cannot leave their properties. And if they're homebound, they cannot bring down the Union."

"And you believe Mr. Lincoln will follow through?" Ted asked.

"The President's terms were clear: If the Southern states do not cease and desist this rebellion, on January 1st the Emancipation Proclamation will be issued in its final form. What's more—"

Thump, thump, thump!

General Saxton fell silent. Ted, Laura, and I exchanged glances, the thought I had was reflected on their faces: A knock on the door this late in the evening usually meant a problem.

"Excuse me." Ted stood and left the table about the same time we heard Rina clomping through the foyer.

"More coffee?" Laura held the pot aloft.

The undertone of muffled voices drifted into the dining room. No loud, frenzied commotion meant no injury needed tending.

Moments later Ted stopped under the archway to the dining room, grinning. Beside him stood a well-dressed, but dusty young woman wearing a tentative, travel-weary expression.

"Everyone," he announced, "our new teacher, Miss Charlotte Forten."

Ted offered Miss Forten his seat at the table and went to find another chair for himself. Laura went to ask Rina to bring in a bowl of soup.

While we waited for Rina, Laura poured coffee. Charlotte explained that she'd been delayed on Hilton Head and landed on St. Helena just before nightfall. Since no one from The Oaks appeared to greet her, she rightly assumed we hadn't received word of her arrival. A soldier from the Army base drove her here.

Rina entered the dining room with a steaming bowl of soup and a warm hunk of cornbread.

Miss Forten glanced up. "Thank you," she said to Rina.

Eyes averted, Rina nodded.

Miss Forten told us she hailed from a free Black family in Philadelphia, all active in the abolitionist movement. Her father and uncle also belonged to an antislavery network that assisted escaped slaves. Ted, if he knew any of this, hadn't mentioned it. The information surprised me, as I had assumed she was White until she arrived.

After finishing her soup, Miss Forten struggled to keep her eyes open. Taking pity on her, Laura suggested she may want to retire. Miss Forten agreed. Bottling my curiosity, along with the others, I wished her a good night. Rina showed her to her bed.

⁂ ⁂ ⁂

In the wee hours, Laura jostled me awake. Rina, in her nightdress, hovered over our bed. A messenger had come to say we were needed at The Hill. Kisse's baby Rose had taken ill. Laura and I dressed and rushed downstairs. Hastings had the wagon hitched and waiting.

Only a few days ago, Laura and I had dropped off blankets for Kisse and Rose. At the time, neither of them displayed any sign of sickness.

We hurtled along the road toward The Hill. Above us, gales lashed live oaks branches. Skeins of Spanish moss soared through the night air. The wooly vines whirled around us like bearded specters.

Did the low rumble of hoofbeats trail us?

Gripping the seat rail, I turned and peered back down the lane. In the carriage lantern's glow, the retreating oaks vanished, swallowed by the night. In vain I searched for someone or something. Berating such fancy, I decided to face forward again. That's when it appeared: a globe with a center bright as a harvest moon. It hovered not far behind our wagon. The iridescent perimeter of the sphere undulated as it kept pace with our progress. In the space between the horse's gallops, the cantering thump of ghostly hooves echoed. I blinked, certain my eyes and ears deceived me, that the thrill of the evening's dinner party or fear for Baby Rose had excited my imagination.

The wagon careened over a rut and I briefly levitated. Falling back onto the wooden seat, I slammed against the rail.

"Are you okay?" Laura called out.

Righting myself, I faced the front of the wagon. "Yes." I moved closer.

Grim-faced, Laura clutched the reins. "We're almost there."

Shivering, I pulled my cloak tighter and fixed my eyes on the road ahead.

⁊ə ⁊ə ⁊ə

Arriving at The Hill, Laura jumped from the wagon, grabbed her bag, and ran to Kisse's door. I followed, entering upon her heels. Assaulted by the reek of vinegar and candle wax, we both hesitated.

Aunt Phoebe, at Kisse's bedside, limped off to make room for Laura. The leg ulcers must have improved.

"The windows," Laura said.

I rushed to open them and discovered each one boarded up. I pulled at the slats without success.

"I can't work blind." Laura called out to me. "Go get the carriage lantern."

I dashed outside to the wagon and returned seconds later with the lantern.

"There," Laura pointed to the table by the bedstead.

After positioning it to do the most good, I stood catty-corner to the bed.

Laura sat on a three-legged stool. "That's better," she said to Kisse.

Kisse scanned the room with wide, unseeing eyes. She cradled Rose, rocking to-and-fro.

"Aunt Phoebe sent word Rose is doing poorly. I'm here to help," Laura said.

The young mother let out a choked sob, shook her head and hugged the baby tighter. One arm poked out from the bundle. The infant's limb resembled a winter-stripped twig.

"May I take Rose for a moment?" Laura asked. "I promise to give her right back."

Aunt Phoebe said something to Kisse in the pidgin the freedmen favored. I sensed her urging Kisse to do what Laura requested.

Laura watched this exchange with a measured, neutral expression that I knew belied impatience.

Head bowed, Kisse gave her baby over and buried her face in her hands.

Laura laid the child on the bed, loosened the swaddling and stiffened. The baby lay unmoving, her complexion ashen except for a rash surrounding her mouth. Laura placed her stethoscope on Rose's thin chest, but I saw no rise and fall of the baby's rib cage or a sign of encouragement in Laura's expression. I prayed my eyes deceived me and for God to spare this poor little mite.

Laura removed the stethoscope. Holding on to one of the tiny hands, she turned to Aunt Phoebe. "When did the baby take ill?"

"Bout three days ago. She took down wid feber and wouldn't feed."

"What did you do for her?" Laura said, her speech clipped.

"Wash her in vinegar, pokeroot and salt," Aunt Phoebe responded.

Laura nodded, her attention focused on the child's mottled face. Opening the baby's mouth, Laura grimaced. "When did the rash appear on her cheeks?"

"'Dis mornin'."

Laura wrapped the lifeless infant and returned her to her mother's arms. "I'm sorry, Kisse."

Kisse received the limp bundle and proceeded to howl.

Laura stood and turned to me. "Ellen, sit with Kisse while I have a word with Aunt Phoebe."

Laura brushed by me and waited at the doorway. Aunt Phoebe hobbled past Laura who shut the door with a *whomp!*

Kisse's wails penetrated my heart like an ice dagger. Not knowing another way to offer comfort, I hiked up my skirts and plopped onto the narrow cot. Kisse radiated a sorrow so raw I questioned if my presence was an intrusion. After a moment, I reached over and covered Kisse's hand with my own. She did not acknowledge my presence, but neither did she recoil from my touch.

On the other side of the cabin door, two voices rose, fell and clashed as the wind howled and moaned.

ءٮ ءٮ ءٮ

The earlier wild wind and echo of phantom hooves did not follow us on the drive home. Frowning at the road ahead, Laura and I remained as silent as the night.

"The child died of the pox," Laura said after a time, her voice thick.

"Surely not!" I said. "There was only a hint of a rash on her face."

"And inside her mouth," Laura added. "Had she survived the fever, those tiny pimples would have spread and postulated."

"But how?" I asked. "Kisse wasn't sick."

"I've been wondering the same thing." Laura sighed. "My best guess is the blanket and clothing donations we gave them were contaminated. Rose's infancy made her more susceptible. Kisse may yet become ill."

"You mean to say the donated shipments from the North carried smallpox?" I felt the color drain from my face. "But *we* distributed those articles to everyone!"

Laura remained silent. The wind still blew, but no fierce gusts impeded our travel.

"This is terrible," I said over the clopping hooves. "Perhaps we can enlist the assistance of a doctor from Beaufort—"

Laura yanked on the horse's reins, bringing our wagon to a halt. "Once smallpox is contracted, nothing can be done. It's pointless to involve another doctor. And dangerous!"

"Why?"

"Too much is at stake."

"For whom?" I asked. "Aren't we obliged to get help when possible?"

"Yes, and that's why we won't elaborate on what we saw this evening."

I shook my head. "If there's an epidemic, won't word get out regardless?"

With a weary sigh, Laura took up the reins and signaled the horse to move forward. "Unless we call attention, no one will care."

Sensing she wasn't finished, I waited.

"Who would come to our aid?" Laura scoffed. "Unscrupulous quacks whose primary interest would be to see pox on Black skin. No, we'll deal with the outbreak that's likely coming; do our best to prevent its spread; comfort and tend the sick. A cry for help will bring nothing but condemnation."

"That's rather a cynical view of your colleagues."

"Early this year there was outbreak in Washington. The doctors, the municipal officials, the Army, blamed it on freedmen who'd recently arrived," Laura said. "All were rounded up and secluded. Under the most deplorable conditions, I might add."

"You think if the authorities learn of an outbreak here our people will be blamed?" I asked.

"Yes! What's more, we risk losing financial support, which would finish our work before it's even begun."

"C-come now, Laura," I stammered. "Surely not."

"Ellen, don't be naive. Those in opposition to the Port Royal project will blame a smallpox outbreak on the freedmen. They'll claim a scourge proof positive of God's denouncement of emancipation. Or the work of the devil! That's all the excuse they'll need to cut off funding and halt the project. Our patriotic duty is to demonstrate progress. In this way, we'll do our part to heal our country."

"I suppose we could get help from the Gullah healers—root doctors, isn't that what they call them?"

"Witch doctors!" Laura glared at me. "The cure is more likely to kill them than the pox."

"If an outbreak is eminent, certainly the people deserve a say in their own care. Especially since there's no cure."

"Aunt Phoebe boarded up the windows. I'm surprised the child wasn't asphyxiated!"

"Surely Aunt Phoebe offered a reason for doing so?" I said.

"She claimed it was to contain the disease. Ridiculous."

"It's not ridiculous. And you know it. In fact, it makes perfect sense." I let out a long sigh. "You're heartbroken by Rose's death, but it's no more Aunt Phoebe's fault than it is yours."

Laura looked at me, but didn't reply. We both fell silent, eyes fixed on the flickering lights of The Oaks in the near distance.

"This is difficult," I eventually said, "and your concerns are valid. Nonetheless, if an outbreak comes, you cannot deal with it single-handedly."

"You're right, of course." Laura squared her shoulders. "We'll do it together."

！▲ ！▲ ！▲

One trying day a couple of weeks following Miss Forten's arrival—or Lottie, as she wished to be called—the three of us arrived home from school hungry. Rina came into the foyer from the dining room carrying a tureen.

"Good afternoon, Rina!" Laura said. "Just the woman we need. Any chance we might dine a bit earlier today? We three are famished."

Rina shifted the tureen onto her hip. "Der be too many folks comin'. Can't magic de food from de pot." Scowling, she stared at Laura.

We three stood silent.

"For goodness sakes, Rina!" Laura finally said. "What a fuss about nothing. We'll have an apple and eat at the regular time, if it's such a bother."

Grabbing Lottie's hand, we made a hasty retreat to the parlor.

"Dey kill me, dey kill me sure." Rina's raised voice followed us. Laura followed Rina.

"Please excuse Rina, Lottie," I said after we sat down. "She isn't normally like this. I can't imagine what's gotten into her."

Lottie heaved a sigh. "Please don't worry, Ellen. I'm sure it'll be fine, eventually."

"Eventually? No, Laura will have a talk with her. This is no way to behave." I sighed. "It's out of character—"

Laura waltzed into the parlor.

"I take it you spoke to Rina?" I said.

"I tried." Laura rolled her eyes, and then flopped onto the chair opposite me. "She's in an ornery mood."

"So we gathered." I glanced sideways at Lottie beside me.

"I'm sorry, Lottie," Laura said. "I don't know why—"

"It's me," Lottie said.

"You?" Laura and I said simultaneously.

"Rina likely resents having to serve me, another Black woman."

"But you're our colleague!" Laura said.

"And you live here," I added.

"Rina may feel serving me is beneath her. Or, she may think I consider myself better than her, owing to my position," Lottie said. "For my sake, ladies, leave it be."

Laura raised her eyebrows at me and I shrugged. "If you're sure."

"It'll work itself out." Lottie managed a wane smile. "These things always do."

☙ ☙ ☙

Chapter 15

Henrietta

Without my prompting, Miss Ellen's perspective and history recedes in a rush of light and whoosh of air. Frogmore's screened porch tilts one way and then the other. I grip the chair's arms…Breathe in…one, two, three, four…the room settles and I exhale, one, two, three, four. My racing heart slows. This journal is spent. I glance at Maum, who remains predictably asleep and blissfully ignorant of where I've traveled and the people I've encountered.

Dear Miss Lottie! How curious it is to see her in the past. For those of us between the colors, the way isn't always clear. Or easy. You never really belong. The moment you think you do, someone reminds you that you're not one of them. Even life's blessings can be a curse when you live between. Although I entered this world Black and enslaved, the moment Miss Ellen took me in for her own, I crossed the rubicon of race. If I moved someplace else, where no one knows me, I'd simply be Black Henrietta. Until I opened my mouth. My voice tells another story.

Yet I recall a time when my lack of speech defined me.

When Maum Cat brought me to St. Helena, her daughter Manners received me with open arms, but her grandchildren did not. At first they tried including me, but when I didn't respond, they gave up. Can't blame them. If only they'd stopped there. But children have a way of poking at things and people they don't understand. Eventually, the children's unsatisfied curiosity gave way to contempt. At school they took to calling me dumb and stupid. Owing to my injury, when I spoke in class my utterances sounded thick and slurry. Of course, my deformed jaw and scars cried out for ridicule. *Ugly. Monster. Hag.* My persistent silence in the face of such abuse further inflamed my tormentors.

Still, I adored school and learning. I caught on faster than others my age and Miss Lottie often complimented me. This enraged my classmates who considered me slow.

On one of the days Miss Lottie praised me in front of the class, Mercy and Dora took to pointing and snickering. Mercy's little brother, Shrimp, spat on me. I'm pretty sure she put him up to it.

In the schoolyard after dismissal, Mercy and Dora blocked my path.

I tried to dodge around them, but Mercy leaned sideways and cuffed my ear with an elbow. I shook off the sting and kept moving. I trekked down the road, shoulders hunched, head bowed, too scared to look back. For a bit I focused on the marsh grass on either side of me. Fiddler crab holes dotted the muddy bottom. Low tide. I slowed my pace and took a breath. Maybe Mercy and Dora got to doing something else and forgot about me, so I glanced back. At the sight of both girls my tummy twisted. I faced forward and kept moving.

"Dummy, dummy," Dora chanted.

"Ugly, ugly," Mercy joined in.

Dora has no right calling me dummy when she never gets a sum. She can't write her letters either. Mercy's not dumb, but besides me, she's the least pretty girl at school. I've even heard some of the boys call her Mutt Mercy. If they stopped being mean, I could help Dora with her sums. Or be a friend to Mercy, 'cause other than dull Dora, she's got none.

"What's the matter? Maum Cat got you tongue?" Dora yelled.

It grieved Mercy and Dora that Maum Cat favored me.

Dora screeched and cackled at the joke about Maum.

I picked up my pace.

A vulture swooped down by the roadside to join others pulling flesh from a dead hound. The dog's tongue lolled to the side; vacant holes stared sightless at the sky. Saliva filled my mouth. I gagged, spat, and stumbled on.

SwallowBreatheWalkSwallowBreatheWalk

"Why you runnin'?" Mercy called out.

I kept moving.

"Eeeww," they chirped in unison. Laughing, they stomped closer.

"You like that dead dog in the ditch. *Ugggly!*" Mercy stepped on my heel.

I staggered, but kept my balance. Tears stung my eyes, but I held them in. I wiped my nose on my sleeve.

"Lookee here, Mercy." Dora pulled up beside me. "The ugly dog-face baby's cryin`." She leaned closer, her mouth twisted.

I reared back.

Mercy came to the other side of me. I looked into her eyes and the hatred frightened me so much I commenced sobbing. They took turns pushing me between them, chanting, *crybabydogfacecrybabydogface*. I didn't know how much longer I could stay on my feet.

But I didn't fall. It's Mercy who goes down. Then Dora hit the ground, hard.

From somewhere, Fairy Jenkins appeared. Tall and strong, she's screaming at them, "You leave her be!"

Mercy and Dora lay sprawled in the dirt. Fairy kicked one, then the other.

As mute as I had ever been, Dora stared up, wide-eyed.

"We were just havin' some fun, Fairy," Mercy whined.

"You call pickin' on somebody and hurtin' them fun?" Fairy's nose scrunched. "You wait 'til I tell you mamas. And Maum Cat. See how much fun you gonna have then! She Root you for sure."

Fairy grabbed me by the hand. "Come on."

Fairy must've told Miss Lottie about me getting beat on, `cause soon after she spoke to the whole class about how we should look out for one another and be kind, especially to those that need it, and quoted the Bible: Matthew 25:40: *Inasmuch as ye have done it unto one of the least of these my brethren, ye have done it unto me.*

After that, I'd've followed Fairy anywhere. And did. Everyone needs a loyal, true friend like Fairy. My difficulties with the other children didn't end that day. But having Fairy by my side sure helped.

How curious to learn all these years later, around the same time I struggled, poor Miss Lottie dealt with something similar. And with Miss Rina, of all people. What a surprise! I never saw her be anything but generous and kind. But those days during and just after the War Between the States confused our folks. Everybody scrambled to find their way.

Miss Lottie eventually found her way back up North. Her leaving saddened me. At the time, they told us she suffered from poor health. Later, I learned she experienced recurring symptoms of tuberculosis. But now I wonder if she just got tired of not belonging.

Both my mothers stayed in touch with her, exchanging letters all through the years. Miss Ellen told me when Miss Lottie married the Reverend Grimke, and how they moved to Washington when he became pastor of a big church. On another occasion, Miss Ellen shared that Miss Lottie had given birth to a baby girl, Theodora, and how the child sickened and died only a few months later. Poor Miss Lottie, heartache pursued her all the way up North. Still, from what Miss Ellen said, she's had a rewarding life, working alongside her husband, and writing poetry, papers, and such. Hard to imagine that by now the sweet Miss Lottie I remember must be coming on seventy years of age.

The break from the journals has done me good and I'm ready to carry on. Maum hasn't so much as turned over. Fixing the quilt around my knees, I use the corner bit of fabric to pick up the next book and flip it open to the title page.

This book belongs to:
Ellen Murray
January, 1863—December, 1863

I hesitate, but for a moment. Curiosity overrides my anxiety, and squeezing my eyes shut, I touch the page and again become one with Miss Ellen's past.

᪐ ᪐ ᪐

Chapter 16

Ellen

Following Baby Rose's death from the pox earlier this winter, Laura and I feared an outbreak in the community. But by the time Christmas came and went with no sign of an eruption, Laura deemed the risk over.

On New Year's Eve, sitting at my desk in our bedchamber with a plate of Rina's molasses cookies between us, I remained skeptical and questioned Laura yet again.

"You're sure?" I asked.

"Yes." Laura smiled and sighed.

"I don't mean to badger you," I said. "I suppose I'm afraid to let my guard down lest the worst happen."

"That's understandable." Laura handed me a cookie and took one for herself. "Smallpox is not new to St. Helena. A few plantations have experienced outbreaks. So some freedmen are resistant—like Kisse and Aunt Phoebe. That's why they never contracted it from Baby Rose or passed it on."

I nibbled the cookie and let Laura's assurances sink in.

"Ellen, I don't blame you for being skeptical or worried. But it is New Year's Eve, and thanks to President Lincoln, we have good reason to feel positive stepping into 1863."

"You're right." I finished my cookie and brushed crumbs from my nightgown. "His Emancipation Proclamation. We need to focus on the future."

"Exactly," Laura said. "As of tomorrow, all enslaved Blacks in the Rebel states are free."

"I'm looking forward to the reading and celebration at Fort Saxton."

"Me too." Laura stood, stretched and headed for our bed. "We should go to sleep. The steamer leaves early."

"Uh-huh." I snatched the last cookie off the plate. "I'm right behind you."

❧ ❧ ❧

"Ellen, wake up," Laura smoothed the hair from my face. "Dress quickly or we'll miss the ferry to Port Royal."

"The ferry!" I sat up and threw my legs over the side of the mattress.

Laura pulled on her skirt. "It'll be going back and forth all day. But they're opening the ceremonies with the reading. We don't want to miss it." Laura stepped into her shoes. "I'll meet you downstairs."

We arrived at the wharf, giggling and breathless, to discover the *Flora* had indeed departed without us and several other latecomers.

"Oh dear," I said, staring at the steamer, already a good distance from shore.

Laura heaved a sigh. "Oh well, there's nothing to be done for it now." She put her arm around me and whispered. "Besides, we needed the sleep."

My face warmed as I looked around to see if anyone heard.

Laura laughed. "It's warm, the sun is shining, and we're together. The ferry will be back soon."

❧ ❧ ❧

Located on the old Smith Plantation, we spotted Fort Saxton from the deck of the steamer. At the shoreline stood the ruins of a colonial fort, and beyond that, the oak grove and picnic area. Savory smoke wafted all the way out to the ferry, and my mouth watered. Rumor was they'd slaughtered ten oxen for the event and prepared vats of sweetwater, which Laura and I love. Rina heard they'd used only the best molasses, vinegar, and ginger in its preparation.

"Come on," Laura said after we disembarked.

Taking my hand, she led us from the pier, around an oak grove, and the regiment's camp. Crossing through a cordon of officers and cavalrymen at the crowd's perimeter, we wove through the throng to the foot of the raised platform. The military band played. I glanced around at the audience and estimated our number to be in the thousands. Freedmen must have come on foot from nearby plantations, others by steamer from the Sea Islands. A number traveled from Hilton Head. All wore their Sunday best. I admired one beautiful woman in a headscarf she had artfully knotted at her forehead. I touched my plain bonnet. How would it feel to adorn oneself in such rich, vibrant color?

A freedman across the way raised his tremulous voice and sang, *My Country 'Tis of Thee.* Two women joined in, followed by others. The song swept through the crowd like a welcome breeze.

Colonel Higginson sat at the front of the platform, holding two flags: the national and the regimental colors. He stared straight ahead, a picture of patriotic stoicism. The hymn finished, Higginson waved the flags and then handed them to a sergeant. I focused on the three men behind the sergeant. They sat huddled in a row like the proverbial wise monkeys; most likely the newly appointed Federal Tax Commissioners. Mandated to either collect taxes on confiscated plantations or sell, their arrival gave us another reason to celebrate. Many freedmen longed to own a piece of land. Their destiny, and that of their progeny, depended on the judicious application of the law by the commissioners.

"Look." Laura pressed closer. "I think that's Lottie, near the back," she whispered. Lottie had left earlier in the day with some younger teachers from neighboring plantation schools.

I stood on tiptoes for a better view. Indeed, Lottie sat beside the Black regiment's doctor who'd recently arrived. It turned out he and Lottie hailed from the same area up North and knew each other. He leaned in to her and, smiling, spoke into her ear. Noting the coquettish tilt of her head, I turned to Laura, who continued to stare at them.

"It's likely nothing," I said. Yet I worried that others, not so generous, may also be watching. Lottie's Negro status, no matter how light her skin, made her a target. Both Black and White begrudged her position as a respected teacher. Some might use her interaction with the doctor to besmirch her reputation.

The sergeant on the platform completed his address and the other flag bearer took center stage. He raised his voice, "Follow Captain Jesus," he exhorted, "who was never defeated."

On that cue, the 1st South Carolina Volunteers stood and broke into song:

The army is gathering from near and from far, the trumpet is sounding the call for the war...

Laura and I joined in:

Marching along, marching along! For God and for country we are marching along…

General Saxton took the stage. Loud cheers punctuated his every statement.

At the conclusion of his address, the crowd broke apart. The band played "John Brown's Body." With raised voices, we followed the scent of roast oxen to the picnic area.

Once we'd joined the line for sweetwater, Laura turned to me. "I made light of it earlier because I didn't want it to mar the day, but I do regret we missed the reading of the Proclamation," she said.

"I know, but look." I smiled.

All around us freedmen chatted and laughed. A few feet from our queue, a group of youth teased one another.

"They're free, Laura. Nothing else matters."

૨ા ૨ા ૨ા

By March, the Federal Tax Commissioners on stage at the Proclamation celebration had settled in to do their duty. We received news that the foreclosed properties in our area—153 plantations—were to be sold off to raise money for the war effort. Those of us involved in the Port Royal project feared Northern speculators would swoop in and buy the lot. Hoping for an update, Laura and I had gleefully accepted General Saxton's request that he stop by for a visit today. Mr. Hooper, having scheduled a previous appointment, told us to proceed without him.

૨ા ૨ા ૨ા

While we waited for Rina to bring tea into the dining room, the general explained that one of the original missionaries with our band, Edward Philbrick from Coffin Point, had aligned himself with a conglomerate of Northern investors. Together, they planned to purchase a number of plantations.

Laura and I did not know Philbrick well. One of my few encounters with the man had been upon my arrived to St. Helena during a forced stop at the chapel due to a rainstorm. There Nelly, her back to him, had rolled her eyes and said my being there meant she needn't accept his offer to escort her home. At the time, her dismissal of Philbrick appeared mean-spirited.

I've since changed my mind. Perhaps Nelly's intuition drove her rebuttal. Still, to think one of our own missionaries would betray the freedmen this way defied belief.

"You are certain about Mr. Philbrick?" I asked the general, my voice pitched low.

He nodded.

"Do you understand what's at stake?" Laura asked.

"Of course I do!" The general's nostrils flared. "Do you take me for a fool?" He glowered at Laura.

"Certainly not," Laura drew in a long breath. "I apologize. It is my fear and disappointment talking."

"Let me make sure I understand this correctly, General," I interjected. "You mean to tell us Edward Philbrick plans to buy up prime properties at the upcoming auction and have the freedmen 'work' for *him*?"

"The freedmen should own the property." Laura smacked the table.

"Mr. Philbrick thinks differently." General Saxton's lip curled.

"I cannot believe he is sticking to his preposterous notion that the freedmen aren't ready for land ownership," Laura paced the length of our dining room, "that to appreciate the *concept* they must first work as free laborers. What utter nonsense."

"It's all too convenient, if you ask me," I said, "not to mention self-serving."

"This is dreadful!" Laura stopped. "Not only will the freedmen be denied the land they've worked without compensation, his scheme also places the entire Port Royal project in jeopardy."

A sudden chill gripped me. Again, the survival of the project, and by extension Penn School, hung in the balance.

"I'm doing what I can," General Saxton said. "The tax commissioners know of the Negroes' desire to own land." One side of his mouth quirked up. "One of the commissioners plans to speak on their behalf. Right now he's en route to Washington. The commissioner believes he can convince the Secretary of the Treasury to amend the tax act with the use of preemption; it's akin to squatters' rights, so the freedmen have a fighting chance at the auction."

"But the first one is scheduled a week from today," Laura said.

"I am aware, Miss Towne."

"Why not postpone the sale?" The general and Laura frowned at me. "Just until we hear back from Washington," I added.

Laura's eyebrows shot up and she turned to General Saxton. "Is that possible?"

"I don't have the authority." Saxton scratched his beard. "If only the land sales adversely affected our military mission."

"They do." I sat straighter. "The Army encampment at Hilton Head relies on local produce to feed the troops, correct?"

"Yes," General Saxton said. "But how does that—"

"If the land was sold, the supply would end. Edward Philbrick certainly isn't going to farm vegetables! His concern is cotton and profit."

"You're right!" General Saxton laughed.

"What's more," Laura said, "if Philbrick offers the freedmen a steady wage and the promise of land for purchase at the war's conclusion, they may rather work for him and not enlist."

General Saxton picked up the thread, "Recruitment for the Black regiment would suffer."

"That's not all," Laura continued. "Philbrick would need armed plantation guards which, in turn, would mean fewer soldiers to protect our borders."

General Saxton shot out of his chair and bolted for the door, almost colliding with Rina and the tea tray.

"Where are you going?" Laura called, accepting the tray from a befuddled Rina.

"To Hilton Head." The general set his hat on his head. "As if you didn't know."

ᕦ ᕦ ᕦ

Thanks to General Saxton, advertising for the tax sales was suspended until we heard from Washington. Word arrived and not a moment too soon: Sixty thousand acres—reserved for military and educational use—would be sold at a later date when no longer required. This land included most of St. Helena and our home, The Oaks. Also, at a federally set minimum price the freedmen would then have the right of first refusal to purchase. Those of us associated with the Port Royal project celebrated the small, but mighty victory.

On the morning of the sale, Laura and I arrived in Beaufort with little time to spare. At 10 o'clock, sixteen thousand acres were going on the block. The streets of Beaufort teemed with people coming and going. We followed others away from the river and up a street to the Tax Commissioners' residence, and the auction's location. To that end, several chairs and a desk lined the upper balcony.

Around us the crowd of predominately freedmen expanded. Off to my left, an old man, his ebony complexion as scarred as his fiddle, struck up "The Swallowtail Jig." For the freedmen, the mere occurrence of this sale offered reason to celebrate.

Laura nudged me and we moved forward. Covering my mouth and nose from the reek of pipe smoke, I searched the gathering for familiar faces. I soon spotted Edward Philbrick up front, presumably here to represent his Northern conglomerate.

"Look." I pointed him out to Laura.

"What's Ted Hooper, of all people, doing with him?" Laura frowned at them.

"How odd," I said. "He's not an admirer of Philbrick's scheme. He told us so himself."

"Look who else is up front," I said, "to the right of Philbrick and Ted."

Laura squinted. "Isn't that Harry from Lady's Island who came to us about the property?"

"One and the same," I said.

Some time ago, Harry had told us he wanted to purchase the Inlet, but questioned the risk.

"I axed Mister Philbrick," he had said, "he tell me no."

Laura had crossed her arms. "Did he now."

Harry nodded.

"What else did Mr. Philbrick say?" Laura asked.

"He say he buy de Inlet fur we, keep it safe de year and we work fur de money he pay."

"And you want to know what we think of this idea?" I said.

"Yessim."

Laura's lips formed a thin line. "If you want to make money, I suggest you hold the land yourself."

"Besides," I added, "Mr. Philbrick could change his mind and keep the property. What then?"

Harry frowned. "Losing de money be somethin'. But if Mister Philbrick own de land, change he mind and don sell back—" Shoulders stooped, he had shook his head and left us.

Today, Harry stood tall, his shoulders back.

Still looking at him, I leaned in to Laura. "Do you think Harry went along with Philbrick's proposal?"

Laura shrugged. "I hope not." A sudden hush fell over the gathering. The Tax Commissioners had stepped out and onto the upper veranda.

For all the initial excitement, the commissioners' task of detailing the particular property up for offer droned on and on. While we waited for land the freedman wanted to go on the block, Philbrick purchased five plantations for his wealthy investors.

"Odious turncoat," Laura hissed.

"Look," I lifted my chin, pointing at the auctioneers with their heads huddled.

A palpable frisson went through the crowd.

"What do you think is happening?" I asked Laura.

Brow ruffled, she shook her head.

Around us, bodies moved and made way. A freedman Laura and I knew from Oaklands Plantation drew up beside us and nodded a hello.

The auctioneer smacked his gavel. All small talk and fidgeting ceased. He then proceeded to detail the length and breadth of Oaklands Plantation from a survey map.

I stole a glance at the man beside me. Generations of his forebearers' sweat, tears and blood had sown, tended, and harvested Oaklands' lucrative crops. Set at the heart of St. Helena Island, its importance could not be understated. Whoever won this bid—consortium or former slave—would emerge victor.

"Four hundred acres of prime land! Who will start the bidding? Do I hear fifty cents an acre?"

Philbrick's hand shot up, his voice rang out, "Twenty-five cents!"

The auctioneer reared back like he'd been slapped.

Philbrick's cocky stance exuded arrogant superiority. Unfortunately, he had good reason to be confident. Despite the proviso that offered freedmen first refusal, Oaklands—due to its size and merit—was likely inaccessible to a recently freed slave.

"Twenty-five cents, from Mr. Philbrick. Do I hear *more?*" The auctioneer drew out the final word. "Oaklands is certainly worth more than a paltry twenty-five cents an acre."

Tension was ripe, evidenced by the skunky pong that hung in air.

A freedman stepped forward. Judging from the huddle of associates about him, he represented an alliance.

"Fifty cents an acre!" he called out. His associates clapped him on the back as though offering of the bid alone made them winners. I suppose in some ways, it did.

Philbrick scowled over at the group. "Seventy-five cents!" he bellowed.

Beside me, the freedman from Oaklands wiped his brow with a handkerchief. He raised his arm. "Dolluh!"

The auctioneer smiled. I shuddered.

"One-ten!" Philbrick countered.

"Dolluh twenty-fibe!"

"One twenty-five from the Black man in the straw hat! Do I hear more?"

Philbrick shooed the suggestion with a flip of his wrist.

"SOLD!"

The auctioneer announced that the winner must put up two-fifths now, the balance upon receipt of the deed.

Where did the freedman get that kind of money? Surely he couldn't have saved all of it in the short period of time he'd been earning a wage. I frowned this question at Laura.

She leaned in. "My best guess is he was lent the money."

The auctioneer announced another sale.

One property after another was declared, delineated, and auctioned off. Some went to freedmen, but Philbrick and his conglomeration purchased many plantations.

A swift bolt of energy surged through my limbs when the Inlet came up on the block. Harry, who'd consulted us whether or not he should buy the land or work for Philbrick, began the bidding. In a clear, confident voice, Philbrick countered Harry's offer. Back and forth they went, the price escalating with each bid.

I turned to Laura. "What's Philbrick doing? Bidding on Oaklands and the other properties made sense. But the Inlet? He knows Harry wants it, can pay for it, and as a former slave he has first right of refusal."

The answer dawned on me and my mouth fell open.

"Exactly," Laura said. "He's spitefully driving up the price."

Back and forth they went, my heart racing faster with each subsequent bid.

"Sold!" the auctioneer finally called out.

A lump formed in my throat. Harry now owned the Inlet.

Ted Hooper pumped Harry's hand, and a thought occurred to me.

I nudged Laura. "Do you think Ted loaned Harry the money?"

"It's possible," she said. "When we arrived, I assumed Ted and Philbrick were together. Which I did think odd."

"Me too," I laughed. "It appears Ted Hooper threw everyone off the scent. Including us."

By the sale's conclusion, Edward Philbrick held eleven plantations, including Coffin Point. However, twenty-five thousand acres now belonged to freedmen in joint ventures, cooperatives, and individually, in great part thanks to the intervention of General Saxton and the plan we cooked up around our dining table

⁊⁊ ⁊⁊ ⁊⁊

Chapter 17

Henrietta

A distant moaning escalates to a high-pitched scream and then snaps, like a thunder crack. Miss Ellen's presence spirals into the shadows of time and, in a flurry of breath, I am back in the present moment.

Across from me on the porch swing, Maum tosses off her blankets, sits, and gazes about, her mouth puckered.

"You're at Frogmore…" I hesitate. My voice sounds disconnected, as though part of me remains in past, "…on Miss Ellen's back porch."

Maum scowls. "Course I am!"

She thinks I'm talking to her.

"You don't have to be so cranky." My own hackles rise and I clam up.

Maum half-sits, half-rolls off the swing, and for a moment I fear she'll topple right onto the floorboards. Eyes averted, she brushes her skirt, raises her head and makes for the stairs.

"You can use the facilities inside," I say.

She waves me off and keeps on toward the old outhouse. The glossy moon lights her path. The night sounds have stilled. The earlier roar of the incoming tide is now a whisper.

Come to think of it, I should probably make a visit myself. Putting aside the notebook, I wiggle out of my blankets, stand, stretch, and put on my gloves. I feel stiffer than Maum Cat looked.

I've kept the stove warm, so while I'm inside I make another pot of tea and grab an extra cup and sugar for Maum. By the time I get back to the porch she's already sitting on the swing.

"Want some?" I hold out the tray.

"Sugga?" Her grin is childlike.

I laugh. "Yessim."

A few minutes later we're swathed in our quilts, sipping hot tea.

Maum lifts her chin at me. "Where you at?"

"In Miss Ellen's notebooks?"

"Mmm-hmm."

"Miss Laura and Miss Ellen have come down during the War Between the States."

Maum nods. "Sumptin' always happenin' back in dem days." She stares blankly over my head.

"I learned the government auctioned off land cheap, for the tax money owed by the Confederates who ran off. Both Miss Ellen and Miss Laura did what they could, so our folks had a fighting chance to buy some of that property." I sipped my tea.

"How'd dey do dat?"

"Well, for one they worked with the generals in charge to make sure the freedman had an opportunity to buy some land. An old man named Harry thought well enough of them to seek their advice about his purchasing prospects. Then they went to the land sales auction to ensure fair conduct. And you'll never believe this..."

Maum frowned. "What?"

"Tommy, Fairy's husband? He figures quite a bit."

"Tommy always doin' and helpin' somebody in dem days." She smiled.

"He's still that way," I say.

"Uh-huh."

For a few moments we just drink our tea.

"You in dem books?"

"Oh, no," I stammer. "At least not yet." Maum's right, though, at some point I'll likely appear, but until now it hadn't crossed my mind. I shiver and push the notion aside. I'll cross that bridge when I must.

Maum drains the last of her tea and hoists her legs onto the swing. The warm drink seems to have loosened her bones as well as her tongue. "Where you at?"

"I just told you."

"No," Maum shakes her head. "When Miss Ellen was helpin' folks buy land, where you at?"

Keeping ahead of Maum sure can be challenging. "With Miss Manners, and you—I suppose?"

"Don't know?" She draws out *know*, like I do and I'm just not saying.

A lump clogs my throat. Maum is well aware my missing memories rankle. I've often thought she knows more than she's saying about *My Time Before*, which we took to calling it when I was a child.

"Why don't *you* tell me?" I croak. "You're the one that found me, brought me here." This isn't the first time I've asked her for more information.

Like always, she prods me with another question. "How old you be when Miz Ellen go to dat auction? Don be rollin' dem eyes at me, Henrietta."

I groan. "It would've been around the time you brought me here, so five or six."

"Mebbe you still in Beaufort."

"Maybe." For a second I'm hopeful that she'll share something. Anything. But all she does is stare at me.

Finally, she asks, "You 'member me comin' to collect you in Beaufort?"

"Maum, I've told you all this before," I whine.

"Den tells me again."

I exhale, close my eyes and try to find the words. "I'm in a kitchen—"

"Mmhmm, dats good. What else?"

"It's hot. I don't feel well."

"People?"

"I don't know—"

The mist clears. A woman's face appears. She wipes my forehead with a cool cloth.

I bolt upright. "A woman. She's washing my face." It's not much, but it's more than I've recollected in years.

"Dat's sumptin'."

"I suppose." Something, but not enough. I slouch back into the chair.

"What you expectin' to find in Miz Ellen's books?"

"Expecting?"

I'm taken aback by both the question and sudden digression. Although, I shouldn't be—Maum's as nimble as a politician.

Her face is scrunched and she stares at me, waiting.

"I'm not *expecting* anything." I rearrange my quilt.

"Then why you botherin'?"

"Land sakes! You're the one who told me to read the notebooks, remember? Saying that Miss Ellen must've wanted me to know her story or she wouldn't have left them for me to find?"

"Don be cussin' me."

"I wasn't—never mind."

Maum carries on, "It's time to tell you own story. `Fore it's too late."

"What does that mean?" I growl through clenched teeth. My jaw throbs.

Maum doesn't answer. Instead, she snuggles down, rolls over, and pulls the blankets over her head.

It's several minutes before I can even think straight enough to pick up Miss Ellen's journal. Now I'm not even sure that I should. I frown at Maum. She's on her side. The outline of her frail body rises and falls beneath the bedding. I release a loud sigh and some of my rage. I shouldn't allow myself to get so flummoxed. I know what she's like. And she's old. For all she irks me, I owe her my life. Where would I be without Maum Cat? I reach over and grab the journal.

A flash of memory: *My nostrils flare and I salivate. In a kitchen, the woman's face, and the smell of roasting chicken.*

Where did that come from?

I look down at the notebook. Something locked inside me just loosened. I don't know what. Or why. But whatever's happening, it's tied to Miss Ellen's writings. I remove my gloves. Maum is right. I am supposed to read them.

≈ ≈ ≈

Chapter 18

Ellen
June, 1863

Laura burst into the bedchamber and announced, "I have a surprise."

Inserting my pen in the inkwell, I turned around. Her hands were primly clasped at her waist, but her eyes sparkled. Looking at me, she laughed.

"What?" I asked, also laughing, but unsure of the joke.

"Does that *what* mean, why am I laughing or what is the surprise?"

"Stop teasing!" I said, chuckling.

"Fine. I'll put you out of your misery."

Silence.

"Laura!"

She grabbed her own chair and pulled it close to my desk by the window.

Her smile faded and she cleared her throat. "Before we get to the surprise, there's something I need to make clear." Her eyes locked mine.

"All right."

"I asked you to join me here, to participate in this work I truly believe is important, not only to the freedmen, but for all of us, our country. What I didn't factor in," she drew a breath, "was the risk to your health." She stopped and swallowed hard.

During the winter, I had fallen ill with a fever, chills, and an unrelenting cough; as had Lottie. Both of us were forced to step back from our teaching duties. Lottie had recovered in reasonable time, whereas I had spent a month and then some, convalescing. Laura had stoically nursed me back to good health, but I know my illness had frightened her.

"We're together!" I said, taking hold of her hands. "And yes, at times I'm exhausted, we both are, but I wouldn't change a thing."

Laura laughed, but her lack of mirth saddened me. "Darling Ellen, I've brought you into the middle of a war zone."

Until this moment I hadn't appreciated the burden of responsibility she carried regarding my well-being.

"Are you suggesting I don't have a mind of my own?" I almost laughed at her stricken expression.

"Of course not. I would never suggest—"

"Good. Let's agree then to set aside your ill-chosen remarks. Coming here has meant I've had the chance not only to teach, which I love, but to establish a school. I would never have had such an opportunity in Newport." With a nod I said, "I'm where I belong and that's that."

She blinked, opened her mouth as if to speak, but when I lifted my eyebrows in warning, she closed it.

"The war," I continued, "will end eventually."

Laura moaned and tilted back her head. Staring at the ceiling she said, "Encircled by Confederates, as we are, some days I feel downhearted. It is as though it's not just us in the Port Royal area who are surrounded, but the entire country."

"Look at me," I said. When she looked straight into my eyes, I continued. "You're dismissing the good. This past spring, within our own circle, we've had two weddings: General Saxton's, then Nelly's."

"If you ask me, I don't know why a fine, intelligent man like Rufus Saxton married that flibbertigibbet Mathilda Thompson, or why Nelly Winsor, so capable and independent, wed Josiah Fairfield. He's mean-spirited and bad-tempered. Mark my words, she'll live to regret that union."

"My, you are determined to be glum!" I said. "We don't always choose who we fall in love with, do we?"

Laura sniffed, but the edges of her mouth quirked. "You've got me on both points, I suppose."

"You're also forgetting that despite their hardships, the freedmen have made tremendous progress. The children attend school and are learning to read. Many of the adults also. They're now able to support themselves and their families and, like other citizens, defend their nation. Do you recall in April, the Black regiment's triumphant march through Beaufort after their victory at Jacksonville? Not so long ago we could never have imagined such an event.

"Speaking of which, what about the proclamation, President Lincoln's proclamation? Our people are free! We had the privilege of sharing that firsthand." Drawing a breath, I recalled another pivotal announcement from our President. "Last April, Mr. Lincoln also said that West Virginia would join the Union this month, on the 20th. That's most certainly a step in the right direction."

"You're right, of course," Laura said. "But I still feel guilty."

"Whatever for?"

"For putting you in danger; for the sacrifices you're forced to make."

"Laura Towne, we've already established you didn't put a gun to my head. I'd be miserable without you. And Penn School." I sighed, "I must say, I am disappointed if this surprise you speak of is a confession of guilt. I do not accept it."

Laura laughed. "No, of course not. I was trying to tell you I'm sorry your life is so difficult—"

"Again, I say, my life is full and happy here with you."

"You win!" Laura threw up her hands. "Regardless, I want you to have a reprieve. Perhaps I need it more than you." She laughed at the admission.

I wiggled closer until our knees touched. "What did you have in mind?"

"Captain Dutch of the *Kingfisher* has invited us to tour the ship and go for an outing to Edisto Island. It would give us an opportunity to visit where our refugees came from, so that we might better understand their loss. Edisto's beach is supposed to be beautiful, wide and deep at low tide, with endless fine sand. Captain Dutch is supplying sailors and boats and suggested we invite some friends to join us."

"The *Kingfisher*? It's stationed in the Sound, isn't it?"

"Do you like the idea?" She searched my face. "I thought, too, it might be nice to get out and about, you know, normally, the way other couples do."

Eyebrows raised, I laughed. "Other couples?"

She shrugged, a hint of pink colored her cheeks.

In truth, I was eager to get back to work. I'd already missed so much because of my illness, and I had a lot of planning to do before school resumed in the fall. And yet—

"It's a fabulous idea." I stood, pulling her up along with me. "Who shall we invite?"

❧ ❧ ❧

Chapter 19

Ellen
New Year's Eve, 1863

In a few hours 1863, with all its blessings and hardships, will be a memory. The year 1864 will surely bring unimagined opportunities. I have resolved to embrace each and every one with a glad heart. The first of which is our move to a new home. If I adopt such an attitude, perhaps Laura will also. Thus with a fond farewell, the moment I am strong enough we will pack up and leave The Oaks, and set up house at the cottage Laura has found for us in the village of St. Helenaville.

ン ン ン

I reread my brief, lifeless entry, and set aside my pen. For the past six months, between teaching and tending other school business, I'd nursed wounded soldiers, and then freedmen sickened by smallpox and typhoid. I'd barely had a moment to myself. When I did, I'd craved sleep and had no appetite to write. Then I had been brought to my knees by malaria. Now, I don't know where or how to resume writing. The once familiar pages of my story are more like strangers than family. I am lost in uncharted territory, searching for a path home. Often, if words fail me, I sketch. And so I took up my pen, not to write but to draw.

As I considered what to draw, a mockingbird whistled and trilled.

Inspired, I sketched outlines of the birds Laura keeps in an enclosure in the yard. Their lilting melodies at times penetrate our closed bedroom window. At full moon, they serenade us. On those nights, the daily concerns and burdens that crease Laura's brow soften and her face is as beautiful as the mockingbird's song.

Stopping, I leaned back and squinted at my work in progress—a bird in flight; another at rest; the pair, caged.

Laura opened the door and, smiling, walked over to my desk. She cupped my shoulders with her warm hands, then massaged the base of my neck. Closing my eyes, I turned my head one way and then the other.

"It's nice to see you up and writing."

She stopped and leaned over me. "Oh, you're drawing," she said, her voice rising. "Our mockingbirds, correct?"

"Mmm-hmm."

"Well done."

I leaned back for another look. "Not bad," I conceded.

"You're troubled that we must move house," Laura said, her lighthearted tone replaced with a somber one. "We'll take the birds with us. Nelly would try to have Rina bake them in a pie."

"What?" I said, choking on a laugh. I pulled my chair out and looked up to meet her gaze, curious as to what I'd find.

She shrugged and turned her head, but not before I saw the flame of anger that burned in her eyes.

"I'm not upset in the least about the move," I said. "Although I don't think that Nelly and Josiah would devour your pets, I do believe they want us gone from The Oaks as soon as possible."

Laura nodded and drew breath.

Poor Laura. While overwhelmed and distracted by a smallpox outbreak throughout the island, and tending me, yet again, bedridden and incoherent with a malarial fever, the Fairfields had taken advantage. Having raised insufficient funds from the land sales in March of last year, the tax commissioners had to sell off or lease another 16,000 acres of the reserved lands.

Although our Penn School remained independent, other plantation schools were absorbed into a government system. Speculators leased the land for up to five years, committing a portion of the proceeds derived to the establishment of a school. For those with money to invest, the arrangement was potentially lucrative.

Nelly and Josiah Fairfield, seeing an opportunity to cash in on their philanthropic work, had leased The Oaks out from under us. The property was now theirs, and Laura and I were not welcome.

"I wouldn't blame you for resenting the move." Laura brought me back to the moment. "We began our life together here."

"Exactly," I said. "Our story isn't over. This chapter ends, another begins."

Her eyes flitted to the drawings. "I thought perhaps you felt melancholy."

"Frustrated is more like it. I don't know where to begin writing. I thought sketching might loosen my tongue, so to speak."

Laura nodded. "I'll leave you to it, then."

I turned my seat back to face the desk.

"May I offer a suggestion?" Laura called from the doorway.

I glanced over my shoulder. "Of course."

"To capture your thoughts, perhaps forgo the details and use a broad stroke." She nodded goodbye and closed the door.

Setting my drawings aside, I reached into the drawer for some foolscap. Rather than disrupt the flow in my notebook, I'd write an addendum. I picked up my pen and thought for a moment. These last six months had been a whirlwind. Even if I hadn't always been able to participate, I still had plenty to say. Certainly enough to create a picture of our lives.

≥ ≥ ≥

Chapter 20

Henrietta

This time, without turbulence, I land in the present. Except for the lap of waves, all is quiet. Maum sleeps on and here I sit, wrapped in a quilt as though I haven't just traveled back in time. I close the journal. That I have returned to the present must mean it has nothing more to share. But what of the addendum Miss Ellen planned to write?

I grip the journal's covers, front in one hand, back in the other, and then lift and open them like wings. Nothing. I give the book a shake. No loose papers flutter out.

I check the dates again. There is definitely a leap. The entries go from *June, 1863* to *New Year's Eve* and then jump to *Spring, 1864*. Miss Ellen said she wanted to document that time. Where would she put the addendum if not with this journal? The succeeding one perhaps? To avoid the next journals' sharing their stories before I am ready, I slip on my gloves. Then I examine the subsequent books. No luck.

I had emptied the locked drawer of her desk. Afterwards, I'd looked and felt all around inside. Besides, storing the loose entries someplace other than with the diaries makes no sense, especially for someone as organized and methodical as Miss Ellen. Wracking my brain on where else to search for the missing six months, I return to the current journal and riffle the pages to the end. There, attached to the inside of the back cover, is an envelope. Because it's thin and pretty much the same size and color as the backboards, I missed it. Lifting the flap, I reach inside and remove a sheaf of folded paper. I open it and two photographs fall onto my lap: souvenir images of Fort Sumter. I set the photos aside and lay the foolscap sheets down on the journal. Written at the top of the first page is the heading, *Early Summer, 1863, Tea at The Oaks.*

I've found the broad-stroke entries she referenced. "Hurrah!" I cover my mouth and glance Maum's way. She hasn't moved.

To make sure the entries are all here, I go to the final page. It's dated, *Fall and Winter, 1863*, which coincides with Miss Ellen's final installment on New Year's Eve.

It occurs to me there are no drawings. To be certain, I stick my gloved hand back into the envelope and wiggle my fingers. Empty. I pull my hand free and the envelope lifts, along with the end sheet pasted to the book board, revealing a narrow opening at the top.

I turn the notebook around so the slit faces me and peek inside. With care, I pry it open and pull out another, slightly smaller envelope.

"Watcha got there?"

The envelope flies through the air. "Maum!" My heart slams my breastbone and I press a hand to my chest. "Goodness gracious!"

Maum snickers and pulls herself up against the end rail of the swing.

Maum's laugh is contagious. I chuckle. "What's so funny?"

"You jump higher dan de tree frog." Maum's gaze trails to the floor by my feet and she stops her guffawing. "Wats dat?"

I bend over and pick up the second envelope. "I think it might be Miss Ellen's drawings. I found it stashed at the back of one of the journals and she made mention of some sketches."

"Watcha waitin' for?" asks Maum.

Reaching inside I pull out the sketches.

There are four of them, each about four by six inches. I place them on my lap.

"They're a study of mockingbirds," I say more to myself than Maum.

I'm not an artist and I can't tell what she used to draw them, but they are detailed and shaded with color. One is a close-up of the bird's face; in the next, the bird is perched on a bare branch; another is in flight; and the final one is looking down from above.

I hold them up for Maum.

"I 'member Miss Laura keep dem birds at de Oaks," says Maum. "Dat it?"

"For now."

She eases herself down and turns her back to me.

I ponder the illustrations on my lap. I had no idea Miss Ellen could sketch. It's a shame she didn't do more. What with Penn School and Fountain and me, I suppose she didn't have time. Chances are she forgot about these, or she might have dug them out and displayed them here, at Frogmore. I suppose we all have bits and pieces of our life we tuck away and then forget.

I put the drawings back into their envelope, get comfortable and reach for the addendum sheets. "Well, Miss Ellen," I whisper, removing my gloves, "what were you up to during the last half of 1863?"

ая ая ая

1863
Addendum

Memories: as slippery as marsh grass when you try to grasp them and as permanent as indigo when you'd rather forget. The queerest thing can trigger a recollection. For instance, lemon loaf reminds me of dear Robert Shaw ever since Rina served it at an afternoon tea held in his honor at The Oaks.

We hoped a tea would provide a pleasant diversion for the young colonel stationed at Lands End and for us some news of the war. Without details, the constant boom of cannon fire echoing across the Sound wore on our nerves. Along with Colonel Shaw, we included Nelly and Josiah. Lottie, Laura and I made six—the perfect number.

Glancing about the table, I felt a pang for our friend, General Saxton, who loved a good tea. Overlooked in a recent change in command, he remained depressed and uncommunicative.

"Tell us about yourself, Colonel Shaw," Josiah asked, the moment Laura finished pouring. "How did you come to lead this regiment of yours?"

Lottie, the epitome of good manners, stiffened. I stirred milk into my cup. Certainly, we all wanted to know the story of the colonel's all-Black regiment, the 54th Massachusetts Infantry, but our guest had yet to even take a sip from his teacup.

With a nod, the colonel did manage to swallow some tea. Staring into his cup, he said, "I can assure you, sir, it is not a position I had ever imagined I'd assume. Nor did I seek out such a command.

"You may have gathered from my speech that I hail from Boston. My family is active in the movement, believing that the Black man must be free in every sense of the word, that he might rightly and justly participate fully in society. So, when Governor

Andrew requested that I form the 54th, after much consideration, I agreed."

"The decision was a difficult one?" Laura inquired.

"Yes," Colonel Shaw sighed. "It was—"

"Did you doubt their ability?" Nelly asked.

"No, absolutely not," the colonel said. "I doubted my own." He ran a finger around the edge of his cup. "I know all too well what is required: the sacrifice and the loss."

"Antietam," Laura said.

Although a strategic win for the Union, the Battle of Antietam had resulted in the deaths of thousands of young soldiers. I couldn't begin to imagine what Colonel Shaw had witnessed, or endured.

The colonel frowned at Laura. "Yes."

"I'm not clairvoyant." She smiled. "We have a mutual acquaintance, Ward Pierce."

Ward Pierce had healed, mind and body, from the terrible beating he'd endured by angry cotton agents and had come back to report the progress of the Port Royal project for the *Atlantic Monthly*. Laura and I had seen him several times since his return.

"Mr. Pierce praised your service," Laura said. "In fact, he sends his regrets at being unable to join us today."

"The governor suggested you form a Black regiment?" Josiah returned to his original query.

"Yes," Shaw said. "Between Governor Andrew and Fredrick Douglass, I had little choice. Each man is formidable." He glanced about the table. "I assume you are aware of Douglass and his work."

"The former slave?" Nelly said. "Certainly! The man is a living testament to The Cause. He's written extensively on the antislavery movement. I also understand his oratory abilities are quite convincing."

"Indeed." Shaw smiled. "He, along with the governor, persuaded me that if the aim of this war is to end slavery, that Blacks must be allowed to fight for their freedom. In fact, Douglass' two sons were my first recruits."

Laura smiled. "You're pleased with your men, Colonel?"

"Yes. A finer, more dedicated group you'll not find. I'm exceedingly proud of them, of their discipline, character and commitment," Shaw said. "They are eager, as am I, to put their training to the test and meet the enemy head-on."

"I understand from Ward Pierce that the Black troops have been relegated to maintenance, functioning primarily as laborers," Laura said, "that there's been reluctance to have them participate in the actual fighting."

"You are correct, Miss Towne." Shaw tilted his chin. "However, my commander has assured me that our regiment will be allowed to defend the Union, as befitting any soldier."

❧ ❧ ❧

Addendum

Independence Day, 1863

With yet another smallpox outbreak behind us, our St. Helena community gathered at the Brick Church for the July 4th celebrations.

After leading the Penn School choir in rousing versions of "The Star-Spangled Banner" and "My Country," Laura and I looked forward to the remainder of the festivities and retired to the platform under one of the oaks. The freedmen planned to sing a few of their own songs.

"Look over there," I said to Laura, "by the vat of sweetwater."

Crouched down, Colonel Robert Shaw of the Massachusetts 54th chatted with several of our scholars circling him.

"What a remarkable young man," I said.

"Let's say hello," Laura suggested.

"Yes, let's."

"Miss Towne, Miss Murray."

Reverend Philips from the Brick Church approached us from behind.

I turned and smiled at him. "I trust you enjoyed the Penn scholars' performance."

"Yes, yes." The reverend shooed off the children's significant accomplishment with a wave of his hand. "Miss Towne, we were wondering—"

"We?" Laura interjected, her tone steely.

Just then his wife toddled up to him. No doubt "she" was the "we" he referenced.

Reverend Phillips nodded her way and ignored Laura's question. He continued, "Our church was only supposed to house your classes temporarily, until you could find a more suitable location."

"That's correct," Laura said.

The Reverend Phillips looked at his wife. She scowled.

He cleared his throat. "Has there been any progress in that area?" he asked.

"Not yet," Laura shrugged.

"It isn't that we don't want to help," Mrs. Philips spoke up. "But the Penn School's presence is disruptive—"

"Disruptive?" Laura's eyebrows almost reached her hairline.

"Yes, the noise and the mess. Your presence requires more cleaning and maintenance of the building and grounds," Mrs. Phillips said.

"I can imagine." Laura nodded. "But you must find solace knowing that the Lord's house is being used to help others. Surely that's what He would want."

"Of course," Reverend Phillips said. "However, the building was meant to be a church, not a school."

"I can assure you, Reverend Phillips, Mrs. Philips," Laura locked arms with me, "we will be more than happy to relocate once a suitable alternative is arranged."

Of course Laura and I wanted a school of our own! The reverend knew our dire circumstances. So did his wife. What did they expect us to do?

"Yes, well—" Pastor Philips stared at his scolding wife like a frightened rabbit.

Just then, the Fairfields appeared and greeted the reverend and his wife. For once Nelly and Josiah insinuated themselves at the perfect moment. Laura and I slid away unnoticed. Leaving the grounds, I spotted Colonel Shaw and waved a quick goodbye. We'd catch up with him another time.

ta ta ta

Addendum

July 18, 1863
The Battle of Charleston

In the space between slumber and wakefulness, a rumbling sounded and I surfaced from sleep. Now another boomed, more distant. Alarmed, I turned to face Laura.

She brushed a curl from my cheek. "Only thunder."

Sighing, I stretched out and scanned the window for signs of rain. "Part of me wishes they'd just get on with it."

Rumors had been swirling for the past couple of weeks that the Union Army planned to lay siege on Charleston. Gunfire, although intermittent, had been constant. Yet no one knew for certain when, or if, it would escalate.

"Be careful what you wish for." Laura yawned and stretched.

"You're right," I replied. "Who knows what the consequences will be."

&a &a &a

Earlier this week, the First South Carolina Colored Regiment had set out on a diversionary mission to capture the railroad bridge over the Edisto River. Unfortunately, the expedition had failed. In retreat, scores of abandoned slaves rushed the troops, desperate for help. These refugees had arrived on St. Helena destitute and hungry.

Thunder rolled again. This time the windows shook in their frames. Sitting up I frowned at Laura. "Are you sure that's not naval guns?"

"Hmm—" Laura rose from our nest of crumpled blankets.

Cannon fire sounded throughout the day, rattling nerves and windows; the ground we trod trembled with the intensity of a battle I could only imagine. Still, I am certain nothing I conjured compared to what the men endured.

While waiting to learn the outcome of that encounter, Laura saw to the physical ailments of the recently arrived refugees, and I handled their practical needs at the store. Upon the third day,

Josiah and Nelly arrived home in the evening and asked the rest of us to join them in the parlor.

Lottie, her cheeks brightly colored, reached for my hand.

Josiah cleared his throat. "I wish to state plainly that this information comes on good authority: Ward Pierce who, in the role of reporter, accompanied Colonel Shaw's expedition." Josiah paused and inhaled. "On Saturday past, in a direct assault, the Union Army breached Fort Wagner. Colonel Shaw desired that the Massachusetts 54th participate actively, and they did. I was told that he led the charge—"

"I'm not surprised," Lottie interjected.

Josiah cleared his throat. "Agreed; he was committed—"

"Was?" My heart stuttered. "Has something happened to Colonel Shaw?"

Laura put a hand on my arm. "Let Josiah finish."

He took a breath. "The colonel sprang upon the fort, leading his men. I was told he was struck by enemy fire almost immediately."

"No!" Lottie gasped.

Josiah winced, but carried on. "Most of the officers of the 54th were wounded or killed. The entire battalion fought bravely. They took Fort Wagner, but couldn't hold it. Fire from Fort Sumter shelled out our men."

Images of their bloody, mangled bodies flashed in my mind. Those young Black men were some of the first of their race to stand with their White brethren-in-arms and fight for their country. Beside me, Lottie sobbed.

"And Colonel Shaw?" Laura asked.

"No word yet." Josiah frowned. "The hope is he's been captured and held prisoner." Josiah looked around. "There's more. Ward Pierce has gone to Beaufort to help set up hospital space and care for the casualties. He's asked for help."

Laura glanced at me, brows lifted in question: Would I accompany her?

A vision of Tommy and his mangled arm stopped me from answering. The memory of his surgery, and those brief moments when we'd questioned if he'd wake afterward, still gave me nightmares. Nursing wounded soldiers meant I would encounter injuries as bad, or worse. Leaving would also affect the Penn School. My stomach soured.

Laura took my hand. "Ellen, you don't have to go."

The image of Colonel Shaw crouched down and engaged with our scholars at the July 4th picnic sprang to mind.

"Yes, I do," I said.

Laura squeezed my hand and turned to Josiah. "We'll leave first thing in the morning."

Lottie sniffed and dried her eyes. "I'm coming with you."

ea ea ea

Addendum

Laura, Lottie, and I left for Beaufort at daybreak. A sense of foreboding swirled between us, heavy and pungent like the morning's marsh mist. It is one thing to hear battle sounds in the distance, it is quite another to witness, firsthand, the results.

A baby-faced soldier waited at the wharf to deliver us to the Barnwell-Gough House, now named Hospital 10, where the injured 54th soldiers had been transported. We'd stowed our bags, boarded the wagon, and set out along Bay Street.

A young fellow, sweat glistening on his Black brow, leaned into a wheelbarrow stacked with watermelons; a slim-hipped woman balanced a bushel basket atop her head, its contents hidden beneath a checkered cloth, youngsters trailed behind, carting bags; others, young and old, strode purposefully, hefting pitchers and buckets.

Over the gallop of horse hooves and rattle of wagon wheels someone yelled, "Make way, make way!"

Laura pivoted in her seat. "Ambulances."

Our driver steered the horses to the side of the road. A moment later, three canopied carts charged past. The racket of cart and animals mingled with the moans and cries of the occupants. Cold dread bloomed within my breast.

Within moments, the ambulances disappeared around a corner in a flurry of dust.

With a snap of the reins, our driver continued on and then turned at Carteret Street, where we drove under a low-hanging oak bough. Here a crosswind blew, but it offered little reprieve. For along with cool the air carried a hot, savory scent, at once familiar. My mouth watered and Lottie's nostrils flared.

"Can you smell that?" Laura asked in a quiet voice.

"Yes," I said, swallowing. "It's making me hungry."

"What do you suppose they're cooking?" Lottie asked.

"Roasted meat of some sort," I said.

The young soldier at the reins shifted around, his expression pained. "Ma'am—"

The horses veered and our buggy slumped into a hollow, jostling us. The driver focused on righting our buggy.

"They're burning amputated limbs," Laura said.

Hand to mouth, I stifled a wretch. Beside me, Lottie whimpered and then fell silent. She withdrew a handkerchief from her pocket and clamped it on the lower half of her face. I reached over and hooked my arm through hers.

Above the jagged line of rooftops, plumes of smoke drifted, charcoal specters against the Carolina-blue sky.

& & &

The three of us stood at the bottom of the hospital walkway, bags in hand. We'd been instructed to report to Dr. Esther Hawks. Although we'd never met, we knew her by reputation. She had come to the Port Royal area about the same time we did, having followed her husband who served as the assistant surgeon to the 1st South Carolina Volunteers. Despite Dr. Esther's medical training and experience in the North, the military did not allow her to practice. Instead, she taught the freedmen's children in Beaufort, like we did on St. Helena.

Under the Hawks' direction, Hospital 10 became the first one of its kind dedicated exclusively to Black soldiers. Shortly after its opening this past April, however, Dr. Esther's husband received orders for Florida. Until her husband's replacement arrived in May, Dr. Esther had temporarily assumed the role of chief surgeon and manager.

"All set to go in?" Laura looked at me and Lottie.

Lottie nodded. I adjusted the grip on my bag and followed Laura up to the door.

A large, two-story former residence of tabby—concrete made from burnt and broken oysters shells, sand and ash—in the Federal style, Hospital 10 boasted an upper balcony over the portico. The front steps flared out like welcoming arms, ready to embrace the Southern gentry. But those folks had skedaddled during the Big Shoot. Now the injured Black Union soldiers in need of medical attention crossed the threshold.

We entered and stood in the foyer. A gangly girl passing by took one look at us and scooted off. She returned moments later, followed by a petite woman about my age.

"Dr. Hawks," Laura said. "We've come to help."

With a round face and snub nose, Esther Hawks' large eyes betrayed little.

She offered us a weak smile.

"I'm Laura Towne," she said and extended a hand. "My colleagues, Ellen Murray and Lottie Forten."

Dr. Hawks glanced between the three of us. "I understand one of you has medical training?"

"I'm a homeopathic physician," Laura said.

Dr. Hawks sniffed. Laura's smile faded.

A brief, heavy silence followed before Dr. Hawks turned. "Come," she said. "I'll give you a quick tour and then we'll set you to work."

Despite Dr. Hawks' initial attitude, she kept Laura close at hand, assigning her the more challenging or gruesome tasks. If Dr. Hawks or the other surgeon needed an assistant, she called upon Laura. This meant I saw little of her.

One of the eight rooms in the house was reserved for surgery. The others were lined with cots: row upon row of men from the 54th Massachusetts recovering from injuries sustained at Fort Wagner. Many had only flesh wounds, others suffered more severe injuries. These silent souls never complained. I surmised they turned all their strength and energy inward in an effort to recover, or let go.

Lottie's kindness made her a natural nurse. Across the room from me, she fed broth to a young man. Although I couldn't hear their conversation, I sensed that, between sips, she asked him questions. Smiling shyly, he appeared to be responding to her.

"Comes easier to some folks, eh?"

I turned to the baritone voice. A soldier sat upright in his cot, his wide back pressed against the wall, his left arm coddled in a sling. Initially assigned to a different room, I hadn't met all the patients in this room yet.

He smiled. "War has a way of makin' us do things that aren't in our nature."

An astute observation; nursing did not come naturally to me. I belonged in a classroom, even a rowdy, overcrowded one.

I smiled back at him, throwing up my hands. "Still, we must all do our part."

"A little conversation would ease my mind." With a heavy sigh he glanced at the unconscious men in the cots flanking his.

I grabbed a nearby stool and settled down at his bedside. "Ellen Murray. What's your name, soldier?"

"George Washington."

He chuckled at what must have been my startled expression. I folded my hands onto my lap. "Where's home?"

"Canada."

"How fascinating." I leaned in. "I was born in Canada. St. John, New Brunswick. My father died when I was a toddler and my mother moved us to Newport, Rhode Island."

"We're further west, near the Great Lakes, in a town called Welland. I left my wife and two boys behind to tend our crops." George stopped for a moment; a wistful expression clouded his eyes. "I was born in Virginia—"

He stopped talking. His eyes followed a small, middle-aged Black woman who'd hobbled into the room. I'd previously noticed her, but we'd yet to be introduced. She'd arrived at the hospital earlier in the day to tend the newest arrivals. She stumbled by the row of cots and went to the far corner of the room where she slid to the floor and drew a shawl about her head.

I rose from the stool.

"Leave her be, ma'am," George said, "she takes time out when the spells come."

"You know her?" I sat back down.

George nodded. "She got me to Canada."

Only one woman was capable of such a feat. "Is that Harriet Tubman?"

"Yes ma'am. You heard of her?"

"Of course," I stammered, "they call her Moses."

Harriet Tubman escaped from Maryland years ago to the free state of Pennsylvania and then, risking recapture, had returned many times to rescue others via the Underground Railroad. With the aid of abolitionists and free Blacks, she'd personally guided or arranged for hundreds of fugitive slaves to secret routes and safe houses in free states and territories, including Canada. These activities had earned her the nickname Moses.

I stole another look at the tiny heap in the corner. Someone had mentioned she'd come to Beaufort, but I had forgotten.

"What kind of spells does she have?"

George repositioned himself on the bed. "Headaches, mostly. And sleepin' jags."

"I wonder why."

"Clubbed on the head while helpin' someone bein' beat. Just a gal at the time. Ain't been the same since," George offered, matter-of-factly.

"How dreadful!" I made a mental note to tell Laura. Maybe she'd be able to ease her suffering.

Since Miss Tubman had settled into her corner for the time being, I turned my full attention back to George. "Why come back to the States?" I asked in a low voice. "Leave your family and risk your life, and freedom?"

George took a deep breath. "Like I said, ma'am, Virginia was my home first. If it weren't for folks like Miz Tubman over there, I wouldn't be free; my children neither. I figured alongside the Army, I could do my part."

"Your wife agreed?"

George gave me a lopsided smile. "She weren't too pleased." His humor faded. "But the Army pays. We do our best sharecroppin', but the extra'll come in handy. We've our boys to consider."

"How old are your sons?" I asked.

From the corner of my eye, I noticed Ward Pierce standing in the doorway. He waved me over.

"Excuse me, George, it appears I'm needed."

George adjusted his pillow. "I'll just rest for a bit."

Laura, Lottie and Dr. Hawks already stood in the hallway.

"What's going on?" I asked.

"Bad news, I'm afraid." Pierce's ears shone bright red.

"It's Colonel Shaw, isn't it?" Laura said.

Lottie choked a sob. Dr. Hawks shifted her feet, but kept her eyes riveted on the floor.

"I'm afraid so," Pierce said. "The Army hoped he'd only been injured and taken prisoner. But the final report states otherwise. They buried him in a trench alongside his men."

"How tragic," Dr. Hawks said.

Beside me, Lottie released her tears. "Such a noble young man! He spoke often of his beloved mother. He was so devoted to her. She'll be devastated. Oh, this is too terrible to bear!"

My throat constricted and I put an arm around Lottie's shoulders.

"Burying Colonel Shaw with his men was meant to dishonor him," Laura said. "Little did the Confederates realize it does him credit! It is exactly what he would have wished."

"Without question," Pierce said, his voice thick.

🐦 🐦 🐦

Addendum

Fall and Winter, 1863
Illness, Loss, and Gratitude

With the wounded stabilized, Laura and I left Hospital 10 after spending almost a month there and returned to St. Helena. The idea of opening school and seeing our scholars buoyed my spirits.

Before leaving Beaufort, I'd paid a final visit to George Washington, the injured Union soldier from Canada.

"I understand you're to be discharged tomorrow," I had said. "You'll be heading home?"

He stood and I had to tilt my head to meet his gaze.

"Yes, ma'am."

To reach Canada he would have to travel through slave states, where he ran the risk of being captured and sold off.

"Godspeed," I said.

"Thank you, ma'am." Smiling, he gave me a little bow.

I pray he made it. Something tells me he did.

ਤੇ ਤੇ ਤੇ

Summer temperatures took hold and rose daily, mirroring our concern for Lottie's well-being. Previously, weak lungs hampered her ability to function. Now debilitating headaches plagued her. Upon doctor's advice, she, along with Ward Pierce, left us and sailed north, out of the war zone. At the outset, Pierce had given three years to the freedmen's cause. Now, with his war assignment for the *Atlantic Monthly* publication finished, he wanted to go back to Massachusetts and resume his law practice. We wished him well.

Lottie, on the other hand, promised to come back once her health improved. In the meantime, we needed another teacher. I wrote to my sister and suggested she take Lottie's position.

Bursts of smallpox no longer surprised or alarmed us. Unless the patient was an infant or compromised in some other way, they usually recovered. For this reason, we assumed with the fall's cooler weather the summer eruption of the disease would retreat. It did not.

Owing to our strategic location, an influx of soldiers had arrived from the North with whom we all interacted. Laura theorized that they'd brought along a new variation of the pox, one to which the freedmen had little defense. Weak and vulnerable, they succumbed. Typhoid also descended and spread its ugly tentacles.

Our days and nights throughout the fall were split between school and caring for the ill, with little time left for sleep. One evening on a trek to the freedmen's cabins, we arrived to discover a previously healthy, active toddler swaddled in his mother's arms, only his face exposed. A rash of smallpox lesions covered the poor child's forehead, nose, cheeks, and tiny pointed chin; encrusted lids ended in dark, velvet lashes. His breath came in halting gasps, a sure sign of pneumonia. His young mother, ripe with the next child, glanced up at Laura, her eyes dark pools of misery.

"My God!" Laura rushed to her side. "How long has he been like this?"

"Jus' this mornin'," the mother whispered.

"That's why we axed dem to git you." The father stepped out from the corner.

We stayed with the family throughout the night. The child died at dawn. Within two weeks, his mother, fevered and pocked, went into early labor and delivered a stillborn child, a girl. We'd later heard that the father, mad with grief, had taken a sickle, gone into the forest and single-handedly cleared a path all the way to St. Helena Sound. His tracks ended at the water's edge.

Dealing with the sheer volume of sick children and adults within our community took its toll on both of us, but especially Laura, who'd borne the brunt of the responsibility for several months now. Soon she'd get a break. She planned to visit her family in Philadelphia for Christmas. For this reason, I downplayed my own symptoms of illness.

&a &a &a

All I know of my bout with malaria, others later told me. Rina related that despite Laura's around-the-clock care, I continued to fail. At one point they thought I might not survive. General Saxton stepped in and sent for a doctor who brought quinine. From my perspective, it was like waking from a night's sleep cut short.

My eyelids felt weighted and I struggled to lift them.

"Look, her lashes are fluttering!"

A voice wriggled through a crack in my consciousness. With Herculean effort, I opened my eyes a fraction. The room tilted; the image, just out of reach, wavered.

Someone drew a cool cloth across my brow, over my eyes, down my cheeks. I licked at the water dribbled on my lips.

"Ellen, open your eyes. Look at me."

Laura's face came into focus.

"Welcome back."

Someone took my hand. I turned my head.

My mother smiled down at me. "You gave us quite a fright."

A hallucination? I turned to Laura. "I sent for your mother and sister." She placed a hand on my arm. "You've been very ill, but the worst is over."

Hattie appeared over Laura's shoulder. Tears streamed down her face, but she smiled. "Welcome back, sister."

"How long?" I croaked.

"A month, give or take," Laura answered.

With a sob, I reached out for Mother.

She drew a chair to my bedside and took my hand.

My mother and sister's presence touched me deeply. I'd do my utmost to recover, that I might share with them the value of our work, the people, and the natural beauty of our island.

"Where are you staying?" I asked.

"Frogmore House," Mother said.

"Really?" I tried to sit up, but failed.

Buried at the end of a tree-lined lane off Seaside Road, Frogmore House sat on the shores of the Harbor River. The Coffin family had fled during the Big Shoot, but a testament of their cruelty stood in the dining room: a scarred post formerly used to whip slaves. If Frogmore's walls could talk I imagined they'd howl with injustice.

A shadow must have crossed my face for Laura added, "We tidied up the house, Ellen. Even the dining room."

Later that evening, seated away from the others, Laura took my hand. "Is there anything I can do that would make you more comfortable?"

Her care-worn expression broke my heart. "You've done enough."

Head bent, she traced the outline of my fingernails with her own. "I was so afraid—" her voice caught.

I edged closer. "I'm sorry I worried you."

"Nonsense. You couldn't help it." She drew herself up and wiped her eyes. "Now then, how about a sponge bath and a clean nightgown?"

♪ ♪ ♪

A few days later, my sister Hattie, while spooning broth into my mouth, announced she and Mother would be staying.

"How wonderful!" I said. "And you'll teach alongside Laura and me?"

"Of course!" she said.

My heart suddenly began to race. I thought it was reaction to Hattie's good news, so I took a few deep breaths to calm myself. But the rapid fluttering continued. "Something's wrong, Hattie." The room whirled around me and I slid down onto my pillows. "Get Laura."

She placed the broth bowl on the side table and hurried off.

The ceiling spun; appeared closer and then farther away. Closing my eyes, I took measured breaths and told myself to settle down. Still, my heart hammered. I prayed that Laura would come soon.

Minutes later she burst into the room and rushed to my side. She laid a hand upon my forehead, my cheeks. Hattie hovered in the background.

"At least you're not fevered," Laura said, her voice calm. "What happened?"

"I'm not sure," I said. "Hattie and I were chatting. Suddenly my heart started pounding and I felt dizzy."

Laura took hold of my wrist, searched for a pulse. "Breathe. That's good. In and out."

She looked at her watch, her face a mask. Finally, she released me. "Are you still dizzy?"

"Not really," I said, grimacing, "but now I have a headache."

"Anything else?"

"I feel a little nauseated, but sometimes that happens if I'm scared."

"Are you itchy?" Laura lifted one arm, then the other. She ruched my sleeves, inspected the inside of my forearms, and the crook of my elbows. "Do you have a rash anywhere?"

I opened the neck of my nightgown and peered in. My deflated breasts and skeletal ribs looked liked they belonged to someone else.

"No rash," I said.

"Good." Laura folded back the covers. "I want you to lie down properly," she lifted my head and adjusted the pillow. "And relax."

"That's easier said than done." I tried to say this with a laugh, but failed.

"She was doing so well. What's going on?" Hattie asked.

Laura pulled the blankets over me and turned to Hattie. "I'm not sure, but I suspect it's a reaction to the quinine."

"Really?" I asked. "But that's the cure."

"It is," Laura said, "but there can be side effects."

"And that's why my heart is beating fast?"

"I believe so." Laura lifted my chin and looked into my eyes. "I don't want you to exert yourself. Do you understand?"

"Will it stop?" Hattie voice trembled.

"Soon." Laura brushed back a loose strand of hair from my brow. Her reassuring tone washed over me.

"I feel sleepy," I said.

"Then rest," Laura said. "I'll be back in a bit."

"Where are you going?" I asked, fear overriding the guilt of my neediness.

Laura patted my hand. "There's something I have to tend to. It won't take long." She rose, walked over to the window, and closed the drapes, shutting out the sun. "Hattie, would you stay with her?"

My sister pulled a chair close to the bed. "Certainly."

Laura had left my bedside to send for another doctor. He agreed that I was reacting adversely to the drug quinine. Together, they recalibrated my dosage.

After the disturbing side effects of my treatment subsided, I discovered Laura had canceled her Christmas trip north to visit family. I felt guilty, but relieved; the thought of her leaving had terrified me.

ɛå ɛå ɛå

The bittersweet Christmas of 1863 came and went. Most in our community had suffered illness or loss, perhaps both. Laura confessed she and the doctor initially feared my heart sustained permanent damaged. Now they believe I'll make a full recovery.

The New Year of 1864 holds promise: Hattie will take Lottie's place and teach alongside us at the Penn School. Mother has agreed to stay. And I am blessed with health, purpose, and my love, Laura.

ɛå ɛå ɛå

Chapter 21

Henrietta

My head bobs, jerks, and my eyes snap open. Back on the porch, I tilt my neck sideways and massage the burning muscles. Catching a scent, my nostrils flare.

Who would be cooking at this hour?

With the force of a charging Fripp Island wild hog, I am pummeled by the recollection of Miss Ellen's ghastly experience when driving through Beaufort en route to Hospital 10.

As though vanquished by my acknowledgment, the phantom odor disappears. I inhale again and am rewarded with the scent of fresh salt air and the sweet rot of pluff mud. No whiff of smoke.

I grew up hearing Miss Ellen's stories of George Washington, the soldier and patient from Canada. Mind, the versions she offered back then omitted the hospital horrors. Miss Ellen and George corresponded for years. Whenever she received a letter from Canada our family would gather round, and she'd read aloud. I wonder if George Washington still lives. I must search Miss Ellen's desk for his letters. Perhaps I can write to him myself, and let him know of Miss Ellen's passing.

Remembering the addendum sheets, I look about and discover they're scattered on the floor at my feet.

"What's all dat?" asks Maum.

I pick up most and duck-walk over to the final sheet. "Some loose papers from Miss Ellen's journal. I dropped them. Did I wake you?"

Maum wriggles to a sitting position. "I wasn't sleepin'."

I smile at her. "Well, while you *weren't* sleeping, I discovered Miss Ellen's 1863 journal ended mid-year and that she didn't have time to write because of a smallpox and typhoid outbreak. Then Miss Ellen got sick herself with malaria. On the eve of 1863, Miss Laura encouraged her to write a summary of the missing months." Holding on to the chair's arm I hoist myself from the floor.

"Folks sick den, plenty die. I thought sure de good Lawd gonna take Miz Ellen." Maum stares out at the night.

"What is it?" I ask.

"Dat year Manners' boy Jethro die in she arms."

My breath catches. "Manners lost a child?"

Maum turns to me. "Mmm-hmm. Jethro look like he spit outta hes daddy mout. Dat boy follow Cyrus closer dan de shadow."

"Manners' man?" The family almost never mentioned him. He left or died—I never understood which—before I lived with them. Other than his name, I knew nothing.

"Mmm-hmm," says Maum. "Den Manners' new babe born dead."

The familiarity of the story sends a chill rolling down my spine. I look at the papers on my lap and then back at Maum. "H-how did Cyrus die?"

Maum shrugs and takes a deep breath. "He walk into de water and don walk out."

ن ن ن

After another toilet break, Maum snuggles down onto the swing, and I am back in the chair. With great care, I return the loose-leaf pages and drawings to the safe-keeping of their resting place within the journal of 1863, and exchange that journal for the next. It sits upon my lap and I hesitate to open it and lay my hands down, acknowledging that whatever lies between these covers will be of a past that includes me.

ن ن ن

ن ن ن

This notebook belongs to:

Ellen Murray
March, 1864—August, 1864

ن ن ن

Chapter 22

Ellen

Meow…meow…meeoow…MEeeoooOOW!

Laura laughed. "Lucky waits until we've gone to bed for the night before asking to come in."

"It's my turn." I sat up and lit the candle. I'd recovered from my bout of malaria and the unintended effects of the quinine treatment, but I still struggled with fatigue.

"If you don't feel well—"

"I'm fine, just lazy," I said.

Laura snuggled down into the covers. "Don't be long."

I headed through the short passage to the sitting and dining area, hesitating at the threshold to get my bearings, our new home not yet as familiar as The Oaks.

After Nelly and Josiah jumped to lease The Oaks and operate a farm school, while Laura dealt with the smallpox outbreak and my malaria, they'd made it clear they desired we leave. My weakened condition notwithstanding, I still found their duplicitous behavior shocking. More so on Nelly's part than Josiah's. Laura and I had lived and taught alongside her, had a friendship, we thought.

While I convalesced at Frogmore with Mother and Hattie, Laura had packed our belongings and set up house here, at what the locals now called the Teacher's Cottage. With Rina's help, Laura had done a fine job. Our new home pleased me, with one exception: the whipping post in the dining room.

Now in the dead of night, accompanied by the screeching of our cat, I crossed into that room where the post stood in shadow. By day I resented it, by night I loathed it. Since my arrival, I'd told Laura—and Hastings, and Rina—that I wanted it gone. Yet here the horrid thing loomed.

I sidled past the monstrosity doing my utmost to avoid looking at it. My candle's light reflected off the metal cuffs and pulleys and something made me turn, and then draw closer. Illuminated by the candlelight the scars inflicted by lashings appeared: fine crannies rusted with blood. *Whose?* I could only imagine.

YeeoooWWWW.

"Is Lucky still outside?" Laura called from our bedchamber. "What's wrong?"

"Nothing."

I stumbled for the door and opened it. Purring, the cat snaked around and between my ankles.

"From now on come in earlier," I scolded. "Or I'll leave you outside for the wild things!"

Tail held high, he trotted off.

With a *whoosh*, the door blew open. I rushed back to shut it. My candle flame flickered out. I gave the door a solid shove and inched my way to the sideboard where we kept the matches.

"What is going on?" Laura shouted.

The answer died on my tongue as I crashed into something solid. I cried out and stumbling backwards, pressed a hand to my forehead. Star-shaped lights exploded behind my lids.

Laura's footsteps reverberated on the floorboards. "Ellen?"

Confused and in pain, I couldn't respond.

A scrape and snap sounded, and sulfur stung my nose. I squeezed my eyes tighter against the candle's bright glow. Laura's arm encircled my waist and she walked me forward.

"Sit down and let me look at you." She pried my hand from my forehead, "Relax your brow and open your eyes."

Slick blood covered my hand and ran down my wrist. The metallic smell curdled my stomach.

Laura clamped a handkerchief on my brow. "Forehead wounds always bleed a lot. Don't be alarmed. Concentrate on your breath…in and out…that's right."

The acute pain dulled to a steady throb.

"Damn it, Laura, I've asked and asked for that post to be removed!"

"I know," she patted my knee.

"Don't patronize me!" Tears sprang to my eyes.

She lifted up my hand. "Hold the hankie in place and stay put. I'll be right back."

She returned with her medical bag and a pitcher of water.

"Let's get you cleaned up." She wiped my eyes and dabbed a wet cloth on the cut.

"Ow!" I leaned back.

"Ah, there it is," she said, "a small gash over your eyebrow." She wadded the cloth. "Keep that on it."

She held the candle up to my face and peered into my eyes. "Good. Your pupils are dilating."

"Will I require sutures?" My stomach lurched at the thought.

"No, nor should the cut leave a scar." She reached for a bandage. "But you'll likely have a black eye."

"I mean it, Laura. I want that whipping post gone!"

"I'll look after it." The dressing hung loose in her hand. "I promise."

Upon returning to bed, I faced the wall and tugged the covers up to my chin.

Moving closer, Laura cupped my shoulder. "Ellen?"

I pulled my knees into my chest.

Laura sighed and turned over. Soon her rhythmic breathing mellowed to a gentle snore. Not long afterward, the cat landed on the mattress. He curled in the bend of Laura's knees and commenced purring. I kept my back turned on the both of them.

Eventually my heavy lids drooped and a dream-vision appeared: a woman's bare back, a man's arm arching and releasing a lash. With a gasp, my eyes flew open. Heart racing, I turned to Laura. Both she and the cat slept on. I lay back and took slow, deep breaths. My hammering heart slowed, but I couldn't banish the dream's shadow that had followed me into wakefulness.

I'd never witnessed a flogging, but last winter Rina fell ill, and I saw the effects of the lash upon a body and soul. Laura had wanted to listen to Rina's chest. She had insisted she was fine. Hastings, in an unprecedented display of authority, put his foot down. Rina's eyes flashed at him before he turned and exited the room.

Staring ahead, back straight, she pulled off her apron and loosened her shift.

"I'm going to lower your bodice." Laura peeled back the garment then turned to me, wide-eyed.

Thick, knobbly stripes riddled Rina's back.

"Right then," Laura cleared her throat, "let's listen to your chest."

I waited in excruciating silence for the examination to end.

At some point during my rumination of the past, exhaustion won out. In the morning, I discovered a note for me pinned to Laura's pillow: "Rest," she wrote, "doctor's orders."

Bone-weary, I didn't have the energy or desire to object. For today, getting washed and dressed would be task enough.

Stepping out onto our back porch, I took a breath of morning air and surveyed our yard, now in early bloom. The sun cast an amber glow on sprouting greens: spring onions, lettuces, and peas atop linear mounds of soil. Budding pomegranate trees and an apple tree stood to the side. Hastings pulled weeds in the strawberry patch, as Rina plucked the ripe fruit. I thanked God every day they'd moved to St. Helenaville with us.

Hastings headed off in the direction of the barn, while Rina made her way to me with a sweetgrass basket of glistening berries.

"My goodness," I said, "they look lovely."

Rina beamed. "I was thinking mebbe I got 'nuf flour for a cobbler. Da rest you and Miss Laura can hab fresh."

She joined me at the little table. With a frown, she peered at my face, but said nothing. Most likely Laura filled her in earlier. Pulling a small knife from her pocket, Rina went to work.

"May I help?"

She shook her head. "No ma'am. Y'all need rest, get you strength back."

I made no protest. I'd be better off to save my breath to cool my grits. Yet I couldn't complain. Our Rina's tenacious spirit benefited Laura and me at every turn.

With nimble fingers, she plucked the strawberry's hull from the soft flesh. Seeing the bloody juice splatter the bowl and Rina's fingers, my thoughts drifted back to the post and our home's previous occupant.

"Rachel, who lived here before us, you knew her?" I asked.

"Mmmhm. Rachel 'n me grow up together at de Oaks."

"Did you?" I settled back into my chair.

Rina put a few berries in front of me.

"She somethin', Rachel," Rina chuckled. "Mmmhm—"

"How so?"

"Smart as a whip. Not like me. I tells it like I sees it." Rina shook her head back and forth. "Rachel be quiet. Always thinkin'. Cunny like de fox. But then she hab to be."

"Why's that?" I popped a berry in mouth.

"She be a skinny chillun gal, all legs 'n arms, big hands 'n feet. Nobody pay her no mind, 'cept to make fun. 'Specially de man chillun. Theys dumb as a stump, I tell her. One day you be growin' into dose feet and put some meat on dem bones." Rina sighed.

"And did she?"

"Yessim." Rina stopped working and rested her hands on the bowl. "My hips spread and bosoms grew, but Rachel, she stay skinny like a stick. `Til one summer she ripen full and juicy, same as dese berries." Rina nodded at the fruit. "Rachel not dark, like me. Dat's how Massa Fripp see her and pick she out. We was hangin' out washin' behind de Big House at de Oaks—you know de sunny patch nearin' de water—we talkin' and laughin'. A boy comin' to us sayin' Massa Fripp need she. I swears Rachel teeth rattle in she head."

"What's Massa Fripp wantin', Rina?" She squeezed my hand tight.

"Forgive me Jesus, but I thank de good Lord it not me he call for.

"We come round and Massa Fripp be settin' in de wagon at de foot of de porch stairs. He holler, 'Get in.'

I tell Rachel be strong and help she into de wagon. But ole' Fripp, he mean."

Rina lowered her voice, mimicking Fripp. "'Not there, you fool, in the back.'

"I start prayin'. Rachel she cryin' so hard she can't talk. She gets in like he say and before I tell she goodbye, he whip de horse and go."

"That's horrible!"

Rina hulled the last few strawberries without another word. Memories and questions marked the silence between us. Clearly there was more that happened, because Rachel came to reside here, in this cottage. But Rina rarely offered details of her life on the island before our arrival and I feared, if pressed, she'd retreat.

After a few moments she smiled over at me. "In da end Rachel, she got da better of ole' man Fripp."

"How so?" I pulled my chair a little closer.

Rina put the bowl of fruit in the basket and pushed them aside.

"Ole man Fripp, he take Rachel for he sons." She raised her brows at me and waited.

"No!"

"Mmm-hmm." Rina continued. "Massa Fripp have three boys, two mean just like him. But the youngun, Clarence—mebbe he like he momma—he love Rachel."

"Did he?"

"Yes, ma'am," Rina nodded. "Massa Clarence, he claim her. He set Rachel here, in dis cottage, so when he gone north to doctorin' school, she and de chillun safe."

"Children?"

Rina nodded. "A boy and a gal. He love 'em just like he love Rachel. Learn both of dem to read, even de gal."

"Oh my!" How wonderful to learn our little home had such a history. Except— "What about the post?"

Rina laughed, "Dats just fo' show, so Massa Clarence daddy and brudders leave dem be."

I recalled the conversations between Laura and me about the whipping post. She'd insisted she *had* requested that Hastings dismantle it. "I'm as frustrated by his procrastination as you!" she'd snapped.

Now that I thought about it, the assortment of barriers had come from Rina: Hastings had too much to do; he'd get to it tomorrow, next week; and my favorite, "'fraid de house gwi' fall down." Her reluctance now made sense.

"What happened to them?" I asked.

Rina crossed her arms and rested them on her bosom. "Den de Big Shoot come. Massa Clarence hole up here with Rachel and de chillun. He hide in de woods and come back at night."

"How long did that go on?"

"I reckon 'til late last summer. De Rebels came up dis a-ways and he ran off fo' good."

"And that's why Rachel left?"

"Mmmhm," Rina frowned. "What if ole' man Fripp come back? He nasty, not stupid."

I took Rina's meaning. Newly emancipated and wary, the people feared that the plantation owners would return and reclaim their land and property, including their slaves. Without Clarence to protect her and the children, Rachel would have been vulnerable.

"Where did she and the children go?" I asked.

"She cookin' for de Army on Hilton Head. Rachel know she be safe there."

Rina heaved herself from the chair, gathered up the strawberry basket and bowl and made for the screen door. Holding it ajar, she turned back to me. "Rachel be pleased you and Miss Laura livin' here."

Before I could ask why, the door slammed shut. From inside, Rina whistled a tune.

ટ. ટ. ટ.

By April of 1864, the Penn School's total enrollment neared two hundred. With three forms, maintaining order, even at the best of times, tried us. The addition of any novelty or visitor increased the volume and chaos. Challenges notwithstanding, my health had improved and I could teach. Many others were not as fortunate.

Last month, Pastor Phillips succumbed to the scourge of smallpox that swept our island. Laura had not been summoned to treat him. This came as no surprise. From the outset he resented the Penn School's occupation of "his" church. Laura's refusal of baptism and adherence to Unitarianism rankled him further. Most likely his wife sent for the new homeopathic physician installed on Lady's Island. Which suited us just fine. For too long Laura had single-handedly shouldered the responsibility for the sick and dying of St. Helena. More and more she preferred teaching the children to doctoring the ill. Another practitioner in our area gave her the freedom to do so.

Soon after Reverend Phillips' passing, we received word that securing his replacement was "in the works." Since the school still had no permanent home, and given his predecessor's desire to oust us, Laura and I planned to make a positive impression upon the new pastor when he arrived.

⋙ ⋙ ⋙

This afternoon a small, elderly gentleman entered the sanctuary wearing a woolen suit. He removed his hat, revealing a bald, gleaming pate. Pulling a handkerchief from his pocket, he wiped his flushed face and cast a critical eye around the prevailing organized commotion. I prayed he hadn't come from Baptist headquarters to impart bad news. I asked my students to take a partner and quiz each other on this week's spelling words. Then I walked forward to greet him.

"May I help you?" I asked.

Laura materialized and stood beside me.

He cleared his throat. "Church headquarters sent me. My name is Parker, I've come—"

I turned to Laura and saw my fear mirrored on her face. Although we had never met the man, we were well aware of Dr. Parker's severe reputation as an agent of the Baptists.

Laura straightened her back. "Well, Dr. Parker, we can only assume that you have been sent to evict Penn School from the church."

Despite his stern repute, Dr. Parker's mouth fell open and he blinked at Laura.

"We are disappointed, Doctor." I drew a breath and spoke around the lump clogging my throat. "Reverend Phillips *constantly* reminded us that our presence was an inconvenience. Still, this space is all we have!" My voice cracked. "With no alternative, our school is doomed. I had hoped that Christian charity would triumph."

"There must be some mistake." He looked from me to Laura. "I have not come to put you out!"

"You haven't?" Laura spluttered. "Why then have you traveled all this way, Doctor?"

"First of all," he said, "why are you calling me Doctor?"

"Did you not say your name was Parker?" I asked.

"Yes, but I am a not a doctor."

"So you are not Dr. Parker, the Baptist agent?" Laura asked.

"No! I forgot about the other Parker." He shook his head, and then smiled. "May we start again?"

"Please do." Laura's rigid stance loosened.

With a slight bow, he said, "I am the *Reverend* Parker. I have come to lead the flock of the Brick Church and have no desire to remove your Penn School from the premises."

My face flushed. "Oh goodness!"

Laura shook her head and chuckled.

"In fact," our new pastor said, "I think it splendid that this building is serving the community in two capacities and said so to my superiors."

"I'm sorry, Pastor." I threw my hands up. "It is just your name...and Pastor Phillips gave us *such* a difficult time...and then Dr. Parker—"

He calmly held up a hand. "The mistake is perfectly understandable."

"Welcome." Laura introduced herself and then me. "Our apologies. We had no advance notice of your arrival."

"But here I am," he grinned. "I will be offering Sunday service this week. For today I simply wanted to introduce myself and, if you would allow, visit the children. Might that be possible?"

Laura and I exchanged a glance. This late in the afternoon our scholars may become excited and misbehave.

Laura spoke up. "Might I suggest you return another time, earlier in the day, to afford you the opportunity to experience each form? For this afternoon, perhaps you could visit just one." She smiled at me. "Miss Murray would be the best candidate, given that she is the most experienced teacher and our principal."

I pounced on her suggestion. "I would love to introduce you to my students." I extended an arm, indicating the direction of my class.

A few minutes later, the pastor stood at the head of my class, eager to engage the students.

"What do you have in your heads?" he asked the children.

Only a few feet from me, I still strained to hear him.

A boy seated at the front answered. "Sense."

"Brains," the pastor corrected. "And how does knowledge get into your head?"

"God put it there!" a girl called out.

The pastor smiled and in a soft voice proceeded to explain how ideas entered their minds, whilst pointing to his eyes, ears, mouth, and nose.

Fairy burst into a fit of high-pitched giggles at the pastor's gesticulations. The rest of my class tittered or laughed outright. Face burning, I darted forward, shushing the students, and took Fairy by the hand. I then ushered her out the door and into the churchyard.

Upon my return the children's giggling had been replaced by chatter. The pastor stared out of the window.

"Please, do not be discouraged," I said. "They are easily excited."

"Think nothing of it, my dear." Hat in hand, he shrugged.

I felt bad for the old gentleman. He meant well. "It's close to going home time," I said. "Let me dismiss the class and I'll walk out with you."

At the door, the children filed past, all wishing our guest a good day, with the exception of one girl who kept her head down, only nodding as she rushed by.

My heart ached for Henrietta. A bright and eager student of about eight, damaged jawbones prevented her mouth from properly opening. Laura and I still need to piece together her story.

With the last of the students dismissed, Reverend Parker and I made our way outside. We ambled through the church graveyard and over to his wagon without speaking. Birds chattered and sang. Dry acorns cast from the numerous live oaks crunched underfoot. Still fresh from the North and full of curiosity, he stopped and looked about the grounds.

"How lovely St. Helena seems."

I sensed disappointment in his wistful tone. He untethered his horse and sighed deeply.

"Is St. Helena like you imagined?" I asked.

"The island itself is beautiful." He stroked the animal's muzzle.

"I hadn't considered the aesthetics of the placement." He continued to pet the horse and I waited for him to say more. He turned to me. "If I am honest, Miss Murray, I had expected to find peace and zeal here; a band of fellow workers living in harmony, engaged in a collaborative effort. Instead, I have discovered friction in every quarter—military, religious, and political."

Given that our school depended on his approval, I didn't wish to overstep. On the other hand, to achieve personal success or satisfaction this gentle man needed some encouragement.

"May I offer you some advice, by way of my experiences?"

He faced me. "By all means, please."

"I cannot dispute your observations. Living and working amongst formerly enslaved people offers unique challenges. While our goal is to empower them, in the process we must take care not to stamp out what little sense of self and community exists. While we lead the freedmen toward independence and citizenship, we must guard against corrupting temptations—"

"How do you mean?" His voice rose.

"Objectives instigated to lift up the freedmen may conflict with the opportunity for personal gain in the community." Edward Philbrick sprang to mind. "I have witnessed well-intentioned people lose their way, even men of God—"

His eyes widened.

"We are in uncharted territory, Reverend. The freedmen are fundamentally intelligent and possess wisdom. Our ways are as confounding to them as theirs are to us."

"I see."

"Laura and I constantly question our desires and motives. However," I lightened my tone, "there is another side to the coin. There are many solid people amongst us who hold firmly to their original conviction that the freedmen can and will become contributing citizens. Seek out their company."

"Thank you for your frankness," he said with a smile. "Wise observations. You do encourage me."

I let out a sigh of relief. "I am glad, I feared offending you."

"Not at all," he said. "You've lifted a veil."

"In that case," I said, with a slight smile, "perhaps, *we* might work together and do some good for the Penn School scholars."

He climbed onto the wagon and took up the reins. "I should like that very much." With a tip of his hat he drove off.

Walking back to the building, the air smelled fresher, the birdsong sounded sweeter, and the prospect of teaching our students within the crowded confines of the Brick Church, much improved.

Despite the initial relief that followed our encounter with the Reverend Parker, our circumstances remained unaltered. Since we taught in a crowded church sanctuary, not a schoolhouse, our final task of the week was to ready the space for Sunday service. With more muscle than necessary, I shoved a bench toward the wall. As bench met wall, the front door crashed open.

"Miz Laura, Miz Ellen…"

I spun around.

Tommy stood in the vestibule.

Laura and I reached him at the same time.

"Good grief, child!" Laura said. "What an entrance. We've only just dismissed school. Why have you come back?"

"Dis." Tommy held an envelope in his remaining hand. He waved it at us.

Frowning, Laura took it. "Who is it from?"

"General Saxton, ma'am." Breathless, Tommy bent forward, hand on knee. "Miz Rina had me bring it."

Smiling, Laura shook her head. "She did, did she? Well, thank you. But in future could you deliver a message without scaring us half to death?"

"Yessim." He smiled and scampered off.

Laura withdrew the single sheet from the envelope. "Now then—"

"I hope it's not bad news," I said.

Scanning the letter, her mouth opened.

"What?" I leaned in.

"I cannot believe it!" Still clutching the note, Laura grasped my arms. Her eyes sparkled.

"Well, don't keep me in suspense!" I laughed.

Releasing me, she cleared her throat. "The Philadelphia Commission wrote to General Saxton enquiring whether there was any necessity for schoolhouses in the department—"

"Truly?" I said.

She handed me the letter. "Look for yourself."

Laura stabbed the note with a finger. "Read this line."

"General Saxton wants us to state our case in writing. He will take care of the details."

I returned the letter to Laura and she tucked it back into the envelope.

"Let's finish up," she said. "We need to get home and draft our response."

ও ও ও

That evening, we signed and sealed our letter requesting a schoolhouse. In the morning, Hastings and Tommy rode out to General Saxton's camp on Lady's Island to deliver it.

ও ও ও

Chapter 23

Henrietta

Lifting my palms from the journal, the past dissolves. A bittersweet aftertaste lingers. "Seeing" my younger self through Miss Ellen's eyes unmoors emotions that I cannot name. Reaching into my pocket, I clutch the smooth rock within. Ballast for my soul.

I recall the day Miss Ellen writes of, the one when Reverend Parker visited the Brick Church and all the other children greeted him. I had wanted to join in, but could not. The pain in my jaw turned my stomach when I tried. Afterwards, I'd gone to Maum's cabin, tearful.

Maum took me onto her lap and held me close. Eventually she asked what troubled me.

I told her about being teased by the other children, the pain that plagued me when I ate or spoke, and how today I couldn't welcome our school visitor.

"I can fix dat," said she.

"How?"

She set me down. "Come wit me."

Maum made a poultice from green cockleburs that soothed my aching jaw and said we'll take care of the rest in three days time.

"Why do we have to wait?" I whined.

"'Cause we need de moon be full." Maum frowned.

This made no sense to me. "Can't we try anyway?"

"Uh-uh." Her frown deepened and I don't ask again, fearing she'll change her mind.

On the third day, after the sun set, Maum told me to sit down on a stool. She pulled another up close to me, and sat herself down.

"Hold still," said she.

Using a pair of tiny scissors, she cut off a few strands of my hair. Then she trimmed my finger and toenails. My front tooth was wiggly, had been for a bit, and Maum asked if she could pull it out.

"Why?" I reared back.

"You want you jaw to stop achin'?"

I took a deep breath and nodded.

Maum got a tiny square of cloth, held it between her fingers and gave the tooth a quick yank.

"Dat hurt?" Maum dabbed the cloth on the gap.

"Uh-uh." I explored the space with my tongue. Tasting blood, I made a face. "Yuck."

Maum chuckled. "You be fine."

With care, she rolled up my fingernails, hair cuttings, and tooth into the bloody patch of cloth. "Come on." She stood and headed for the door.

Trotting beside her, I asked, "Where we goin'?"

"To find us a willow tree."

"What for?"

She just kept moving. I didn't bother asking again, knowing she won't tell me 'til she's good and ready.

After a bit Maum sighted a willow. She stalked up close to the trunk and beckoned me over. Cupping my shoulders, she pressed my back against the tree trunk and bid me stand still. Then she took some kind of tool out of her apron pocket and raised it just over my head.

I looked up at her face, all crunched like she's thinking real hard. "Whatcha doin'?"

"Measurin' how tall you be." She put her arms down and with a wave, shooed me. She took the tool and started drilling into the trunk.

"We gonna put all dem bits rolled up in dis cloth in de hole." She stood back and nodded. "Good 'nuff."

Taking the cloth from her pocket, she stuffed the package into the bored hole.

"We needs a twig," said Maum.

She rummaged in the willow's foliage. By and by, she tugged at a branch. It came free. She threaded it into the hole, leaned back, squinted, then wiggled and turned it some more. Staring at her handiwork, she tilted her head this way and that. If I hadn't known better, I'd've thought the branch belonged there. The way Maum brushed her hands together, I knew the job pleased her.

Maum pointed to the twig and told me, "When you taller than dat branch, you jaw stop achin' all de time."

"How much taller?" I asked.

"Tall as dem hairs and nails are fine."

"That's not much," I said. "You sure this gonna work?"

"Mmmhm, if we do it right."

"Right?"

"We gonna come back when de moon be full—"

"To see if I'm taller?"

"Mmm-hmm."

"And if I'm not?"

"We try again."

I heaved a sigh. "So we gotta wait."

Maum put her arm around my shoulders and turned us toward home.

In the weeks following, Maum had me sip swamp-colored tea. Bits floated on top like frog spawn.

"Bleck! What's in it?" I'd asked.

"Shoots 'n roots. Mek you grow and stop feelin' sick."

Holding my nose, I took a swig. It tasted earthy and sweet, so I gulped down the mug.

"'Member," said Maum, "you gotta try talkin'. If you keeps drinking de tea and talkin', it gonna be better. Dat way, when you grows past de hole in de tree, you jaw gonna loosen up and stop hurtin' so much."

While we waited for me to grow, Maum took to massaging my jaw with a salve of lard rendered from a buzzard's carcass. It stunk real bad, but Maum said it'd be worth it.

During one of those sessions she handed me a stone about the size and shape of an oyster shell.

"What's this?" I asked.

"A buzzard rock," said she.

"What's it for?"

"To stop the chillun from tautin' you," said she.

"If I carry this rock the others won't jibe me? I'll be safe?"

"Mmmhm," said Maum.

"How's it work?" I asked.

"Dat rock like hen's teeth."

"Hen's teeth?" I leaned away, arms crossed, sure Maum was teasing me.

"Hold still." She held onto my chin and turned my face, so she could keep working the foul-smelling grease into my sore jaw.

"Gettin' a buzzard rock ain't easy," says Maum. "First off, you gotta know where to look. Dem birds hide de nest way up, mebbe de top of de lightin' pine. You gotta watch and wait 'til de mama buzzard leave de nest to feed. Dat's when you scramble up de tree and steal de egg—"

"Egg?" I frowned at Maum.

"I'm gettin' to it," said she. "You gotta take de egg home, boil it up 'til it's good and hard, go back to de tree, and when de mama buzzard fly off again, you put it in de nest. Now," said Maum, "when dat egg don hatch, de mama buzzard she gonna fly off and get de rock to break it open. After she give up, you gotta climb again and take de rock."

Maum released my chin, sat back and wiped her hands on a rag.

I still thought she was teasing me. "You didn't climb up no tree," I said.

"'Course not," said Maum.

"Where you get the rock then?" I asked.

"Doc Fishbone," said she.

"Fishbone?" A face with beard stubble flashed in my head. I wasn't sure if it was a memory or just something I'd made up. "Did that man tend me back in Beaufort, after I got hurt?"

"Mmm-hmm. There only be one Fishbone," said Maum.

I imagined the bent scrawny old man who came to the kitchen house climbing a tall pine tree and stealing buzzard eggs. "You sure that old man climb a tree?"

"Where else he get dat rock?"

I shrugged.

Maum huffed.

"Wait," I said, "what's all that got to do with hen's teeth?"

"When de last time you seen hen's teeth?" asked Maum.

"I ain't never seen hen's teeth."

Maum smiled. "And buzzard rocks be just as hard to find."

On the full moon, Maum and I headed out to our willow. I pressed against the trunk, beside the twig plugging up all the bits of me.

Maum shook her head, no.

"You sure?"

"You drinking all dat tea?" asked Maum. "You eatin' all Manners give you for supper?"

"Mostly. But it hurts to chew."

"You eat more, you grow more," said Maum, and then she turned for home.

We returned the following full moon, and I'd grown a sliver past the twig.

"What now?" I asked.

Maum took out the twig, pulled the little parcel from the hole and gave it to me. "Sleep with dis under you head tonight. Tomorrow you jaw be loosened and it don' grow crooked."

୬ ୬ ୬

I open my fist and I stare at the smooth, warm rock in my palm that Maum gave me all those years ago. After that moonlit night, I did all Maum asked of me and it worked. To this day it's a mystery. Which charm cured me? The green cocklebur poultice or root tea? The buzzard grease? Might it've been my own wishful thinking or Maum's juju? Whatever the reason, I have Maum to thank.

Maum moans *Mmm-hmm* in her sleep, like she knows I'm thinking of her. I look over, but she doesn't stir. Her breathing levels out, her chest rises and falls, rises and falls.

The one and only thing I've asked of Maum that she made no effort to help me with concerns the answer to another mystery: my injury. For the life of me, I cannot remember. God knows I've tried. Maum says I just need to bide my time. Well, I've been bidding it for forty-some years. Seems to me if my memory could be jogged, it'd've done so by now.

Miss Ellen claimed the not remembering might be for the best. She said this soon after Miss Rina passed. Miss Ellen told a story—the same one recalled in her journal—of how years back, Miss Laura and she had tended Miss Rina when she was sick.

She didn't want Miss Laura to examine her, and how her man Hastings had insisted, and Rina relented. Turns out, her back was a woven mess of scars and stripes. Afterwards, Hastings told my mothers Rina still woke crying and thrashing in the night with memory nightmares.

Learning that our Miss Rina had been treated so cruelly made me sad. Even so, I didn't agree with Miss Ellen about the not knowing what happened to me. Maum Cat helped fix my sore jaw, but even back then I knew I couldn't stop hurting inside until I understood what caused my pain. I had stayed quiet, though. I recognized Miss Ellen meant to comfort me.

I set memories of Miss Rina and my mother aside, and glance at Maum's sleeping form. It occurs to me that Rina is another person Maum has outlived. And now *both* my mothers have passed. And still Maum carries on. She even outlived her daughter, Manners.

Although I tease Maum about having nine lives, whatever her age, she can't live forever. What will I do when Maum passes?

The notebook on my lap slips and I pin it with my elbows. Where did I leave off? *Ah yes!* The news that my mothers would be getting a schoolhouse of their own.

I smile, knowing how well that turned out. What I don't fully grasp is how it all came together. Closing my eyes, I once again press my bare palms to the page.

ta ta ta

Chapter 24

Ellen

Not to keep us on tenterhooks, the Philadelphia Commission responded to our request for a schoolhouse building before the end of April. We'd since secured a location. All that remained to be done surrounded finishing the partially constructed three-room structure itself, once it arrived. Supervising the construction would fall to me. Laura was finally going to visit her family in Philadelphia.

Earlier this morning, Hastings had carried out Laura's nearly empty steamer trunk and loaded it onto the wagon. Laura planned to bring back whatever comforts or essentials she discovered on her visit which eluded us on St. Helena.

Laura closed the clasp on her carpetbag and set it on our bed. "Ellen, I feel terrible leaving you here alone to deal with the arrival of the school building."

I groaned. "We have been over this several times—"

She held up a hand. "I know."

"I'm just thankful the schoolhouse is coming," I said.

"Me too. It's not that I doubt your judgment if there are problems. It is just that—"

"You cannot help fretting." I tried to sound understanding, less impatient. I also didn't want to give in to my own fears.

She exhaled. "Exactly."

I drew closer. "We both know that your delayed visits have resulted in some hurt feelings. It's high time you went to Philadelphia to visit your family."

Laura nodded.

"What's more," I continued, "your worrying about events out of our control won't change a thing. The building will arrive, albeit partially constructed, and I'll make sure it's deposited on the property, whether it's flawed or perfect, cavernous or a cottage."

"This is true," Laura chuckled. "And I believe we made a sound decision regarding the location."

"We did." I picked up her carpetbag from the bed.

After touring the island, we decided to purchase a central and familiar area for the children: the plot of land across from the Brick Church.

"Come now." I turned to leave. "I'll let Hastings know we're ready."

"Ellen, wait."

I looked back. A flurry of emotion crossed Laura's face. I dropped the bag and went to her. Pulling her into my arms she sobbed, "I'll miss you." Not trusting myself to speak, I closed my eyes and held her.

ʃʃ ʃʃ ʃʃ

The moment Laura embarked on the steamship *Flora*, I found it difficult to draw breath. Still, I refused to weep while waving her off from Beaufort's dock. I repeated to myself that she deserved this break, that she and her family needed this reunion. I had Mother and my sister, Hattie, at Frogmore House; Rina and Hastings nearby; and a fine assortment of neighbors, friends, and acquaintances all within a short walk or buggy ride. I told myself, *time will fly.*

And it did. Summer days folded one upon the other until a month had passed. Keeping busy helped mitigate the hollow ache of Laura's absence. I always had something to do, someone to see, or some problem to solve. With school out, I also caught up on domestic chores. To date, I had relocated our library from the bedchamber to the dining area, mended some clothing and, under Rina's tutelage, baked a pie.

In her absence, Laura had arranged for my giggle-prone student, Fairy, to deliver prepared treatments to an elderly patient who would accept medicine from no other White doctor but Laura. At the time I thought Laura's choice of emissary curious. I believed Fairy to be a flibbertigibbet, but I resisted the temptation to object. If Laura saw something in the child, I did not wish to prejudice her choice. Today, however, Fairy neglected to show at the preassigned time for the delivery. The task fell back to me.

Maum Cat lived a stone's throw from our cottage. I had not accompanied Laura on a visit, so we had never met. But I knew her story. Of indeterminate age, Maum arrived here from Africa. Stolen as a child, she purportedly recalled parts of her life there, including worshiping an African god.

To avoid the afternoon's sweltering heat and blazing sun, I set out early for Maum's cabin. Ten minutes later I arrived.

"Maum Cat?" I rapped the cabin door. "Ellen Murray here with a delivery from Doctor Laura." I waited and listened for the old woman to call out.

With a rush of air the door opened and I took a step back. My young student with the malformed jaw, Henrietta, moved aside to allow me entry.

Waiting for my vision to adjust to the cabin's dimmer light, I recognized the lemony-sweet perfume of magnolias. I spotted a glass jug on the table overflowing with the creamy teacup-sized blossoms.

"Come here," the old woman said, her deep voice crackled with age and good humor.

Ensconced in a rocking chair, she wore a multi-colored patchwork quilt around her shoulders, and another quilt lay across her knees. A headscarf the color of crushed cranberries topped her ensemble. Given the heat, I marveled at the mantle and crown of fabric.

"Maum *see* with she hands." Henrietta wiggled her fingers. She had stepped in behind the chair.

What did she mean? The old woman didn't appear blind.

Maum stretched out a weathered hand with untrimmed, yellow fingernails.

Swallowing my distaste, I stepped forward and took the proffered hand.

She tilted her head back and gazed up at me. Her skin, a study in wrinkles, reminded me of well-worn, tooled leather.

Maum turned her head toward Henrietta.

"It be best if you kneel down, so Maum can touch your face," said Henrietta, her questioning tone indicating my permission was required.

It entered my mind that Laura must have submitted to this inspection. However unorthodox, if she passed muster, so must I. Gathering my skirts, I knelt before the old woman.

Maum rubbed her hands together, making a dry, chafing sound, and then cupped either side of my chin with crevassed palms. I stiffened. Wearing a calm, inward expression Maum stroked my cheeks with the edge of her thumbs. At her touch, the taut muscles capping my shoulders relaxed. Only Laura had ever caressed me thus. I closed my eyes and recalled the night before Laura's departure, how we had faced each other in bed, the way she had touched my brow, my cheeks, and finally my lips. Whereas Laura's hands had been playful and tender, Maum's were searching and purposeful. With a satisfied exhalation, Maum released me. I opened my eyes.

She leaned back in her chair and rocked, one, two, three—"You are beloved."

I cleared my throat. "Thank you." Unsure of what to do next I looked to Henrietta, still at her post behind the old woman.

"Sit here, Miz Murray." Henrietta brought around a little chair.

Maum cocked her head to the side. "You happy *now*."

Her inflection on *now* insinuated a resolution to a previously held state of mind. Before Laura, before coming to St. Helena, my life had been one of general dissatisfaction and loneliness. This truth, however, I had shared with no one.

"You from de nord?" Maum brought my attention back to her.

"Yes."

"Where 'bouts?"

"Newport," I answered, "Rhode Island."

"No." She fixed a hard gaze on me.

Unnerved and bewildered by her tone, I tried to make light of her declaration. "Surely, you don't think me untruthful?"

Her expression relaxed. "You brought medicine?"

"Yes." Relieved at her shift in focus, I searched the floor around me.

"Here, Miz Murray." Henrietta held out my parcel.

"Thank you, Henrietta."

The girl's eyes met mine for a moment.

"No lazy bones in dis gal," Maum cackled.

Henrietta's little mouth formed a thin, sweet smile.

"Henrietta keep me company and give me medicine. She bide with Manners."

Maum's daughter, Manners, I knew. Tall, with broad hips, I never saw her without her signature headscarf. The woman could take any scrap of fabric and fashion it into something extraordinary. Middle-aged and widowed, her small home overflowed with children. Such a large family must have presented challenges, yet whenever our paths crossed she was jovial and chatty. Still, with Manners having so many mouths to feed already—

"How did you come to live with Manners, Henrietta?" I asked.

Henrietta slunk back to her place behind Maum's chair.

"Never mind dat," Maum waved off my question.

During the beat of uncomfortable silence which followed, I bent over my parcel and unpacked the contents.

Unscrewing the lid of a jar, I showed them the shiny green salve within. The honeyed fragrance of beeswax and herbs surfaced. "Comfrey ointment." Working alongside Laura, I knew most of her remedies. "Rub it in to ease your aching bones."

Maum reached behind for Henrietta. "Dis gal have strong hands."

"Wonderful," I said. "So you know what to do, Henrietta?"

A small nod, but no eye contact.

"Next, we have some willow bark tea. Brew and drink for pain." I looked up. "Have you taken it before?"

"Mmm-hmm," Maum said.

I held out the final item, a small pouch. "And here we have the huckleberry powder to help with your vision. Mix it in sweetwater."

Maum frowned.

"The purple potion," Henrietta offered.

"Do you have any questions?" I stood and put the treatments on the table beside the jar of magnolias.

Maum spoke to Henrietta. "Run 'long. Find out if Manners finished cooking de soup."

Henrietta hesitated, but then headed for the door.

"Thanks for your help," I called after her.

With a backward glance and a tentative, lopsided grin she trotted out into the sunshine.

The moment the child was gone Maum fixed me with a look.

"Henrietta a good gal," she said.

"Yes." Her determined tone and expression made me suspect she had dispatched the girl for reasons other than soup. I returned to my chair.

"Why does Henrietta wears gloves?" Along with her disfigurement, the unusual habit afforded the child unwanted attention from her classmates.

Maum frowned and lowered her voice. "De gift be too strong."

Chapter 25

Henrietta

A jarring re-entry to present-day steals my equilibrium. Squeezing my eyes shut, I cling to the arms of my chair as the back porch tilts to, fro, and around. With focused inhalations, my breathing and heart rate eventually return to normal, if such a word applies to me. The "gift" Maum speaks of to Miss Ellen—my ability to touch something or someone and "see" their story—added to my misery as a child. Despite the ridicule, had I not worn gloves I would have been under constant assault from the emotions and histories of the objects and people I encountered. I am heartened, but not surprised, that Miss Ellen recognized my distress, even if she didn't fully understand. Maum had a different take. By my side when it first appeared, she celebrated this peculiarity and deemed it a blessing, a gift.

We had only just arrived on St. Helena. Maum took me directly to her daughter Manners' cabin. The place was overrun with children and people coming and going. Outside, the youngsters played a game with a stick and pinecones to see who could hit the cone the farthest. Not yet well enough to join them, I wandered about inside the cabin as Maum and Manners chatted. Near the windowsill, a pipe sat in a bowl. I do not know what possessed me to pick it up, but the moment I did a man, tall with a broad chest and big hands, appeared.

My expression must have shown on my face for his eyes widened. "You see me?" He pushed his wide-brimmed hat back from his forehead.

I opened my mouth to answer, but nothing came out. I nodded.

I turned to look at Maum and Manners. They sat talking as they had before the man appeared.

"Dey kent see me." His shoulders drooped. "Kent hear me neeber."

"W-who are you?" I whispered.

"I be Manners' man." He tipped his chin to the window. "Dems me chilluns."

He took the pipe from me and smiled. "Been some time since I sees dis." He stuck the stem between his teeth.

"So you've come home?" I asked.

He shook his head. "Tell Manners I try. But you kent outrun a bloodhound and a bullet."

I looked over at Manners. "Why don't you tell her yourself?" I heard a clatter and turned back. He'd vanished and his pipe lay on the floor.

I ran to Maum. Pressing my body against her side, I told her what had happened.

Maum clasped my arms gently and pulled me in front of her. "Wat he look like?"

"Big hands—he wore a floppy hat."

"Otis?!" Manners bolted from her chair. She scanned the room as though hoping to discover the man hiding in a corner.

I gave her Otis' message. Manners commenced wailing.

Tears filled my eyes. "I'm sorry."

"It be fine, Henrietta." Maum held my hands. "You done good." She stood and turned me to face the cabin door. "Run along for a bit."

Glad to escape Manners' woeful sobs, I ran outside and sat in the shade of the yard's big palmetto.

The mood in and around the cabin that evening remained somber. Folks came and went. All wanted to hear the news about Otis. Turned out he'd been missing for some time. No one knew if he was alive or dead. Maum claimed my sighting of him suggested the latter.

The next day, she sat me down and asked more questions.

"Least aways, Manners knows." Frowning, Maum said this more to herself than to me. A second later, she pinned me with a look. "Dis neber happen afore?"

I shook my head. "No, never."

"Sometin' else happen, tell me straight away, you hear?" Maum said. "We figure dis out together."

Once a day Maum gave me a different object to hold or touch. Sometimes I'd glean a sense of the owner, other times something about the history of the object. Shoes, scarves, hair combs. The last item she handed me on this particular day was a cooking pot.

The pot's owners had been many and varied, the last one blind.

"You sure?" asked Maum.

I shrugged. "The woman scrubbin' the pot is feeling the bottom for stuck-on bits, angry she don't see no more."

"Why kent she see?" asks Maum.

"Somebody hurt her." I commenced trembling and my teeth set to chattering.

Maum took the pot from me, put it aside, and pulled me close. "You got a special gift, Henrietta. Powerful strong."

Clinging to Maum, I sobbed, "Why this happening to me?"

"Blue Root used to heal you powerful, Henrietta." Maum nodded. "Root like dat sometime leave a mark."

"I'm scairt, Maum."

She squeezed me tighter. "We gonna get you some gloves."

ба ба ба

Chapter 26

Ellen

De gift be too strong—

The old woman's conspiratorial tone gave me a chill.

Moments later, Maum commenced rocking. The *thump-thump* of my heart kept time with the *creak-creak* of her chair. Suddenly she stopped, reached over, and gripping my thumbs, flipped my palms up. She then kneaded the bones of my hand and stared into the distance as though another faculty swam behind her irises. With a repressed shudder I recalled Laura saying many freedmen considered Maum a seer or prophet.

Part of me wanted to pull free. Christian doctrine forbade participation in supernatural practices. But curiosity, and an indefinable authenticity in the old woman's bearing, held me fast.

"What do you see?"

Releasing my hands, she sat back and adjusted her patchwork wrap.

"Where you from?" she asked for the second time.

"I already told you, Newport, Rhode Island."

She frowned. "You born there?"

"Oh, actually no, I was born in the Province of Canada."

She made a small grunt of triumph.

"I was only a toddler when we left. I didn't know you meant my birthplace," I explained, desiring to dispel the notion I had lied. "How did you know I wasn't originally from Newport?"

Maum didn't answer, but instead reached out for my right hand. Pressing the flesh below my pinky finger she said, "Soon you be a mama."

"That's not possible."

Maum shrugged. "Neber too late to be who you suppose to be."

A tamped flame within me flickered and I leaned forward, hoping she would tell me more. Instead, Maum adjusted her wrap and closed her eyes.

"Sure you want to hear what dey done?"

"To Henrietta?" I asked, taken aback by the sudden shift. "Yes."

"We do this together den," she said. "Give me you hands."

I pulled my chair closer and reached out. She shimmied forward, pressing her knees against mine and hooking her bony feet around my ankles.

My cheeks flushed. "Wh-what are you doing?"

"Hants feed on evil talk."

After being on the island for some time now, I'd become somewhat familiar with the people's version of the supernatural. As a consequence, Maum's warning conjured images of ravenous, slavering ghosts. A cold shiver skipped up my spine. I glanced about the cabin half-expecting to find the hants Maum spoke of.

She regained my attention with a squeeze. "Henrietta gift be de mark of a powerful healing. She wear gloves for protection. It all happen before de Big Shoot. Henrietta tasked in Beaufort, in a fancy house on de Point. One day, when Henrietta dustin' de mistress bedchamber, she see de dish o' peppermints and tek one."

&ca; &ca; &ca;

Chapter 27

Henrietta

"Peppermint!"

I clap a hand to my mouth and look over at Maum, but she hasn't stirred.

A fancy cut-glass dish, with a lid. Round lozenge the color of fresh milk. The smell of sugar. And mint. I thought it heavenly. Now I cannot abide the smell or taste. But back then I sure wanted one of those sweets. I remember holding the lid in one hand and reaching in with the other.

Just one.

I glance behind to make sure I'm still alone in Mistress' bedchamber, pluck a single candy from the top of the mound and place it on my tongue. It's hard and smooth. Water fills my mouth and I swallow, careful to keep the peppermint tucked in my cheek. I don't want to swallow it whole.

"*What* are you doing?!"

I drop the glass lid. There's a *thwack* when it hits the floor, then a *crracck* as it bounces and breaks into three pieces.

The mistress' nails dig into my arm, but the fear that gripes me is much sharper. Her eyes bug at the glass dish and then at me. Her beaky nose wrinkles. I don't know what to do about the candy, so I keep swallowing my minty spit.

"Mama?"

I peek around Mistress at Miss Lucy. She ain't mean like her mama. She's pretty, like those porcelain dolls on her bed. Cook told Pearl that Mistress beats Miss Lucy, but on her legs so Master don't see the bruises. That makes me sad, so when I see Miss Lucy, I make sure to give her a smile, hoping that eases her hurt feelings. Sometimes she smiles back. I hope she takes pity on me. But she ain't looking at me. She's staring at her mama.

"Thief! That's what she is," Mistress screeches at Miss Lucy and gives me a shake, clawing her nails deeper. "Stole my candies. Then broke my crystal dish."

That's not true, I think. *I dropped it because you scared me.*

Like she knows what's in my head, the slap I get is so sudden and fierce it knocks the peppermint from my mouth. For a moment no one says anything. Bawling, I wipe blood and spit from my face. My legs are shaking so bad I'm afraid I'm gonna fall down. Worse of all, I gotta pee real bad.

"Please, Mistress, I'm sorry. I shouldn't a done it," I beg. Sobbing, I cross my legs and hope I don't shame myself.

Mistress shoves me away.

Miss Lucy's hands are clenched by her side. She don't move; she don't glance at me. "Let her be, Mama. She only dropped the lid because you startled her."

"Well, well," Mistress' voice is real soft now. "I'm not surprised you're taking the nigger's part. You're spineless. Always have been. You were a feeble infant, a puny, dim child, and you're growing up to be the weak-willed woman I always knew you'd be."

Miss Lucy draws a big sigh and looks heavenward. I shove a hand between my legs to keep from wetting myself.

"Sigh all you want, it's the truth and you know it." Mistress sneers. "You're just like your mother."

This confuses me. Ain't Mistress her mama?

"That woman died trying to spit you out. From what I hear, she was soft on the niggers too."

Miss Lucy says nothing back, just stares. Mistress' face goes all red. I hop from one foot to the other. I look at the door, and wonder if I can make it outside. Mistress sees me and says, "Oh, no you don't." So I stay put.

Then she turns back on Miss Lucy, crosses her arms and sniffs. "I told your father we'd sheltered you too much, but would he listen? No, he's insisted on spoiling you. Well, I say it's high time you faced facts. Dealing with the niggers is like breaking a horse or training up a hunting dog, you gotta show them who's in charge. Today you're gonna learn that."

Miss Lucy finally looks my way. Her face has gone right pale. Even her pink lips have no color in them.

Mistress reaches into her dress pocket and pulls out her leather strap.

"No, Mama—" Miss Lucy tries to grab hold of Mistress' arm, but she keeps her eyes fixed on me and pushes off Miss Lucy.

Before I know it, Mistress has my neck trapped in the bend of her elbow.

"I have to go!" I scream.

"Go?" Mistress laughs real mean like. "You're not going anywhere."

I can't hold it no more. Warm pee gushes between my legs.

Mistress brings the strap down, but I'm wriggling so much she misses, whips her own legs, screams, and lets go of me.

"You. Disgusting. Creature." Mistress' face looks purple now.

Mouth moving like a fish gasping for air, she stares at her pee-soaked shoes.

Now she's whipping at me with the leather strap like she's swatting flies. I leap around trying not to get hit. Miss Lucy is crying and screaming for her mama to stop. But there ain't no stopping her.

Mistress backs me into a corner and grabs hold of my arm so tight I think my bones gonna snap. "Since you won't stay put on your own—"

She drags me over to the rocking chair, tosses me flat on my back, and puts her foot on my neck so I can't get free. I can't draw a single breath. She lifts the chair up. I squeeze my eyes shut, thinking she's gonna slam it down on me. But she doesn't. Instead, she lifts her foot off my neck. I roll onto my side and while I'm gasping for air, she presses something across my cheek and over my ear. My eyes fly open. The rocker rail.

"Stop!" Lucy screams.

"If you don't do as you're told," Mistress growls, "you'll be next. Now sit down!"

"No!" Miss Lucy yells.

"Sit! If you know what's good for you," Mistress growls.

I think she's trying to get Miss Lucy to sit down on the bed, but then Lucy says, "I'm sorry, I'm sorry—"

With sickening clarity I recall the crushing weight of the rocking chair and the high-pitched crack of my jaw breaking. Astonished by the sudden memory, I sit back and try to gather my thoughts.

I had concluded years ago that my injury must have had violent origins. If I'd had an accident of some sort, Maum wouldn't have kept it a secret. Still, an intellectual deduction is one thing. Reliving the terror and pain of that trauma, quite another. To confirm the point, I swallow the taste of peppery mint and fresh blood lingering on my tongue.

My entire body trembles. Pulling the quilt around me, I take deep breaths, *in out in out*. I close my eyes and Jakob's face swims before me. Under normal circumstances I might reject such a vision. Not tonight. I welcome his tender expression and allow thoughts of him to soothe and quiet my troubled spirit. Eventually, the trembling subsides, my teeth cease their clacking. I open my eyes and Maum is sitting up, staring at me.

"What come first? You 'member what happen or find it?" Maum nods at Miss Ellen's journal.

I glare at Maum. "Does it matter?"

"Mmm-hmm," says Maum, the corners of her mouth lift.

"If I tell you, you have to tell me something." I don't care that I sound like a whiny child.

Maum frowns. "Tell you what?"

"If I tell you whether I remembered or found it, you have to tell me the parts I don't recall."

"So you do 'member." Maum smiles.

Snapping the notebook shut, I let out an exasperated sigh. "Yes, I remember. And Miss Ellen's account was almost identical."

"Must be time." Maum nods, stares straight ahead.

My scalp tightens. "Why didn't you tell me?" My voice catches.

Maum looks at me. "Keep you safe." Her tender tone implies she wants me to understand.

I scowl at her.

"You 'member what de Mistress and she daughter done."

My stomach churns. I nod.

"Anythin' else?"

I touch my jaw and share the memories that cascade—

My mouth, and the whole side of my face, throbs. I'm stretched out on a pallet of soft blankets, with the fireplace hearth within arm's reach. My hand, flat against heated stone warms my palm. Flames crackle. It's dark. The fire gives off a golden glow.

How did I come to be in the kitchen house? Voices. Hushed and low. Whose?

I open my eyes and squint into ceiling rafters. Turning my head, the walls of the room wheeze in and out like a squeezebox. I shut my eyes for a moment and try again. A haze, like mist on the marsh, parts, and three people come into focus.

"Tell me again," Cook says. "I want to make sure you didn't leave nothin' out." She's speaking to Pearl, the skinny gal that works inside with me.

Pearl's whimperin' and sniffin'. "I did already."

"Come on, best you tell Cook again." Now Chains is talking to Pearl. His voice is low and rumbly, like thunder movin' on. What's he doing in the kitchen house? Chains works with the horses.

Pearl takes a big breath. "Like I told it, I hear Mistress and Miss Lucy squabblin', dey shoutin' and bangin'. You know how mean Mistress get when she in one of dem moods."

"Mmm-hmm," Cook says. "So what you do?"

"I run to de stairs. Mistress chamber door be full open. Henrietta lyin' still as can be. I thought sure she dead. Dat's why I holler."

"And de Mistress in de room? Miss Lucy too?"

"Mmm-hmm." Pearl nodded.

"What'd dey do?" Chains asked.

"Mistress told me to clean up de mess. Miss Lucy bawlin' and run off," Pearl said. "Mistress go after dat."

"And you?" Cook asked.

"Like I told you, I run for help," Pearl said.

They're still askin' Pearl questions when Cook's mouser, Smudge, sits down right by my head. His golden eyes flicker with firelight. Maybe he feels bad 'cause I'm hurt. Thing is, I don't know how I got hurt. Pearl said she found me in Mistress' chamber, but I don't remember being there.

Meow. Smudge rubs his forehead against my face and then hops on top of me. I groan 'cause everything hurts. The cat pays no never mind and plops himself down on my belly.

"Shoo, shoo—" Cook shoves Smudge off and crouches beside me. "How you feelin', baby? It's me, Cook," she says, like maybe I don't know her. "Chains and Pearl here, too."

They're both standing off a ways. Chains got his arm around Pearl and she's chewing on her nails. Cook strokes my hair all tender-like and I look up at her. I want to know what happened. I try to ask, but it hurts so bad I can't talk. Tears roll down my cheeks; my nose runs.

"Hush," Cooks says, even though I didn't say nothin' at all. She pulls a hankie from her apron pocket and dries my tears and drool. I frown at the blood on it and glance up again. I try real hard, using my eyes to ask what happened to me. But she don't see my question. Instead, she hollers at Pearl to bring the bowl. Chains grabs Smudge who's still tryin` to get at me. He slips out the door, taking the cat with him.

"Doc Fishbone here yesterday," Cook tells me in a soft voice, "he says you gotta rest, and no speakin'."

Yesterday? I just woke up. And yesterday I wasn't hurt and lyin' here. So I don't know what she's talking about.

Pearl holds out the bowl Cook asked for. Before taking it, she cradles my head on her lap. There's a cloth floatin' in water. She squeezes the cloth out some and uses it to put a few drips on my mouth. Parting my lips, the cool droplets land on my tongue. I raise my eyebrows at her, asking for more.

"Good gal," Cook says, "that's right, nice and slow."

After a bit, Cook decides I've had enough. She hands the bowl back to Pearl and tells me to rest. I try to shake my head *NO* `cause I want to hear what happened. Cook is singing a real pretty song. My eyes be so heavy—

"That's about all I remember," I tell Maum.

"You 'member Doc Fishbone?"

I shake my head.

"You never saw him again?"

"I don't even remember seeing him when he tended my injuries. Why? What's he got to do with anything?"

"Fishbone come back `cause Cook ask him. And he brung me `cause sooner or later dey both know we gotta get you safe."

"Safe from what?"

"De hex we put on Mistress and she daughter."

"I don't know anything about a hex."

Maum frowns and shakes her head. "No, 'course not."

I take a deep breath. If I am to learn more I must be patient. "You said, *it must be time.* Is that what you meant? That I'm safe now?"

"Mmm-hmm." Maum nods.

Who-cooks-for-you? Who-cooks-for-you?

I glance at the pines. A shadow of wings vanishes. The owl gives me an idea. "Why don't you start by telling me about Cook."

Maum sits up a little straighter and struggles to rearrange her blankets. She's spry in some ways, but truth is, she's old. Real old. It's also the middle of the night. I feel bad for getting so riled.

"Here," I say, "let me help you." I fluff her pillows and do my best to make sure she's comfortable and warm. "Would you like a cup of tea?" I ask after she's tucked in.

She smiles up at me and shakes her head, *no.* I go back and sit down. Once settled, I look her way and raise my brows.

"Doc Fishbone tell me 'bout you, how de Mistress and she daughter put you under de rockin' chair and crack you head like a pecan. Den he say Cook wanna Root dem. He ask me for help."

"There's a Root for punishment?" I ask. Although my knowledge of Roots is limited, I do know there are different kinds, depending on the intent. They're usually sachets made from cotton or flannel. I know of the Money Root and the Follow Me Love Charm, so why not a Root for revenge?

"Mmm-hmm," Maum nods. "De Blue Root powerful strong."

"I've never heard of that one."

Maum shrugged.

"So you and Doc Fishbone went to the kitchen house together to administer this Root? I don't remember any of that."

"You not suppose to. Cook make a tea help you sleep. Blue Root sometime bounce back. What you don' know won' hurt you. Fishbone make a Forget Root to keep you safe. Inside he put something from all we, and pinch o' salt."

"Salt?"

"Hants. Keeps dem away." Says Maum, all matter-of-fact. "Den he say sumptin' and toss dat Root in de fire."

"So I was there and slept through all of this?"

"Mmm-hmm," Maum noded. "Den Fishbone make two more Roots. One for de Mistress, 'nuther for Miz Lucy. He sew de two

191

packets 'bout the size of a camellia blossom and put in 'em a pinch of goofer dust—"

"Graveyard dirt?"

"Dat's right. But this goofer dust he get after midnight 'cause he gonna hex dem."

"Hex, you mean curse them?" My scalp tingles.

"Uh-huh," Maum nods. "Den he stuff a crow feather, hair from de women and sumptin' dat belong to dem, a button from Miz Lucy and a hairpin from she mother. Den he take bits of cloth with you spit and blood on it, and sew dem up tight. Fishbone shut he eyes say de hex words."

"What'd he say?" My heart speeds up.

Maum shrugs. "I don' understand."

"Another language?"

"Mebbe. Cook say he talk backward."

"If that's so, how'd you know he hexed them?"

"He say so." Maum looks at me like I'm dim-witted.

I leave it be. "What'd he tell you, then?"

"He tell Pearl to put dem Roots inside de Mistress and Miz Lucy pillow covers." Maum sits back.

"That's it?" My temper simmers near boiling, but I keep my voice even. "You've kept me in the dark all these years because of a superstitious belief in Root magic?"

Maum's eyes fly wide open. "'Cause of dem Roots, you safe and get to come to St. Helena. I brung you!"

"What are you talking about?" The volume of my voice rises to match Maum's. "The Union Army came into Beaufort. There was no one left to stop you."

"You come before den." Maum crosses her arms.

"But my birthdate? Manners told me you gave me that birthday because that's the day you brought me here, after the Big Shoot."

"I say that so nobody know," says Maum. "Mix up de spirits."

"Know what?"

"Dat we kill de Mistress and Miz Lucy, and set you free," says Maum.

"You killed them?!" My scalp is prickling again. "You said you Rooted them."

"Same," says Maum. "Dey die."

"How?"

"Fever," says Maum. "Mistress sweat and moan all de day and night. Say she bones hurt. Miz Lucy bad too, say she head gonna blow off. Pearl run 'tween the two of dem. Blood come out everywhere. Mistress blue all over. She die first. Next day, Pearl find Miz Lucy stiff as de starch shirt, she face swollen and purple like a plucked berry."

I wince at Maum's description. "Is that why it's called a Blue Root?"

Maum shrugs. "De Massa real sad 'bout Miz Lucy. He go north to see family. When he come back, we say you die too."

"And you brought me here when he went north?"

"Mmm-hmm."

"You still think the Root caused my affliction?"

Maum smiles. "You blessing. De good Lawd find a way to mek up for wat you lost."

I roll my eyes. Maum and I have been down this road many times. I leave it be and return to the conversation at hand.

"You must have been scared. I see why you kept things secret at first. But I don't understand why you didn't tell me once we'd safely arrived here, or later on when I begged you to tell me how I ended up like this." I turn my head so my disfigured jaw is in full view.

"I want to." Maum sighs. "I know how much it bother you. But Doc Fishbone warn me de hex might bounce back. De Forget Root what keep you safe."

"Safe from what? No one knew I was here, or cared. The Union Army came and all the White folks ran off. What would have been the harm in telling me then?"

"Doc Fishbone say mebbe Mistress and Miz Lucy spirit come back and trouble you. He say if you 'member, you safe 'cause dey give up lookin'."

"Trouble me? Maum, I was troubled anyway, I've been troubled for years. You should have told me. I don't think anything could have hurt me more."

"Blue Root too powerful." Maum frowns and shakes her head. "After we leave Beaufort, Cook go blind. Pearl's man, Chains, he run off with 'nuther gal."

"Nothing happened to you! And you saw fit to tell Miss Ellen." Realizing this, I'm angry with my mother as well. "She could've told me."

"You ever ask her?" Maum's eyes are wide and her forehead crinkles.

"Why would I?" I volley back.

"If you need to know so much, why you don' 'member? Tell me dat."

"You're saying it's my fault that I don't remember!"

"No, not you fault. You job. I can't carry all o' it."

Crossing my arms, I look down. Tears nip my eyes. I sniff them back.

"Do you 'member de fire? De one dat burn down de cabins?" asks Maum.

"Yes," I face her again, "but don't be telling me that was the Root turning back on you. If it was, you'd be dead. Ever think of that? You're still here."

"I here 'cause you need me," says Maum in a small voice.

Turning my back to her, I snatch the notebook and in a flash of anger return to the past.

❧ ❧ ❧

Chapter 28

Ellen

With a groan, I shove the cat off of me. Since Laura went up North, he had only me to pester.

"I'm awake, stop."

Through the window, amber light flickered amongst the tree leaves.

"Looks like it is going to be a lovely day." Lucky meowed and then poked me in the face with a soft paw. "All right! I'm getting up."

I threw off the bedsheet and stood. The back door screeched open and Rina called out, "Miz Ellen, come quick!" Her footsteps reverberated across the floorboards. She arrived at the bedroom door, chest heaving.

"Goodness! What is it?" I reached for my dressing gown.

"Manners' cabin on fire!" Rina burst into tears.

"What?" I turned back to the window. "What time is it?"

"Just past three o'clock." Rina wiped her face.

The glow was not the rising sun. I tossed my dressing gown onto the bed, grabbed my skirt and pulled it on over my nightdress. "Did they all get out?" I asked, buttoning on a light jacket.

"Don' know. Friday woke me and Hastings."

"Friday?" I asked, and then recalled the little bandy-legged fellow from the village, Manners' eldest grandson, whom Rina favored.

"Yessim. Dey grab de buckets and run off. I come get you."

⁂

Through the trees, a line of flames danced. Smoke stung my eyes and clawed my throat. Pulling a handkerchief from my pocket, I wiped the tears and covered my nose. Head down, I ploughed on. Rina coughed and spluttered behind me.

Manners' cabin, along with Maum Cat's and two others, sat in a jagged row near a clearing not far from the road that snaked its way from one side of the village to the other. By the time we arrived, Manners' home had collapsed into a smoldering heap. The two other cabins had also crumpled and caved. Flames ringed Maum's place. Chairs, tables, a bedstead and pots and pans littered the packed, sandy earth at the edge of the clearing. Tears, having nothing to do with the smoke, pricked my eyes.

Heat forced me to back up. Beside me, Rina followed suit. A line of people crossed the sandy courtyard and continued through the brush that led down to the water's edge. Hand over hand they passed sloshing buckets and pots of water.

"Come," Rina took my elbow. "We best see to de folks yonder."

A safe distance off, Manners' extended family and neighbors huddled. Some prayed, others wept. At the core, someone wailed, a heart-wrenching cry that rose higher than the violent flames. We walked forward and goose pimples rippled up my arms and needled my scalp. All eyes turned our way. I had no idea what to do or say. Oh, how I wished for Laura.

Rina squeezed my hand and we joined the group.

A tearful young woman shook her head at Rina before moving aside. "Let Miz Rina by." She grabbed hold of a little boy's elbow.

The ring of people parted. Rina clapped a hand to her mouth. "Dear Lawd!"

Encircled by family and friends, Manners sat on the ground, her legs splayed out. On her lap she cradled Maum Cat's lifeless body.

"Mama, Mama!" Manners rocked her mother with a force that matched her grief.

Rina rushed to Manners.

The circle of mourners closed. Unsure of what to say or how to help, I took a step backwards, and then another, stopping a safe distance from the fire, near a thicket of trees.

"Get back!" someone bellowed.

The ring of people scattered. Manners stumbled up the road, carrying her mother's body.

As though constructed of corrugated paper, Maum Cat's cabin folded and collapsed with a crackling crash. The burning embers rained down on the space where only seconds before friends and family had gathered around Manners and Maum.

Something rustled to my left. I wheeled around. A cluster of fan palms quivered. A raccoon?

"Shoo" I called out. "This is no place for you tonight."

"Yessim—"

"Wait!" Stepping toward the palm, I parted the fronds. Henrietta, her face sooty and tear-stained, tried to extricate herself from the tangle.

"Dear child, come here!" I drew her free and to my side.

Henrietta clung to me, her eyes squeezed shut, and sobbed.

I glanced back at the charred bones of Maum Cat's cabin. The men continued to douse the flames. Amongst the crowd, Rina gathered the homeless and neighbors, no doubt pairing them up so everyone had a roof over their head.

I crouched down, eye level with Henrietta. Removing the handkerchief from my skirt's pocket, I wiped the child's tears.

"Come dear, let's go home."

❧ ❧ ❧

Chapter 29

Henrietta

Removing my hand from the journal, I relax my shoulders. *How strange it feels to see myself through Miss Ellen's eyes.*

I blink at the swing cradling a sleeping Maum Cat. What did I expect, that she'd vanish as I read?

When Miss Ellen recorded the cabin fires, she thought Maum perished. Thank goodness that wasn't the case. Underscoring the point, Maum snorts in her sleep.

My outrage with her for not sharing the truth behind the reason of my coming to St. Helena vanishes. Relief floods my limbs. Resentment is such hard work to maintain. Especially against those we love.

I am amazed by Maum's sleeping habits. Not only can she nod off wherever, whenever, several times during this night she has woken up, carried on a conversation with me and then fallen back to sleep with the ease of a babe drunk on mother's milk. At this time of my life, sleep often eludes me. Maybe when I'm old, like Maum, I will also sleep like the dead. I swallow, wishing I hadn't drawn that particular comparison.

My mind turns back to the fire and what I recall of the event.

First, someone hollered at me to wake up. Wouldn't have been Kit. He was too little at the time. Might've been Friday. Hard to say, Manners having twelve children, plus me. Next I remember rushing outside. Flames crackled and whooshed out of cabin windows, leaped from rooftop to rooftop. Men who'd formed a line down to the water's edge shouted instructions over the clamor; women who'd come to help milled about the clearing, comforting each other, screaming children clinging to them. I wanted Maum. But I couldn't see her anywhere. Even if I could've gotten through the crowd to look for her, the fire itself and the heat it gave off frightened me. So I ran into the bushes.

That's where Miss Ellen found me hiding and took me home. Lucky for me. Not so for the others. That fire was a big setback for Manners and her brood. Now I'm guessing Maum believes the Root came back on her and her kinfolk, retribution for hexing my mistress, like she fancies happened to Cook and Pearl.

Unbidden notions of Maum dying that night push up like toadstools after a rainstorm. I wrack my brain trying to recall the next time I actually saw her. All things considered, it might've been awhile. But I can't remember. I don't even know where she went to live during that time. Never asked, even later. Why didn't I seek her out?

Maum likely kept her distance so I'd settle in with the Misses. Even so, she appeared later, at some point. Probably when I was troubled. Which I was a lot.

I here 'cause you need me.

An icicle of foreboding rises within me. I am fastened to the chair. A cold sweat beads my brow. With a trembling hand I reach into my pocket for my buzzard rock and stare at Maum. I try to banish this ill-defined fear by drawing one deep breath and then another.

As loud as a trumpet's blare, Maum passes wind.

She wakes, wild-eyed, and looks around. I receive an accusatory glance and then she harrumphs, whisks the blanket up over her shoulders, and rolls over.

The chilling fear within me shatters. The next moment I am seized by a soundless belly laugh. I can scarcely breathe. My body shakes and tears flood my eyes. It takes a few moments, but I eventually regain control. Still giggling, I dab my eyes and blow my nose. Time to return to Miss Ellen's pages. Hopefully they will clarify Miss Ellen's belief that Maum Cat died the night of the cabin fires. Closing my eyes, I inhale and press my palm to the page.

ᶻᵃ ᶻᵃ ᶻᵃ

Chapter 30

Ellen

While I lounged on the back porch, Rina unpinned laundry from the clothesline. Henrietta trailed alongside, folding and stowing each item in a basket, all the while chatting.

In the weeks since Henrietta's arrival, she exhibited no reaction to Maum's passing in any obvious way. Perhaps the old woman had prepared the child for her eventual death. Maum apparently told everyone that she was looking forward to being reunited with her African ancestors and prophesied that when her time came Henrietta would join a family that needed her as much as she needed them. Perhaps this accounted for Henrietta's response. Or lack thereof. I am certain the girl loved Maum Cat. One only had to spend a few minutes with them to appreciate their mutual devotion.

Rina laughed and I turned my attention back to her and Henrietta.

They folded a bedsheet with the grace of seasoned dance partners. Rina set it on top of the clothing basket and then headed back toward the garden shed. Henrietta bent to pick up the basket and a slight breeze lifted her kerchief. Adjusting her scarf, she sniffed, and a flurry of expressions crossed her face. I, too, had caught the bitter scent of ashes on the wind. Henrietta lifted the basket and made her way up the path to the house. I stood to greet her, and the child's misshapen little mouth curved into a smile.

Pointing to the corner, I said, "Stow the basket over there for later." I pulled another chair around to face me. "Come, sit. I have some good news."

Brow creased, Henrietta set herself down.

"Why do you look so worried?" I chuckled. "I said I had *good* news."

Head down, she picked at her fingernails. "'Bout Miss Laura?"

"Yes, she'll be home before school starts, thank goodness." Henrietta looked up and managed a weak smile.

"Stop your fretting." I leaned forward and covered her fidgeting fingers with my hands. "I told you before, I wrote to Miss Laura and explained about the fire. She fully supports you moving in."

Henrietta's big brown eyes filled. "What if she don` like me?"

My throat tightened. "Come here." I pulled her onto my lap. "Miss Laura is going to love you as I do."

ê. ê. ê.

On the day of Laura's homecoming, Hastings went to fetch her so Rina, Henrietta, and I could make a celebratory meal. Despite Henrietta's nervousness about Laura, she joined in on the preparations.

At the rumble of wagon wheels, we all three ran out into the yard. Moments later, Laura and I embraced. I closed my eyes, and inhaled. How I had missed the earthy, sweet scent of her skin; the solid feel of her in my arms; the steady rhythm of her breathing as she slept beside me.

She leaned back, still holding on to me. "My, how hale and hearty you look, Ellen!" She smiled at Rina, beside me. "You too, Rina. Perhaps I should leave more often," she laughed.

"Never!" I pulled her in for another hug.

"It not be de same without you, Miz Laura. Dis be your home. We be family."

"Thank you, Rina." Laura drew back. "We certainly are. But someone is missing," she looked around. "Where is Henrietta? I had hoped she would also be here."

Henrietta, who had tucked herself in behind me, stepped out. "Here I am, Miz Laura," she said in a small voice.

"My goodness!" Laura put a hand to her chest. Henrietta giggled, something I had not heard her do before.

Hastings, who had strode off to secure help unloading the trunk, returned with an extra pair of hands.

"Let's go in." Laura smiled at me. "Put everything in our bedchamber," she called back to Hastings and his helper. Linking arms with me, she held her hand out to Henrietta. "It is wonderful to be home."

The next day, Laura and I headed to the site of the schoolhouse.

"It's good to have you home." I inched closer.

She smiled, her eyes teasing. "You missed me, did you?"

"A little," I said, laughing.

Past the Brick Church a ways, Laura steered the buggy onto our property and down the lane. Live oaks, thick with Spanish moss, lined the path like sentries. I liked to think of them thus, offering us both welcome and protection.

My scalp tingled. More so, the closer we got. Managing the erection of our schoolhouse did not suit my personality or skills, but I had done my best to supervise in Laura's absence. We stopped in front of the partially completed structure.

"It's only two weeks until school begins," I blurted. "I know we had hoped to begin the year here. Perhaps if you had been in charge—"

"The outcome would be the same. You told me the government contractor and his crew haven't been paid in six months. You're fortunate they completed the framing. The interior will be done when they are compensated."

"The contractor managed the best he could. He knew I wanted the project finished for school's commencement. To his credit, he kept the crew working for as long as possible. But—"

"He could not keep asking the men to labor without pay." Laura finished my thought and then jumped down from the buggy. I followed.

Hands on hips, she smiled up at the half-completed building.

"Often, I doubted we would get this far," I said.

"I have an idea that might hasten the process."

Laura turned to me. "Go on."

"General Saxton. Perhaps he could use his influence to get things moving again."

"Excellent. Have you contacted him?"

"He has always been so fond of you—"

"Ellen Murray!" she chuckled. "Now I know how you charmed the contractor and his crew to forge ahead without pay."

I suppressed a smile. "Nonsense, I simply observed that you and the general are more like-minded."

"Indeed?" Laura smiled. "And you think I can give the general marching orders, so to speak."

"Absolutely," I laughed.

"If it will get our scholars out of the Brick Church and into their own schoolhouse sooner, I'm willing to try." She took my arm. "Come, you can give me a tour of the building."

૨ા ૨ા ૨ા

Chapter 31

Ellen

After the summer break, we resumed our chaotic and cramped classes in the Brick Church. Although grateful Penn School still had a place to convene, we needed funds to complete the schoolhouse. To that end, Laura had inveigled General Saxton to appeal to the powers-that-be. Now we waited. Something I did not enjoy and Laura abhorred. A few weeks later, the general appeared at our doorstep after church. My heart sped up.

"What a pleasant surprise, General." Laura opened the screen door. "Come in."

The general entered and removed his hat.

"Have a seat at the table," Laura said.

General Saxton sniffed the air. "Do I smell Miss Rina's apple cake?"

Laura and I exchanged an amused glance. General Saxton always managed to turn up at mealtime.

After settling the general with a thick slice of cake and mug of coffee, Laura leaned in. "So, what brings you by?"

An anticipatory thrill ran the length of my body and I wiggled my toes to release some nervous energy.

The general dabbed his mouth with a napkin. "I have some news about your schoolhouse." His eyes crinkled and danced.

"Do go on, General," I said with a laugh. "We've had quite enough suspense."

Stroking his beard, he chuckled. "The funds required to complete the interior have been approved. You can resume work immediately." He thumped the table.

Laura clapped her hands and turned to me. "Your vision of a schoolhouse for Penn is about to become a reality, Ellen. Congratulations!"

"Congratulations are definitely in order," General Saxton said. "You've worked hard, Miss Murray. As have you, Miss Towne. The people of St. Helena owe you both a debt of gratitude."

"I appreciate your sentiment, General," I said, looking at Laura. "But the people owe us nothing."

General Saxton smiled and nodded. For a moment no one spoke. Then Laura asked, "How soon can we put up a belfry?"

"A belfry?" the general and I blurted at the same time.

"Why of course." Laura blinked. "I set aside $100 last fall to buy a bell, but I was afraid we would need it to finish the school's interior. So I deferred the purchase." She looked from me to the general and grinned. "Every school needs a bell."

"That it does." The general said, then hesitated and put down his mug.

We waited as he stared into the depths of his coffee. The clock ticked off the seconds.

"General," Laura said, "is there something else on your mind?"

Nodding, he looked up.

"What is it?" Laura asked.

"You may recall," he said, "that we captured the city of Atlanta in September."

"May recall?" I spluttered, having choked on my coffee. "After the Union Army burned its way through Atlanta, the former slaves had attached themselves to the Union troops. Hundreds of men, women and children landed on St. Helena. Surrounded by Confederate territory, where else could they to go?" To date we had done our best to clothe, feed, house, and doctor them, which the general knew full well.

"Of course," he nodded and moved on. "The city's loss is sure to be a turning point in our favor and bring us closer to the end of this dreadful war."

The general stated the obvious. Atlanta had kept the Confederates supplied with essentials. But this was old news.

"Has something changed? Did the Confederacy regain ground?" I asked.

He shook his head and averted my gaze. "The Union Army continues the campaign east, across Georgia. Their final destination is Charleston. I am told, however, another column of Negroes follows the troops and that it grows larger with each passing day."

Neither Laura nor I reacted. All resources—food, shelter, clothing—were strained to breaking. Now to learn more people would be arriving.

"I thought it best to prepare you." The general drained his cup.

"Thank you for letting us know." Laura heaved a loud sigh. "We'll do our best to be ready."

"War, ladies." The general toyed with his empty coffee mug. "Honor, heroic victory in bloodless battles—the reality is a far cry from these romantic notions."

"This we know." Laura's tone was crisp.

"Yes, I daresay." He had the good grace to look abashed.

Laura and I may not have participated in battle, but we had firsthand experience with the aftermath. Memories of our volunteer time at Hospital 10 in Beaufort still give me nightmares. The pain and disillusionment of maimed young men; the mangle of amputated limbs heaped in the back garden that fed the ever-present bonfire. To this day, I recoil at the smell of grilled meat. I also worried about my friend, George Washington from Canada. Had he made it back to his family?

The general's hands formed fists. "We must destroy the Rebel forces, cut off their supplies, and destroy their communications. The people of Georgia must be thoroughly convinced of the personal misery which attends war. The Army's success in Georgia is vital to the preservation of our Union. No matter the cost!"

I noticed Laura had crossed her arms.

"So," she began, "the end justifies the means?"

"To a point, yes."

"But surely they go too far," I interjected. "Will they likewise burn and terrorize the folks of Savannah? Beaufort after that?"

"Please understand," the general's voice softened. "War, the deprivation and suffering it imposes on our soldiers, takes a toll. Not only on the body, but also the soul."

"That justifies soldiers' inflicting wanton pain upon innocent civilians because they themselves are wounded?"

"The civilians in this case are not innocent. They aid their husbands, sons, and brothers in thwarting our advance. But that is neither here nor there." He waved away this defense. "As a leader you can set an example and punish offenders. War, however, releases a wolfish spirit in some men who are otherwise sheep. We must pray for a quick resolution."

"We will," I said.

"May I also suggest that we pray that those who lead are morally and spiritually equipped to shepherd the flock with whom they are charged. 'For unto whomsoever much is given, of him shall much be required.'" Laura quoted a portion of Luke 12.

"Amen," I whispered.

The general squirmed in his seat.

After a moment, Laura said, "General, may I ask you a question?"

"Certainly." He stopped squirming, perhaps believing the conversation finished. From Laura's measured tone, I suspected not.

"What do you know of the soldiers' inappropriate behavior toward women within the ranks?"

My stomach collapsed into a mound of jelly.

"What women?" The general reared back. "There are no women with the troops."

"You do not consider Negro females who accompany them for safety, women?" Laura's eyes narrowed

The general's confused expression transformed to one of comprehension.

"Certainly!" he spluttered. "I didn't understand your meaning."

"Were you aware?" Laura pressed.

"No! But I am not naive." His distress was palpable. "You are certain?"

I placed a hand on Laura's arm.

"Yes. I am certain," she said. "I treated a young woman violently used by several men."

I held my breath. A girl of no more than sixteen had arrived with the first round of freedmen from Georgia. In pain and terrified, she eventually allowed Laura to treat her injuries. Doing so, Laura discovered that she had been brutally raped by several Union soldiers. Not one to often shed tears, in relating the girl's story to me, Laura had broken down.

"Several men!" The general's eyes widened. "Surely not!"

"If you doubt my word I will elaborate," Laura said.

"That won't be necessary. You, and Miss Murray, are women of unfailing character; I will always accept what you say. I hope you believe the same of me." He raised his brows.

I nodded and Laura said, "Certainly."

"I will follow through on what you've shared with me," he said. "I'm confident we can put measures in place to curb such behavior. You have my word."

The clock ticked off several seconds and then chimed the quarter hour. The general stood and pushed in his chair. "I best be going." He retrieved his hat and, with a nod, departed.

ᶦᵃ ᶦᵃ ᶦᵃ

Chapter 32

Ellen

Today, Laura held the reins on our drive home from school. I tucked in the wool carpet and snuggled closer to Henrietta, who sat between us. She looked up and gave me one of her sweet, lopsided smiles. A good sign, as I hadn't seen one of those since her friend, Friday, disappeared. One of Manners' brood, the boy had gone fishing with his little brother, Kit, and never returned. The three-year-old had come home alone excitedly repeating, "Fish carried Friday." Manners had assumed Kit scrabbled his words and meant Friday caught some fish for supper. That was three days ago.

Other than her understandable anxiety about Friday, our adopted daughter thrived. We three, along with Rina and Hastings in their own cabin out back, were a family. Happy and content in a way I never believed possible, I had to remind myself that war had brought us to St. Helena.

"Ellen?" Laura's voice rose a notch.

I looked around. We were home.

"Sorry—daydreaming." I climbed down from the wagon and then helped Henrietta, who ran off to Rina for a treat.

Laura smiled. "What were you dreaming about?"

I took her arm. "How fortunate we are."

Just then Henrietta came running back from Rina's cottage, her eyes bulging, like hens' eggs.

"What's the matter?" Laura asked.

"Miz Rina's crying. They found Friday."

Rina doted on all of Manners' children and grandchildren, but none more so than Friday. Rina had clung to the hope he would be found safe. Henrietta's horrified expression told another story. I took her hand and together the three of us crossed the yard to Rina's cabin.

Cheery afternoon sunlight streamed through the windows, alighting on a glass jar filled with wildflowers, a stark contrast to the forlorn demeanor of the occupants. Hastings sat at their small table, looked up, and shook his head to our unasked question. Rina cowered in her chair, apron over her face, her wet sobs a sorrowful lament.

Henrietta positioned herself at Rina's knee and placed her cheek upon her lap. "Miz Laura and Miz Ellen here."

Rina wiped her face with edge of her apron. "I miss him too much." Her voice caught. "He was de bandy-leggedest little fellow in de village, but I did love to look upon him."

"I am so sorry, Rina." I walked forward. "We all are."

"'Member when dem cabins burn down?" Hastings said. "Friday come git me." He shook his head. "Dat boy work all night to put out dem fires."

After alerting us, Friday, albeit slight for a ten-year-old, had labored in the bucket brigade alongside the adults.

"Don' seem fair," Hastings continued.

"Where did they find him?" Laura asked.

"De marsh," Hastings said. "Dey was pickin' oysters at low tide. Friday got bogged and de tide come in—"

Rina commenced wailing again. Hastings covered his face with his big hands.

Fish carried Friday. Little Kit's phrase echoed in my mind.

ﻊ ﻊ ﻊ

For good or ill, we had little chance to mourn dear Friday's passing. That same evening a wretched crowd of displaced and destitute freedmen—men, women, and children of all ages, who had trailed the Union Army from Georgia—arrived by steamboat. The adults wore rags, many of the children wore nothing at all. Most appeared ill, broken down with fatigue and deprivation of food. Our residents, many themselves refugees from Edisto only two years prior, took in these poor folks. The remainder crowded into the Brick Church.

Laura and I, along with others, helped distribute food, blankets and clothing. The weary crowd eventually settled. The lucky ones fell asleep. Others lay awake, their bodies wracked by wet coughs.

From the back of the sanctuary where I stood, I spotted a lithe young man making his way toward me.

"Hello," I said. "It was good of you to come and help."

He smiled shyly and nodded. "Evenin', ma'am."

"Did you find any friends or family?" I pointed at the space with my chin. With so many on the move, plenty of the sojourners had become separated from dear ones.

"All friends tonight. But hain't found no family," he said, crossing paths with Henrietta on his way.

What our Henrietta lacked in years she made up for in compassion. Comforting child after child, she made certain each one received what little we had to offer. Figuring she must be tired, I walked back into the sanctuary to collect her, and Laura, so we could head home. I spotted Laura and raised a hand. She walked forward and Henrietta followed with her arm across the shoulders of a bedraggled boy of about three, who reminded me of Friday's little brother, Kit.

"Who is the lad with Henrietta?" I asked Laura.

She did not respond, but stood beside me, waiting the few seconds for Henrietta to catch up.

"This here boy's Fountain," Henrietta said. "His mama dead. Can we bring him home, Miz Ellen? Miz Laura said ask you."

Open-mouthed, I turned to Laura. "Fountain?"

Laura cleared her throat. "Henrietta was helping me when we came upon a young woman with a set of twin boys about a year old, and a newborn girl, along with this boy, Fountain. The newborn's mother died giving birth somewhere in Georgia, leaving the babe and this little fellow orphaned." She nodded at Fountain. "Her two boys are still nursing, so she has been able to suckle the dead woman's baby." Laura drew a breath. "But the twins' mother asked if we could take Fountain. I did not have the heart to refuse her."

I looked down at the trembling, wide-eyed waif who stuck his thumb in his mouth and nudged closer to Henrietta. Barefoot and filthy, he wore a tattered shirt that skimmed his knees.

"He can sleep on a palette in my room, Miz Ellen," Henrietta pleaded.

I took a deep breath. "The first thing we'll do is get home and fill the tub with hot water." I crouched down and peered into his vacant eyes. "Would you like a nice, warm bath?"

He responded by looking up at Henrietta. "I'm not sure he talks," she said.

"I know you're frightened," I said to the boy, who continued to stare at Henrietta, "but you're safe now."

Henrietta smiled at him. "You come along with me." The two of them headed for the door.

Laura took a step and I grabbed her arm. "We'll be there in a minute," I called out. "You go on ahead to the wagon."

Once Henrietta was out of earshot, I faced Laura. "Know this: He may be with us for some time."

"I don't blame you for being upset with me," she said.

"More surprised." I shook my head and chuckled. "I thought our adoption of Henrietta had fulfilled Maum's prediction. Now I wonder."

She shrugged; the lines crossing her forehead relaxed.

"Come on," I said, taking her arm. "We'll figure it out. We always do."

Outside, Henrietta was already seated on the wagon. Fountain stood in profile by the front axle, a stream of urine arched through the air and splashed onto the ground.

"I believe we now know how he came by his name," I said.

ফ ফ ফ

Chapter 33

Ellen

With the construction completed outside and in, our schoolhouse stood waiting for her scholars! During the Christmas break, Laura and I arranged for all the desks to be installed and the chalkboards set up. Rina found a couple of gals to clean so everything would be move-in ready for the commencement of classes in the new calendar year.

On an unseasonably warm, sunny day at the beginning of January, Laura and I packed the wagon with the few textbooks we owned; dip pens and ink bottles, extra nibs; and several boxes of chalk, all of which we'd been storing at home. Rina added a picnic basket and an old patchwork quilt to our load. Leaving the children in the care of Rina and Hastings, we set out midmorning to visit Penn School before the scholars returned.

"Can't you hurry Rufus along?" I sounded sharper than I intended.

Laura looked at me. "Pardon?"

"I'm sorry." I laughed. "I'm so excited I can barely contain myself. I woke up before dawn."

"Forgiven." She patted my leg. "I tossed and turned myself. It's a big day for us."

After we passed the Brick Church, the sprawling oaks scattered on the school property came into view. Tears pricked my eyes. Why now, I couldn't say. I turned my head, but there was no fooling Laura. She loosened Rufus' reigns and laced her arm over my shoulders and pulled us together.

She signaled Rufus to turn down the laneway. "There it is."

Raised several feet off the ground, the whitewashed clapboard building stood tall and proud. Multi-paned windows with painted shutters ran the perimeter. Wide, railed stairs led to the front door's veranda. A ladder leaned against its side railing. This allowed the ringer access to Laura's bell, housed inside a wood-frame belfry atop the portico.

"I am so proud of you, Ellen. You made this happen."

I leaned into her. "We both did."

For Rufus' sake, Laura halted the wagon beside the entrance near a patch of grass. Both of us carrying a box, we headed for the stairs.

Under the portico I turned to say something to Laura before opening the door. But instead of being behind me, she was scaling the ladder up to the belfry. I leaned over the railing. "What are you doing?"

"What does it look like?" she laughed.

"If you ring that bell, everyone within three miles of us will come running!"

Perched on the final rung, she smiled. "I'll just clang it lightly, to make sure it works."

The toll deafened me for a moment.

"Content?" I yelled.

Wearing a huge grin, she climbed down, picked up the box she set on the bottom step, and joined me at the door.

"I hope we can eventually have a rope attached so one of us doesn't have to climb up there every day."

"I'll look into it," she said.

With the knell of the school bell reverberating in my head, I pushed open the door.

We walked through the vestibule to the narrow cloakroom where hooks lined the walls. Directly across stood the closed door to the office.

"Go on then," Laura said. I opened it and Laura peered around me.

A desk was directly ahead. Underneath the window stood a file cabinet and a bookcase with three shelves.

"Nice." Laura turned in a small circle.

"Leave the boxes in here." I was anxious to look around. "We can sort them later."

Shutting the office door, we made our way into the front classroom.

Sunbeams, filtered through leafy boughs, lit up the polished furnishings.

"Does it look the way you imagined?" Laura asked.

"Yes and no," I said, still surveying the space. "Before, I focused on what wasn't done."

"And now?"

"It's better than I imagined. It's—" I swallowed a lump in my throat.

Laura put her arm around me. "I know."

We strolled up and down the aisles. Wooden desks, meant for two, were pieced together with scrolled wrought iron and bolted to the floor. The iron section held one desk top to the back of the next chair. Laura stopped and ran a finger round the rim of an inlaid inkwell. Smiling, she walked forward and examined the framed chalkboard.

I peered out the side window. Not far off loomed a massive live oak with cascading greybeards of Spanish moss. The tree's old limbs reached out toward the school as though conferring a blessing.

The Blessing Tree.

We made our way to the door at the back of the room and entered a short hallway to the two remaining rooms. The scholars here would come and go by the back entrance.

"Are you pleased so far?" Laura asked.

"Oh my, yes," I said, opening the door to the class on the left. The windows looked out onto a stand of pine trees. We wandered through, and then crossed the hall for a peek at its counterpart. Satisfied, we returned to the front classroom.

I stood behind the teacher's desk, running a hand across its polished surface.

"I'll take this room," I said, "because of the office. It's a bit larger and better for the older scholars."

"It's also nearest the front door. If we have a visitor, you'll be right here to receive them."

I thought of my Blessing Tree. "Why don't you take the back classroom on the right? It has a nice view of the yard, and the laneway. I'll assign the other to my sister, Hattie."

"It's settled then," Laura said. "Let's go eat. I'm famished."

ea ea ea

Around back of the schoolhouse, we discovered an area cleared by the contractor's men. After tossing aside several pine cones and acorns, we threw down our picnic blanket and set out lunch. Rina had packed us boiled eggs, apples, cornbread freshly baked this morning, and a jug of sweetwater. Laura dug in before we'd finished assembling the lot. Not that I blamed her. My mouth watered at the fragrant aroma of Rina's cornbread, always as comforting and nourishing as its maker. Finally, I dug in and we ate in comfortable silence, passing the sweetwater back and forth.

Once we'd had our fill, I began to pack up. "I suppose we should head home."

Laura stretched out onto her back. "Leave that be for a bit," she said. Rolling onto her side, she patted the blanket. "Come lie with me."

With a luxurious groan, I too stretched out and closed my eyes.

Laura stroked the side of my face.

Rising on my elbows, I looked around. "What if someone comes? The wagon's out front and you rang the bell."

"No one is coming. And if they do we'll hear them," Laura said.

I settled back. "I suppose—"

"Are you happy?" Laura whispered, her sweetwater breath warm against my cheek.

I rolled over to face her, our bodies aligned one to the other. "Yes," I said, my lips brushing hers.

ɜ₳ ɜ₳ ɜ₳

Two days later, the mild winter weather did an about-face and assaulted us with relentless thunder, lightning, and freezing rain. This morning's dreadful storm finally let up about midday, although the sky remained a stubborn shade of gunmetal.

While Laura mended a pair of Fountain's britches, I read to the children. At the back door, Hastings knocked and called out, "Miz Laura?" Odd, since Rina usually acted as intermediary.

"Come in." Laura set her sewing on her lap. "Is something wrong?"

Hastings stopped at the entrance to our parlor, "I just got word a tornado touch down by de cotton exchange. I'm headin' over."

Laura stood, her mending falling to the floor. "Is anyone hurt?"

"Neber said." Hastings shrugged.

"The school's just down the road from the exchange." My mouth dried with fear.

"I ain't heard nothin` about de school, Miz Ellen," Hastings said.

"We'll come with you." Laura stooped to pick up her sewing. "I'll bring my medical bag, just in case."

The children, who were tucked on either side of me, drew closer. Henrietta reached for my hand. "Please don't go."

"It'll be fine." I gave her little hand a squeeze and smiled at each of them. "Hastings, please tell Rina we're going with you and that' I'll send the children over for her to mind."

With a nod, Hastings turned and left. Laura had gone into our bedchamber, I presumed to retrieve her medical bag.

I smiled down at the children again. "Run along. I'm sure Miss Rina will give you a treat."

Fountain hopped down from the settee and tugged Henrietta's hand.

Henrietta resisted. "You'll come back, wontcha?"

Poor child. She knew the sorrow of loss. "Of course." I gave her a quick hug. "Now go have fun with Miss Rina."

Henrietta let Fountain lead her to the back door.

Laura rushed back into the parlor just as I finished tying up my work-a-day boots. Holding her bag in one hand, she tossed me my old cloak with the other. Together we ran out to the waiting wagon. Climbing aboard, I prayed our new schoolhouse wasn't destroyed.

꿈 꿈 꿈

Hastings navigated the spongy roads, steering Rufus around puddles and through soggy muck. Downed pine branches and palmetto fronds littered the ditches and road. Farther on, snapped and twisted tree limbs dangled from their trunks.

"The cotton exchange is still standing," Laura said as we neared the Church Road intersection. Not far along Church Road, Hastings slowed the cart.

"Oh my goodness," Laura moaned.

What had previously been a cabin on a familiar piece of land now resembled a heap of giant matchsticks. In the midst of this destruction, people worked to clear up the mess.

"Would you look at that!" Laura said. On either side of the destroyed cabin stood two others, perfectly intact.

Hastings brought our wagon to a standstill and jumped down. "I be back," he said and trotted off.

"Ask if anyone needs medical attention," Laura called after him.

We watched and waited while Hastings spoke to a man stacking timbers. I hoped no one was injured, or worse. I suppressed my desire for Hastings to hurry. I needed to know if our schoolhouse sustained damage. Laura gripped my hand and exhaled a stilted breath.

Hastings jogged back, hopped on the wagon and picked up Rufus' reins. "Nobody hurt. I tell dem we come back after de school."

Under the circumstances Hastings drove fast, but it felt like a snail's pace. Laura hadn't let go of my hand and every few moments she gave it a squeeze.

Just before the Brick Church, we came upon a loblolly pine stretched across the road and Hastings halted the wagon.

"Can we move it?" I asked.

"No, Miz Ellen." Hastings pointed to the root ball of the upended tree. "I'm gonna try goin' 'round."

Laura lifted her bottom off the seat and looked. "Are you sure there's room?"

"We be fine, Miz Laura."

To his credit, Hastings took it slow and steady. Gentle old Rufus drudged on. Horse and wagon squeezed through and I released my breath.

Minutes later, we arrived at Penn School. I spotted the roof's ridge through the trees and a wave of relief flowed through me. Finally, we drew close enough to view the building.

Hand over mouth, I turned to Laura. She stared straight ahead, her face ashen.

A pine, even taller than the one blocking Church Road, had crashed through the portico, porch, and stairs. The tree's dense branches hid the entire front of the building, and any destruction. The crown almost reached the live oak I'd secretly christened our Blessing Tree.

We all jumped down and rushed to explore the extent of the damage.

"The roof is intact," I said. Although, I couldn't see the belfry.

"The bell!" Laura groaned. She took off at a sprint, circling the Blessing Oak to get around the fallen pine.

Hastings and I followed.

Splintered planks poked out from under the branches. Pieces of railing and broken remnants of the stairs had been catapulted to the side of the building. Thankfully, the clapboard was unscathed; the glass windowpanes, intact. Fortunate, since we hadn't shuttered them.

"Where's the bell?" Laura lifted branches.

"Lemme do it," Hastings said.

Folding himself in half, he crawled underneath in search of the bell. Branches snapped and cracked like bones breaking.

"Dere," he backed out of the prone tree.

Laura and I crouched down and peered in. Sure enough, our bell sat encircled by splinters of the belfry.

"It looks all right," I said after we'd wiggled out from underneath the prickly needles.

"The earth is sandy," Laura sighed. "That saved it."

"Let's walk around to see if there's any more damage." I plucked pine needles from my chignon like it was a pincushion.

"We'll be back in a moment," Laura told Hastings.

We walked around back, circling to the opposite side of the building. Finding no further damage, we entered the schoolhouse through the rear door. Thankfully, not a raindrop had made its way inside.

We returned to the wagon and set back down Church Road.

"After all the work and planning, to see our schoolhouse scarred, before we've even moved in, is a shock." Laura sat with her arms crossed.

I turned to her. "Disappointing, certainly. We were lucky—"

"Lucky!? The bell might be cracked."

"It looked fine."

"Perhaps," she said. "We won't know for sure until it's up and we ring it."

"Goodness! It's not the Liberty Bell. The entire building could've been blown down," I snapped, "like the cabin on our way here. That's what our school might've looked like if we weren't lucky."

Hastings turned in his seat. "Don worry, I'm gonna round up some fellas and we have dat porch fixed and de bell up real soon."

"Thank you," Laura said.

He nodded and turned back to driving.

"You're certainly taking all this in good stride," Laura said.

I shrugged. "The best laid plans of men and mice often go awry."

Scowling, she cocked her head.

"Robert Burns, the Scottish poet."

"I know who said it!" Laura said. "Right now it doesn't offer much consolation."

"Laura!" I said in a loud whisper. "What is wrong with you?"

She blinked and stared into the distance.

I said no more, deciding to leave her be.

We neared the cabin razed by the tornado. Since we discovered earlier that no one needed medical attention, Hastings suggested he'd take us home and return on his own.

"We might just be in the way," I said in agreement.

"Nonsense." Laura looked askance at me. "Surely we can offer some comfort."

I hesitated, unsure if I had the energy to comfort anyone.

"Ellen, if we go home all I'll do is mope."

"I suppose."

"Besides," she nudged me with an elbow. "Pleasure and action make the hours seem short; Shakespeare."

"I guess I deserved that," I said with a laugh.

☙ ☙ ☙

That night in bed Laura said, "I'm sorry for the way I spoke to you today."

"You don't have to apologize."

"Yes, I do."

I wiggled closer. "Do you want to tell me what was going through your mind?"

Her mouth open and closed. Finally, she said, "Penn School is yours."

"Ours."

"But the concept was yours; you found space for the scholars; you're the teacher. You developed a curriculum; and you oversaw the schoolhouse's construction."

"Why are you saying this?" I pulled myself up against the headboard. "I couldn't have managed any of that alone! If it weren't for *you*, I wouldn't even be here."

Laura sat up and joined me against the headboard. "I'm proud of you. I wouldn't change a thing. It's just—"

I took hold of her hand. "Please, tell me."

"The bell," she chuckled. "It seems silly now that I have to say it out loud." She turned to face me. "You were right. We were lucky. That pine might've landed on the roof and caused extensive damage. But I thought of, arranged for, and purchased the bell with my own money."

"And the one and only thing damaged by the tornado. Oh Laura." I shook my head. "Here's the irony."

I slid down onto my pillow and Laura followed.

"Unbeknownst to you, I spend a great deal of time and energy worried I'm not contributing enough to our relationship. That you're the one in charge, the stronger of the two of us."

"That's not true."

"No, it's not. I now realize that. But neither is the reverse." I pressed my hand against her cheek. "We must resolve to live the credo you coined for us when we first met. Do you remember?"

She smiled. "Stronger together."

"Exactly."

Cuddling closer, I gripped the edge of our bedding. In a whoosh of blankets, I shut out the world.

ða ða ða

Chapter 34

Henrietta

Blinking away Miss Ellen's past, I return to my here and now. After a few breaths, I set the notebook face down on the side table. Across the way, Maum Cat still snores. A breeze blows in off the water and her swing-bed sways and creaks. I look toward the shore, but can no longer see the moon.

With a yawn, I stretch my arms. Even if I wanted to, I couldn't sleep, and I don't. Miss Ellen's story beckons like a bright light. I pull out the bolster at my back, tuck it behind my head, and close my watery eyes for a moment.

I always considered Miss Ellen steadfast, but I didn't appreciate the breadth and depth of her love for Miss Laura and our family: Fountain and me, along with Miss Rina and Hastings.

I'm equally astonished by how much she relates which I have forgotten or did not know. Are all daughters this blind? Or would any woman bumping up against her past through the eyes of her mother feel like I do?

Some of my memories do cross paths with Miss Ellen's; particularly the day of the tornado, and how the rain and wind had lashed our cottage that morning. Miss Ellen's perspective mirrors my recollection: Fountain and I snuggled in as she read a story about a rascally brother and sister who ran away and got lost in the woods. Hastings arrived during the telling and announced a tornado had touched down on Church Road near the new schoolhouse. The Misses prepared to leave and I stood stock-still, with a throbbing ache in my jaw that rendered me mute.

What if they don't come back? What will happen to me? How will I look after Fountain by myself?

Bless her kind heart, Miss Rina tried to comfort me after they left, saying, "Don't you worry, dat school gonna be fine."

Not long after I'd moved in with Manners, her cabin burned down. Friday drowned once I settled in with the Misses. In my child-mind, I was convinced that if something good happened, something bad must follow, Miss Rina's well-meant, but incorrect assurances left me feeling misunderstood and lonely. So much so, I couldn't stomach the warm biscuits and cool sweetwater she served up.

Hours later, Hastings and the Misses came home and shared with us what had happened. I sensed tension between the Misses. Only now do I appreciate the insecurities they singly bore.

My, how we bend and twist the truth to protect those we love—and ourselves.

I am reminded of my conversation with Jakob earlier; how I let him leave, hopeful for a future I know we will not share.

I open my eyes and toss aside the bolster beneath my head. Sitting up, I scooch back in the chair and reach for the journal.

ِ ِ ِ

Chapter 35

Ellen

"Hallelujah!" The Confederates evacuated Charleston without a fight, and the Union Army reclaimed Fort Sumter. Here on St. Helena, Laura and I did our best to stay ahead of one crisis after another. On the same eve we discovered our poor Friday had perished, boatloads of freedmen from Georgia landed. Besides our usual work, we helped care for these latest refugees. Despite our best efforts, both old and young succumbed at an alarming rate.

Adding to the disorder, a new teacher assigned to the Coffin Point school, and by extension Frogmore house, meant Mother and Hattie needed a new place to live. Until Laura and I located something more permanent, we put them up in the empty, but somewhat run-down cottage next door to us.

On moving day, Laura and I took our wagon to Frogmore and commenced loading up Mother and Hattie's belongings. After sliding one of the larger boxes onto the cart bed, I stole a moment and walked down to the Harbor River. The marsh grass grew thick and the water ran deep. Not far from shore, a pair of freedmen fished in a small boat. Wispy clouds blew across the sky and I breathed in the briny scent of pluff mud.

"It is lovely."

I jumped at Laura's voice.

She chuckled and rubbed my back.

I laughed. "Daydreaming—"

She circled her arm about my waist and we both gazed across the water toward Hunting Island.

"The house here *is* roomier than our cottage," Laura said.

"It is." I turned and faced her profile. "What are you suggesting?"

Still staring out over the water, Laura shrugged. "Only that if the opportunity—" she stopped mid-sentence and scowled. I followed her gaze.

About eighty yards off, two armed soldiers stood at the shoreline watching the men in the boat.

"Not again," Laura said.

Goose pimples raked my forearms. They were Union recruitment officers.

The taller, bearded one yelled at the men, "Come ashore!" He beckoned.

From the boat, one of the freedmen waved a sheet of paper. He hollered something I couldn't understand. The other fisherman also flourished a note.

"Exemption papers." I turned to Laura. "I hope the officers accept that and go."

Laura shook her head. "I doubt it." She cupped her mouth, "Leave those freedmen alone!"

The officers looked over at us, then at each other and guffawed.

My sister Hattie appeared at my side. "What's wrong? I heard yelling."

Seconds later, Mother joined us. Taking in the scene, her brow puckered.

"Recruitment officers," Laura said. "They're trying to get those fellows ashore, but the men are refusing."

Hattie stared out over the water. "Mother, are they the freedmen who gave us their catch the other day?"

"Maybe." Mother squinted. "I can't say for sure. They're too far off."

"They need to come in and present their papers," I said.

"Do you think that would matter?" Laura asked.

Suddenly queasy, I pressed a hand to my belly.

"It's a known fact the freedmen *want* to fight for the Union," Mother said. "If these men required an exemption and have the papers to prove it, certainly the officers will leave them be."

Laura opened her mouth to say something but Hattie jumped in. "I heard that if the freedmen have a health issue or an injury, they're excused. Or elderly or sick family depending on them."

"The recruitment officers don't care about any of that," Laura said. "They carry off whomever they please, whenever they want."

"That's why these fellows are refusing to come in." I sighed.

"That's horrible," Hattie said.

"And then some," Laura said. "It's no wonder the freedmen choose to go into hiding or run away."

"You should tell General Saxton about this," Mother said.

"Ellen and I have already discussed the issue with him," Laura said.

Mother's brows rose and Hattie's jaw dropped.

"The general took measures to address the abuse," I offered. "Unfortunately, it appears to have fallen on deaf ears."

"Look." Laura lifted her chin.

Having picked their way through a patch of thorny burweed, the recruitment officers now teetered at the water's edge on sandy hillocks. The shorter officer waved a fist. "Git back to shore!"

"This is your last warning," the tall, bearded one yelled, then stumbled and cursed.

The fishermen lifted their oars, but rather than row ashore they turned the boat to open water.

The tall officer, having found his footing, raised his rifle and fired. One of the fisherman, his back to the shore, slumped forward. The boat rotated, exposing his mate.

Hattie's high-pitched scream echoed the blast. My hands flew to my ears. "*No! No!*" I shouted.

My sister threw herself at me, whimpering. Wordless, I held her. Laura's eyes darted one way and then the other. Beside her, my mother stood ashen-faced.

"We have to do something." Laura lunged in the direction of the soldiers.

"Wait!" Mother reached out too late.

Releasing my sister, I ran after Laura.

"I'll have you reported for this!" Laura bellowed at the officers.

The tall one cupped his ear. "What'd ya say?" He turned back to the water, again raised his rifle, and fired.

The second fisherman gripped his arm and then slumped down into the belly of the boat.

Gasping, I reached Laura, her fists clenched at her sides.

"This cannot be happening," I moaned.

From the shoreline, the short officer looked our way and spat. "This here's military business," he hollered. "Mind yer own." Both men stomped into the underbrush that led to the road.

Out on the Harbor River, the little boat turned in circles.

"We must get help," Laura made a dash toward our wagon. I lifted my skirts ready to follow her.

"Wait!" Mother shouted, and stabbed a finger toward the water.

Another boat floated alongside the one with the injured men. One of the two crewmen tied a rope to the bow.

"Hold up, Laura," I cried.

Already by the wagon, she turned to me.

"Help's come," I yelled.

She sprinted back and dropped her medical bag at her feet. "Don't just stand there," she said, windmilling her arms, "wave them in."

❧ ❧ ❧

Chapter 36

Henrietta

"Not done yet?"

At the sound of Maum's voice, like a startled tortoise, Miss Ellen's history retracts within the pages of the journal. I struggle to meet the present.

Maum Cat's blankets carpet the floor and she stands amongst them, crooked as an old pelican. Without waiting for my response, she groans, straightens and shuffles off to the privy. Taking her lead, I close the notebook and go into the house to use the toilet.

We arrive back on the porch at the same time and Maum returns to the swing. I help her rearrange her blankets and then I settle into my chair

"I shouldn't have gotten so angry earlier," I say. "Even if I believe you should have told me how my injury happened, I realize you meant well."

She shrugs and looks at me in a way that says she's not bothered and that I shouldn't be either.

For some reason this chokes me up. I try to control my wobbling chin. Maum ignores my effort and pretends not to notice.

"You find what you lookin' for in dem books?"

Swiping at my eyes, I think about that. "Can't say I was looking for anything in particular, but I sure learned a lot about what Miss Ellen and Miss Laura got up to during the war."

"You 'member dem days?"

"In a way. My memories are like shards of a broken mirror. I can see my reflection, but only in bits and pieces."

Maum tilts her head. "What you learn 'bout the Mizzes?"

I smile. "*The Mizzes* were bold and brave. I always knew they were influential in these parts, but I learned a lot of what went on behind the scenes that they directed."

"Like what?" Maum shifts and leans into my answer.

"'Member near the end of the war our folks were on the move? Hundreds followed General Sherman north; some landed here."

"Sure do," says Maum. "Dat's how we got Fountain."

"Miss Laura treated one of the women that traveled with that column, a gal the Union soldiers violated. The Misses spoke to General Saxton about our soldiers doing such things. He promised to take it up with General Sherman."

"In dey own way, both de Mizzes try to right what wrong." Maum nods.

"That's true," I say. "Another time they helped a couple of freedmen, exempt from enlisting, who were minding their own business fishing out back here," I point toward the water. "Recruitment officers showed up and shot them because they wouldn't do what they wanted." My voice quivers.

"Bad everwhere. You know dat," says Maum. "You gotta look for de good. If you lucky, it find you."

I let out a slow breath. "I was lucky, that's for sure. Pearl found me after the Mistress beat me. You found me in Beaufort. Then Miss Ellen found me during the cabin fires."

"Dat what Miss Ellen want you to learn?" Maum lifts her chin in the direction of the diaries.

I shrug. "Maybe…except—"

Maum cocks her head. "'Xeptin' what?"

"Now I have more questions than answers." I try to laugh, but it comes out dry and hoarse. "This is going to sound mad—"

Maum stares and waits for me to tell her whatever's on my mind.

"The cabin fire." I clear my throat. "You mentioned it earlier, asking if I remembered."

"Uh-huh."

"I do remember." Suddenly my stomach is a nest of nerves. Ignoring it, I carry on. "Problem is, Miss Ellen's viewpoint is different than mine."

"How's dat a problem?" Maum's voice goes up a notch.

I take a breath and say what I must all at once. "Because Miss Ellen implies that you *died*. At first I thought she was just confused; that she'd mistaken you being overcome by smoke for having passed on. But she continues, saying that I didn't mourn you like she figured I would, and so on."

"Why would you mourn losin' what you still got?" says Maum, calm and cool as a summer sea breeze.

I try another tact. "Do you recall seeing Miss Ellen after the fire?"

"'Course I do."

I shimmy to the front of my chair. "That's my point. Then why does she refer to you in the past tense? It's downright disturbing."

"Dat's it?" says Maum. "Dat's what's botherin' you?"

"I don't know what to make of it," I say.

"Folks believe what dey want. Trust youself, Henrietta. Den you see clear." Face scrunched, Maum yawns long and loud.

"I don't understand."

Maum's eyes are closed. "You will. Soon 'nuff." Her voice is thick with sleep.

Before I can say another word, she's down and under the quilts. A few heartbeats later, she's softly snoring.

I'm so frustrated I can't return to the journals. Instead, I try to puzzle out what Maum Cat said. To me, her explanations are meaningless—platitudes that do not account for Miss Ellen's detailed memories, especially those surrounding the cabin fires.

The next time I saw Maum Cat after those fires comes to me in a flash. I recall standing in the far corner of the Teacher's Cottage's yard one morning, behind the barn with a ripe plum from our tree. I took a big bite then spat the sour fruit into my hand. A fat worm wriggled in the rotted, brown flesh. That's when Maum showed up.

"How you doin'?" she'd asked.

"Fine." With a shiver, I tossed the putrid plum onto the ground. "Where you been?"

"You don' look fine," says Maum. "The Mizzes treatin' you bad?"

"Oh no," I say, "they bein' real good to me."

"Why you face lookin' like a chewed boot, den?"

For some reason I don't tell her about the bad fruit. Instead, I tell her, "Everybody's worried 'bout Friday. He went fishin' with Kit and didn't come back." In the next breath I say, "He drowned in the creek."

Maum's brows scrunch together. She chews on her lip like she's thinking real hard. "Says who?"

"Me." I stare at the mess of fruit at my feet and don't tell her what's in my head. "But I still want him to come home. So does his Mama. And Miss Rina too."

Maum comes closer and lifts my chin so I'm looking up at her. "How you know sumptin' like dat?"

I shrug. "Just do."

Maum's warm hand slips onto my shoulder. "Tell 'em to look near de crooked oak."

I look down at the rotten plum. The worm is still wiggling; I stomp on it and then glance back up at Maum. "You tell 'em."

"You think dey gonna listen to me?" says Maum. "Manners know where dem boys go fishin'. Jus' tell 'em to check de creek near de crooked oak. Friday like dat spot. He keep it special for him 'n Kit." Maum shoos me. "Run 'long. Miz Rina waitin' on you."

I dash toward Miz Rina's cabin like Maum Cat tells me to. I'm almost there and turn to wave goodbye. But she's already gone. I round the cabin. Miz Rina's scrubbing clothes in the big tub. I tell her where they should look for Friday.

Miz Rina stops her scrubbing. "De crooked oak?"

"Mmm-hmm," I say.

Miss Rina looks real hard at me. Maybe she's trying to figure if I'm making up stories. Finally she dries her hands. "When de tide's low, I gonna get Hastings to ride out."

Sure enough, late that day they found poor Friday, drowned in the creek right where Maum Cat had said he'd be. His little legs still been stuck in mud, his lifeless body folded back and his arms stretched out just like the picture in my head. His mama, Manners, and the rest of his kinfolk mourned him sorrowfully. Grieving the boy seemed a darned sight better than hoping one day he'd show up home looking for his dinner.

My memories align with Miss Ellen's. A crowd of freedmen landed here and the folks of St. Helena put them up at the Brick Church. Everyone that could went to help. Maum sat cross-legged on the floor talking to an old man. She looked up, caught my eye and waved her skinny arm like the metronome on Miss Ellen's piano. I remember these details because of her unusual request.

"Henrietta, be a good gal and find de yellow boy. His mama gone, and he need you help."

I stood looking at her for a second. I'd seen all different kinds of black and brown folks, and buckra that pinked up in the sun, but I'd never laid eyes on anyone yellow.

"Yellow boy?"

"Dat's right."

I shrug. He'd be someone worth laying eyes on. I check the groups huddled in the corners. Then I move up and down the rows of people stretched out on the floor. In the middle of an aisle, Miss Laura sits crouched talking to a tired, hungry-looking woman holding a baby. I walk closer, thinking maybe the baby is yellow. Beside them, I spot a boy sucking his thumb. He isn't yellow, at least not like I imagined. He's brown, like me. All around him is a shimmery, golden light.

Apart from the child in her arms and the shimmery boy, two baby boys sit alongside the woman. I hear her asking Miss Laura for help, saying how the baby's mama died and how she's been feeding that baby plus her own twins. The woman wants Miss Laura to take the thumb-sucking shimmery boy because she can't look after all of them.

The more the women talked the harder the shimmery boy sucked his thumb. I went over and put my arm around his shoulders. He leaned into me and that golden light just up and disappeared. I knew then and there we had to take him home. He belonged with me. That's what I told Miss Laura.

My mothers committed all their time, energy, and what little money they had to Penn School and our St. Helena community. Even so, they took me in, and at my request, they opened their arms and home to Fountain. They loved both of us with their whole hearts. All of this speaks to Miss Laura and Miss Ellen's steadfast character, which brings me back around to the exception of Miss Ellen's recollections of Maum Cat. Those observations just don't make sense. I grab the journal.

ঌ ঌ ঌ

Chapter 37

Ellen

Arms linked, Hattie and I walked along the water's edge behind The Oaks plantation house. The setting sun streaked the sky pink and frosted the green marsh grass gold. Snowy egrets, one after another, flew to roost on a loblolly pine branch across the creek.

"Are you pleased with your move to The Oaks?" I asked.

"I am thrilled. So is Mother," she said. "Odd, isn't it, how one incident leads to another?"

I laughed. "Might you be more specific?"

Eyes wide, she stopped walking. "If the government hadn't made changes to the leadership hereabouts, after leaving Frogmore House, Mother and I would be likely still sleeping in that decrepit cottage in St. Helenaville."

I chuckled. "Come, now. You had fantastic neighbors."

She laughed and we walked on.

"Fate did intercede," I said. "However, so did you."

"Oh." She shrugged. "The letter."

"Yes, the letter. You set the ball rolling when you wrote to your friend in Massachusetts and told her how the recruitment officers shot the freedmen on the water out at Frogmore House."

"And you believe *my* letter actually influenced the changes?" Hattie searched my face.

"Definitely. Your friend sent it in to the *Springfield Republican;* they published it, where the Secretary of War read it. Your letter prompted the investigation—"

"That resulted in General Saxton taking charge of the freedman's affairs," Hattie finished my thought.

"Exactly," I said. "In turn, the general exercised his authority and sent the Edisto refugees back to their island. Two years is a long time to be gone from home when it wasn't your choice."

"Not everyone approved of the general's changes," Hattie said. "Josiah and Nelly Fairfield left."

"That outcome did not disappoint me," I said.

"Nor I." Hattie turned and looked back at plantation house. "Especially since their departure led to Edwin Ruggles taking their place to run things here, and his kind offer to share half the house with Mother and me."

"So you like having a tall, dark, handsome housemate?" I teased.

Hattie suppressed a smile. "I never said he was handsome. I said he was kind."

"Oh, look," I pointed at the huge, pink sun on the horizon.

Hattie gazed at the skyline for a moment and her face relaxed. A smile lifted the edges of her lips.

"I suppose we better get back," Hattie sighed. Arms still linked, we turned and strolled toward The Oaks.

Mother, Laura, and Edwin Ruggles greeted us at the porch.

"Were you worried?" I asked Laura as we climbed the steps.

"No," she said. "We have exciting news."

"We've only been gone half an hour," Hattie said.

Laura shrugged, and looked to Mr. Ruggles. Mother's face was a mask.

"Well," I said. "Are you going to share this news or keep us guessing?"

"Let's go inside, shall we?" Mr. Ruggles stood and opened the door.

We filed into the parlor, sat down, and waited.

Mr. Ruggles remained standing and looked from Hattie to me "You two had no sooner left when General Saxton arrived."

"At this time of day?" I blurted.

"He was out this way on military business, but wanted to stop by to give us these." Grinning, Laura held up tickets. "Passes to the flag reinstatement ceremony at Fort Sumter on Easter weekend."

The Confederates lowered the Stars and Stripes when they took Fort Sumter. The ceremony would put it back where it belonged. We had requested passes from General Saxton, but hadn't heard back. Until now.

"I told the general I am quite happy to stay here," Mother said. "I'd rather not traipse around Charleston."

"Oh my goodness!" Hattie exclaimed. "I can think of nothing more exciting!" She turned to Mr. Ruggles. "Did the general also bring a pass for you?"

"Yes, indeed." He straightened his back. "In fact, he requested I escort you ladies, and several other teachers from the island."

ѯ₳ ѯ₳ ѯ₳

A few days later, we crowded onto a steamer in Port Royal and headed for Charleston. Unfortunately, rough weather made the voyage difficult and Laura seasick. The bumpy carriage ride through the shelled-out section of the city didn't help. Eventually, we arrived at our accommodations. Edwin Ruggles hopped down and hurried ahead, presumably to announce our arrival to the house staff.

I stepped down ahead of Laura. "Give me your hand."

She sighed, but didn't protest. I led her through a wrought iron gate into a courtyard hidden from the street by tall shrubbery. Farther back stood a stout kitchen house, its roof caved in. The main house also bore the scars of battle: random holes in the walls where cannon balls had shot through.

The other teachers from our group milled around the yard, surveying the damage.

"Such a shame," Hattie said, coming up beside us.

"Not a high price when you consider the stakes," Laura said.

"Would you look at that." I pointed to the jessamine, jonquils, and daffodils heedless of the destruction around them.

"It's a miracle they survived," Hattie said

"Deep roots," Laura stated, and turned toward the house.

ѯ₳ ѯ₳ ѯ₳

Still unwell the next day, Laura insisted I go with Hattie and the others to tour the city. With reluctance, I agreed.

Mr. Ruggles took his position of escort seriously and also assumed the additional role of tour guide.

"We are now entering the burnt part of town," he narrated. "Note the charred homes; the street, devoid of foot traffic. Very bleak indeed."

The acrid air reminded me of Maum Cat's doused cabin after the fire. Cloud cover contributed to the somber atmosphere.

Regardless, Laura and I had witnessed so much deprivation and suffering in recent years that the sight of ruined brick and mortar failed to disturb me the way it might have done before coming to South Carolina.

After roaming the meandering back streets, we came out onto the road that followed the harbor shoreline. The horses picked up their pace, clopping over the cobblestones still wet from an early morning drizzle.

"A curious fact," Mr. Ruggles said, "the stones that pave these streets were once ships' ballast."

My interest piqued, I glanced over the edge of the carriage to take a closer look.

"That island in the distance is Fort Sumter, where we will be going tomorrow for the Flag Raising Ceremony." Mr. Ruggles slowed the carriage. "What do you think, ladies?" He gestured to the stately homes, one more magnificent than the next, lining the street.

"They're beautiful," Hattie agreed. "Aren't they, Ellen?"

I smiled politely and bit my tongue.

The allure of these mansions was a facade; one that concealed the ugly truth behind their origin. I could not admire residences built by mercenary cotton planters from wealth accrued on the backs of people robbed of kith and kin; held without consent, and forced to labor without reward; generations of their progeny likewise condemned. For me they were not anonymous slaves, their value comparable to that of livestock, but people I knew. Those like the ill and destitute refugees from Edisto and Georgia. Or poor Maum Cat, who'd yearned to be reunited in death with her faraway ancestors. Some were my students, others family, whom I loved, like our Henrietta and Fountain; Rina and Hastings. The greed and unwillingness of these men to consider anything but an economy upheld by slave labor had divided our country. It brought war down upon all of us.

Moments later, we continued our journey up, down, and around the side streets, passing more vacant, elegant homes, largely unscathed. Many of the ornate gates leading to courtyards stood open. Mr. Ruggles explained the homes' private status had been revoked by military decree, hence the unlocked gates.

He drew our carriage to a stop. "This single house design," Mr. Ruggles instructed, "is typical in Charleston. One room wide and two deep.

"Let's have a closer look, shall we?" Mr. Ruggles offered a hand as we climbed down from the carriage. At my sister Hattie's turn, he blushed pink.

I walked on ahead of them, following the others through a filigreed gate. Visitors like us wandered in and out as though touring a shop or museum. Although my intuition (or my conscience?) bade I do otherwise, I entered the courtyard. Stairs led up to the house's piazza where glass-paned doors ran the length.

A luxuriant garden surrounded all. Tourists marred the vision. A stout girl, with a long, pointed nose, snapped a pink blossom from its stem. Confederate slaveholders or not, violating the deserted home's garden struck me as inappropriate.

Making my way out, I encountered Hattie with Mr. Ruggles. "I'll meet you back at the carriage," I said, and kept walking.

Rushing out the gate, I collided with two women crossing by. "I'm sorry," I stuttered at the taller one. "I shouldn't have—"

"Trespassed?" the shorter, dark-haired one said.

Although most of the White citizens fled Charleston, a few stubbornly shuttered up their windows and remained. Judging by their sour expressions, these women belonged to the latter group.

The taller woman shook her head in disgust, and then addressed her companion. "Nasty Yankees! How'd they like us pokin' round their yards?"

Both glared at me.

Although the truth of their words stung, I held their spiteful gaze until they gave up and walked on.

Eventually my companions ambled out of the courtyard and everyone settled back into the carriage. We drove the cobbled streets to another part of town and halted across the road from a bricked enclosure. The upper ledge of the high wall sported impaling bars. Broken glass studded the brickwork. A chained iron gate prevented entry or exit. The building, crouched within the courtyard, reminded me of a stone lion in its lair. A chill flowered in the pit of my stomach.

Moments later, we dismounted our carriage for a closer look. I let the others cross the road ahead of me. Having recalled Mr. Ruggles' earlier comment about the cobblestones once being used for ships' ballast, I wanted a closer look. Unfortunately, failing to mind the uneven, slippery surface, my foot caught and I skidded, wrenching my ankle. I turned it this way and that without pain. Satisfied, I walked on, using more caution.

Upon reaching the wall at the other side of the road, I discovered my shoelace had come loose and stopped to retie it. I tottered, and to steady myself, placed my hand on a section of the wall's brickwork. Immediately dark emotions of extreme intensity gripped me: Fear, anger, futility, loathing and loss collided, spun and swirled with sickening speed. I pulled my hand free and the sensation stopped, but I remained lightheaded.

Sensing someone's presence, I straightened and looked into the bright eyes of an ancient Black woman, head wrapped in an indigo scarf. In the bend of one arm hung a sweetgrass basket.

"You sick? I seen you bent over." The woman pivoted toward my friends and appeared about to summon them.

"I'm quite well, thank you," I said in a rush. "Just retying my shoelace." I lifted my foot.

She frowned.

I forced a smile. "Is this the old Sugar House?" I wanted to distract her. However, I also wanted to confirm what I suspected: that this was the infamous workhouse for recalcitrant and runaway slaves. Rumor had it the dungeon's whipping cells had double walls filled with sand so the cries and screams of the tortured couldn't be heard on the street.

"Dat's it." Her scowl deepened. "It's all played out now. De suffern's trapped in dem bricks. I feels it." She drew closer and rasped. "You feels it too." With that she walked on.

Shaken, I rejoined my companions.

Throughout the remainder of our exploration of Charleston, I found it impossible to think of anything but the Sugar House. My visceral reaction to the mere touch of the brick wall surprised and confused me. And what of the old woman's pronouncement? Each time I searched my mind for an explanation, the memory surfaced of sitting, rocking with Maum Cat, our legs entwined, our hands clasped. Had my communion with Maum left an indelible mark upon my spirit? And perchance bestowed upon me the gift of second sight?

ﺫ ﺫ ﺫ

Chapter 38

Ellen

Good Friday morning, Laura and I were amongst the first to arrive at Fort Sumter for the ceremony to reinstate the American Flag. Excited for the occasion, I wore my new pink-stripped cotton dress and straw hat, which the wind almost blew from my head the instant we stepped foot on the island.

"I knew you'd regret wearing that." Laura shook her head, but smiled. Although she owned several hats, today Laura wore her most serviceable bonnet with wide, strong ties.

I laughed. "Yes, you did."

Laura helped me fiddle with the chinstraps. Bonnet corrected, we started our walk toward the fort.

❧ ❧ ❧

Behind us, a great cheer rose up from the crowded harbor. Stopping, we turned. On the water, from rowboat to packet and steamer to paddleboat, roars of pleasure and great hurrahs drew closer. A band on board one of the steamers struck up "Battle Cry of Freedom." Singing commenced amongst the hurrahs.

Laura and I looked at each other. "What do you suppose this is all about?" I asked. "An early start on the celebrations?"

"I don't think so," Laura said. "It's too spontaneous."

Just then a group of chattering men and women disembarked and hurried onto the wharf. One of the gentlemen climbed upon a wooden shipping crate, cupped his mouth, and hollered, "Attention!"

While he waited for people to gather round, he summoned one of his mates with a whistle. After a brief exchange, the fellow ran off in the direction of the fort's entrance.

A murmuring crowd gathered, curiosity etched on their faces. I linked arms with Laura and waited.

"The news has been relayed from the steamer, *Diamond*, that five days ago at Appomattox the Army of Northern Virginia surrendered!"

Laura and I joined in the cheer that went up and over the crowd, then rushed like a wave along the wharf. Moments later, shouts rose up from within the fortress.

"Does this mean the war is over?" I asked Laura.

"Not officially," she said, "but I'd wager the Confederate cause is doomed."

Once inside Fort Sumter's walls, Laura and I spotted a souvenir booth where I purchased a photograph of the fortress, which I planned to share with our scholars. At my left hand, Laura browsed, and on my right, another woman completed her purchase. With the grace of an elephant, a man shouldered through, dislodging the woman who, thankfully, had finished buying her souvenir. And who was this man? None other than Edward Philbrick! He rifled through the merchandise, oblivious of me beside him. I glanced at Laura, still engrossed in the display. She despised the man's contorted views of philanthropy, and to be honest, I did not respect him either. His alignment with a Northern conglomerate during the tax land sales of '62 had undercut the freedmen's ability to purchase. Although not illegal, the morally questionable scheme had proved personally profitable. Recent revelations surrounding his plans for resale underscored this point.

Philbrick straightened and looked at me. Surprise flickered in his eyes. I nodded a polite hello, and turned, keeping myself between him and Laura.

"It's getting late, Laura. We should find a seat."

She stared at a photograph in her hands. "What do you think?"

Just then Philbrick addressed the vendor. Laura's head snapped in the direction of his voice. A scowl darkened her face, and without glancing down she replaced the photograph on the counter.

"Let it be," I whispered.

The flinty look she gave me said she would do no such thing. I stepped aside.

Philbrick, apparently done browsing, left the stall. Laura followed him, with me not far behind. She called out his name.

He stopped and faced her. "Miss Towne, how are you?"

"I fare well," Laura said. "Although I daresay not as well as you, Mr. Philbrick."

His eyes narrowed. "I cannot complain."

"I should think not!"

"Clearly you have something you wish to say, Miss Towne." He rolled his eyes. "Why don't you impart whatever it is so we can both move on and enjoy this lovely day?"

My cheeks burned with indignation for Laura. Although tempted to intervene, I pressed my lips together.

"As you wish," Laura said, her tone calm. "Is it true you plan to sell, for profit, the land you acquired at the tax sale?"

"At the time of the land purchase I made clear *my goal* was to prove the output of free men would be better than slaves. *My goal* was not personal profit. Unfortunately, this assertion regarding profit has given rise to the mistaken notion that I would, at some future point, sell the properties to the freedmen at cost."

"How, pray tell, can the freedmen purchase land at $25 an acre—as opposed to the $1.25 you paid—when you pay them only 55 cents a day? You have shamelessly put personal gain ahead of the freedmen, whom you ostensibly came to help."

He took a deep breath. "Miss Towne," he said, as though talking to a young child. "I do not, nor have I ever, believed in the success of an economic system whereby property is sold at an amount incongruent with fair market value. To do so would only hinder the freedmen's success. They would be demoralized to obtain the land for less than it is worth."

"As you were demoralized?" Laura asked.

"It's not the same." His voice rose in volume. "My vision was broader in scope. Its success has proven to Northern investors that it is safe to put their money into Southern agriculture. No small feat. It will go a long way to benefiting the Black community. Not to sell to the freedmen now, at cost as you suggest."

"No, Mr. Philbrick, this is what you suggested when you stated you wanted to *ease* the freedmen into the free labor system before assuming the awesome responsibility of land ownership."

"It would not be good to coddle the freedmen in such a way. To do so would hasten failure in the future when he must function independent of our support."

Laura's eyebrows shot up. "On the contrary, Mr. Philbrick, I wonder if it has been good for *you* to have gotten rich at the freedmen's expense."

Mr. Philbrick made no rejoinder. They stood glaring at one another.

"It's almost 11:30," I said, hoping to break the impasse.

After a quick glance my way, Philbrick turned and fled in the direction of the amphitheater.

ea ea ea

We found excellent seats near the draped pavilion meant for the speakers. All around us people surged in, and the tiers soon filled. Laura appeared none the worse for her confrontation with Philbrick. The band struck up the triumphant tune, "Victory at Last," at which point I chose to put the Philbrick incident aside and turned my focus outward. An opening prayer and psalm reading followed. General Anderson rose to his feet. A hush fell over the congregants.

"I am here, my friends and fellow citizens, and brother soldiers, to restore to its proper place this very flag which floated here during peace before the first act of this cruel rebellion."

A lengthy discourse, delivered in an unrelenting monotone, followed. My eyes grew heavy. At one point I drifted off, snapping awake when my head drooped. General Anderson continued to drone on and my mind wandered. What would the near future look like for all of us? The end of the war would not eliminate the acrimony between North and South. What plans did President Lincoln have to heal our country? Would the freedmen be able to move about without fear of capture or persecution? What of the Southern landowners who'd fled? Many would likely return. And if they did—

Loud applause broke my reverie, and joining in, I promised myself I would give the next speaker, Henry Ward Beecher, my full attention. A Congregational clergyman, renowned and respected in abolitionist circles, Beecher would doubtless address society's reconstruction.

Having imagined a robust, imposing figure, this man with a middle-aged paunch, thinning gray hair, and bulging eyes disappointed me.

Pushing aside this uncharitable thought, I straightened my back, determined to listen.

Gripping his fluttering sheaf of papers, Reverend Beecher began, "Dear citizens of Charleston—"

Citizens of Charleston? Certainly not the bitter women I encountered in the city or their neighbors.

"The condition of peace in the South—"

I perked up, eager to hear.

"—acceptance of our Constitution, its laws, and the national government. One nation, under one government, without slavery, has been ordained, and shall stand. On this base reconstruction is easy, and needs neither architect nor engineer."

I gaped at Laura, who shook her head.

When Southern Whites come home, I doubt their willingness to toe the mark and allow the North to dictate their relationship with the freedmen, or simplify reconstruction. All hope of a plan for peace and reconciliation rests with President Lincoln.

I turned my attention back to the podium.

Reverend Beecher announced, "In conclusion—"

Clearly, what the man lacked in insight and zest he compensated with brevity.

Suddenly, the crowd quieted. General Anderson walked to the flagpole. Forced to surrender here four long years ago, he now had the honor of pulling the halyard and resurrecting the flag. The Stars and Stripes flew up the pole and a thunderous cheer resounded throughout the amphitheatre. Naval guns fired, one after another. I covered my ears. Blue smoke curled, rose up over the ramparts, and drifted out to sea.

At the conclusion of the gun salute we sang "The Star-Spangled Banner." Back where she belonged, our dear old flag joyfully fluttered, free at last.

❧ ❧ ❧

The day following the festivities at Fort Sumter, Laura and I headed for the celebration of the Confederate retreat and surrender at Appomattox being held at Zion Presbyterian, the church established for and attended by Black families.

We enjoyed a luncheon as colorful and varied as those in attendance: fresh fish and oysters, grit cakes, collards flavored with pork fat, red rice, and shrimp boiled with potatoes and fried with rice.

Afterward, speakers, engaging and encouraging in their discourse, addressed the crowd of both Blacks and Whites, all excited by a new, inclusive vision of our shared future. Our General Saxton received a loud, extended cheer at the conclusion of his speech. Only President Lincoln's name elicited a greater response.

The final speaker, James Redpath, especially fascinated both Laura and me. A publisher, antislavery activist, writer, and war correspondent, he had recently been appointed first superintendent of public schools of the Charleston region. But it was his sympathetic biography of the infamous rebel, John Brown, that most captured our attention. Hanged for treason back in '59 for seizing the arsenal at Harper's Ferry, Brown became a martyr for the antislavery cause. Laura and I wanted to know the author's view of the times in which we now found ourselves.

He satisfied our curiosity at the end of his address when he invoked the martyred Brown and concluded the day's celebration with the rebel's favorite hymn, "Blow ye the Trumpet."

Ye slaves of sin and hell,
your liberty receive,
and safe in Jesus dwell,
and blest in Jesus live.

Swaddled in the lyrics of this prophetic refrain, we eased into the crush of congregants making their way from Zion's sanctuary toward an expectant tomorrow.

&a &a &a

Tired from our trip to Charleston, but glad to be home on St. Helena Island, I sat at the edge of our bed. Already up and dressed, Laura appeared ready to take on the day.

"Ready yourself," she said. "I'll go and see to the children."

I sniffed the fragrant air wafting in through our window. "Smells like Rina is frying corn fritters."

Laura laughed. "There won't be any for her to take along to the village if Henrietta and Fountain get to them first." She left and closed the door behind her.

The visiting Northern dignitaries who had attended the Charleston festivities afterward traveled to Beaufort. Today, they planned to tour Saxonville, the freedmen's village south of the Brick Church. General Saxton wanted the visitors to witness, firsthand, how well our Black community had responded to the Port Royal free-labor project.

Perfect for an outdoor assembly, the sun shone bright and clear while a warm breeze tamed the humidity we often experienced, even in spring. The six of us piled onto the wagon and Hastings took up the reins. With a groan and a lurch of the wagon, we set off.

Once on the road, Rina chatted to Hastings and the children about this and that. Eventually she turned to me and Laura. "Y'all had a good time at Fort Sumter?" Without waiting for an answer she added, "It's too bad 'bout all our folks not gettin' in."

"What folks?" I asked.

"All them on Cap'n Smalls' boat. It ran aground at the wharf."

We had noticed *The Planter* on the crowded harbor that day. Celebrating freedmen filled the decks to capacity.

"Are you certain?" Laura asked.

"Smalls is an expert pilot," I added.

In '62, back before being freed, Robert Smalls had commandeered that same paddle wheeler and piloted it through Confederate waters to the Union blockade.

"Sure am," Rina said. "No one could get off."

"What a shame," I said. "That means all the freedmen aboard *The Planter* missed the Flag Raising Ceremony."

Rina shrugged. "Suppose they got what they went for anyways."

"How so?" Laura asked. "They couldn't even disembark."

"From de decks dey saw our Stars and Stripes rise like de sun over dem fort walls."

Laura chuckled. "Well put, Rina."

I drew a deep breath and stared sightless at the passing scenery. Rina's pragmatic view aside, I questioned if a White war hero piloting White folks would have been left to his own devices had he ran aground.

🐦 🐦 🐦

Established by the military to settle the refugees, Saxonville stretched along one road for about a mile and a half. We trundled through the settlement, stopping at the intersection of the oak. Thick limbs, gnarled with age, brushed the earth. On its vast canopy of branches, long layers of crepe-like Spanish moss hung, the strands crimped by sorrow and loss. The packed, sandy earth beneath and around the tree stretched out in all directions, making it the presumptive meeting place of the village. At the far end, tethered horses and wagons, tended by military of lesser rank, clearly belonged to the entourage from Beaufort.

Hastings dropped us off and then went to park the wagon.

Engaged in conversation, Laura, Rina, and Henrietta walked ahead toward the row of cottages. I offered my hand to Fountain. For the first time ever he took it without hesitation, and my heart skipped. The bedraggled, skinny little man we'd taken in now appeared almost unrecognizable in his clean shirt and breeches. He still clung to Henrietta or Rina at times, but more and more he turned to Laura and me with a question or need. Grinning down at him, I swung his arm. He rewarded me with a smile that could melt an ice cap.

I spotted Manners in a cottage yard across the way. At six feet, on any occasion you couldn't miss her, but today she also stood out for another reason. With great skill and care, she'd fashioned the most beautiful headdress from bright, multi-colored cotton. Her large, boisterous crew, including Kit, followed in her wake. Having spotted him, Fountain wriggled and looked up at me. Both boys had suffered terrible losses: Kit his brother, Friday; and our Fountain, his mother, and for all intents and purposes, his newborn sister. I thanked God the boys had each other.

"Go on then," I said. Fountain scampered off and joined Kit.

In tacit agreement, they immediately commenced herding the poultry in the yard. They'd soon stop when the hens' cluck-clucking alerted the resident rooster.

Hastings had returned from parking the wagon and joined Rina. Now they joined Manners' crowd. Henrietta stood off by the cottage, talking to Fairy. Even at a distance Fairy's high-pitched giggle grated. An unlikely pair, the two had become friends.

Henrietta appeared to be a steadying influence on flighty Fairy. Fairy's lively, if impetuous, spirit made her fun to be around. And Henrietta deserved a little fun.

I headed toward a vegetable garden patch to where Laura stood. On my way, I glanced about the similar properties, noting that behind each cottage lay individual cotton fields to help supplement the homesteader's income.

I drew up beside Laura. "Do you think our Northern visitors will be impressed?"

She smiled at me. "Why wouldn't they?" She nodded at the neat row of collards sprouting. "All of these plots are lovingly tended."

"With all they've endured, it's strange to think that the freedmen on St. Helena are the lucky ones."

"Hopefully the Port Royal Experiment's success will be obvious to today's visitors and they'll carry the message back North," Laura said. "Then we can retain our funding, and the lessons learned from us will benefit less fortunate freedmen elsewhere."

A few minutes later, Hastings, Rina, and the children came alongside us and we six ventured back out to the main road now bustling with activity. One after another, our friends and neighbors arrived—on foot and atop wagons or horses. Before long, a fair number of us who called St. Helena home milled about the oak glade. Having noticed friends across the way, Rina and Hastings carried on. The children trailed them, kicking the sand and giggling. I stopped and took in the bustling scene around us.

Laura nudged me. "What are you grinning about?"

"Just happy to be here." I shrugged. "And it looks like the war's over."

Laura linked arms with me. "Rending the country in two was easy. Rejoining the frayed edges, now that is going to require some skill."

"If anyone is up for the task, it's President Lincoln," I said.

Laura looked past me. Curious, I turned. My sister Hattie, at Edwin Ruggles' elbow, was almost upon us.

"Ellen, Laura." Hattie sounded pleased. "I hoped to find you."

"Oh, hello," I stuttered, looking from Mr. Ruggles to Hattie.

Hattie's cheeks reddened and her placid eyes conveyed a fiery warning. I had suspected a budding romance between them, and I wasn't displeased, but somehow the reality took me aback.

"Did you two enjoy our trip to Charleston and Fort Sumter?" Laura asked.

I stood stalk-still and tongue-tied.

Laura cocked an eyebrow at me. "Ellen and I certainly did."

"Yes," I forced a grin. "It was good of you to escort us, Mr. Ruggles."

Hattie's wary expression softened.

"Edwin, please." He smiled at Hattie. "It was my pleasure."

Hattie, her cheeks aglow, held his gaze.

Just then Rina, Hastings, and the children returned.

After they all said hello, I asked Hattie if Mother had come with them.

"Yes." She looked about. "We left her talking to Reverend Parker. What a gentleman! I imagine everyone is grateful he assumed the post at the Brick Church."

We all nodded, leaving any well-deserved criticism of his predecessor, Pastor Phillips, *may he rest in peace*, unstated.

All at once, a buzz of chatter moved through the crowd. Everyone around us parted like the Red Sea. General Saxton with his wife, Mathilda, made their way to the base of the oak, and the entourage followed. Amongst them, I recognized two of yesterday's speakers.

General Saxton stopped and turned to face us. A hush fell. The Black preacher from the Praise House near Eddings Point emerged from the crowd. "A good afternoon! Yessir, General," he called out.

Several "Amen!" and "Hallelujah!" rose like a welcome breeze, eventually ebbing to a "Praise de Lawd" conclusion.

All eyes turned to General Saxton.

"I am certain I speak, not only for myself, but for our honored guests, in congratulating the residents of Saxonville on your accomplishments," the general said. "Individually and in community, with great effort you have cleared the land, built your homes, planted your gardens and cotton fields. Hard work and pride of ownership is evident at each and every homestead."

He paused, smiling at the eruption of chatter and friendly jostling. No doubt the freedmen were pleased, and justifiably so. But the general's compliments were also intended for our visitors' benefit, in the hope that they would convey the freedmen's industry and success to the decision-makers up North, that they might loosen their purse strings.

The gathering settled and hushed; the thud of distant galloping the only sound.

General Saxton continued. "I would like to take a moment to—" The general frowned toward the entrance to the clearing.

A cavalry officer pulled up on a black horse and picked his way through the mumbling crowd.

General Saxton separated himself from his entourage and signaled the rider with a raised hand.

The man dismounted, saluted, and with his back to the crowd, relayed his message. During the interchange, the general's eyes widened and his body stiffened.

My heart pumped double-time.

After saluting General Saxton, the officer led his horse into the shade. The general, his posture erect, returned to the oak. He took a step forward and the muttering crowd fell silent.

"My friends," he paused and swallowed. "I have just learned that, on Friday evening, a cowardly assassin entered the theater where our President and First Lady were attending a play."

Collective gasps arose; someone screamed; several people wailed.

General Saxton held up a hand. "Please! Allow me to finish."

A tense silence descended and the general went on.

"I am most grieved to report that our President was shot in the head and mortally wounded." General Saxton's voice cracked. "He died the following morning, surrounded by—"

Laura gasped and clutched my arm. "My God, Ellen!"

I turned to her, but could not utter a response.

General Saxton continued talking, but between the uproar of the crowd and the ringing in my ears, I could not comprehend anything else he said.

A cacophony of screams and wails grew to an almost deafening crescendo.

Trapped beneath the massive, mournful oak, their laments echoed around the clearing. Across from where we stood, a woman crumpled to the ground in a dead faint. Rina! Hastings kneeled beside her. Laura rushed over to them.

Remembering the children, I spun this way and that. Where had they gone? Just then Fountain launched himself at my legs. I bent down and picked him up, uttering words of comfort I did not feel, all the while searching the roiling crowd for Henrietta.

Yellow ribbons.

Rina had dressed Henrietta's hair this morning, pulling the long, curly coils together and plaiting them with yellow ribbons.

There!

At the edge of the chaotic crowd, with her back to me, Henrietta's yellow ribbons blinked in a ray of sunshine. An old woman, crouched before her, drew Henrietta into an embrace. A second later, with an unsteady lurch, the woman stood and turned the child to face me. I waved, relief washing me from head to toe. Until I locked eyes with Maum Cat. With a gasp, I squeezed my eyes shut, blinked and refocused my gaze.

Henrietta stood alone, waving back at me.

Holding Fountain in my arms, I forced my trembling limbs to move and ventured into the grief-stricken rabble to collect my daughter.

☙ ☙ ☙

Chapter 39

Henrietta

In one breath, I am my younger self waving at my mother and Fountain, and in the next I am a grieving, grown woman with the living past scattered around me in Miss Ellen's journals.

To be sure, seeing Maum Cat that day at Saxonville shocked Miss Ellen. No wonder, considering she believed Maum perished in that fire the year before. Also, I am struck by how often Miss Ellen mentions Maum Cat in her writings. To my knowledge they weren't close.

More happened that day Miss Ellen visited Maum's cabin than I realized. I have a distinct memory of opening the cabin door and experiencing a heady rush of surprise at finding my beautiful teacher on the stoop. For even then I loved Miss Ellen: how she fashioned her smooth, brown hair, the little hats she wore, how she smelled of soap and chalk. Oftentimes I drew near her just to breathe in that scent. After Miss Ellen gave Maum the medicine from Miss Laura, I recall Maum Cat shooing me off. I knew she wanted rid of me, that she needed to talk to Miss Ellen on her own, but I had no idea why. Even so, to "see" the two of them sitting knee-to-knee, their ankles looped, surprised me. Miss Ellen believed their communion changed her, maybe even gave her the second sight. Miss Ellen's eerie incident at the Sugar House in Charleston implied just that.

Until now, I would've sworn Miss Ellen didn't believe in such things. And I certainly never saw evidence of her having the sight. Nor did she speak of it, although that would've been difficult, living with Miss Laura. She would've put a stop to any of that talk right quick. I suppose just because Miss Ellen never mentioned having the sight doesn't mean she didn't possess it. In any case, that she chose to write about it and attributed the receipt of it to Maum Cat signifies it held value for her. A gift, that's what she called it. One thing's for certain, wherever Maum Cat goes, mystery follows.

Thinking about Charleston leads me to remembering the two postcard-size photographs of Fort Sumter that fell out of the other notebook earlier. Rummaging through the pile of notebooks, I find them underneath the last book and set them on my lap. Without question, these are the photographs Miss Ellen bought at the Flag Raising Ceremony. I run my finger along the edges. Nothing happens. They have no additional story to tell me.

Yet, gazing at the images, a sad yearning wells within me for the Misses. They were still young women then and had good reason to feel hopeful, especially on that day. Fort Sumter was back in Union hands, and they'd learned the war was coming to a close. But while they celebrated in Charleston that Easter weekend, Mr. Lincoln met his maker. Miss Laura always said that any hope of healing our country's war wounds died with him.

Maum grunts, turns over in her sleep and faces me, pulling the quilt with her. She thrashes about, but when she settles her scowl eases, smoothing out some wrinkles. Unlike the Misses, I don't ever recall Maum looking younger. Even back around the time we went to Saxonville. And when it comes to that day, my memories differ from my mother's. Especially about Maum.

Miss Rina got up early that morning and made corn fritters, this much is true. She sang while she worked, something I hadn't heard her do since Friday had gotten bogged and drowned. Without us asking, she gave Fountain and me some of those cakes, still hot from the grill, and poured molasses all over them. I don't think I've had better since. After we finished eating, she fixed my hair with the brand-new yellow ribbons the Misses bought in Charleston. I recall thinking, *this the best day of my life.*

Done up in our Sunday best like everyone else, we roamed the neat little cottages and gardens at Saxonville. Kit and Fountain chased chickens and I met up with Fairy. I remember laughing with her although I can't recall what set us off. Mind you, we're still like that. One-armed Tommy just shakes his head and leaves us be when we get that way. As in Miss Ellen's account, she eventually gathered us up and our family headed over to the clearing with the big oak. Then the general and the visiting folks arrived. The general spoke, that I remember. Miss Ellen recorded the details, but I have no recollection of the specifics.

Mockingbird Diary of St. Helena Island

In my mind, the chaos began when a soldier on a black horse arrived. Even though the sun continued to shine, it felt like a big, black thunderhead had rolled in. Grown men commenced crying; women screamed and pulled at their clothes. I must've wandered off from the Misses because I found myself alone amongst all those frantic adults. I started pushing my way through and around them, desperate to find Miss Ellen or Miss Laura. Relief rushed through me when I recognized Miss Rina. Before I reached her, she crumpled to the ground in a sorry heap. I screamed—or tried to—but nothing came out. Just then, someone from behind grabbed me by the shoulders and spun me 'round. My eyes immediately alighted on Miss Ellen, holding Fountain and frantically waving.

Moments later Miss Ellen came beside me and dropped to her knees, her skirts puddling on the sandy earth. I must've been crying because I have a distinct memory of her drying my face with a handkerchief, saying, *hush, Mother is here.*

Spotting my mother in that frenzied crowd was a lucky accident. Or so I thought. After experiencing Miss Ellen's version, I wonder. For I am certain that day I never once laid eyes on Maum Cat.

ᘓ ᘓ ᘓ

ॐ ॐ ॐ

This Book Belongs To:
Ellen Murray
January, 1869–

ॐ ॐ ॐ

Dearest Ellen,
On wings of love I offer the best of birthday wishes,
Laura

ॐ ॐ ॐ

Chapter 40

Henrietta

January, 1869? That can't be right.

This final notebook of Miss Ellen's, the leather one with the tooled mockingbird, is not dated weeks or months later than the one I just read, but years. Putting it aside, I pick up the previous installment and re-check the date: *April, 1865.*

Of course! President Lincoln's assassination. I close the notebook and place it with the rest.

But why the four-year interruption?

Reaching for the journal, I lay it, unopened, upon my lap. A carved image of a bird is traced onto the nut-brown leather.

A gift, perhaps?

I am only delaying this journey. Taking a deep breath, I open the book and step in.

🐦 🐦 🐦

Chapter 41

Ellen

Trembling, I hesitated by the front door of the Teacher's Cottage. The deluge hammered our roof and walloped the windows. In the distance, thunder rolled and rumbled.

Yesterday, hired hands barged the last boatload of our furniture along the shore of Port Royal Sound and down the Harbor River to our soon-to-be permanent home, Frogmore House. Good thing, for today's downpour would have prevented its departure. All that remained were a few personal belongings, books, letters and such which I preferred to transport myself. Laura purchased Frogmore last year, but it needed extensive repairs and we wanted a second story added. Although the renovations still remained incomplete, we concluded they were now far enough along to move in.

Outside on the porch, Laura held open the door. "Ready?" She raised her voice over the din of the storm. Behind her a gray wall of the pelting rain obscured the yard. I could barely make out poor Rufus or our drenched wagon.

"Perhaps we should leave later, once this storm has let up," I suggested.

"And when might that be? This afternoon? Tonight?" Laura shrugged. "Or tomorrow? We have nothing here. No food, and I refuse to sleep on that pallet again." She rubbed her hip. "I think we should go and get the day in at Frogmore."

"I suppose you're right." Basket in hand, I pulled up the hood of my cloak and slopped to the wagon.

At first I thought we'd be forced to turn back. But no sooner had the village disappeared behind us, the rain stopped and the clouds parted. Soaked to the skin and chilled to the bone, we tarried forward at a snail's pace through a river of muddy channels, some so wide that even ever-ready Rufus needed coaxing from Laura. Otherwise, we drove in silence. Not that I could have carried on a conversation with my teeth chattering.

Just as well. Cold I might be, but my temper simmered at a ready boil. I regretted not insisting we wait.

I tilted my face toward the weak sun. No matter how cold or wet, I still preferred a South Carolina winter to the snow and ice up North, although, I did favor the North's warmer attitude toward our country's ongoing Reconstruction. At least for now. Men with power could be as mercurial as the weather. I hoped Ulysses Grant, when he assumed office in March, would be a better president than Andrew Johnson.

I couldn't help but wonder what life would be like for all free Blacks—not just our sea islanders who'd had the benefit of the Port Royal project—if President Lincoln had lived and if General Saxton hadn't been forced out of the Freedmen's Bureau. Our Black community never had a better advocate than General Saxton. He would have stood up to the demands of the Confederates who President Johnson had allowed back to our state after the war. The election of President Grant has rekindled hope things will improve for us. I know Laura believes in him. "He's a Republican," she said, "a war hero and a fine man. I dare say anyone will be better than that vengeful racist Andrew Johnson! The man couldn't lead a parade, never mind a country divided."

At the intersection leading to Frogmore, the wagon stopped short. "Oh!" I slide sideways.

Laura clicked her tongue.

Rufus snorted, but refused to move.

Frowning, Laura reached for the buggy whip and clicked her tongue again. "Rufus, walk on."

Mired in muck, his hooves made a sucking sound as he tried to obey. Moving again, Laura snapped the whip over Rufus' head and then slapped the reins down on his rump. This spooked poor Rufus; he tried to respond but failed, and so we rounded the corner at an odd angle. Laura yanked the reins and snapped the whip again, but to no avail. I prayed while Laura struggled to maintain control. But the wheels on her side lifted, the wagon tilted and I skidded down the bench. I told myself to hold on and stay seated.

That was my last conscious thought.

I regained my senses in a swampy ditch, Laura's face inches from mine. "Wake up, Ellen, please wake up."

Eyelids fluttering, I tried to bring her features into focus.

"Oh, thank God," Laura said and burst into tears.

Questioning why I lay prone on the ground, I attempted to sit up, but searing pain shot through my arm and I fell backwards. Laura's face again blurred, and I closed my eyes against the gyrating trees and contorted sky.

A moment later (or was it minutes?) I heard Laura calling me from a distance. In a split second my mind cleared and I remembered.

"You took quite a fall." Laura propped me to a sitting position and cradled me to her chest.

I held my aching arm against my body. "I must have fainted."

"Does it hurt much?" Deep lines of concern etched Laura's face.

I shrugged. "Ow!" A lightning jab bolted from my shoulder to my elbow.

"I am so sorry, Ellen." Laura's eyes shone with tears. "How could I be so foolhardy?"

"Don't, please." Seeing her distress, I felt guilty for my earlier frustration with her. "It was an accident—"

"An avoidable one!" She stroked my brow. "Are you able to sit on your own? I want to get you home."

After assuring her I could manage, Laura hastily gathered the items that had likewise been tossed out in the mishap, repacked them and returned, carrying her scarf.

Crouched beside me, she fashioned a sling and then helped me stand. "Come, let's get you to Frogmore."

Wet, cold, and filthy, Laura and I arrived at Frogmore. Rather than track muck through the house, we trudged around to the back porch. There we stripped off our outerwear and boots. My sodden wool cloak had doubled in weight. Laura helped me remove it, while I cradled my injured arm. My poor cloak! I doubted even Rina's ability to remove the gooey pluff mud stains.

Just then Rina, followed by the children, rushed out the door and onto the porch. The screen door slammed behind the lot of them. At the mud-splattered sight of us, everyone commenced talking at once: Rina chattered on about the laundry she'd have to do, Fountain chirped gleefully about the vast quantity of mud.

"But what happened?" Henrietta asked. Waiting for an explanation, she stared at us, picking her nails.

Rina crossed her arms over her bosom. Fountain stopped talking and looked from Laura to me.

Laura stepped forward, cleared her throat and explained that I'd been thrown from the wagon, how the soft mud, and my heavy cloak, had prevented serious injury, but that I'd hurt my arm.

All three turned and stared at my arm, which I held against my breast like an injured bird's wing. Rina threw her apron up and over her head, and started keening as if I hovered near death. Henrietta's brows shot up and Fountain's eyes bugged out. Clearing my throat, I asked Rina to calm down and go brew us some hot lemon tea. Sniffing, she wiped her eyes and ran off.

I turned my attention back to the children.

"Miss Ellen," Henrietta said, her voice timid and lips trembling. "Your arm—"

Laura grabbed a wooden-backed chair from the corner and brought it over for me. "I don't think it's fractured." Laura leaned over, probed my bended arm and then straightened up. "As I thought. It's sprained and bruised. I'll need to wrap it with gauze."

"So it ain't broke?" Fountain asked.

"Isn't broken," I corrected, with a smile.

A sudden pain made me wince and Fountain gulped. "You sure you gonna be all right?"

"Of course she is!" Laura walked over and rubbed Fountain's back. "I'll take care of Miss Ellen, I promise. Why don't you scoot and find out if Hastings needs you?" She smiled at Henrietta and softened her voice. "Would you help me get Miss Ellen to bed?"

᠁ ᠁ ᠁

Laura had insisted I rest, at least for today. And although I thought it unnecessary, to appease her I had agreed. After I was changed, my arm swaddled in a gauze sling, and settled in bed with a hot cup of lemon tea, Laura drew up a chair. She exhaled and sat up straight.

"What is it?" I asked, unease tingeing my voice.

She looked me in the eye. "One of your baskets was tossed out of the wagon and your diaries—"

"Are they all ruined?" I tried not to sound disappointed.

"No...not all. I was able to salvage five of them."

"Do you know which ones are gone, the years, I mean?" I asked.

"I didn't flip past any of the title pages where you marked the dates, but I figured you'd ask, so I did open them," Laura said.

"And—"

"From what I can tell, the last three years are spoiled."

I nodded.

"You told me it was unwise to drive over today, but I wouldn't listen." Laura's voice caught. "Now you're hurt, your precious diaries are destroyed, and it's all because I was too pigheaded to listen to reason."

"It's true; you are stubborn," I said. "Nor will I argue with your suggestion of pigheaded." I stopped momentarily for effect and we both smiled. "But I won't lay the blame for today's misfortunes at your feet."

"Why not?" she asked. "I'm the one at fault."

"Because it would be too easy. The accident was just that, plain and simple. But us, and the way we relate to one another, is more complicated."

"Ellen, I know at times I run roughshod over you—"

"That's rather harsh." I laughed. "This is my view: At school, I'm the leader. But in our personal lives, you tend to be the decision-maker. I have implicitly consented to this arrangement, content to follow your lead. I confess I don't always like it. Especially, when you forge ahead without heeding my advice or warnings."

"Like today," she said, heaving a sigh.

I smiled at her. "Stop castigating yourself and just hear me out." She nodded and I continued. "It is *also* true that I have enjoyed the benefits of your decisive, bold nature in our relationship. It has allowed me to invest my energies elsewhere, in areas more suited to my own strengths. Having said that, I do have a mind of my own. Leaning on you has perhaps made me somewhat lazy in that regard. I could have protested more today. If I'm honest, part of me was also eager to get here. And like you, I had no desire to sleep on a hard pallet another night." I reached for her hand. "We're home, we're safe, that's what's important."

"But your diaries—"

I swallowed. "It is a sore loss, I admit. But a minor one compared to what could have happened."

"I suppose." Laura's brows remained clenched, her mouth a thin line.

"We've been together for eight years," I continued. "None of them easy. But with each one that passes I grow to love and appreciate you more and more. We have so much to be grateful for. And still so much to look forward to. Our new home, here at Frogmore; the children; maintaining Penn School, and our teaching. Of late, writing has become a chore. I don't have the energy I once did. I'm now tired at the end of the day."

The worried expression on Laura's face eased a bit, and she grinned. "I have almost ten years on you, Ellen."

"I never think about that," I said.

"Well I do." She laughed. After a moment she said, "Won't you miss writing?"

"For years, unburdening myself on paper has been cathartic; it's given me peace. I will still write, but the desire to document the minutiae of my life has vanished. Recently, I've continued more out of habit than need."

Laura stared at me for a moment. Releasing my hand, she stood. "You rest. I'll get some unpacking done."

"You don't believe me," I called after her.

She turned back and smiled. "I do. But I know you well, Ellen Murray. You are also doing your utmost to ease my conscious."

≈ ≈ ≈

My arm healed by the time my birthday rolled around at the end of the month. To celebrate our move and my turning the grand age of thirty-five, Laura and Rina planned a dinner.

Our family gathered around the table for my birthday celebration, along with Fountain's best pal, Kit, and Henrietta's childhood chum, Fairy. Henrietta's newer friend, Jakob, also arrived bearing a bouquet of wildflowers for me, and a posy for

Henrietta. Tall and broad-shouldered, Jakob possessed striking features and a ready smile. More importantly, his wit and intelligence matched Henrietta's. For anyone with eyes to see, Jakob's lovelorn, soulful gaze revealed his feelings for Henrietta; but whether she harbored anything more than platonic interest in him, only time would tell. I recalled my own mother's intrusion in this area and had no desire to repeat history.

After a delicious meal of oyster stew and cornbread, we gathered around the fireplace in the parlor.

"Something special arrived for you." Laura handed me an envelope.

I recognized Hattie's handwriting at once, although it still gave me an odd sensation to read *Mrs. Edwin Ruggles*. Holding the envelope, a familiar hankering for my sister and mother returned. After their marriage, Hattie and Edwin, along with my mother, had moved North. Although I missed teaching alongside Hattie, she and Edwin remained committed to Penn School. These days we needed their financial support more than ever.

"You gonna open it?" Rina asked.

I returned my focus and unsealed the envelope. Seated right next to me, Laura rubbed my back. She understood how much I missed my mother and sister's presence.

I unfolded the letter within and a banknote fluttered out. I glanced at the amount, said nothing, and handed it to Laura. Then, with all eyes on me, I read Hattie's note aloud.

> *Dearest Ellen,*
> *I hope this birthday finds you well and happy! Mother and Edwin send their love and best wishes, as do I.*
> *Knowing full well you would balk at any trifle I might send, we have enclosed a donation, in your honor, for Penn School, which is something I know you will appreciate. It breaks our hearts that funding for our beloved school ended along with the war. How bitter the reward of peace!*
> *Be on the lookout for a small package Mother posted.*
> *Your loving sister,*
> *Hattie*
> *P.S. Our love to Laura, Henrietta, Fountain, Rina, and Hastings*

"What a kind gesture." Laura passed the banknote back to me. "And very generous."

With a lump in my throat, I nodded.

"I think this is your mother's package." Laura handed me a small, soft bundle.

Inside I found half a dozen monogrammed handkerchiefs. I held them out for the others to see, and then Rina took them off my hands. "Real nice," she smoothed the fine cotton and set them aside.

Fountain jumped to his feet and offered me a gift wrapped in old newsprint. "Open mine and Kit's, Miss Ellen."

"What could this be?" I made a show of feeling the package all over. Then I shook it and turned it up, down, and around. Both boys sat at the edge of their seats. Ripping one tiny piece at a corner, I peeked inside.

"Come on, Miss Ellen!" Fountain said, "don't tease us so."

I ripped open the parcel, laughing. Upon the sight of the boys' gift my laughter turned to awe. "Did you boys make these?" I asked. I held up the pair of wooden bookends: one carved in the likeness of a heron in flight; the other, a heron at rest.

"I did one, Kit the other," Fountain explained. "Hastings helped us."

"I promise you dat dem boys did all de work, Miz Ellen," Hastings said.

"Laura, would you look at these?" I handed her a bookend.

Laura examined the sculptures, her lips parted. "Astonishing." She looked at Fountain and Kit, both beaming at the praise. "You have a gift, boys. Use it well."

Their smiles broadened. "Yes ma'am," Kit said.

Fairy slipped out while we fussed over the bookends, then arrived beside me holding out a beribboned sweetgrass basket.

"For you, Miss Ellen. My gran'mammy helped me," she said.

I held the basket up by the handle, admiring the skill and time that went into its making. "Oh my, it's beautiful, Fairy." I said, setting it down on the table. "A fine basket like this deserves a place of honor and I shall display it proudly. Thank you, dear girl."

With a smile, Fairy nodded and returned to her seat. I watched her go, grateful our daughter called this sure-footed, steadfast young woman her friend. And to think I'd once considered her flighty!

"I wish I'd given mine first," Henrietta said. She passed me a slim hankie-wrapped package.

Nestled within lay a bookmark, cross-stitched with the phrase, *Love Makes a House a Home.*

Tears filled my eyes. "Oh, Henrietta." My voice cracked. "Thank you."

Henrietta gave me one of her sweet, crooked smiles. By the grace of God, her rosy bow-shaped lips and smooth skin, a rich shade of cinnamon, overruled her disfigured jaw line. The physical traces of the beating she'd suffered as a child receded as she'd grown. Hard to believe our girl turned fourteen on her last birthday. Still, emotional scars ran deep. Laura and I had done our best. But was it enough? I prayed that she would come to realize her beauty and worth.

Rina stood. "Birthday cake be my gift. Who gonna help me serve it up?" she asked.

Fountain and Kit jumped to their feet, one racing the other to the kitchen.

ða ða ða

Later, as I prepared for bed, it struck me that I hadn't received a present from Laura. I instantly felt guilty and looked around my bedchamber. Her funds alone purchased this house. Me, our family, Penn School, and the people of St. Helena consumed her every waking thought. A gift-wrapped token paled when compared to all of that. Picking up *Wuthering Heights*, I went to our sitting area. I had just settled in nicely when Laura walked in.

"Ah, you're still up. Good."

"Is everything all right?" I closed my book.

"I have something for you. Did you think I'd forgotten?" Her eyes held a glint.

My face flushed. "Maybe—"

She pulled her chair closer to mine, and reaching behind her cushion pulled out a paper-wrapped package. "Happy birthday."

Putting my novel aside, I took the gift and peeled off the wrapping. "Oh my!"

"I cannot replace the diaries you lost, but I thought you might like this one," Laura said. "I had a friend of Hastings tool the leather binding."

"It's stunning. Thank you!" I ran my fingers over the delicately wrought mockingbird on buttery leather. "It's almost too beautiful to write in."

"I hope you will," Laura said. "Otherwise I shall feel your stopping was my fault."

"Very well," I said, "I will christen it by documenting our move to Frogmore House and this wonderful evening. Otherwise, I will write in it only when I feel compelled."

"Whatever you wish," Laura said. "I'm glad you're pleased."

"How could I not be?" I asked.

Laura cast her eyes over to our bed's tarpaulin canopy meant to shelter us from our incomplete, leaky roof. She choked out a laugh. "I can think of a few reasons you may be less than pleased!"

"An inconvenience to be sure, but that is all." I got up from my chair. "Let's go to bed."

Laura smiled and my pulse quickened. In two steps I bridged the gap between us. Reaching out I took her hand, delighted by its familiarity. Her fingers, shorter than mine, her palms wider, and her strong grip that assured me she would never let go.

ᵹ� ᵹ⁊ ᵹ⁊

Chapter 42

Henrietta

In the gentle way of morning marsh mist, the past evaporates in all but my mind's eye. There, the Misses sit side by side in the reading nook of their bedchamber, hand holding hand. Across the room stands their tarp-canopied bed. The leather cover of the notebook and etched lines of the mockingbird blurs. Removing a hankie from my pocket, I press it to my closed lids.

The tender, vulnerable side Miss Laura reveals to Miss Ellen comes as a surprise to me. I'm equally astonished by Miss Ellen's boldness; how she took the lead in appraising the discord in their relationship and established a path forward.

This is not to say I never witnessed both disputes and affection between the pair. I did. Miss Laura fretted when Miss Ellen worked too many long hours, if she didn't get enough sleep, or picked at her dinner. Heaven help us if Miss Ellen caught so much as a head cold! Such an event would throw Miss Laura into a fluster. As for Miss Ellen, she quietly supported Miss Laura in all ways. Of the two, I believed Miss Ellen to be the more solicitous. In private, perhaps not as much. I suppose from the outside looking in, one never knows the whys and wherefores of lovers.

Let's go to bed. The image of the Misses about to embark on such intimacy fills me with curiosity. I never fully considered the breadth and depth of their union. The notion also highlights the yawning gap in my own life. Considering my mothers' shared, abiding affection evokes a longing within me. And dare I admit, envy. How wonderful it must be to align your desires, passions, work—your entire life—with another. A partner to walk with through the day in, day out drudgeries, along with the successes and failures; to share a bed.

The idea of lying beside Jakob through the darkness of night quickens my pulse. I close my eyes and imagine the heat of his body, the salty-sweet scent of his skin. A tightness in my belly unfurls, a restlessness and unease; a sudden and irrepressible desire to have him here beside me now, touching my face as he did last evening.

Jakob and Minette, their naked bodies entwined.

I grimace at the invented memory and bury it in the boneyard of my recollections, along with hundreds of other similar, skeletal remains.

A future with Jakob was, and remains, impossible. How could it be otherwise? Even the Misses, perfect for each other, experienced conflict and struggles. What chance would Jakob and I have, considering the avalanche of debris blocking our path? How would we avoid the pain if we trod forward? Such a step would only lead to disaster.

I am reminded of another disaster, that of the overturned cart during the Misses' final trek from the Teacher's Cottage to Frogmore House. Their incident demonstrates that even a well-suited couple court trouble if they're not on the same page.

Now I imagine the pages of Miss Ellen's diaries strewn in the mud. The cart episode accounts for the missing years. An old guilt rises within me. I wish I'd said something. Warned them ahead of time. Maum Cat wanted me to. I can only explain my reluctance to speak up to that of stubbornness; the type of defiance common in young people rushing for independence while railing against the wisdom of their elders.

Days before our move to Frogmore House, Maum Cat came to me. "Henrietta," said she, "you tell the Mizzes to go or stay."

I reared back and repeated, "Go or stay?"

"Mmm-hmm," says Maum.

"That makes no sense," I counter.

"The rain's comin'. Wind too," says Maum. "Tell the Mizzes no travelin'. It be dangerous."

"You don't want them to move to Frogmore House?"

Crossing her arms, Maum shakes her head.

I throw up my hands. "What then?"

"Tell 'em don't linger. Go or stay. The rain's comin'."

I stare at her. "Fine," I say.

I forgot Maum Cat's request the moment we parted. It wasn't until the Misses arrived on the porch here at Frogmore, soaked through and mud-splattered with Miss Ellen's arm injured, that I remembered, too late to do any good. To her credit, Maum Cat never ground salt into my guilt-wound. Just like Miss Ellen forgave Miss Laura for insisting they travel that day.

What if I'd done likewise for Jakob? Forgiven his indiscretion with Minette? At the least, I could've heard him out. It's easy to misconstrue meanings and intentions. Like yesterday. I all but accused Jakob of avoiding me at Miss Ellen's funeral when the poor man was simply too scared to approach me. I cringe at the recollection of the strained expression on his face when I insinuated he avoided me: how his eyes glistened before he turned, shoulders slumped.

Jakob mentioned our Sunday dinners with the Misses, back in the old days. Miss Ellen's account of her birthday party surprised me. I knew both the Misses thought me intelligent. Their assumptions about my education and ability said as much. But Miss Ellen revealed she considered me beautiful. My throat tightens and I swallow. If only. How different my life might have turned out had I shared her view.

One thing she sure got wrong. Even then I loved Jakob.

If I misread my own mothers' relationship, is it possible that I also misunderstood what transpired between Minette and Jakob? He has always maintained this is the case. My mothers faced their issues head-on and held true to their motto, *Stronger together.* What if I had done likewise with Jakob?

Again, I envision Jakob last evening, the moment when he held a hand against my face, the longing in his eyes. Could he be mine? Or do too many obstacles, too much damage and pain separate us?

I glance at Miss Ellen's mockingbird notebook on my lap. I lay a hand upon it and close my eyes.

ða ða ða

Chapter 43

Ellen

This morning, after our leisurely Saturday breakfast, I told Laura that I planned to do mark papers on the back porch.

"I think I'll get Whit from Hastings, and go for a swim." She squinted out our kitchen windows toward the Harbor River. "See if he likes the water."

"What puppy wouldn't love a romp in the river?" I laughed and shook my head.

"What is so funny?" She frowned and blushed. "You never know—"

I giggled some more. "Dear Laura, you are perfectly smitten with that frenzied ball of fur."

Her stern façade cracked and she laughed. "I suppose I am. But I do want to make sure he can manage on his own should he venture—"

Rat-a-tat-tat-tat—

We both turned.

Jakob stepped inside the screened porch. Spying us through the kitchen window, he waved.

Crossing the room, Laura opened the back door. "Good morning! Fountain and Kit are off fishing. And Henrietta got up with the birds to go help Fairy tend her sweetgrass patch."

"Yessim." Jakob took off his cap and stepped over the threshold. "I hoped to have a word with you and Miss Ellen."

Laura side-glanced me, her eyebrows arched. "Certainly, Jakob. Come on in and have a seat."

"Would you like some sweet tea?" I asked.

"No, thank you, Miss Ellen." He pulled out a chair from the table, but remained standing.

"Right." Laura walked over and sat down. I followed.

Jakob folded his tall frame down onto the chair and clasped his hands on the tabletop. Adam's apple bobbing, he looked from Laura to me and back again.

"Come now, you needn't look so ill at ease." Laura smiled. "What's on your mind?"

He drew in a long breath. "It's about Henrietta—"

My stomach clenched. "Has something happened to her?"

"No, no, ma'am." Jakob waved away the suggestion. "It's nothing like that. I wanted to talk to you and Miss Laura about Henrietta and *me*."

"Oh." I leaned forward.

"Henrietta and you?" Laura asked.

"I've a mind to marry her, and I'd like your blessing before I propose," he said in a rush.

Laura opened her mouth, closed it, and turned to me.

"Haven't you missed a step?" I asked.

"Step, ma'am?" His brow crinkled.

"Courtship?" I said. "Where you woo the young woman so she knows you're interested?"

"Henrietta's not like other gals." Jakob shook his head. "We've been friends for too long. Should I start bringing her presents or flowers and such when I come round, she'd wonder why and start asking all kinds of questions." He looked from me to Laura. "So if I have a mind to marry her, it's best I just say so and be done with it. Any courting can come afterwards."

"I see." I blew out a long breath and looked across the table at Laura.

She cleared her throat. "You make a good point, Jakob. Perhaps you're right about our Henrietta. But any decision must come from her."

"Agreed," I said. "However, if it's a blessing you're after today," I glanced at Laura who offered a brief nod, "we'll happily give you ours."

ta ta ta

I hastened to the parlor windows, gathered the drapes a tad, and peeked out as Jakob rounded the house. Arms swinging, he strode on toward our lane leading to the road.

"Well, what do think of that?" I asked Laura the moment I returned to the kitchen.

With her arms crossed, she pointed with her chin. "Let's chat on the porch."

"Is something wrong?" I asked, once we sat down. "Why aren't you pleased? I thought you liked Jakob."

In the loveseat opposite me, Laura leaned back. "Of course I like Jakob," she smiled.

"Is it that you think he's an unsuitable match for our girl?"

Laura laughed and shook her head.

My cheeks burned. "What is so funny?"

Bright eyes dancing, Laura shifted forward. "Answer me this: In the time it took you to cross the length of our house, did you, or did you not, concoct a detailed plan for Henrietta's trousseau, wedding, and honeymoon?"

I picked at a fingernail. "Honestly, Laura?"

Laura remained silent.

I looked up. She stared at me, one eyebrow raised.

"Okay, the dress. If you must know." I suppressed the urge to smile. "I did give that a thought."

Laura reached for my hand. "Feeling happy and excited for Henrietta is natural. We're mothers. I share your enthusiasm—"

"Jakob adores Henrietta, he has done since they were children," I said. "I know he'd love and respect her."

"Agreed." Laura shrugged.

"What is it then?" I released her hand and folded my arms. "You don't seem pleased."

"Henrietta deserves to be cherished and appreciated. She needs someone who will respect her individuality and accept her flaws."

I got up from my chair and joined Laura on the loveseat. "You don't believe Jakob could be that person for Henrietta?"

"That's not what troubles me." Laura stroked the back of my hand. "I believe he is a perfect match for her."

My eyes moistened. "Why then do you hesitate?"

"What we believe isn't important. It's what Henrietta believes. What she is willing to *receive*," Laura said.

"Receive?"

"Henrietta's view of herself does not align with ours. And likely not Jakob's."

I took a deep breath. "Owing to the injury, you mean. She has struggled with her self-worth."

"*Has* struggled, Ellen?" Laura paused.

"Her jaw's malformation receded as she grew. By the grace of God her permanent teeth were spared." I added, "Henrietta is now beautiful in every way. And I might add she is an accomplished scholar who will soon to be a teacher. That terrible episode is far behind us."

"It may be behind *us*, Ellen. But the question remains, is it behind Henrietta?"

"You think not?"

Laura sighed. "I am not convinced."

"Why do you say that?"

"For the same reason Jakob feels it necessary to propose first and court later," Laura said. "He sees all of her, which makes me love him even more." She looked away, blinked.

"Oh, Laura." I squeezed her hand.

"Time healed and faded her physical scars. But the internal beating she sustained? Those scars are more difficult to gauge." Laura swiped at her eyes. "What's more, she continues to suppress all memories of the event."

With a long exhalation, I stared at the cheerful sunshine blinking off the trees. "Do you still think we did the right thing? Not sharing the details of the beating, I mean."

"I do," Laura said. "Even if I didn't agree with Maum Cat and her daughter Manners' superstitious Root nonsense about danger, I did—and do—accept their insistence that it's Henrietta's place to unearth those buried memories."

"It bothers me, though," I said, "withholding information that affects her." I straightened and faced Laura. "Has enough time passed? Might telling her now perhaps expedite her emotional healing?"

"We've been over this many times, Ellen. Henrietta's mind locked out the beating for a reason. Who are we to open that door?"

"But if she asks—"

"Yes," Laura said. "We agreed, that's different. But that she has never requested specifics from us is telling."

I put my head down on Laura's shoulder and took a deep breath.

"We must both curb our enthusiasm about Jakob, dearest, and allow Henrietta the space to make her own decision," Laura said. "And whatever the outcome, we must accept her choice."

"It's just that I want her to have a full life, to experience the kind of bond and love you and I share."

"I want that for her as well." Laura tipped her head to mine. "But something tells me our Henrietta hasn't yet come into her own; to accept and love herself as she is. Until that happens, she won't be able to fully give herself to Jakob. Or anyone, for that matter."

꧁ ꧁ ꧁

Chapter 44

Henrietta

The porch of present day materializes around me and tears stream down my face. The tooled mockingbird stares up at me; head cocked, its beady eye taunts. I knock the book and bird off its perch and it hits the floor with a flutter and thud.

I glance at Maum. She sleeps on, oblivious to my distress.

Useless tears simmer. I lean over, pointed elbows grind into my thighs, I press closed fists against my eyes.

Why did he go to all that bother and then not—

A chill slithers and squeezes my rib cage. I retrieve the journal from the floor and flip back to the beginning of the entry.

May, 1873.

Just before I graduated from normal school. Round about the time I overheard Mercy behind the bookcase tell someone Jakob was using me. That same evening I had ended things between us.

Jakob never said a word about getting a blessing from the Misses. Never said much of anything. He sure enough held back his proposal. But he didn't hold back when it came to Minette. He took up with her right soon after.

A banked fire in the pit of my soul stirs to life.

Jakob, the Misses, Maum—their secrets amounted to lies! What other deceptions remain hidden? I leaf the journal, searching for the next date, a place to lay my palm. A blank sheet. I flip the page. Nothing. This can't be.

I straighten and fan the entire sheaf. A whoosh of paper and gust of air hits my face. Every page unmarked.

My chin quivers as I stack the incomplete journal on top of the others.

A *shoosh* from the shoreline reaches me, a farewell sigh of the receding tide.

With a grunt, Maum Cat rolls onto her back. I wait to see if she'll wake. After a few moments, the steady rise and fall of her chest indicates she's drifted back into a sound sleep. A smile plays at the edges of her mouth. *What are you dreaming about?* I wonder.

I stand and straighten. Stiff and sore, I lift my arms over my head and reach up, up. Hands on hips I twist from the waist. Squaring my shoulders, I look across the property and beyond the Harbor River, to the open marshland. A thin streak on the horizon shimmers. Above it the purple bruise of night has faded to pink and yellow. Soon dawn will break the skin of night. A bird chirps, another whistles. Draping myself in the quilt that's kept me snug throughout the night, I tramp through the damp grass toward the shore. I take a deep breath of salt air and the earthy undercurrent of pluff mud.

Partway to the shore I stop and admire the mottled haze that dances just above the water's surface. The mist swirls and parts. On rare occasion, dolphins feed close to our shore. Standing as still as an egret, I wait.

From out of the mist, a boat emerges. A single person rows, their outline smudged by the remnants of night and morning fog. A fisherman perhaps? But the boat heads straight for shore with no apparent intention to stop and cast a line. The rhythmic splash of the oars' dip and pull grows louder. The boat draws closer. But before it makes shore, a woman appears at the water's edge, her back to me.

Where did she come from?

Tugging up my quilt, I wrap myself tighter and walk at a quickened pace. I am almost upon them when the woman on shore turns to face me.

My breath hitches and I freeze. Miss Ellen smiles.

The skiff is now only a few feet from shore. I know the boat's pilot before I lay eyes on her. Miss Ellen wades in, the drenched hemline of her skirts trail behind. Miss Laura reaches over to help her into the hull. Miss Laura only has eyes for Miss Ellen. I am like a ghost. The moment Miss Ellen takes her seat, Miss Laura plunges the oars back into the river and commences turning the bow toward open water.

I toss the quilt from my shoulders. "No! Wait!" I run to the shore.

Miss Ellen twists around and lifts a hand. Miss Laura continues to row.

I kick off my shoes and rush into the water, but I cannot match the boat's speed. Seconds later it disappears, swallowed by the churning mist. Knee-deep, I am still close enough to hear the whoosh and splash of the oars, feel the tug and pull as they cut through the rippling waves.

Choking back sobs, I yell, "Please. Don't go."

Elbows raised, I pump my arms. Water rises to my hips, breasts. For a moment, the Misses come back into view. My skirts swirl and drag with the ebbing tide. My legs fail to do as I bid. The murky water will soon be over my head. The craft glides across the surface and into the marbled fog.

Bright, orange light bursts over the horizon.

I stop, my gaze drawn to the presentation of the risen sun. I look back to where the retreating skiff should be. The mist has cleared, taking the boat and my mothers with it.

The tide pulls as I slog back onto dry land. Shivering, I stumble up to where I dropped the blanket. Shaking, I struggle to untie the bow at my neck, and the buttons of my shirtwaist and skirt. Sloughing off my sopping undergarments, I wrap myself in the blanket. Although chilled and trembling, I am nonetheless compelled to look back to the water. Overhead, seagulls soar and squawk; a chevron of pelicans passes, en route to fish in the deeper water of the Sound. In the distance, past the open water and marsh grass, stands a silhouette of treetops on Hunting Island. Nowhere in this vista can I find the Misses' rowboat.

Seeing Miss Ellen one more time—the recent lines of sorrow etched about her eyes and mouth, smoothed—warms me within and my shivering abates. With the sun at my back, I tromp up to the house. Now more than ever I need Maum Cat's Root wisdom.

Arriving at the porch, I fly up the stairs and stop at the swing. Maum is stretched out on her back, mouth slack in slumber. Although desperate to talk, I hesitate.

While I dither, a broad sunbeam floods the porch, casting lemony shadows on the wicker chairs and side tables. Growing ever stronger, it glints off the windows, and for a brief second, it blinds me. Palm slanted to forehead, I shield my eyes and look back to see if the blaze disturbed Maum. The sunbeam's focus shimmies and shifts. I am reminded of the lighthouse beacon on Hunting Island, and how it signals danger.

Maum's face glows and glimmers, as do her hands and arms, resting atop the quilt that covers her torso and legs.

Fear grips my belly. "Maum?!"

I rush forward and do my best to hold on to her, but it's like trying to grasp motes of dust. The quilt collapses in my hands and crumples in upon itself. I gasp for air and rummage through the folds of the blanket. Standing tall, I shake it out with a snap, as though somehow Maum Cat will magically reappear.

"Why would you leave me?" I sob.

I go where and when I'm needed.

The porch tilts and reels. A high-pitched thrum buzzes in my head. I flop down upon the swing, clutching the quilt to my breast. Fearing I'll lose consciousness, I take a long, slow breath in through my nose; pursing my lips, I exhale slowly. I repeat this until the porch rights itself and the buzzing fades.

I stare at the blanket pressed against my bosom, still warm from the heat of Maum's body. Lying down, I bury my face in it and inhale Maum's dried apple and rosemary scent. My eyelids flutter and droop; my arms tingle and my legs feel like anchor weights. The moment before I can no longer resist sleep's call, I hear Maum whisper, "Ain't neber too late to be who you suppose to be."

&a. &a. &a.

Chapter 45

Henrietta

"Henrietta? Wake up."

Fairy sounds far away.

"Now Henrietta!" She jostles me.

Surfacing from the quagmire of sleep I pry open my eyes. Her blurred face is close to mine.

Blinking, I sit up. Mindful of my nakedness, I grab and pull the quilt with me.

"Good Lord, what are you doing out here?" Frowning, she throws up her hands, "Like…like this?"

I heave a sigh. My eyes fill. A tangle of thoughts and feelings rise in my throat. I try to swallow them, but I cannot. The burden of last night's events is too great to carry alone. *But how can I tell her?*

Fairy's frown softens, and she nods at a basket looped in the bend of her elbow. "I brought some biscuits and fresh eggs to scramble."

Burying my face in my hands I give in to the loss, fear, and loneliness that chokes me, and I weep without restraint. Fairy sits down, the swing creaks, and teeters. She puts her arms around me, holds me close, and lets me cry. "There, there," she says, rocking me like a child.

Between sobs, I grip Fairy's hands and tell her in a jumbled rush. "We found them…Miss Ellen's diaries…I walked to the water…a boat…I saw the Misses…I came back. Maum Cat, she…" I form two fists and throw them open with a burst, "…vanished!"

Fairy's brow crimps. "Come." She helps me to my feet. "Let's go inside. You get dressed. I'm gonna make us some breakfast."

With my face washed, hair combed, and dressed in clean, dry clothes, I head downstairs. My mouth waters at the aroma of percolating coffee and cooking eggs. I walk into the kitchen and Fairy looks up with a smile. "Almost ready."

I sit down at the table and Fairy pours the fragrant brew into the mugs she's already set out for us. Seconds later, my plate is full of scrambled eggs and two hot biscuits with melting butter. I'm ravenous. Fairy joins me and I gobble forkful after forkful of the fluffy eggs.

Fairy laughs. "I'm glad you like 'em."

I swallow and nod, take a gulp of coffee. "I don't remember when I last ate."

She pats my hand. "You enjoy, Baby."

My hunger abated, I slow down and savor the hot, buttery biscuits. Fairy tops off our coffee.

"Now you're awake and your belly's full, tell me again what you were sayin' earlier on the porch?" Fairy asks. "I had trouble understandin'."

"I must've sounded insane." I dab butter from my lips.

"Now don't be talkin' like that." Fairy shakes her head. "I just want to hear exactly what went on. From beginning to end."

I detail the events of the previous night and earlier this morning. Fairy crosses her arms; uncrosses them; grunts occasionally; her brows rise often, but she says nothing until I stop speaking.

"That's why I found you sound asleep in nothin' but a blanket," Fairy says more to herself than me. By the way her eyebrows are scrunched I know she's thinking things through.

Beneath the table, I wipe my sweaty palms down the length of my skirt.

"Wanna know what I think?"

"Mmm-hmm," I croak.

"This was Miss Ellen's way of letting you know she was ready to go and happy to be joined up again with Miss Laura."

"So you don't think I'm losing my mind?" I ask.

"'Course not! Ain't nobody more sane than you." Fairy flicks her hand. "Miss Ellen led you to them diaries, didn't she?"

"I suppose—" I hesitate, recalling how Maum helped me find the diaries and encouraged me to "read" them.

"What?" Fairy asks.

I draw a ragged breath. In the minutes that follow, I tell Fairy about Maum Cat and how she stood by me throughout the years when I've needed her most. Finally, I share how she vanished earlier this morning.

"You must be someone special to have Maum Cat's spirit tagging you."

"You *knew* Maum Cat was dead?" I ask.

"'Course," she says.

"But you never let on; never corrected me."

"Would you've believed me?" Fairy stares over the rim of her coffee mug.

I open my mouth to protest then clamp it shut.

Fairy smiles and continues. "The Misses didn't put their faith in the Root and they didn't raise you up to, either."

"Then why me?" I ask. "Why would Maum Cat, or her spirit, visit me, of all people?"

Fairy tilts her head. "After all you told me, I wonder if it had something to do with you almost gettin' beat to death." She shrugs. "Might've been back then you saw the other side and 'cause of that, they can see you."

A chill rushed up my spine.

"It's a gift." Fairy reaches forward and covers my hand with hers. "Nothing to be scared of. Means you're special."

"If special means seeing people that aren't there, no thank you. That's a gift I don't want."

Fairy chuckles. "Do you remember when my girl Sassy was about three or four years old? Her goin' on and on about her friend Mary."

I nod. "Sassy compared her friendship with Mary to ours."

"Did you ever meet Mary?" Fairy relaxes back into her chair.

I struggle to remember. "Now that you mention it, no, not that I recall."

"Well you didn't, 'cause that child lived only in Sassy's mind."

"Oh."

"Don't mean Mary's friendship with my girl didn't count. Mary was as real and important to Sass as you are to me."

"But I'm an adult! And at one time Maum Cat actually lived outside of my imagination."

Ignoring my comment, Fairy continues. "My man Tommy has only the one arm, right?" Fairy stares at me.

"Well...yes...obviously."

"He lost it to that gator before you and me even met each other. Yet to this day, in his dreams he always got two arms. In the winter when it gets damp and cold he complains the fingers on his missing hand ache."

Fairy's meandering explanation makes my head hurt. Closing my eyes, I pinch the bridge of my nose. "What's that got to do with me seeing and talking to a dead woman?"

"Just 'cause she's dead doesn't mean she still ain't part of you. Same with Miss Ellen and Miss Laura."

I open my eyes. "You think so?"

"Mmm-hmm."

"So you really don't think I'm crazy."

Fairy throws up her hands. "Stop sayin' that. You're one of the smartest people I know. 'Course not."

The icy fear buried in my chest eases. "Thank you for coming this morning. I don't know what I'd've done without you."

"I can't take all the credit," Fairy says. "Jakob asked me to check in on you. He doesn't like you being out here grievin' by yourself. It's no wonder you're surrounded by spirits. In times like these, the folks who love you gotta gather round."

"And that includes Jakob?" I scoff.

"It does." Fairy's voice rises. "I can't understand why you're so sure he don't care?"

Truth in what she says burrows beneath my skin. Even so, something else bucks inside me.

I lift my chin. "Why you so sure he does?"

"Even a blind man can see Jakob loves you."

"But not just me!" I fire back. "Easy for you to say. Tommy never had eyes for anyone else."

"Maybe so." Fairy says with a laugh. "I still don't see how you're any different from me. The way I recall it, Jakob only ever wanted you, Henrietta. You only ever pushed him away. What'd you expect?"

"That's not true! I loved Jakob. You know I did."

"Why y'all not together then?" Fairy juts her chin out." Tell me that?"

"You've got it all wrong. He let *me* down."

"You talkin' about Minette?"

"No...yes, but even before. Back in normal school." I toss off the years with a flip of my wrist.

"When y'all was training up to be a teacher? What happened? And why don't I know nothin' about this?"

I shrug. "I heard Mercy and some other girl talking—"

"Mercy? Same gal that always taunt you with Dull Dora back when we were schoolgirls at Penn?"

"Mmm-hmm."

"Why you listen to anything she say? That gal was always jealous because you smarter than her, and a whole sight prettier."

Fairy's comment about my looks catches me off guard. But I leave it be. "From behind a tall bookcase I heard Mercy talking to someone. I don't know who, but she said, 'Jakob's not interested in Henrietta,' and my ears perked up.

"The other girl said, 'Really?' Mercy laughed and said, 'He's just using her, if you know what I mean. He told my brother Shrimp just that. Only makes sense. Why would Jakob marry that dog-faced Henrietta?'"

"Why'd you never tell me any of this? Fairy asks.

I shrug. "Too ashamed, I suppose."

"You sittin' here tellin' me you let that mean, jealous Mercy decide who you are, who you gonna love, or who gonna love you? Didn't you learn nothin' growin' up? You gotta stand up for yourself. Problem ain't Jakob not lovin' you enough, back then or now. You gotta believe in yourself, Henrietta. Show yourself some love and respect if you want other folks to do the same."

At Fairy's reproach, my eyes fill. "What if you'd heard the same about Tommy? Bet you'd be whistling a different tune then!"

"What I'd been doin' is whistlin' the death march at Miss Mercy's funeral after I spoke to Tommy and found out it was a lie! Did you bother goin' to Jakob and askin' him about what you heard?"

I stare back at her and swallow. "Jakob went to the Misses and asked their blessing to marry me."

"What?"

I nod my head.

"You mean after all that business with Mercy?"

"No, before."

"You tellin' me you turned down Jakob's marriage proposal?" Fairy slumps back in the chair and crosses her arms over her bosom. "Why you kept all this from me?"

"I never. I wouldn't...I just found out." I draw a shaky breath. "The Misses never told me. Jakob never got around to proposing before I—before I broke things off."

Bursting into tears, I fold my arms on the table and bury my face.

Fairy comes around, sits down, and rubs my back.

"Why didn't the Misses tell me?" I lift my head. "Why didn't Jakob fight for me?"

Fairy hands me her handkerchief. "Dry your face."

"Everyone I love lied to me, Fairy." I sit up and blow my nose. "Or a' least didn't tell me things I had a right to know."

Fairy tilts her head.

"Don't look at me like that!" I say. "Withholding information is a form of lying."

"You might look at it that way," Fairy says.

"What other way is there to see it?" I smack the table.

"You feel betrayed." Fairy's voice is real soft. "You're angry."

"Wouldn't you be?" Fresh tears spill down my cheeks.

"I 'spose." Fairy nods. "Question is, who you angry at?"

I throw out my arm and point nowhere, everywhere. "Them...Maum. The Misses. Jakob—" I sob his name.

"I never told you Maum was a spirit," Fairy says. "Ain't you mad at me?"

"No." I sniff and dry my eyes. "What you said makes sense. If you can use spirits and sense in the same sentence." I laugh.

"It's no different with the Misses, or Maum, or Jakob." Fairy raises her eyebrows. "Could be you're angry at yourself?"

I stare at her. "What did I do?"

"Nothing, Henrietta. And that's the point." She scowls. "You gotta take some of the blame that Jakob took up with Minette."

"Me? How's any of that my fault?" I splutter. "She didn't hold a gun to his chest."

"No, but you left a big hole in his heart for her to fill. Not that I'm sayin' it all falls on you or Jakob. Think about it. Something about them two getting together never sat right. Did it?" She gave me a kind look.

"What do you mean, not right?" I ask.

Fairy chews her lip the way she does when she's thinking real hard. "First off, Minette shows up here, from New Orleans of all places, not knowing anyone exceptin' that wicked crone, Maum Gull. I never liked that woman—her daughter neither. Folks say the both of them conjure evil. Who's to say Maum Gull didn't have something to do with those two meetin' up? And why you have no confidence in Jakob's feelings for you? Maybe she hexed the both of you."

"Maum Cat once said something similar about Minette and Maum Gull, although she never suggested anyone being hexed."

"After all the damage is done," Fairy brushes one hand with the other, "Minette leaves."

"Not just her," I say. "Jakob ran off too."

"It's not like he vanished," Fairy says. "He took the signalman's job at the lighthouse on Hunting Island."

"I still never saw hide nor hair of him for years."

"If you wanted him you could've gotten word out," Fairy says. "Minette sure managed, when it suited her needs."

"Esme." I sigh.

"You ask me, that gal's the only good that came outta those two gettin' together." Fairy stops talking and stares inward for a few seconds. "Something special about that gal. It's in them blue eyes of hers. Can't say exactly what, though." She shrugs. "That said, I'm not so sure she's Jakob's."

"Fairy!"

"Come on, Henrietta, don't be coy with me. You know I'm not the only one that thinks that. Most of the island feels the same way. You can't blame folks for wonderin'. Minette comes; she goes, and then she shows up—three years later, pretty as you please—with that sweet child, bearin' no resemblance to Jakob, I might add, and just hands her over to him like a puppy she didn't count on being such a bother. What kinda woman gives up her child like that?"

"We don't know why she did what she did," I say.

Fairy shakes her head. "You're always willing to give everyone the benefit of the doubt, everyone 'cept Jakob, that is."

Resting my elbows on the table, I cover my face with my hands.

Fairy pulls her chair closer. Softening her voice she asks, "Why didn't you two get together after Minette dumped off Esme and left? Nothing then stopping you."

I lift my head and look at Fairy. "He tried."

"You mean to say you turned him down that time too?" Fairy blinks.

I shrug. "I thought he just wanted a mother for Esme. Hex or no hex, I don't have your confidence, Fairy. Never have."

Fairy sighs. Something I don't hear her do often.

"I should've spoke up. Told you what I was thinkin' at the time." Fairy slaps her thighs. "I'm not gonna make the same mistake again."

"How'd you mean?" I sit up straight.

"You took what Mercy said about Jakob for true 'cause *you* believe you're not good enough. That evil woman in Beaufort crushed your jaw. But you let her wickedness break your spirit. Lord knows the Misses gave you all they had; Maum Cat too, from what you say. Still not enough. Nobody can make you believe in yourself. That's a choice you make. So what's it gonna be?"

"It's not that easy," I stammer. "I can't just snap my fingers and change how I see myself."

"Why not?"

"Because I don't *feel* that way!" My raised voice is strangled by the urge to cry.

"So what?" Fairy shrugs.

I blink at her.

Fairy lowers her voice and says, "You don't have to feel, you have to act. Believin' will come."

"Now you're the one that's talking crazy."

"That so?" She raises an eyebrow. "Even though you're smart and beautiful, you've acted like you weren't worth nothin', and that's what you got. Why can't it be the same, other way 'round?"

I have no counter to Fairy's logic. "I don't know why you always say I'm the smart one."

"I said you were smart. Never said nothin' about you bein' smarter than me." A huge grin crosses her face.

We both laugh for a moment and then a hush falls upon us. I avoid her gaze. The tick-tock-tick from the hallway clock underscores our silence. Fairy, I sense, is watching and waiting for me to speak.

Eventually I look at her. "I can't change the past, Fairy. No matter how much I'd like to."

"No, what's done is done. But you still got today, and, God willing, tomorrow and the day after that."

"That's funny. Maum Cat said something similar."

"You don't say—" Fairy's brows rise.

"Did I mention Jakob came round here last night?" I tell her. "He wants us to be together."

"What you gonna do?" Fairy asks.

I offer Fairy a tentative smile and quote Maum Cat. "Ain't neber too late to be who you suppose to be."

Fairy leans back and crosses her arms. "True 'nuff."

❧ ❧ ❧

At the wharf, Fairy stands on one side of me, Fountain and his family on the other. Most of the St. Helena community gather behind us. The steamer, with Miss Ellen's mortal remains aboard, sails away.

I recall Miss Ellen's first impression of our island: her awe at the maritime forest on the shoreline, her excitement at the prospect of reuniting with Miss Laura and the future they planned together. I look up at the blue sky, the sun now high above us. No downpour today, like the one Miss Ellen experienced on that long-ago afternoon.

I ponder all of this, not with a sense of sadness, but rather one of satisfaction, a consequence of Miss Ellen's parting gift: her diaries. From them, I've gained a deeper appreciation of her love for Miss Laura and their shared passion and commitment to protect and educate the freed people of St. Helena, the love they both had for Fountain and me, and the family life we shared. Although Miss Ellen's final few years were challenging, I believe they did not negate all she had accomplished. The many people gathered here this afternoon to send her off assures me this is so.

The ship, much smaller now, will soon be out of sight.

A few folks break apart and turn to home. The steamer is now only a dot on the horizon. I look at Fairy. She puts her arm around my shoulders and pulls me close.

"She's not really gone, you know," Fairy whispers.

I nod, and picture Miss Ellen sitting in the hull of that rowboat with Miss Laura leading them both on to some new adventure.

A hand alights on the small of my back and I turn to face Fountain. "You okay?" he asks.

There are smudges of grief under his eyes. "I'm fine," I tell him. "Fairy and Tommy will take me back to Frogmore House. You go on home." I lean around Fountain and offer goodbye to Olivia and the children. Looking back at my brother, I say, "I need to talk to you soon, just the two of us, all right?"

His brows furrow and he tells me he'll come by tomorrow. After hugging me tight, he gathers up his family and walks off. Watching the slump of his shoulders, I hope that sharing Miss Ellen's diaries, and telling him of my communion with her at the shore, will offer him a measure of comfort and peace.

Jakob and Esme cross paths with Fountain and his family. They stop and exchange a few words. Fountain and Jakob shake hands. Fairy squeezes my arm and says, "I'll wait with Tommy."

I open my mouth to ask her to stay, but her quick frown and headshake tell me she'll tolerate no argument. Fairy says hello to Jakob and Esme in passing and walks on toward Tommy, who stands gabbing with a clutch of men.

Jakob removes the wide-brimmed hat he's wearing and twirls it round with his fingertips. Esme steps forward and hugs me. She leans back. "Such a beautiful send-off, Miss Henrietta, don't you think?"

"Perfect." I smile at her and then look at Jakob. "I'm pleased you both came. Miss Ellen would want you to be here. And so do I."

Jakob smiles, the tension about his face relaxes a fraction. "We're honored—"

❧ ❧ ❧

A high-pitched yip sounds. Someone yells, "Grab him!" Kit, I think.

From down the wharf, a black puppy charges toward us. The few people milling about step clear; some try to catch the dog, but he easily slips by. I fear he'll run off the end of the dock and into the water, but he stops in front of Esme.

Laughing, she bends down and picks him up. "Hey, fella." The pup licks Esme's face like she's a long-lost friend.

"He yours?" Kit calls out.

Esme glances at Jakob.

Jakob's eyes dart from Esme, to the dog, and back again.

Unlike me, Esme does not hesitate to take what belongs to her. "Sure is," she shouts back to Kit.

"Better tie him up. Near knocked me off my feet." Kit's voice is laced with humor and feigned outrage.

"Yessir," Esme calls back. With a giggle, she buries her face in the puppy's velvety fur. The little fellow snuggles into her.

Rubbing the back of his neck, Jakob shrugs at me.

To hide my amusement, I focus on the pup. He's a common enough mutt, except—I lean over for a better look.

"His eyes," I say, "they're...unusual."

We all three peer at the dog.

"Same blue as yours," Jakob says to Esme.

"So they are!" Esme smiles at us. "Look at his coat. It's so shiny and black, just like coal." Her eyes widen. "That' what I'll call you, Coal!"

The dog squirms. "I'll wait for you in the wagon, Pap. Take your time." Esme grips the pup tighter.

"There's a bit of rope under the seat," Jakob says.

Esme smiles at me. "Bye, Miss Henrietta. I hope we see you real soon."

Without Esme between us, I am shy. I dig deep and garner strength to say what I know I must.

Jacob looks sideways and heaves a breath. "Henrietta, there's so much I want to tell you." Jakob's eyes are pleading, yet he keeps his distance from me. "So much has happened. I can't explain it all. But one thing I'm sure of, it's always been you I love."

I step forward. He smells like fresh air and warm nights.

"Hush," I whisper.

I take off a glove and place my bare hand against his cheek. Surprise and pleasure flash in his eyes. He opens his mouth to speak, but before he can say a word, I stand on the tips of my toes and silence him with a kiss. In an instant, his strong arms surround me. Drawing me close, he smiles before his lips meet mine. I am where I belong.

"Ain't neber too late to be who you suppose to be."

🐦 🐦 🐦

Acknowledgments

A special "Thank You" to my much younger sister, Nora Trpcic, whose passion for the Lowcountry proved contagious.

Retired Lieutenant Colonel Meridith Marshall arranged access to the Military Base in Port Royal, South Carolina where the Emancipation Oak still stands. Friends, food, and wallop of history. Doesn't get any better.

The village of St. Helenaville was swallowed by time and I could not determine its exact location on the island. Super Librarian, Grace Cordial of the Beaufort Central Library, went above and beyond, going so far as to scout the area and report back to me.

Judy Ann Pearce, my most stalwart Southern supporter, accosted a gentleman at the gates of Frogmore House, and obtained information that I might contact the current owners. Caroline and Bill Hatcher graciously invited me into their home and gave me a grand tour. Looking out the back windows facing the water, taking in the same view as Ellen and Laura, was a research highlight.

This story would never have been completed without the input, advice, and encouragement of my writing group, B.A.M., Jennifer Maruno, Sharon McKay, Claudia White, Jill Bryant, and Nancy Hartry. Likewise, beta readers, Natalie Hyde, Louise Johnston, and my "favorite" cousin Andrew Maxwell read early drafts of the manuscript. My dear friend, Alicia Snell, patiently read several versions. Each offered invaluable criticism.

A special "Thank You" to Nadine Laman of Cactus Rain Publishing. I am most appreciative of her enthusiasm, guidance, and support.

Family is everything and I am grateful to mine for riding life's waves with me. Ali, Andrew, and Dri; Kyle, Lydia, Cohen, and Hailey; Jennifer, Rob, Sean, Andrew; and last but definitely not least, Luke. Y'all are treasures.

&a. &a. &a.

Dear Reader,
If you enjoyed this book, please tell your friends,
and write a review on GoodReads.com and Amazon.
Thank you, Deborah